BY SANDRA HOCHMAN

POETRY
Voyage Home
Manhattan Pastures (Yale Younger Poets Award)
The Vaudeville Marriage
Love Letters from Asia
Earthworks
Futures

NOVELS
Walking Papers
Endangered Species
Happiness Is Too Much Trouble
Jogging

NONFICTION
The Satellite Spies
Streams

FOR CHILDREN
The Magic Convention

FILM
The Year of the Woman—A Documentary

PLAYS
Walking Papers
The Whore and the Poet

PLAYING TAHOE

A novel by

SANDRA HOCHMAN

Wyndham Books
New York

Copyright © 1981 by Sandra Hochman
All rights reserved
including the right of reproduction
in whole or in part in any form
Published by Wyndham Books
A Simon & Schuster Division of Gulf & Western Corporation
Simon & Schuster Building
Rockefeller Center
1230 Avenue of the Americas
New York, New York 10020
WYNDHAM and colophon are trademarks of SIMON & SCHUSTER
Designed by Irving Perkins

1   2   3   4   5   6   7   8   9   10

Library of Congress Cataloging in Publication Data

Hochman, Sandra.
Playing Tahoe.

I.   Title.
PS3558.034P5   813'.54   80-28668
ISBN 0-671-25358-1

I WISH to thank Irwin Small, Steven Hochman, Chuck Neighbors, Lucia Nevai, Sybil Wong, Richard Hochman, Jo Anne Roberts, the Searby family, Alan Olinger, Gary William Friedman, Jerry Wexler, Arthur and Alexandra Schlesinger, Bill Targ, John Brock, Judith McFarlan, Lanny Myers, Donald Townsend, Alan and Susan Patricof, Dorothy Butler Farrell, Eric Javits, Rene Schwartz, Anna Thornhill, Mark and Susan Strausberg, Judy and David Auchinchloss, Sherry and Jerry Lynn, and my mother, Mae Barnett, for their constant friendship and help while I was writing this book.

AND WITH gratitude to Neal Travis and Teddy and Richard Rosenthal.

FOR MY DAUGHTER, ARIEL. FOR DERBY.
AND FOR JACQUELINE KERSTENS.

Come down off your throne
And leave your body alone;
Somebody's got to change.
You are the reason
I've wasted all these years.
Somebody's got to change.

—*Steve Winwood, from the* Blind Faith *album*

1. Disco Was Dead

DISCO WAS dead. Nick Dimani heard the frippertonics, the new solar sounds, and they frightened him. Nick had made his first comeback with disco. He had been in the business, of course, long before disco was hot. Dimani was no fool. He had *legs*. He had survived. He had crossed over, like a needle in a weaving loom, from black jive to white jive, back to black jive so many times you would think he'd be sure of his survival. But in his business, the music business, there was money and fame but *never* any assurance of survival. Nick knew you were only as good as your last album. He had hit it big with disco and, before that, rock and roll. Nick had reached the charts again and again. He had played God. An American hero. And like a god, he had inhabited the Elysian fields easily, forgetting what it was like to topple from the pure air and scent of flowers back into the purgatory of boyhood where there was nothing but ghetto smells, ugly billboards, bad vibes. When you are born in emptiness and urine the way Nick Dimani was born on Brighton Beach's dirt streets in Brooklyn, forty-three years ago, when you are able to reach millions of people all over the planet who have your songs in their throats, when everyone looks at you with awe, it is painful to slip down the cragged mountain, falling from the heights of wealth and fame. This had happened to Nick many times during his career. Once he had even been *dead* in the business. But Nick Dimani had always climbed back up on the charts. Now he was falling again. Now, somewhere inside the chambers of his brain, hidden by his shaggy nineteen-eighties hairdo, inside the dry look he made with his blowdryer was fear. Nick had to make another comeback.

He felt like a hero who had been wounded in the back with an arrow. As a hero, he knew he could bear the pain. "That's what heroes are," he told his wife, "people who can tolerate terrible suffering." Still, often in his dreams, he was still the kid from beggars and gypsies and addicts and street people. He dreamed of empty kitchens and the smells of rotten food. He knew streets with condoms and cots and screaming radios that hurt your eardrums. He was still, in those dreams, the accordion kid from Brooklyn, hungry and scared. Scared that this time he was really finished. Upon waking, he realized, as he dressed, either he made a new album, the way he wanted to make it, or he'd better forget it. Somewhere inside this part-Italian, part-Jewish man in the perfect pure-red silk shirt and custom jeans, this man who walked around the planet earth being *recognized,* this kid who *had it all,* in his mother's words, who, in her words, too, *lacked for nothing*—he was now aware that unless he created a new hit album, it was all over.

His latest song, a single called "Roller Queen," was nowhere and slipping. It wasn't number three with a bullet. It was number twenty-five this week according to *Cash Box:*

All night long
I have this dream:
I'm gonna be a roller queen.
Sound inside me
Day and night,
Rolling me,
Rolling me,
Rolling me,
Out of sight—
Keep moving,
Keep moving on me,
Moving on me.

"Outasight."

"Outasight, outasight," everyone—all the baboons with golden chains around their necks—said at Mecca Records when he first played it for them. If it was so fucking outasight, how come it was falling on the charts? If it was such a fucking big single, how come when he turned on the box he saw Donna Summer singing somebody else's song? How come he didn't hear it on the radio? How come it was *slipping?* "Roller Queen" was slipping. Dimani was slipping. Disco was slipping.

And so Nick skied obsessively that winter in Lake Tahoe. At night in his bed at Harrah's villa, he was sweating out his nightmares. He was falling from Olympus. He was in a box he couldn't break out of. After all, he wasn't Houdini. His hero, Houdini, had started out life as Ehrich Weiss. He had become the magician whose escapes were legend. Wasn't that what every song was? An escape? Houdini had been born in Budapest, Dimani in Brooklyn. They were both small men. They both had black hair and large dreaming brown eyes. They both had broken out of the straitjackets of their lives. Dimani had been born Nick Dubinsky. He had made himself *Dimani* the way Weiss had made himself Houdini. According to Patti Smith, Houdini had "broken the heart of every locksmith in America." Wasn't Nick able to break out of his pain, out of his box, the way Houdini did?

One more hit. One more escape. That was all Nick Dimani wanted. One more album. Not just a single. But an album. He had six new songs. He wanted to record them on an album he would call *Playing Tahoe. Tahoe* had a great sound to it. It was an Indian word. Meant "Cold Water." Tahoe was America. It was the West. It was freedom. Tahoe was the high Sierras. It was pure air. It was everything that was right for now. He was now writing cool, galactic Sierra melodies that nobody could touch, his own high-tech surf sounds, bird sounds, and beatific nature caws, the new Nick Dimani sound, cooler than The Plastics. It was his *best stuff*. All he needed was Sylvia to put some new-wave existential lyrics to the music. Her little verbal playlets of alienation. And he would have six killers. Sylvia inside her guts always knew what was right for his songs. Nobody could write lyrics for him the way she did. That's why he needed her. Just for this album. They would hit it again. One more deliverance. One more escape from the inferno of the bottom of the charts. Lundholm was the angel that could lift him from the fire. All he needed was Sylvia Lundholm to come out to Tahoe, create the words for the new album, and then he'd be home free. He needed her laments. Her confessions. That was *all* he needed. But Lundholm didn't need him. Lundholm was now oddly aloof. Lundholm wouldn't write another fucking lament or confession. That was what she told him before Christmas. Could you imagine if Houdini needed a partner? If he had to ask *permission* to escape? If, in order to get out of the box, he had to ask someone to help him? He couldn't get out of the handcuffs without Sylvia.

The problem with his life, Nick Dimani thought, was that he was always dependent on someone else. In order to *create* he needed a partner. He needed to depend on Sylvia. It was a need that was driving him to despair. He could create the melodies. But without her words they didn't work. And he couldn't write words. Only songs without words. And that was the trouble. That was the kicker. He had tried to write his own words. They were no good and he knew it. He had even yoked his sound with other writers. The combination never worked. Not one song that he wrote with anyone else ever went *anywhere*. That's why he needed Sylvia. It was more than a marriage. It was symbiosis, a need so strong it was almost a joke. He, Nick Dimani, was a freak. A Siamese twin. He couldn't be cut off from the body of his partner or he would die. He, Nick Dimani, who was supposed to be such a tycoon of the earwaves, who was one of America's major composers, who was a legend in his own time, was a nada, a nothing, a zero, without Sylvia Lundholm. He needed her. And now she didn't need him. *Need* him? She was *finished* with him. She was walking out. Not just on him, but on music. When he listened to her voice over the phone, cold sweat poured into the silk armpits of his three-hundred-dollar shirt.

"I don't care about music anymore," she said.

He could have crushed her, he could have thrown her against the wall he was so angry. "Angel, please," he pleaded. Angel, my ass. She was a piece of neurotic furniture. He was crazy to have her as his partner. His life-line. He couldn't control her anymore. Nick felt nausea when he thought of Sylvia. It was worse than the nightmares he had in Brooklyn in his boyhood. He dreamed over and over again that someone was stealing his pointed blue suede shoes. He would run after his suede shoes in a dream every night. But now Sylvia was stealing more than his shoes. She was stealing his life. She was stealing his soul. His lungs. His arteries. Without her he couldn't breathe. He couldn't work without her. He couldn't write without her. The world wanted his songs. And his songs meant Sylvia with her particular talent. Her goddamn fucking life alchemized with his into plastic discs. And now she was walking out on him. After twenty-three years of being in the business together, she was walking out. Nick was more than frightened. He was in pain. He had to stop her. He would crush her to bits if she left. He would really like to kill her. But, as his wife Rita said, "You'd better be nice to her, Nick. She's the goose who lays our golden eggs." Ha! Ha! Ha! Ha, ha, Houdini. Ha, ha, Rita. But it wasn't funny. His need had become an agonized obsession.

"Please, Sylvia," he whispered over the phone, "give me one more album." Nick was sweating it out. That demonized Swede didn't care that he had made her his life. He had given that Swedish neurotic bitch the only dignity she had ever known. He had taken her words and made them into world messages. He had taken her words and spoon-fed them into the mouths of Sinatra and Presley and Elton John. He had sung her words himself, in his act. He had given her a *life*.

"Sorry, Nick, there's no more magic," she had said in return. Now she was saying that she didn't care about their career. She called him a trickster. He was a cup-and-ball man. She was throwing away his natural magic; she was putting him into an open-air straitjacket and forbidding his escape. He had taught her Houdini's tactics religiously over the years; he had taken their lives and magically cre-ated a legend, and she was telling him now she *didn't care*. But this wasn't a dream. This wasn't Brooklyn where he dreamed of his blue suede shoes being stolen. This was happening now and he knew that without Sylvia Lund-holm there were no more albums. There was only a drowning death.

"I need you," he told her simply.

"I'm sorry," she said compassionately.

"Sorry? Is that all you can say? You're sorry? You've just finished me and you say you're sorry?"

"I dream of change. I must change. I'm sorry. I might even want to try writing something else. Alone."

"Our autobiography?" he asked sarcastically. He could have strangled her. He could have mangled her. He wanted to lock her hands into handcuffs and manacle her. He wanted to hold her down so that it was she who was drowning, it was she who could not escape. She was taking his earliest dreams and destroying them. She was making his natural magic disappear. She was turning him back into Nick Dubinsky.

"I don't know. I want to write a book."

"Write a book. Who's stopping you?"

"It's not that. I'm tired of the business. I need a rest. Nick, I've met someone. He's changed my life."

"So what? You've met a lot of men. I wish I had a nickel for every man you've met over the last twenty-three years who you thought you loved. I'd be a fucking millionaire."

"This is different."

"That's what you always say."

"I mean it this time. This man—doesn't want anything from me. He has no ambitions."

"So what? I've heard he's a freeloader without a career. So you're getting nookie from Adonis, what does that have to do with our new album?"

"I'm changing——"

"Come off it, Sylvia." (At first he thought it was a joke.)

"No, it's true, Nick. I'm changing. I have been over this so many times in my head. I've been thinking about it and I have found the man who has given me wings. Try to understand. I love him. And more than that, he's showing me how to be unknown, how to twist and turn *down* the ladder of success. How to climb down the sky like a clean white airplane without need of propeller or parachute. He has taught me that it's not important to show my clippings and to be a legend. I don't need anymore to have fans or to stay in the heavens. He has taught me how to walk on the planet like an ordinary human being and I've learned for the first time how to take great pleasure in unimportant things. He is teaching me how to be *ordinary*. He was born with everything that you helped me to strive for and he turned against it. Downward mobility is his specialty. With him, I'm more than airborne, I'm earthborn." She laughed. "You see, Nick, with him, I don't need *anything* to be happy. I can just eat a meal, take a bath, drive in a car, and realize how false my life has been. He's teaching me to be Sylvia again, and I adore him. I really do, and I always will, no matter what happens."

He couldn't believe this bullshit, this Swedish neurotic shit about airplanes and parachutes. She was getting laid for the first time in years. So what?

"He sounds like a fraud," Nick said as he spit and watched the phlegm fly from his mouth. *I'll kill him,* he thought. He wasn't going to let Sylvia dump him.

Yes, Nick Dimani suddenly understood that winter of 1979 in Tahoe that disco was dying. Ironically, it had been proven by a certain ear specialist to destroy the human nervous system and a kinesthesiologist had recently come to the conclusion that because the beat was frantic, it went against the regulatory system and affected muscular mobility. Exposure to disco had resulted in a nation of potential spastics. *So what,* Nick thought, but it bothered him. Charts and graphs, these crazy ear doctors and asshole psychologists were only pointing to what he already knew. You didn't have to be a genius to know that. Taste was always changing. Music was a business of change. America was a country of change. By the time America absorbed its product, the product had already self-destructed. Disco was dying and his partner was getting laid by someone who wanted her to give up her career.

Punk groups like The Plastics were the new wave. They rejected surf music and golden oldie rock. Their music was surreal and subreal. It had fun with harmonics and hypnotics. It had a new range with banshee and pop tones. It combined an exotic dub dance pulse with pulsar wails and apocalypse tones and a great prose vocal. It was electronic software music, not hard-core disco, but slightly funked with a monothump hypno-beat. It was filled with frippertonic loops that were originally performed at a planetarium. This new funk-a-matic format rising in intensity, which was cool, made use of subdisco footage but now had a mean cleanness, and was music designed for passive listening, which allowed for the option of active listening without demanding it. It was what he was into also. Eno and Blondie, The Talking Heads and The Plastics were all now using long tones like himself, experimenting with modulating waves of upward mobility. Shit! He had tried that years ago. What was coming in was Sistine Chapel Muzak, holy tones, tonically conversing in a quiet and formal manner, featuring perpetuality splitting into different tones, sometimes in sync and sometimes with unilateral variations. Rock had shifted into cosmic tones with existential lyrics. It was as if Camus' actual voice was coming across the air and was influencing the messages and the lyrics. Music had changed to songs with confessional tales of lifelong alienation. Nick thought about these things. They depressed him. Because he was able to do the same thing, only better.

Nick brooded. Winston Tong of Tuxedo Mood sang laments which kept asserting, "It's not my fault, it's not my fault that I'm strange." Disco was now being transformed by cool beat and more messages of optimistic hopelessness. Big deal. Oddball flat funk became riffs revolving into rivulets of high tech funk. He could do that. Only better. A jungle feel collided with space age tech in a dense tropical rainforest which might actually be plastic and riddled with fake insect and bird noise, the roar of space shuttles and other horrifying apparatus. In this new music, voices entered, discussed the facts of love, and levitated the hell out of there. Lyrics now discussed love and no hope, machines and mutant plants took over, and the remaining human voices were echoing laments like unenergized ghosts singing back up. The new music blocked out emotion and everything began to take place in note plunks out of clock time in rapid rhythm attacks that were shockingly cool. The new music had rhythm sections playing along at a disco pace, but the feel was now heavy industrial overkill with the disco thump seeming to be less of a heartbeat than a machine tool stamper in Detroit. He thought about this. New instrumentals such as Eno's *No Pussyfooting* album were more into discotronics, in fact discotronics were becoming the combination of disco and frippertonics created specifically by Robert Fripp and his small mobile and appropriate technology, the Frippelboard and two Revoxes. Disco was being throttled to a slurring halt by neoclassical chamber pieces with sedate existentialist lyrics sending people into space. Dimani knew that disco was being replaced by space shuttle dirges with guitar grooves and a Sartre-Brecht beat, the mischievous skulk of the synthesizer, and high tech.

Fuck all that, Dimani thought. 1981 was going to be the year in which America listened, spellbound, to his new music, to Dimani and Lundholm, to electronic rhythm sections which created a different kind of energy, a toned-down series of biorhythms which were written by the new Nick Dimani and Sylvia Lundholm.

Yes, America was the culture of the *new.* Yes, America chewed up its greatest artists and spat them out. Well, they weren't going to spit out Nick Dimani. He wasn't finished. 1981 was going to be *his* year. If only Sylvia would give him the words. If only she would give him his new album and deliver him from evil.

2. *Porsche Driving*

NICK DIMANI drove his sleek new black Porsche through paradise. Yes, he drove through Tahoe, over the snow-covered summits, around the mountains and winding snow routes. The trees, mostly gigantic tamaracks, were covered with brilliant white snow clusters. In spite of people's attempts to destroy the Sierras, a few special places remained. The Tahoe Basin was such a place. The alpine lilies which shot up in the summer and covered the California and Nevada mountains were under the snow. He loved playing Tahoe. On the 8-track stereo tape in his car was Grover Washington blowing sax. The music, as always, was loud and wound out of his ear and through the mountain like a huge scarf of sound wrapping the lakes, Highway 89, and Emerald Bay in its sound. It was not quite nightfall. The lake gave a perfect mirror image of the snowy Sierras and trees. It was as if the world were reflected perfectly in the deep lake, a lake so cold that when people drowned, no one ever rose to the top. Dimani

raced his car over Mount Tellac, named from the Washo Indian word *tellec,* meaning "great mountain."

Tahoe has a split personality. Its region is divided into two sides, the Nevada side and the California side. On the Nevada side, all the action takes place. That's where the big casinos jut out of the mountains like baby fortresses made of brick and neon and glass. Within the fortress, behind the walls of the fort, a royalty of green felt and numbers secretly exists, knights of the gambling table win and lose and pass the time in a dimension made possible by the royal games. He arrived at the hotel and a valet parking attendant took his car.

"Good evening, Mr. Dimani," the boy said respectfully. "Would you mind giving me your autograph for my sister?"

Nick smiled. "Sure," he said. "What's her name?"

"Sue."

Nick took out his Tiffany ballpoint pen and lifted a publicity sheet from the dashboard. On the sheet was his photograph. He looked ten years younger. He always looked ten years younger in every publicity shot. It was as if his public self were always ten years behind who he really was. "To Sue. Go the distance," he wrote. He always wrote that.

Nick got out of the car. He was wearing his ski pants and a tight white turtleneck, and he strode into the men's room at Harrah's. He took out a vial and his silver spoon and snorted the white powder into his nostril. Suddenly he was lifted as if by helium out of the men's room and onto the floor of his own life. Within minutes he was walking around the casino. Cocaine made him feel good. Made changes in his head. It was as if he had six nostrils and they all felt good. Radiant. Now get thee to a phone, he said to himself. He would be his zany, uninhibited, penetrating, satirical self and nobody, not even his partner, could resist him. He would lay out reality, let her know how much she was needed. He would say it with love, "One more album, Sylvia."

And then he would describe to her *Playing Tahoe,* the album he was composing. "It will be about men and women and the winter snows. It will be about mountains. And standing alone on top of the world. It will be about Tahoe. And nothing on earth will be like it. A new album. About the height of things. An album that will tell the world about how love appears and disappears." And Sylvia, the great poet, would know how to write these things, to say them in a way that everyone would be moved by. She could take his ideas and make them into songs. She could do this because she was some kind of miraculous angel. She was a miracle-maker. "Please God, make her write for me," Nick said to himself. "One last time, God."

When he got to his room, he picked up the phone. "Give me area code two-one-two and thank you, Jellybean," he said to the operator at Harrah's. "Thank you sweetheart." Everyone loved Nick Dimani in Tahoe. Everyone was his *sweetheart.* Sweetness and jellybeans. He could get anyone to shuffle by calling her sweetheart. He would project his voice into the remote island of Manhattan where Sylvia lived in her penthouse. He knew he could move her. Her flaw was loyalty. Also, she was maternal. Perhaps he could get her, one last time, to pity him. She might still be his cosmic angel. One more time.

He dialed. "Hello sweetheart," he said into the white plastic telephone, desperately trying to cram charm into that equipment, talk into that plastic phone that connected the high Sierras to New York City; he held on to her through the digital life-line.

3. *Lamborghini Blues*

WHEN REV met Sylvia, sitting at the bar in Melon's, a hang-out on East Seventy-third Street, her first words to him were, "I'm a rock poet."

"Don't give me your credits; I'm not in show business," he said. He wasn't impressed.

"What business are you in?"

"Transportation." As they left, he puffed on a joint. "Want one?"

"No thanks."

"You should try it. You'd like it," he said.

"I've tried it. I've tried everything," she said.

Walking down the street, he talked to her only about cars. Later, to amuse herself, Sylvia wrote his portrait: America, land of the car, speed land, sedan land, America, built on legs that became wheels by Ford, Chevrolet, Chrysler, America crisscrossed by Airflow, scarred by Imperial Eights, Phaetons, Nomads, Club Coupes, Pickups, Impalas, Camaros, and Corvairs, America, world of the automatic transmission, front-wheel-drive world, Packard-with-a-swan world—you, America, created a guy called Revson Cranwell. He was born in you, coming out of his mother's stick-shift womb with a steering wheel in one hand. He cried oil, howled gasoline, burped tires, crawled to play with expensive engine toys. And at the age of enlightenment (sixteen), got his driver's license in California: a blond Buddha on wheels. She read the portrait to Rev when she saw him again, just for fun.

"That's you," she said.

"Yeah?"

"You like it?"

They were driving in her Lamborghini.

"Don't be so intellectual," he said in his bored, flat voice.

A week later they were driving on the Long Island Expressway. Rev combed his hair in a blond pompadour, nonchalantly fluffed over his forehead, the ideal model of what a pompadour should be. In the car mirror, he could see without a particle of dust or roughness, and with the most beautiful reflections, his black Carrera Porsche sunglasses. Driving with a fluid grace such as drunken men do not ever possess, he handled her Lamborghini as an instrument of precision. His aristocratic hands had calluses on them and he didn't wear driving gloves. As he drove, he felt slightly intoxicated, a con man with his girl, out for the afternoon. They were speeding to New York from Southampton. He was driving her red Lamborghini at a not-give-a-shit eighty miles an hour. The radio played Dion Dimucci.

"Get rid of Nick. He's a creep," Rev said in that cool Wasp voice that he reserved for people he didn't like. He eased the Lamborghini into ninety.

"Why?"

"Why not? You're the genius, not Nick. Whadya need him for? Haven't you had enough of that guy? You can make up the music yourself. What's the big deal? He's a has-been. You have a young head, Sylvia. There are plenty of other musicians to collaborate with. Get that girl Tina Weymouth from The Talking Heads. Write songs with her."

"I can't."

"Why not?"

"Don't be crazy, Rev. I write with Nick. He's my partner."

"So? You're not married to him. He's a creep. Go on to the next."

"I can't just dump him."

"Why not? He'd dump you when he wants to."

"Loyalty. He's my partner. We've worked together for over twenty years."

"Don't be so charitable. Dimani's not loyal to anyone. He's a snake. If it wasn't for your lyrics, he'd be nowhere. His music isn't hot anymore. His head isn't where yours is. I'm telling you, you can find some other patent-leather boob to work with. You don't have a contract with him. Find someone else."

"Who?"

"Paul McCartney. See if he's available. Start at the top. Trade up, not down."

"Paul McCartney? Are you kidding? You're talking like

a civilian. Rev, I have to tell you something. When I'm with you, I realize how tired I am of the business. Sometimes, writing out my guts is like the drudgery of a day in school. What if I stopped writing and just devoted my life to you?" She laughed. "What if I gave up working?"

"Sounds good, but you couldn't afford me," Rev said. "I don't come cheap."

"What do you want?"

"Toys," he said in that bored voice. She didn't know him well enough to tell if he was serious or joking. "A Riva. It's the fastest speedboat. Made in Italy. Costs half a mil. Race cars. *Two* white Excaliburs, in case one breaks down. A staff of twelve mechanics to travel around the country, and just the maintenance of that is about a mil a year. Not to mention a thousand dollars in my pocket every week for spending money. I could be very expensive. You better stick to writing songs. But not with Nick. Find someone else." He was really speeding now. And laughing.

What did Sylvia know about Rev? Nothing. He loved cars and motorcycles. He looked like he belonged in the fifties, a rebel without a cause. He was supposed to come from an old rich Philadelphia family, which in itself lent his figure of a "street person" a certain absurd charm. He always appeared in a succession of blue-collar costumes, snow-white garage-mechanic jumpsuits, ancient jeans, imitation black leather pants and jackets, a red plastic belt, a full-dress teddy-boy uniform, and yes, the complications of true origins were audacious, adventurous, and risqué by turns. But he never managed to look like a street person. He always looked like a gentleman or a prince who was slumming. His class followed him the way a scent follows a dangerous animal. You could smell that Rev Cranwell came out of a monied and aristocratic background. The more he denied it, the more you heard it and smelled it. Part snob, part thug, he was extremely careful and capable. He was a mystery. Sylvia thought about him all the time.

His sense of humor touched her. He laughed a great deal. Nobody knew who he really *was* and he seemed indeed not to belong to the world of the very rich, but to be an alien blond gigolo or a well-born con man who now lived in the world of cheeseburgers and used cars in the Bronx. He came on like a gigolo, an expensive stud who wasn't pushing, just suggesting, underselling himself the way a great salesman does, but Sylvia knew that he was a smart cookie with the staggering fluid grace that only great con men possess. He was beautiful to look at. His head seemed to be sculpted by a Greek artisan striving for perfection. He was thin and six foot three with bronzed golden skin, and thin little gold hairs all over his arms, thick tufts of blond hair on his chest, and around his god-like neck was a thin gold chain with the Mayan calendar sign. It was as if he had once been a Mayan god and stepped out of the sun. His looks dazzled her. She had to blink because she had never seen a man so externally and internally beautiful. When he spoke, there was wit and dry intelligence. Later, when he loved, he knew every trick in the book. She marveled at the way he made her feel. He conjured up her most secret feelings of trust and sensuality. Nothing about him was false. Or everything about him was false. He was so beautiful to look at she didn't care. His voice was what she loved most of all. It was flat and bored, but it had a certain cool hijack-proof authority.

Rev Cranwell, who was he? He was aloof, alienated. He had more masculine strength than any man she'd ever known, and yet he didn't fit in anywhere. He was just a little too charming, a little too distant, and a little too educated to totally bring off his tough-guy image. The backs of his hands were white as milk, but the palms of his hands were strong and rough, so that even his hands, which she loved so much, were a contradiction. When they were alone, he was cool and yet affectionate. He was like the new music Nick was so afraid of. He was kind to Sylvia in a way that was private and almost touching. His normal mask was aloofness. But they were plugged into each other the way a fuse is plugged into an electric receptacle. He was the wall. She was the fuse. They were electrically attracted.

To Sylvia, Rev was perfect and always would be. Because he did not belong to her world or any other world. And in some way she knew he would never belong to her. And so she wanted him. Because she couldn't ever have him and they both knew it and laughed. How long they would be together never came up. She loved his blue eyes and his graceful way of moving. And so it happened that her desires encountered no serious resistance. In America, the land of deodorant, where the rich and the poor smelled the same, no one could sniff out who Rev really was. But she intuited everything about him, electrically connected to him from the second she saw him, the way one always is to a lasting friend. He was a prince who sold cars at First Olds in the Bronx, telephone number 299-6600, and all her sorrow was forgotten.

And now, Sylvia, seated next to her new buddy in her red Lamborghini, was hearing Rev give Nick the ax. And she agreed with him. Whatever he said, she now agreed with. Not because she was a yes-woman. She was *hardly* that. But because, quite simply, from the very beginning, before he even made love to her, Rev Cranwell had changed her life. When he met her, a few months before, she had been what Nick constantly called *neurotic furniture.* She was going through the zigzag of growing older, wondering if she was still attractive.

"Stop that self-pity," Rev said. He didn't like her when she wasn't tough and cheerful and laughing. He laughed at her. "You're not old. You're still sexy. A lot of women in their forties are sexy. Who's that woman, the speedboat champion? Betty something? She's hot. The sexiest woman in America. For God's sake, you're not old, Sylvia. *Stop that.*"

That weekend they had made love for the first time. She

had come alive and afterward, it was as if they were mag-
netized. The white scottie and the black scottie on the mag-
nets she had when she was a little girl. She was hot and he
was cold. She played with the scottie image in her fantasies. Whenever they were together, which was quite often,
she had taken a lot of Rev's practical advice. He was king
of common sense and he had a sense of humor. Whatever
he said made her laugh. He liked to nuzzle in her own
blond hair which she wore in a carefree, tomboyish shag.
She was hot. She turned him on. And now they were
speeding and he was telling her to jap Nick Dimani. It all
filtered through Sylvia's mind quickly like a million light-
year shadows, an invasion of thoughts and questions.
Some people said she was the brains behind Nick Dimani,
but she denied it. He was her collaborator, her partner.
She: words. He: music. But now it was going to be what
Rev Cranwell wanted. All over. Rev was her music. She
thought about him now, not her career. She could afford
to, after all those years, she could finally afford to love
somebody. New things were happening to her. She was
beginning to spend all her time now at the Pierson's Swedish Book Nook in the East Eighties where she ferreted out
all the Swedish poetry in her father's language, the language she loved. She would read Swedish poetry now. She
would bury herself in Swedish sagas. She would read
about Queen Christina and Gustavas Adolphus. She
would read Swedish history, Swedish poetry, Swedish
sagas. With Revson she always had peace, and when she
wasn't with him, she had that solitude that she had never
had while she was creating her career with Nick.

Now, she didn't have to think about herself. She could
allow herself this secret and delicious reverie of daydreaming about Revson. She could imagine his rough hands running up and down her body exciting her in a way that she
had never been excited before. He was her drug and yet
he made her feel stable in a way that Nick Dimani could
never understand in his quest to make them both air-

borne. She had shaken hands with the heavens long enough. Rev was real and he had qualities that made her feel safe. He was honest about being a con man. He never gossiped. He always told the truth. He was punctual, reliable. He was careful about everything. Almost too careful. She could rely on his word and on him. She didn't mind if he didn't really talk very much or if when he did, he spoke very slowly. He belonged nowhere. He was a free soul who would never belong to her, but she grasped onto him from the moment he drifted into her life. She couldn't imagine life without him.

They were speeding out of Southampton, where she kept her summer house open even in the winter. She could see his perfect face in the mirror as they drove on the Expressway. A slight flurry of snow fell on the red Lamborghini. For once, there was little traffic.

She was in love. He wasn't.

"Don't be stupid," Rev would laugh, "there's no such thing as love. We have a good *working* relationship. Don't make a big deal out of it."

"I love you, Rev," she would say. He made it into a joke.

"I don't want to become involved. Don't make a big deal."

She got the picture. But who *was* Rev Cranwell? Was she shaking hands with an angel or a devil? There was always a trace of the Philadelphia mainline background in his speech. There was in him the gentile coldness of the snobbish proper Cranwells that he rebelled against and tried to erase. His family were cousins to the Boston Brahmin Cranwells and the Palm Beach Cranwells, the Peabodys and the Saltonstalls (weren't they all *related?*). There was no trace of the bad boy, the black sheep of the Cranwell family who was now a car salesman but who had been everything else in his short span of thirty-four years driving around the planet Earth, eating junk food, saying "How ya doin?" and sitting in bars waiting for a pickup with big boobs. There was no trace of the young prince who would one day inherit if not the earth, well then a few million bucks, an estate outside Boca Raton for polo, a house in Palm Beach, a landmark "cottage" in Northeast Harbor, and his grandmother's perfectly maintained red 1929 Essex Speedabout.

She liked him instantly. She'd never liked anyone the way she liked him. She liked him in that way that had meaning, the way a forty-year old woman who has been through every dialogue, every scene and every song, every impressive seating arrangement, but never found the right man or the right seat, could like someone new. She was a Swedish fuckup. This was her last chance for what she laughingly called "a relationship." Indeed, he did not belong to this world. He lived on the edge. But then, so did she.

"So what's happening?" he asked as they were nearing New York.

"What do you mean?"

"Are you getting rid of him?"

"Who?"

"Dimani."

"I have to go out to Tahoe to help him with this last album. I want you to come with me, Rev. Don't worry. I'll pay for everything. Nick will pay. He's writing a new album called *Playing Tahoe*. He needs me. The words. He needs my pain to go with his music."

"If you help him out one more time, he's going to hate you."

"He's always hated me. In the industry, you don't have to go very far under love to find a song of hate. Hate is like a graduation certificate. Everyone hates everyone. I don't understand why. I don't hate anybody. I love flowers. I love my friends. I love men. I love children. I love old people. I was with a composer yesterday and I wrote a lyric for him to help him get a gig and he was so grateful. But I was more grateful than he because I was so happy to help him. I don't envy anybody. Because you can't really steal anything from anybody. Nothing is ever really yours and nothing is ever really lost. All that I know is I am who I am and nobody is going to give me a key to another cupboard. My key only opens up myself. And on this shelf, there's always the same thing, Sylvia Lundholm, with every day of her life piled neatly in a row, like Swedish sweaters, one on top of the other. Still hanging in, but still suffering."

"Stop suffering," he said. "There's no percentage. It doesn't pay off."

He kept his eyes on the road. He was born driving. His concentration and ease in the car excited her. She remembered how bad she wanted him the first time. She never needed to make love like this, never needed to make anyone want her as much as she wanted Rev to want her. The excitement that she felt when she touched his golden hair was more than she could bear. The first night they had made love, she remembered, she had fed him dinner. She had eased him into her bedroom where the huge television was. She lit some scented Swedish candles that she had found in a Swedish pot-pourri shop, and she watched him lie down on the bed. She lay down next to him as he watched television. Slowly she began holding him. Suddenly, like a panther, he grabbed her mouth. He pressed his lips against hers and sucked her mouth into his. He held her with a strength she had never felt before. He began ripping her clothes off on the bed. He tore her sweater off and began sucking her breasts. He buried his mouth on her breasts until the nipples ached and he bit her as if he were going to devour her. His hand reached down between her legs. "Not so hard," she whispered. He didn't hear her. He ripped off his sweater and jeans. She felt suddenly as if she were with a wild animal. His cock was enormous and he came into her with a power she had not known, ever.

"Rev, you're hurting me." She couldn't speak. She suddenly no longer had a voice or even a body. He was taking her life away. Eating her up. She looked at his face and saw in it only the wildness of a feline animal. Her body shook. He was going to fuck her to death. He came inside of her like a force and she gave herself to him completely. She could feel his life, his body, his weight. She had quite simply never experienced sex like this. It hurt to have him inside of her because he was shaking loose her life-lines. He was taking everything inside her and breaking her apart. It was the first time she had allowed herself to be totally taken out of herself. She felt his body and her body almost vibrating. It was as if together, they were lifted to another place, levitating to another place where bodies could melt. His cock felt as if it were made out of hard rock. It knocked against her. He was stoning her with his cock. He was tearing her apart and making her new. She felt he was breaking her body. And at the same time that she felt this, she felt his arms supporting her. They were rocking together. Slowly she came and then she fell back on the bed. He began kissing her head, her hair, and her arms. She had never imagined that he would be as passionate as he was. The man that was so aloof when he was with her was a great lover. She shook afterward. And wept.

"It's good," she said softly.

"Thanks," he said. He lay back and watched the images on the screen. She lay close to him. And found herself feeling *whole* for the first time in her life.

4. *What's the Deal?*

IT WAS raining in the Bronx. Rain came down on the lots of used cars, falling over the lonely automobiles whose faces were chalked, like ancient whores, with white chalk marks, their prices showing. On the rainy dirt streets, covering their heads with newspapers, were the derelicts, the people with angry faces whose frustration and reduced humanity came running out of their eyes and noses like mucus. It was the Jerome Avenue world of old tin lizzies, the beastly babel of motors where the el, a huge machine on stilts, groaned out its great insulting noise. The rain came down.

Rev sat inside the front office, in the showroom. His buddy, John, who worked with him, looked out at the rain. No one bought cars. Especially in the rain. Rev, the blond giant with no emotions, looked at the Cutlass shining on the First Olds showroom floor. "I wish she'd buy me a car," he said to John.

"Who?"

"Sylvia. You know. The woman I sort of go out with. I told ya. I met her at Melon's."

"So what's the deal?" John asked. For John and Rev, everything was a deal. Rev had just given up Carltons and played nervously with a pencil on the table where his order book was open in case some dude with a few thousand dollars or some credit came looking for a fully packed Oldsmobile on Jerome Avenue. The rain stopped.

"What's the story?" John repeated.

"It's not breathtaking," Rev said in his calmed-down voice, the words coming slowly out of his mouth.

"I thought you liked her."

"I do."

"What's the deal?"

Rev looked out at the ghetto characters, sniffing glue and walking nowhere special, poor blacks who got caught in the rain. Some cars passed by his vision, banged-up joy wagons that once were sweet rides. "The deal is," he said slowly, "that she has a lot of bread. She's an odd mixture. She's Swedish. Her parents were born in Stockholm. She's thrifty. Another part of her is generous. She gave me a watch from Cartier on the second date."

"What kind of watch?" John asked.

"A Santos. It's being initialed. She's funny. She's hyper and sort of warm-hearted. She is good to people. She has telescope eyes. Big eyes that see everything. Big you know —breasts. She's not as casual as she could be."

"Did you score?"

"Yeah."

"And she's got a lot of bread. You've done worse. Sounds like a good deal."

"I guess. Too bad I don't like show business."

"What's the big deal?"

"I guess there isn't any."

"It sounds like a good deal."

"Yeah. Well, the deal is, we're going to travel together. She wants to take me on a trip. She'll pay for everything."

"Sounds good," John smiled.

Rev and John worked in the Bronx for fun. They loved, in a perverse way, the *poverty* high. There was an energy on Jerome Avenue you couldn't find on the Upper East Side gentile streets where everything was missing a life beat. It wasn't a nitty-gritty place. And the soul was smeared. It shocked his mother in her Philadelphia mainline mind to know that her only son, Revson Cranwell, was selling cars in the Bronx. His mother didn't understand guerrilla energy. She didn't understand ghettos. What she understood was Middleburg, Virginia, Philadelphia, Palm Beach, Northeast Harbor, Fisher's Island, martinis, yacht races, manners, thank-you notes, and horses. She once said to Rev with tears in her eyes something he would never forget. She looked at him and said with the emotions that had gathered ever since her forefathers had demolished the Indians and enriched Philadelphia with horse manure—"You know, Rev, you have no idea the sacrifices I've made for my horses." His mother never rode Oldsmobiles, Trans Ams, Chevies. She rode stallions. She rode thoroughbreds in Virginia. She rode herd over her children. Rode. And asked questions. Over the telephone she asked questions such as, "What do you see in that job as a car salesman?"

And he would answer, "It's a living."

"But Rev, you're so intelligent. You could be doing something else. With all your Geneva and Harvard Business School education."

Into the phone he would say, "I tried that, Mother. I worked on Wall Street."

And she would answer, "But there are so many *undesirables.*"

"Where?"

"In the Bronx, darling. Can't you move into a better set?"

"I like it here."

"On the streets?"

"Yeah. I see tap dancers. Old black vaudevillians challenging each other. People who have nothing better to do than dance."

"Why did you have to be an oddball, darling? Daddy and I still think you're bananas."

"I hope so," he said in that dull, empty voice. The voice with no emotion.

"Can't you be like your sisters and do charity work?"

"No."

"Daddy promised you a 1932 Marmon Convertible Coupe, the kind you wanted, if you would only come back to Philadelphia to spend one summer with him going over important details of the family."

"The family doesn't need me."

"You don't have to put yourself in that jail of the car salesroom."

"I'm a lifer," he said, laughing back at his mother.

For Sylvia, Rev was her sun king, the universe's great mystery, her new heat and life and love. Is the sun pulsating? Dimming? Shrinking? She looked to him as to the upper atmosphere, her helium man, her man whose temperature made him a million degrees and white-hot. She looked to him for her light. He was her new energy. It was more complex than that. Her new love. He was more than even she could say. He was her silence and her new magnetic field. Her corona. She had never felt such energy as she felt with Rev. He was cool. Her electric white man. He was now the world she lived in.

"I love you," she would say. They would be lying on the woolen orange Swedish blanket on her bed. "I can talk so easily to you."

"That's good."

"I can tell you everything. I can spill all the rose petals and thorns and the whole pot-pourri of my imagination and memories out to you, Rev, and we communicate. You rescue me from what I was. It was as if I was drowning, a victim of my own greed and ambition and yes, even my success, and you put your strong arm around my head, you rocked me gently on a wooden rescue board, and you took me ashore, covered me in warmth, and saved my life. We communicate. I often wonder what you and John talk about."

"We don't talk much."

"Don't you communicate?"

"We don't *have* to communicate," he laughed.

"Why not?"

"We just understand each other."

"You mean you share the same interests?"

"We share the same *lack* of interests."

She looked at him.

"Sometimes I think you're crazy," she said.

"I hope so."

5. *Lionel*

WITH HIS deep elegant voice, his dark good looks, his natural power, and his well-informed mind, everyone knew

Lionel Colesman was a tycoon. But the only person Lionel could get to share his monument to himself—his show-place house in East Hampton on West End Road—was Ron Thimble. His house had recently been redecorated with raw silk, blue and yellow furniture. The house looked exactly as it did when it was featured on the cover of *Architectural Digest,* but no one in his family had time or interest to go there. His wife, Karen, an Irish beer heiress with a talent for management, was in the city attending a seminar on Women in Business. Attending? She was leading it. His two teenage girls, who went to Brearley, were going to the Bottom Line to hear the Ramones. His secretary had a cold. And he couldn't get Sylvia Lundholm to join him. She was acting strangely recently and never was available on weekends. That left one person. Ron E. Thimble.

Who was Ron E. Thimble? And what was he? He ministered to the disease of loneliness in rich people the way plastic surgeons ministered to the bags and wrinkles of vain, aging women. Cutting away the wrinkles of loneliness from the lives of the very bored and very overly privileged was Ron's specialty. You could find him among a select circle of people eating lunch at Le Cirque. He would be there—tall, well-dressed, black hair brilliantined back, smiling, his perfect manners and perfect diction charming everyone. He was like the cuckoo who came predictably out of the clock at every hour to make his high-pitched little sound. Every hour Ron could flatter, praise, understand, laugh. Cuckoo! He could quote accurately from *Interview.*

Yes, Ron was a lackey for Lionel. And the rewards? Funding for his entrepreneurial projects—funding—endless funding. A Woolworth or a Mellon here, a Whitney or a Rothschild there, a rich heiress from Monte Carlo, and a prince from Caracas—all friends of Lionel Colesman—these were the social rewards of Ron Thimble's enterprises. His twenty-minute documentary, *The Tantric Mysticism of Tibet,* had won the Locarno Film Festival. He had even been nominated for an Oscar. The nomination meant that funding would be available for the next few years, that invitations would ensure his presence at charity dinners, and that women on Park Avenue whose husbands were away would invite him as a fill-in. As a filmmaker, he liked being seen with the very rich. And the semifamous.

Ron Thimble was not a normal hustler. He was a cultural ornament. He was tall, amusing, and witty and had at least *gone* to Harvard. He referred to most of his friends as "lovey." Unlike most hustlers, he had actually "done something."

"What is he trying to squeeze out of Lionel?" was the question often asked by the envious entrepreneurs in tennis shorts sipping Perrier water at the East Hampton Tennis Club as Ron Thimble sat drinking vodka on the rocks waiting for Lionel to finish his set.

"They are working on a project. Thimble's his house guest," was the reply.

"Another film?"

"Did you see his Tantric documentary?"

"Since when is a hustler into Buddhism?"

"It won some kind of an award. But it was *the pits*."

"Is Thimble a fag?" Perrier gurgled. No one was *sure* what he was.

"He's everything. Right now, his specialty is arranging whatever needs to be arranged for Lionel Colesman."

Actually, unbeknown to the voyeurs at the East Hampton Tennis Club, Thimble was working on a new project with Colesman. He was restless because his feature film was taking a long time to get financed at Paramount. And he had come up with an idea that flattered Colesman. He would create a documentary on the life of Sylvia Lundholm, knowing that Colesman had the hots for Sylvia. They discussed the project that weekend in East Hampton when the leaves were turning and the ocean cast its blue shadow on the empty beach. Birdsong and touristsong had disappeared. The town was empty except for its faithful.

Lionel Colesman, multimillionaire, sat in the house that his wife's money had bought, surrounded by butlers and maids, beautiful antique Georgian furniture, and modern art. Acrylic paintings by Helen Frankenthaler, Jules Olitski, Picasso, Kenneth Noland, and Ellsworth Kelly floated on the walls. Amid the strains of *Don Giovanni,* amid the huge jungle plants from Kind and Company, amid the tinkling glasses filled with the best champagne from Sherry-Lehmann's cellar, he talked with his buddy, Ron.

"I think she's a modern *heroine.* I like the idea, Ron. I *really* do."

The truth was, Lionel was desperate for company. What was the point of having this masterpiece of architecture, this status symbol near the Juan Trippe house on the ocean if nobody came to visit? What was the point of a *showplace* if nobody showed? "It's too much *house,*" his wife had said over *The Wall Street Journal* at breakfast in her lovely and lilting Irish voice so capable of meaningless cruelty.

"Believe me," Lionel answered, "everyone will beg for an invitation." (Why was he *always* wrong lately?)

"Not in the fall. Everyone's busy. Besides, it's too long a drive."

"In a chauffeured car?" Lionel asked dryly. Yes, he adored her in a financially sound way.

"Take Ron Thimble. He is a yes-man," she had suggested. And he did.

As Thimble and Colesman sat there looking at the ocean from the raw silk sofas, listening vaguely to Mozart as if it were Muzak, Lionel considered the mess he had made of his life. Financially lucky, he had married a young heiress after his first divorce and went immediately into the world he always wanted, a world of multimedia, records, real estate, transportation, and commodity trading. The commodities and real estate weren't glamorous, but they were profitable. They paid for the "glamour" businesses. If you owned stock in Colesman Enterprises, you not only owned

Nick Dimani and Sylvia Lundholm, you owned a shopping mall in Palm Beach, a fuel silo in Iowa, a meat-processing plant in Australia, a burgeoning domestic airline in Tampa, a gasohol enterprise in Nevada, a utilities company in the Northeast, and investments in certain nuclear industries which now had been erased from the annual report since many of the artists he owned under the Mecca label were helping to organize no-nuke rock concerts (for public-relations purposes some things had to be disguised). Oh yes, he owned a lot of commodities, a lot of capital. Gold bricks sat waiting for him in banks all over the world like silent yellow paperweights. They were piles of his wife's affection. But Lionel Colesman did not own the souls of his wife and children. They were not loving to him. "They piss me off," he admitted. He and his wife slept mostly in separate households. What bothered him was that his children were indifferent to him. They laughed at him. He thought of this looking at the ocean. He and Thimble were locked together in mutual need.

"I'm going to Tahoe," Colesman said.

"Super," said Thimble. You could always count on Ron for enthusiasm.

"Dimani and Lundholm are going to make an independent record for Arthur Morris. I don't think that's a good idea."

"Is it in their contract?" Thimble asked. He helped himself to sugared walnuts from a silver dish and drank Lionel's Dom Perignon in slow sips, savoring the rim of the iced goblet.

"Yes. The contract was written so that Dimani could go independent whenever he wanted. But whoever thought he'd *want* to. He's got leverage. My lawyer, Lavits, couldn't do anything. Now he's writing an album called *Playing Tahoe*. But he wants Morris to produce it independently."

"Can you talk him out of it?"

"That's what I'm going to try to do. I'm going to Tahoe. Why don't you come?"

"I'd love to, lovey," Thimble said. That was all Lionel

wanted. The purpose of this weekend was to assure himself of no loneliness out West. Loneliness in the East was bad enough, but out West it was unbearable. He couldn't take the Sierras by himself. The Sierras gave Lionel a renewed case of anxiety.

"You'll come?" With all his business smarts and millions, tycoonery had not kept Lionel from attacks of self-pity and insecurity.

"Yes."

It was then that he had allowed Thimble to make love to him. "Do it," he said to Thimble. Thimble obeyed like a faithful servant, which, in a way, was what he was to Lionel Colesman. And so it happened that Lionel, the aging billionaire boy who once read T. S. Eliot and now read *The Wall Street Journal* and *Cash Box,* sat in his home on the ocean thinking of Tahoe, while Ron Thimble administered to his sexual needs. Tahoe? He was glad Thimble was coming along. Sylvia. Would she be there? Ah, yes, Sylvia.

6. *Revson*

WHEN THEY met, he sold Oldsmobiles. He had a card that said, "Rev Cranwell. First Olds." Sylvia met him by accident just before going to Tahoe. Before the new year of 1980. He came into town. Found a job through *The New York Times.* Selling cars in the Bronx at First Olds. For her, Rev Cranwell had carried absurd logic to its conclusion. He had a total absence of hope. That's why he sold cars in the Bronx. Or moved around the country. Unlike most Americans, he wasn't ambitious. He didn't want to get ahead. He didn't want a career. He thought all of that was absurd.

"Don't ever give me your credits," he said, laughing. He

meant it. He was an existentialist in his own way. *Fame*
bored him. *Why bother?* He didn't give a fuck if she was
famous. He liked her. And he liked to laugh with her. He
liked her body. His own was in good shape. And that's
what interested him most in Sylvia. Large breasts. A good
sense of humor. And a certain emotional craziness. He was
attracted to high-strung passionate women, whacky nuts
like Sylvia, who were wild and hyper and nervous and
emotional. They made up for his lack of emotional flair.
His own life was cool, it was a continual rejection of has-
sles, emotional ties, disturbances. He owned nothing but a
car, a white beaten-up callously painted old Eldorado Cadillac convertible. A small wardrobe. And a toothbrush. He
had a passion for cars. And boats. He bought *Yachting*
magazine and *Road and Track* whenever a new one came
out on the newsstand. He rejected *anxiety*. Had no guilts.
Was oddly cut off. A loner who accepted love and money
from others. But a man without *feelings*, without any emotional connections. And he had no *need* to own anything
for the moment. He liked toys. Powerboats and cars. He
liked movement. He liked some people. And he didn't
bother with assholes. If he was your friend, he was your
life buddy. But he didn't want anyone's friendship. He was
electric. At least to Sylvia. He visited her dreams.

From the moment she saw him at the bar in Melon's,
she was fascinated. Whatever that meant. Because she was
his, she wasn't his. He didn't want to own her. And so he
did. He set her straight from the beginning. "You're not
my type. I like short, dark women. But I like you." The
absurdity of that turned her on. The fact was, she didn't
want to be anyone's type. Not anymore. She no longer
believed in marriage. She was having a nervous breakup.
Or breakdown. She was in a life change. Carrying logic to
its conclusion, she wanted to detour from the direct path.
And Rev met her at that time. She had tried to discover
meaning in Swedish transcendentalism, then mysticism,
then analysis. And had found none. The only thing that

remained was her kinesthesiologist, her muscle doctor who understood the body's behavior through muscles. Then, when she was almost forty, when she was most vulnerable, Rev came along by accident. The kinesthesiologist said that Rev had seemed to take away her nervous condition. After meeting him she was suddenly peaceful. "He has given you strength and calm," the doctor said. Was his *confidence* and *cool* a virus she had caught? The masseur told her, after she met Rev Cranwell, that her body had changed. He was the antidote to all those years of straining for fame; he was her medicine man. Her tranquilizer. Her "upper" and "downer." She loved him beyond any wisdom.

7. Permissions

"GOOD MORNING, Mr. Morris's office," a voice said on the phone.

A soft frantic voice said, "Is Peter there?"

"Peter who?" the secretary said. Was *she* kidding? There was only one Peter. A disgusted sigh. Peter was always impossible to find. That was the name of the game. Finding Peter. It was always a search.

"Is Peter Hampton there?" the sexy, dark-haired girl, dressed in a white sweater, white pants, and white cowboy boots asked. She was holding the phone with one hand and drying her artificial nails with her free hand. She had just had long red false nails applied at Dinmar, the beauty parlor on Sixty-fifth Street across from Le Cirque. She was making a call that would set up her evening. "Is he *there?*" She paused for a moment. "This is his *girlfriend,* Barbara. I'll hold." She was often on hold.

The real Peter Hampton, rock star, crossed his long

denim-covered legs in Arthur Morris's office. He was in
the office of the Chief Guru. He was in the Cedar Communications building located at Rockefeller Center. Morris's office was decorated in perfect Cedar taste. There
were couches, expensive paintings. Yes, it was decorated
in Cedar Communications homelife. That was this year's
style at Cedar. Everything in your office was supposed to
look like it did in your home. Providing, of course, that
your own home was worth over a million dollars. And
Arthur Morris's home was. Both his homes. His home in
the Hamptons and his home on Park Avenue. They were
both beautiful and had been decorated by his lovely young
French wife, who was an interior designer. Now, he sat
there in his huge office listening to the new Nick Dimani
tapes.

"What do you think, hey Peter?"

"I'm jealous," Hampton said. And he laughed.

The secretary came in. "Mr. Hampton, a Barbara is on
the phone. Says she's your girlfriend."

"I'm not here," Hampton said softly. The secretary re-
treated like a whooping crane back to her own exotic and
mysterious nest filled with blue telephones instead of blue
eggs. "What's up?"

Morris was enthusiastic as usual. "I'll tell you what's up,"
he said. "I'm producing the new Dylan album and I'm
crazy about these Dimani tapes. Listen." He played the
tapes. His enthusiasm was that of a child. The sound was
muted.

"How'd he ever get started?" Hampton asked, while the
tapes played.

Morris's mind always was a file cabinet of detail. "Dimani
started writing music for black artists in the fifties. Hooked
up with a young girl from a rich Swedish family who wrote
great lyrics, Sylvia Lundholm. Rhythm and blues stuff.
Then rock and roll. All kinds of music. Her words were
unusual. Their big pop number was 'White Trash.' At
first, they worked in the Brill Building. Then Columbia

signed them. Later, Lionel Colesman bought up the whole
Nick Dimani/Sylvia Lundholm catalogue for twenty million bucks."

"I grew up on their songs," Peter Hampton said without
jealousy, but wistfully. Dimani was his idol. "I used to love
them. All the rhythm and blues artists of my generation
did. What's this *new* music?" Hampton asked. "It doesn't
sound at all like Dimani. It sounds too quadraphonic. Too
laid-back and surreal."

"That's what I like. It's a *breakthrough*. It's going to be on
the new album he wants to make. Lundholm hasn't laid
down the lyrics yet. Nick always starts with the sound and
Lundholm writes the lyrics later. Can you believe it—
they've been together over twenty years."

"I heard they're having problems."

"Who *isn't* in this business? Listen, the Dimani/
Lundholm style is always unique. They write together.
Publish together. Produce together. They've been able to
create and maintain over the years a loyal group of fans
that includes every market. The youth audience, the soft
rock audience, pop, disco, the country kids who smoke
dope and get off on the black subculture, the guys in pink
and green suburban jackets who like middle-of-the-road.
Their wives in beehive hairdos. All of them still flock to
hear Nick perform wherever he goes. And now he's going
for the new wave, the same audience that buys The Talking Heads, the B-52's, and The Plastics. He has fans of
every generation. He really crosses over. You should see
how Dimani sells in *Japan*."

"This new sound blows me away. It's so different from
what he used to write."

"That's why I love it. Look at Dylan. The melodic
changes and new harmonics of the last album. It seems to
borrow from everything—from Gregorian chants and in
some way even from seventeenth-century baroque music.
That's what makes him Dylan. He grows and changes.
Same thing with Dimani. When I first met Nick, he was an

energetic kid from Brooklyn like all of us. In love with the whole black culture. The rhythm and blues artists. Melodic blues. Even though he was white, Nick at that time identified totally with the blacks. He moved through a night world populated by jazzmen, hipsters, and other stylish, creative, economically marginal types. He spoke their language. So did I. We were all oddballs. We were considered crazy. Then, he met a rich girl from Sarah Lawrence. A skinny tall blond with huge eyes that were frightened. It was Lundholm. Those two kids used to crawl in the black ghetto. Listen to bebop and early rock and roll. And write together.

"You could find both of them, two kids, devoting themselves to studying jazz. God, those were the last days of the great bebop saxophonists. Guys like Dexter Gordon and Wardell Gray."

"Yeah."

"We all grew up at the Apollo listening to the Ravens. Yeah. To Jimmy Ricks. Those were the days."

"Now what?"

"Dimani is a genius. This is *new stuff*. He is creating an album called *Playing Tahoe*. That's what these tapes are. He wants to write a new kind of nature-covered soul with Lundholm, a combination of The Plastics' high tech and ecology. Sound nuts? Just like Dylan found Jesus, Nick found nature. It may sound simplistic, but so what? I think it will go over with the granola and vitamin-pill set. I think it will sell. Western soul. It's interesting. I want to play it for Richmond."

Morris, the Merlin of music, was about to go into his act. Hampton disappeared from Morris's office like a rabbit dropping out of a hat, a frightened rabbit, mobbed by hundreds of young women outside the entrance to Cedar Communications, who had heard he was there and tried to catch him. As Hampton left, tapes in hand, Morris moved magically to another part of Cedar. He was now in the office of his old partner from Dune Records, Richmond Schneider. If Morris was the magician of the industry, Schneider was its hypnotist. They were both part of the same mind-reading act. They could spot talent in its mother's womb. They had sold coal to Newcastle so many times that Cedar had bought their act and now kept their wisdom immured in their Rockefeller Center building. Morris and Schneider: the Arthur and Richmond Show. They were the industry's two greatest entrepreneurs. They were, indeed, the proven white genies; they could really shuffle. Dune Records had proven that they could sell black to the whites, or, as things had turned around now in the industry, white to the Blacks. They invented crossover. Quite an act. They gave you the permissions. They had the ears. Ears were power. They were the kings of soul and what sold. Corporate king-pins with sleight-of-hand and illusions.

Schneider's office was also designed in Cedar homelife. Schneider's beautiful wife, like Arthur's, was *also* an interior designer. Only she was Venezuelan, not French. Waiting to hear the new Dimani tapes, the Great Richmond stood in front of a huge Jasper Johns target painting. Jasper Johns' targets were the logos for the nineteen-seventies. Schneider would soon have to remove the pop art and redo his office in nineteen-eighties chic. But no one knew what that *was* yet. So the $500,000 targets remained as his backdrop. Richmond, a bearded legend with an Oxford accent, dry wit, and sensual charm, stood patiently waiting in front of his quadraphonic sound system for his old magic partner from Dune Records, Arthur Morris, to appear. Inside the art-filled pop-art office, a cassette played. A cassette *always* played. It was the heartbeat of Cedar Communications. Tape was the bandage and suture of communications. The winding sheet of America was in *tape*. And the cassette was the heart of America. Schneider and Morris and Dimani and Lundholm were all bound to each other on eight-inch reel-to-reel tape. The philosophical question of the nineteen-seventies was not, "To be or not to be?" but "Is it on cassette, or reel to reel?" Everything worth living, worth keeping, was on cassette or reel to reel. Nobody made *records* anymore. They scratched. Nobody played twelve-bar blues. Nobody identified themselves with the black subculture. Except the Cherokee Indians. Thanks to the Richmond and Arthur Show, black and white lifestyle had crossed over so many times it was confusing. According to Arthur, America in the eighties was going into nature, into cool. Dropping acid rock, disco, and The Bee-Gees. And that's what Arthur the Brooklyn prophet wanted to tell Richmond, the prophet. It was all about profit. They couldn't sign Bruce Springsteen. But they *could* sign Dylan. And Dimani. *Only great magicians could pull hits* out of nowhere. *Singles* were not miracles. They were all part of the magical act.

"I have the new Dimani tapes," Arthur said.

"I'm not really dying to hear them," Schneider remarked.

"You will be impressed," Morris shot back. "I want you to listen to them."

"Leave them on my desk. I'll take them home," Schneider said without enthusiasm.

"Good. I think I want to produce his new album."

"Have you heard the lyrics?"

"No. But I like the concept," Morris said.

"Well." Schneider, like the wizard he was, reached into his mind for some pertinent facts. He always remembered what everyone else had forgotten, which is why he was At The Top. "The best thing Dimani and Lundholm ever wrote was 'Bateaux Mouches.' Back in seventy-one. It was never released. But it could have been a great single. I'm not a fan of Dimani and Lundholm, as you know. Her lyrics are plausible. But his music? Frankly, it's never been groovy enough for me, Arthur."

The phone rang. Schneider the prophet answered his own phone. Now he became Schneider the diplomat. A combination of Othello and Machiavelli, his soft deep voice, not unlike the voice of Nat King Cole, played into the phone. The *voice.* It was his instrument. Then his laugh came booming out, a laugh like a bass roll. It began quite low and then slowly filled the Cedar office with its boom, boom, boom. He hung up the phone.

"What a prick. Now. Where were we?" Schneider asked.

Morris said, "I've left the new Dimani tapes on your desk. I'll talk to you tomorrow, Schneider. I think I'll produce this album. It's in the Mecca contract that they can do an outside album every three years. Dimani wants me as his producer. He heard what I did with the new Dylan album. And heard what I brought it in for."

"Fifty-two thousand dollars." Richmond smiled. "That was amazing, Arthur. Even for you. Well, if he wants you for his producer, he has more taste and brains than I ever gave him credit for."

"I'm leaving the office now. There's an auction at the Parke-Bernet this afternoon. Some new Picabias are being sold."

"Which period?" Richmond asked without much interest.

"Early."

"Pick one up for me, if they're under ten thousand. I'll pay you later."

"Will do, Richmond," Arthur said warmly to his old pal as he left. "And don't forget to listen to the tapes."

The tapes. The tapes. The two magicians had created jazz and rock and roll records as discreet as works of art. Tapes as artforms. If Jesus Christ were to come back to earth, they would probably have his second coming on tapes. Christ on 8-track. But since he couldn't get Jesus for his second coming, he had to get Dimani for his third coming. Or was it his fourth? He had made his comeback so many times, it was hard to tell. "Nick Dimani is not over the hill at all," Arthur had said to Peter Hampton. Comeback and resurrection were the name of the game in the industry. But how many times could anyone come back? Time would tell. Look at Bob Hope. He had come back seventy-four times. Too bad he couldn't sing and play the guitar. What did young juggernauts like Peter Hampton know anyway? Did they have legs? Had they ever gone to the well? Did they have any real staying power? Where would Hampton be in five years? Morris was interested in *art*. Not trends. And Dimani and Lundholm were great artists. They just needed a hot new album. And *he* could produce it. He would love to produce it. He loved Nick's music. Of any period. He would love to pull *hits* out of the chambers of Nick's brain the way a prestidigitator pulled a bright red silk scarf out of a hat.

Somewhere in Tahoe, Nick was saying his prayers. Now, in New York, Arthur Morris was going to give his prayers permission.

8. *The Best Act in Tahoe*

NICK DIMANI, eyelids drooping, one of the great composers of the sixties and seventies, entrepreneur of loneliness, arrived in Lake Tahoe. He called his new girl, Laurie, from the airport. Her mother said, "She's working at Harrah's," and hung up. Laurie's mother was a Jesus Freak and didn't approve of Nick Dimani, a *very married* singing star and composer, aging celebrity, party boy, lounge lizard, playing around with her daughter. He could tell all of this from her voice on the phone before she slammed down the receiver. He knew that she walked around South Tahoe with a battered paper-back copy of *The Number One Way to Kill the Devil*. She had given him a copy when he came to call on Laurie. He had thanked her politely and taken the book on an airline trip. He had even looked at it. It was written by a Janwell Haymaker. Who was Janwell Haymaker to be so *pure!*

"Your mother sees *me* as the devil," Nick said to Laurie, teasing her. They were making love at the time.

"So what? She doesn't run my life. She can only suggest what she wants me to do. I'm twenty-one and I do as I please." Now that Laurie was working at the clubs, she had become fiercely independent. She was one of the blackjack dealers at Harrah's. The rules at Harrah's were always strict. There were no phone messages during work. But for Nick Dimani, at least in Tahoe, there were no rules. Nick phoned Harrah's and spoke to management. Soon Laurie came to the phone. She knew it was *Nick.* Only Nick could charm a pit-boss at Harrah's into risking his job and breaking the strict rules.

"I'm in Tahoe," he said.

"I've missed you," she said softly.

"Baby, here I am. I'm here over New Year's. I plan to finish my new album while I'm out here. And Laurie." He paused for effect. "I want to dedicate the new album to you."

"The new album?" Laurie was so excited, she could hardly say anything at first. She was crying. He could tell. He got a kick out of how excited her voice became. "Yeah, honey." *Shit.* That was the only happiness he had these days, the *newness of life* through Laurie's eyes. She was so trusting and receptive to him. Even if he couldn't marry her or take her out in public, he could buy her a whole new life. Clothes. A career as a model. Or an actress. He *wanted* to help her. He could make sure that she met interesting people. Not just show people, but some of the rich cattle and horse people who lived in Tahoe. He loved to see her eyes light up. At forty-three, as the husband of Lady Rita, whose snobbery was becoming paranoia, with three teenage daughters who were always either going to extravagant parties or having them, Nick was not having much fun in the "personal life department." Lady Rita was an aging English socialite whose credentials in society were Nick Dimani's fame and money. Just recently, she had bought her way into being chairman of the Jerry Brown for President cocktail party which was to be held at May Thornton's Carlyle apartment after New Year's. He could just imagine who would be there. Linda Ronstadt, looking good. Louis de Rothschild, just looking. It would be one of those fund-raising parties of the beautiful, the social, the talented, and the very lost. He used to enjoy them. Now he couldn't care less. He wanted youth, not Jerry Brown. Rita's political charities bored him. His wife, Lady Rita, had become a not-so-royal pain in the ass.

His music, the Dimani/Lundholm catalogue, had brought him entry into the best parties in the world. The chic dinners in the grotesque charity gatherings in London, Paris, New York. Where he would sing, not for his supper, but for the *perks* that came with being useful to the other celebrities and impoverished rich women whose checks often bounced at their bank. Nick Dimani singing at the Sloan Kettering Cancer Ball gave him access to the horsey set. Suddenly the Vanderbilts were his asshole buddies. His singing for President and Mrs. Sadat in front of the pyramids netted him world headlines and the chance to talk with all the Arab dignitaries who were so important to his wife. This year it had been Monte Carlo and the Red Cross. Charity had paid off in prestige. And yet, under tiny puffbags surrounding his eyes, under the secret heart which was still a rock and roll heart, he wanted the shot of adrenalin that came with sex. He needed that. Sex was his addiction. His drug. And he found it with Laurie, everything he wanted, for the moment. The *high*. His own biofeedback was Laurie's ability to make his body shake with dizzy elation. He needed the pulsar rays, the *pulse* she gave him.

Whenever the hotel limousine drove Nick to Harrah's villa where he was staying as a guest of the hotel, Nick felt the elation of being turned on to Laurie and being in the

Sierras again. Through the opened window he breathed in the fresh air. At night, Tahoe was a secretive place of dark pines, white mountaintops gleaming in the Sierra dark, and the lights of the huge buildings shining in town. The lights of Harrah's Hotel could be seen towering out of the mountains. But the late Bill Harrah's own house was low and flat and long. It was a gray flat palace, half brick, half bunker, a one-story building that blended beautifully into the rocks and hills. A new butler, one who had never worked for Harrah but now worked for the corporation, opened the door. He looked like a penguin welcoming a stranger to a gray brick iceberg. The villa was a bunker of money. The cost of the bunker, some people said, was over twelve million dollars. The moment Nick walked into the villa the lights were turned up automatically. Songs from his last albums rose out of discreet speakers. Nick was in the world of Harrah now. It was soothing, as soothing as the Brandenberg Concertos, the Bach Partitas. There was almost the feeling you were inside three levels of a stone womb.

Bill Harrah had been a man who had carved hotels into the Sierras. Hotels and gambling parlors. He had made hundreds of millions of dollars. And had died two years ago. Harrah, a Mormon tycoon whose passion had been antique cars, hydroplanes, duck hunting, and beautiful women, had been a man who was willing to spend thousands of dollars to have miniature Bugattis made for his own sons when they were little. He had been a great gentleman and tycoon. A tycoon whose self-control was a legend. An elegant anticowboy who was dressed by English tailors and lived like a king on ranches in Tahoe and Sun Valley. A quiet man who was unassuming, kind to his workers, and who had enough money to buy anything or anyone. On the walls of the villa were plastic Perma Plaque pictures of all the great celebrities who had ever played Tahoe. Everyone—Frank Sinatra, Sammy Davis, Jr.— everyone had signed their pictures, arms around Bill Harrah, with love. There was Harrah with Connie, with Totie, with Frankie, with Wayne, with all the Johns, all the Jacks, all the Barbaras, all the Dianas of show business. Thousands of entertainers had put their arms around his shoulder for an instant and then been placed on a wall inside the villa forever. The villa smelled of fame, neurosis, and history. Masses of money were responsible for its comfort and its wood-paneled perfection and natural rock *Western Sierra chic!*

Inside the villa, plants suspended by macramé were everywhere. So were sliding glass doors, beyond which the huge, dramatically lit swimming pool could be seen. The long house built out of local rock was about a block long and had been built on five empty lots looking over the lake in Skyland, right near Zephyr's Cove. It was surrounded by pines and snow on one side and the deep blue lake on the other. When Harrah had been alive and lived in the villa, it had also been surrounded by bodyguards. Harrah had always been "security conscious." Inside the villa had been hidden guns and sophisticated weaponry. The day after Harrah's death, the weapons had been quietly removed as the villa changed from a private home to a tax write-off for the Harrah corporation. It was now a showplace for the entertainers to stay if they chose, when they played the South Shore Room. They also had available to them the top floors of Harrah's Hotel. It was a matter of taste. Mac Davis, John Denver, and Frank Sinatra preferred the hotel. Nick loved the villa. Harrah's villa was his favorite hangout. In the villa he could wander by himself from one oversized room to another. He could warm himself in front of the huge fireplace in the livingroom, play with the Telex in Harrah's office, black out the world in the master bedroom with the blackout shades. In the bedroom he could watch the Rose Bowl Game on an oversized television screen. The electric drapes could be pressed to reveal the lake or pressed to shut the lake out. The huge mirror in the living room reflected the sunsets and sunrises over the lake. The mirror, reflecting the lake, had been Harrah's idea. It was what he was most proud of. The powder rooms were made of marble and filled with oils and perfumes for the guests. A projectionist was always on duty in the projection room to show guests almost any film, including films that were not yet released. Two bored French chefs were on duty night and day. Best of all, Nick loved to wander in the basement of the villa, right where the foundation was. There, amid the boilers, extra power machines, extra generators, he knew this was what *power* was. It was something hidden, something you kept in the basement to be used in emergencies. Harrah admired all kinds of power. Harrah's personal auxiliary power was as much a secret and as unseen as these generators. But it was always there. Nick was in awe of Harrah, dead or alive.

When Laurie arrived the villa was dark. The penguin let her in. Nick's voice reached her from the darkness. "Laurie?"

"Yes?"

"Come over here." She walked into the dark living room trying to avoid the overstuffed and oversized furniture. "Why did you sit in the dark?" she asked.

"I like candles. And a fire." He lit a candle so she could see him clearly. The soft light illuminated his face. He hoped the bags under his eyes didn't show.

"What's wrong, Nick?" she asked.

"Everything," he said. "I'm glad to be back, but I'm thinking about the album. I have to finish the album. It's a killer."

"Why are you sitting in the dark?"

"I look younger in the dark," he said without emotion. Then he started laughing.

"All right, see if I care," she said happily. She was genuinely glad to see him. "I missed you," she said again. Her enthusiasm escaped from her in short words. "Wow."

"Wow what?"

"I've never been in here before. When old man Harrah was alive, the security in this place was tighter than a rubber band."

"You know why?" Nick asked.

"Why?"

"Because there are things here more valuable than things in the White House."

"Oh sure."

"You don't believe me?"

"What's so valuable? What could be here that's so valuable?" she asked.

"The American flag that was planted on the moon by Neil Armstrong."

"I thought that was still on the moon," she laughed.

"No. It's here. In the dining room downstairs. Documented."

"How'd it get here? I mean, doesn't it belong to the Smithsonian, to the American taxpayers and stuff?"

"Harrah had his own world. His own kingdom. If he wanted the flag planted on the moon to be planted in his villa, he got it. No one is sure exactly how he got the flag. Some people say a powerful entertainer like Wayne Newton gave it to him as a gift. Anyway, you'll see it at breakfast. Who knows? Maybe there were two of them."

"Am I staying here tonight?"

"That's what I was planning on."

"What's the scoop? Why didn't you tell me?"

"Come here," Nick said. "Tell me all the things you love."

"Hot tea on a cold day. Starlight. Cashmere. Bubbling champagne. Broomhilda. Lemonade. Dogs. Rain. You."

"Then stay with me."

"First I have to call my mother. She'll be expecting me in the morning."

"Don't wake her. She'll ask you if you're with the devil."

"All right. I'll call her early before church."

"Laurie?"

"Yes?" Her loose hair came down to her waist. She was so beautiful he wanted to touch her.

"Come here." She moved in the semidark closer to Nick.

"Turn the stereo on." She did. A Nick Dimani song with the Sylvia Lundholm lyrics the world knew by heart unfolded through the house. The song was called "Tears." It was a combination of Nick's piano, kettle drum, and steel guitar. An oldie from the sixties. He was singing on that album, monosyllabic lyrics coupled with a spare narrative chorus that followed the opening of the song.

Tears.
All these years.
Tears.
All my fears.

Her appreciation was what Nick liked. She was turning him on. Was it her? Or his own music? For the ultimate turn-on for Nick was a combination of Laurie and himself. It was almost as if sex for him had to be dubbed over his own soundtrack.

"Help me," he said, sitting on the chair and leaning back. He could see her taking off her sweater in Harrah's mirror.

"You could say something more romantic than that," she said.

"What can I say, Laurie, I have a lot of problems."

"What are they?" She stopped undressing. She was really concerned. He loved that.

"I'm frightened. I want a new album. I don't have any idea if my writer, Sylvia, will come out to Tahoe to work with me. Without her, forget it. And my kids have terrible problems. My wife's having a midlife crisis which seems to be what women have right after they stop wanting to go shopping and spend all your money. God, Laurie, I think sometimes that I'm totally alone."

Oh Jesus, help me. I can't fuck anyone with problems, this is turning me off, she wanted to say. But instead, she said, "Quiet. Lie back. I love you."

"Laurie, you're the best act in Tahoe," he said as she made love to him. "You weren't voted Most Likely To Succeed, darling, for nothing."

Laurie was, and she knew it, a turn-on, for Nick Dimani. And luckily, for both of them, she *wanted* to see him happy.

"I like your face," she said.

With Laurie he felt good. His heart was a tiny hammer now, knocking against his bones, nailing him to life.

9. Sylvia's Make-believe

"DON'T HURT me too much," Sylvia said to her Swedish masseur. She loved this masseur, this ancient man who healed. A tax writeoff, he was a necessity in a frantic business. For Sylvia, his hands were the hands of a giant, but somewhere way back some seventy years ago in a cold country he had also been born with a beautiful instinct for silence and understanding. Although he was a masseur, she felt he was also a poet, someone who just with his own hands understood her struggle from darkness to light. His only accomplishment seemed to have been to have lived to be his age and to have strong hands. And yet his fingers could immediately pick up her pulse, her visions; and where her body was missing in vitality, he advised her from some deep muscular logic which was based on knowing her body and never offending her sensibilities. The wild Norse king of knots. He knew by instinct how to allow her to talk during their session. The massage was a fleshy miracle of relaxation and deliverance from tensions.

"I want to ask you a question," she said. "Is it too late to *change*? To change my life?"

He didn't say anything.

"I can't *reason,*" she continued. "I separated my imagination from commonsense so long ago, I feel frightened. I am frightened. I'm a child in a grown-up world. A pigmy in a world of giants."

"You are," he said, his healing hands working on her muscles. "You're childlike. Why change? At least you can write about it. That's more than most people can do." His touch felt familiar, secure.

"I desperately want to get out of this business. Don't you understand? I don't want to be known as the *girl* who wrote 'White Trash' when I'm forty-two."

"How old are you now?"

"I'm almost forty."

"You'd better hurry," the masseur said with dignity. "You'd better think fast. You have a good chance to defend your femininity."

"I don't care about that," Sylvia said. "I don't care about these tidbits of blistered half-undressed genders. However frightened I may be, I know that I have to get out of this industry before I become too hard, too desensitized, and my life is lost. *I have to change my life again.*"

He held her right foot and massaged the toes one by one.

"At night," she went on, "I dream of entering a healthy sports arena. I don't know where that arena is. There is no locking up of one's ideas in a vault. There are no accountants. There are no lawyers there who look at contracts and at you with a magnifying glass. There are no hustlers there who want to sleep with you and get into your bank account. There are no twenty-four-year-old boyfriends who want to boogie with you if you can only help their singing or modeling careers. There is only a healthy body."

He was Swedish. He understood.

She went on, "Put it this way: Like a common zinnia, I want to grow out of the earth. I really want to record my vision seriously instead of in lyrics. I know there is no plucking radishes from top hats. But I love life. I want to change. Now, more than I can say. I am so tired of records, of agents clutching at my hands. Of all the tent-talk. Sometimes when I wake up and fumble for my dream diary—I keep one, you know, the way Kafka kept one—I want to live in a childlike moment, aware of the wonder of the world the way I used to be when I was a young girl visiting Swedish towns on the cold dark sea with my father in the summer, just able to take care of myself, when love came easy and the world seemed to have an open wishing well in every garden, a world filled with colors like bright yellow and blue, a world filled with butterflies that weren't pierced and under glass the way they are in the record business."

It was almost as if the masseur's magnetic touching of her body brought out her heat and light. She kept talking.

"Right now, I feel like an old soldier," she said, "aware of my rank, alert to obey orders, watching with binoculars the movement in the record industry and waiting for my own ambush. I stand there with my gun, the pistol cocked, the code word committed to memory; I am the youngest soldier there, standing with Nick, who is beside me as my comrade in arms and yet somehow my enemy. I know that the drums will begin and I know that the real question that I keep asking myself is: 'Which *side* of this war am I supposed to be on?'

"I remember one morning when I was a child and I was riding on a white horse. When I fell off the horse, my father laughed and said, 'Just like a girl.' I have lived my whole life trying to eradicate those words, 'Just like a girl.' I've supported myself, but managed to seem feminine and polite; I wanted and won success in a man's world on my own talent. But now that I've found the door to fame, I want to throw away the key. Cash exploded in my face like gunpowder. I want to walk away now. To ride away. I want to follow a friend who seems to understand the anxious marrow in my bones."

"A friend?" the masseur asked. "Who is the friend?" He was working on her legs.

"My new buddy. His name is Rev. He's my energy man. Rev. How can I describe him? He's my solar buddy, my new happiness. There is a casual life I want to lead. With him. I want to be near him and forget charts and hits. I want to get rid of the knots in my body and be a woman in the street once more, a woman with string parcels. Get down off this throne, off this table for good. I want to shout against the wind, to get rid of all my ghosts and be free to find my own condition, whatever that is. I am tired of collaborating with Nick. This thought, like a dream, keeps after me: the thought that time will say nothing but 'I told you so.' This time the price seems too much to pay. I see my life in shadow and when I see the shadows on the wall, I start to weep because it was *I* who made those shadows. I made them as a child. And it was I who put on their show. I am the shadow I made. I want to be childlike. I want to be wiser than a child. I want desperately to get out of this industry. I don't want to be known for the rest of my life as the girl who wrote 'White Trash.' "

The masseur was working on her spine, her thoughts running on under his fingers. "The men I've met in this business divide themselves into three realms. First: those who see you as a winner and want part of your profits. The others are the losers. They'll fuck for anything. The winners and the losers. Like the Guelphs and the Ghibellines in Dante's Florence. They see your cunt as a magical door that will open up the universe of profit. They need your power to open the doors. But the losers are worse than the winners. The hustlers. They'll do anything. The winner-wanters. They are all looking for a step up. In this group are models. Directors. Actors. Failed record producers. Agents. Arrangers. Sports trainers. Singers. Other musicians. Any loser who has made it. Or wants to make it. Would-be stars who are still starfuckers. It's all in that song by Leiber and Stoller:

You used to look so cute
In your white sailor suit
Aboard that big white yacht
That you no longer got—
Don Juan, your money's gone,
And when your money's gone,
Your baby's gone.

"Well, I've played Don Juana over the years to just about everybody. Everyone has come aboard my yacht and I've taken them where they wanted to go."

"Why did you do it?"

"I had the money. And I thought, *why not?* It's also impersonal, to be generous. It doesn't demand too much of your feelings."

"Did you want people to care about you?"

"I don't know," Sylvia said, feeling the pressure of his hands in the kinks of her body. "I guess, like Jimi Hendrix, I wanted to kiss the sky."

"Are there any people you love?" he asked sadly.

"No. Only Rev Cranwell. He at least doesn't want ten percent of my work. He hates music. He doesn't read. He's casual. He doesn't even *know* my songs. I like to drive with him."

"What does he like?"

"He likes me. I think. We have fun. At least, it's not harming anyone."

"It might be harming you."

"How?"

"By taking up all your energies." The masseur wondered if he was going too far, especially after he had just told her the previous week that Rev seemed to have calmed her down.

"Where else should they go?" she asked.

"What about political activities?" the masseur suggested.

"Political men and women are a whole different ballgame," Sylvia said. "They have a world to save and that keeps them busy. They're like Jesus Freaks. Only at least they're doing something good with their lives. Listen, yesterday I met a guy who was a combination communist and sports trainer. You would have liked him. He's about twenty-seven. A Marxist who runs with people for a living. Not just runs. He'll skate with you, ride with you. As we were running, he asked me what my goal was politically and weight-wise. These people are into hunger, humanity, and weight loss. All at once. They have a *holistic* approach. This guy was a combination of Karl Marx and Saint Francis of Assisi. A young Marxist Yogananda. I said I wanted to free Chile and lose ten pounds. He offered, for a fee, to take me to a course on alternative Marxist cinema at the Free University, or show me around the health food supermarkets in New York.

"I told him I already knew my way around Marxism *and* sunflower seeds. Then he asked me if I had ever had a colonic. I said no. He told me that if everybody would just have a colonic, there would be no more imperialism in the world. The capitalist system was anal. You had to attack it by any means necessary. From without and from within. A tank. Or an enema. A colonic was as good as a hand grenade. And cheaper. You could tap a phone, but you'd be better off tapping a body system. If only the leaders of the imperialist world would relieve themselves of all their poisons they would find that they were free to love, he told me. Love and shit went together. The political movement had everything to do with the bowel movement. Freud had it right: Money is shit. He had combined Freud with Marx and Gaylord Hauser, who said *you are what you eat.* This man's unusual concept was that this system is what it shits. Something like that. We were running at the time, so it was all a little confusing. Capitalism could benefit by a huge demonstration called colonic day. The heads of all the large corporations should be given a pottie to poop in. He said this as we were jogging around the reservoir. The great powers should all have a colonic. It would relieve them of greed. Not explosions of buildings. Explosions of capitalist bowels was his method of having a better world.

It was interesting. But in his own way, he was still a capitalist. He hit on me to go shit with him.

"He said to me, 'Sylvia, if you'll pay for *my* colonic, I'll go and have one with you. For you, it will be thirty-five dollars because it's the first time. *My* colonic will be only twenty dollars. I'll be right there to support you. We'll have colonics together.' "

"What did you say?" the masseur asked. He was often amazed by her experiences.

"I said, 'I don't have to pay anyone to shit with me.' And then I thought about it later and I started laughing. Boy meets girl. Boy tries to politicize girl. Girl is already politicized. Boy propositions girl for free colonic. Girl doesn't need colonic, thank you."

The masseur stopped. The massage was over.

"It's so depressing," Sylvia said, getting down from the table. "That's fame. This man offers himself to me for a political conversation and what he really wants is a free colonic."

She whispered, "I'm *tired*. And I've had it with the multiple drum kits. Pop little playlets. And cool. I'm tired of pushing Marxism, colonics, and romance. I'm tired of movements of any kind. It all adds up to control. I don't want to be controlled. And I don't want to control. I'd just like reality for a change. The make-believe ballroom was what I grew up on. Then I loved it, *then*. All the make-believe. Only when I saw deep into the ballroom, when I was fifteen, I wrote a poem about it. It was never published. It was about finding another landscape. Want to hear it?"

"Still know it?" he asked. He was folding the white sheet and moving the table away.

"Listen. It's called 'Footprints in the Mud.' " She stood there, still in the nude, reciting to him like a little girl.

I've grown tired of the water tap,
The bowing maids, the telephone messages,
    the crap—

From now on, I will praise the water
That flows down me and to me and from me,
Marl, turf, red seed, pine tree,
And barbed root are mint and sacrimint.

"Those were my thoughts then. Oddly, those are my thoughts now, so many years later. Now that I'm forty, I'm going to recycle this." She laughed. "I'm going to give it to Nick for his Tahoe album. Let him set it to music. You see, in some ways, I feel just as innocent as I was when I was fifteen. I've paid my dues. I'm not losing my engine. I've gone through the wheel and fire and birth and endless death and I'm beginning to feel reborn. All I can say is that I've learned to love. I've learned to be tolerant. I can even tolerate the business. It's just that Rev is my pal. My new best friend. And I want to hang out with him for a while. Because he's reached what the truly hip have reached: He's so turned-on he's not even attached anymore to a lightbulb. He's just attached to himself. He doesn't have to *do* anything. Or *be* anyone. He just is. Really. He likes his buddies, likes women—once in a while. But he's a detached person. He has a secret and it's that secret I'm after. What frightens me doesn't frighten him. Oh yes," she said, "he has a great sense of humor."

"I understand," the masseur said.

She was always sad when the massage was over. She hated to get down from the cool white metal table. When she lay there, Sylvia thought that one day she would learn to see clearly the world as it was without all the blurs and zigzags. She wasn't sure if she wanted to be nearsighted or farsighted. She just wanted to see things as they were *not* —as well as how they were. She was buying insight. She would risk her life for this. Jimi Hendrix had played guitar with his teeth, but all she had was her vision. She'd have to make it all up, her new life.

Somehow the muscle doctor, who knew every bone and nerve of her body, who knew where her energies were, knew where her stomach was flat, where she perspired, somehow this man whose palms and life-lines she depended on, this man who knew her flesh, also knew and understood the wounded skin of her deepest secrets. He had felt her. He had touched her. He knew what she was made of. To all the rest, she was the different Sylvia Lundholms she tried to portray. To him, she wasn't a *talent*. (That's all she was in the business. They talked about her as The Talent, the way you talk about art if you are going to sell it, record it, or freeze it.) But the muscle doctor was different. He knew her naked in some ways more than she would ever know herself. He was the only person she allowed to come near her and touch her, outside of Rev. Like the masseur, Rev had a wisdom of his own, an ancient wisdom. He made her feel warm as well as smart and powerful. Who was Rev? He was a map. On the map were regions of desert she could never enter. On the map were places that were closed off, dangerous lands, swamps where no one had ever been. Forests where she could never go. But the places she entered were so beautiful, she didn't try to penetrate the off places. She didn't try to voyage where she couldn't survive. Her love was to let him have his own boundaries. To accept him as he was, but to try and create a different landscape. To imagine him as he was *not*. She was an explorer and he was the map. She read him, an authentic cartographer of the stranger called Revson Cranwell.

Here was the amazing thing: By not stepping over the lines of the map, the black lines she was not supposed to enter, by not spilling over her feelings like the colors on a map, she was able to voyage deep into the center of who Rev was. He was an unknown person. And he didn't want anyone explaining him. She knew he would be her friend forever, but she could never possess him; she could never marry him, live with him, have children with him, or have any commitment from him. There were never to be signs to the world of their love. But she would have something else. His company. At least for a while. And the excitement of *not* having him. This for some reason was what attracted Sylvia to Rev, this alienated stranger. He would never give up his freedom. He could always drive away, leaving her alone. And in some way, she fiercely wanted to be alone. So she loved Rev. She thought he was funny. He was *nuts*. Was there a better reason to love someone? And in many ways his alienation matched her own. She wondered if there was anyone else on earth outside of this ancient Swedish masseur who understood her, anyone to whom she could connect in an earthly and still transcendent way.

It flashed through her mind as she dressed after her massage, that she was not really *lonely*. She realized how much she loved her women friends. The girls from college now were mature women scattered all over the country like seeds, growing and blossoming like different trees. Some had flowered. Some were bonsai women. With her friends she could share her secrets, her political dreams which sometimes would fade and then grow bright again. The girls from school, she thought, were more than friends. They were secret family that provided the warmth missing outside the belly of life. Her best friend, Nancy, where was she now? Nancy was a different kind of species. She was not an oak. She was not an elm. She was a tough little pine that could grow and blossom anywhere.

Nancy! She had to find her. And, getting dressed, Sylvia realized, in a new way, with clarity and fear, that she was beginning to feel Rev was not only her friend, but her teacher.

10. *Sex and Drugs and Rock and Roll*

WAS FOCUSING all your faculties on yourself, the definition of a narcissist? Nick often wondered about that. Mir-

ror, mirror on the wall, who's the best cowboy of all? That
snowy morning in Tahoe, Nick looked into the full mirror
at his red Western silk shirt, his black jeans, his seven-
thousand-dollar yellow and white cowboy boots. He liked
what he saw. The boots were his peacock feathers. They
had been made to perfectly fit his feet by an obscure Italian artisan in some remote corner of Texas. Nick knew he
was a dude. He secretly called himself the Brooklyn cowboy. Once he loved music. Now he loved good clothes and
he loved snow. He loved Tahoe as much as he loved sex.
And drugs. And rock and roll. He loved everything about
his life in Tahoe. The mountains. First of all, the mountains. Everything that Tahoe was began with the mountains. It had been a place where once lumber was cut,
where miners followed an Indian trail, where survival was
once the primary thought. The lumber camps had
changed to hostelries. Where Indian squaws walked up
the Truckee River and Western Sierra Nevada. Tahoe!
Nick felt good in Tahoe.

Nick would get up every morning and watch the sun
rise on Lake Tahoe from his bed in Harrah's villa. He
could talk for hours about the Lake Valley and the Sierras,
about the beauty of Zephyr's Cove. He knew the history of
Sumner Station and Summit Cap, Agate Bay, the Ponde-
rosa Ranch at Incline in the North End. He could tell you
the history of Lake Tahoe from the time of its discovery
by Captain John Frémont on Saint Valentine's Day, February 14, 1844, down to the present day of Harrah's gambling casino on the public stock exchange, and all the
gossip behind its recent sale. He had pored over early
magazine articles, county court house records, musty di-
aries, letters, and photographs in his effort to get to all the
material on Tahoe. He knew about the Great Bonanza
road to Washo, carrying a floodtide of animals, the pack
trails and wagon roads used by the emigrants, the Washo
and Paiute Indian tribes fighting for control of the "Big
Waters" fishing and hunting grounds, the armadas of sailing boats.

Mountain men, emigrants, lumberjacks, gale-whipped peaks, innkeepers, timber barons, steamer captains—Nick felt as if he could almost hear them all as he skied down the mountains. He could listen to the snowy peaks and they told him something. He was in love. Tahoe's voices became his music. The music he had written for *Playing Tahoe* was different from anything he had written in the late fifties, the sixties, or the seventies. He had created a new kind of rolling snow music, a sound that was in sync with Tahoe and was fast and outrageous. It was a sound nobody expected from Nick Dimani. No one understood what he was doing except for Arthur Morris. He had sent the tapes of the first music he was writing to Morris, the one person in the music business whose ears were really his own. Morris knew how to hear music in the midst of things nobody else heard. And Morris had called him right after he got the tapes.

"Listen, Dimani, I won't waste words," the bearded mystic said into the phone from his office at Cedar Communications. He, Arthur Morris, legend, the great angel of Dune Records, had said into the phone in his quiet Brooklyn scholar's voice, "I give you permission to work with me." But he hadn't literally said that. What he said was, "I love it. This is your best work, Nick. It's authentic. I want to be your partner in this album. I want to produce this record for you. I'll give you a while to think it over, but I think we can go to Muscle Shoals and lay down a whole different kind of sound track. This album is a classic. A whole new kind of American sound. Have you got the lyrics?"

Nick had told Morris that Sylvia was flying out to Tahoe to create the lyrics and that he was going to create with Morris the new Tahoe sound the way Morris created a new sound for Dylan. And now, Nick Dimani was going to have to do the one thing on earth that really meant something to him. He was going to recreate Tahoe, the place he loved the most, in music. Nick was going to take everything he loved and lay it down in zinc. *Playing Tahoe—*

ballads, an homage to earth, to health, to purity, to snow and pines. What Morris had said that morning gave him encouragement. Morris was never wrong. Finally, Nick was going to have an album that was, in the words of the industry, "today." If Morris produced it, it was a shoo-in to go platinum. That was Morris's genius. He wasn't just one of the *founders* of rock and roll, a record genius. He was also an artist. He could take his knowledge of talent, his knowledge of music, and make any kind of music sound better. Most of all, he dug the new sound. He understood Nick's need to come up with something better. Nick felt optimistic again. Hope!

With Sylvia he was going to create a new kind of electronic software, music that made use of strings and that related to the snow, to dreams and reunions that were not impossible. He could imagine music in which he managed to capture a bird's footprints, the rock and the hills with no junk in between. He could even imagine music with a patch of blue lake, a lake with drowned bodies that never returned. Music, an ideal darkness, all of the intense feelings about nature that he was familiar with. He had spent the early part of his life being a ghetto kid. But he had dreamed of living with the yellow harvest moon and sleeping in a place with curving snowdrifts and a team of horses hauling a bobsled of wood. A Brooklyn boy who loved the tumbles of the rapids going white, going green, going brown over the rocks. A boy who loved the sight of the water. The stones. He wanted all this in his new album.

Slowly he had taught himself the names of flowers and in Tahoe in the summer, he could pick out the brown-eyed Susans, the white asters, the buttercups that came in a yellow rain, the Johnny-jump-ups with their blue mist, and the wild azaleas with their low spring cry. He had spent so many seasons in nature now that the ghetto memories crossed and crisscrossed into the winters of Tahoe and he tried to make himself believe that he, Nick Dimani, had never had pointed blue suede shoes, that he had never spent summers in a tenement wearing an undershirt and looking at the billboards of nothingness that grew like huge synthetic messages of despair and consumption all over Brooklyn.

He made himself believe that this was how it had always been, the whispering sprigs of buds in the spring, the hired man driving a manure spreader in the summer, the woodpecker beating his tattoo against the trees in the fall, and the moon on the shores of Lake Tahoe in the winter, the night's unraveling clean black yarn.

All of that he wanted in his music now, the miles of lake with its blue fingers, carrying the blue into everyone's poems. He heard the melting snow and the snow-born children fighting and throwing snowballs in the winter winds, and all of this he wanted in his music. He could never express these things. He could feel them and he could write a melody about them. But they couldn't come out of his mouth. When he spoke, there was only this gross Brooklynese language which his wife Rita had tried to correct with speech lessons but it hadn't worked. He was a fighter, not a poet. And that's why he needed Sylvia. Without his balls, she would have been nothing in the business. But without her language and her insight into what he felt, he was a silent mirror without anything except the abstract expression of music. His mother had once told him when he was a little boy in Brooklyn and they had taken the subway to Coney Island and looked out over the ocean that the trouble with seagulls was that they had no song. Nothing but a croak came from their throats. He was a seagull. His melodies were his flight, but he needed Sylvia's throat.

"Please God, let her come!"

11. Designs for Living

CHANGES. CHANGES involved the minutiae of dreams. Even in her sleep, Sylvia thought of Rev. She awoke one morning in her depression-proof apartment in New York, wondering if she should live in Hawaii. Her dream? To go to Christy's auction of collectors' cars and vintage airplanes (The Los Angeles Convention Center, Saturday, March 29, 10 A.M.–noon) with Rev and buy each of them a 1930 SS Mercedes Benz Cabriolet. What the hell? It was only money. If she liked him, why not make him happy? One day they could drive their cars in Hawaii. He would like that. The laid-back center of the world. Soft water. Windsurfing. Underwater world. Where speedboats sped through the black water like dangerous sharks. They could stay at the Mauna Kea, play tennis, scuba dive, surf, water ski. Speed in Rivas. Live in sun. Hang out. Pal around. Rev was the best friend she ever had. He was more than a friend. He was perfect. He could do no wrong. She didn't care if he had other girlfriends, or if his alienation didn't allow him to make too many friends. Whatever buddies he had, he kept.

"I don't need anyone, you know what I mean?"

"Then what are you doing with me?"

"I like you." They were at Orsini's Restaurant. Her treat. Rev was eating quickly. He ate like a child, pushing food quickly, so quickly into his mouth. He ate in exactly one minute. Wiped his mouth with his hand, and looked up to see who was coming into the restaurant. She had tried to turn him into a slow eater. Once she had invited him to "21." When the appetizer came, clams casino, she told him: "Take a bite. Eat with your fork. Put your fork down. Talk. Say something pleasant. Then another bite. Slowly. Try to take at least sixty seconds to eat your first course.

Draw it out. Don't just gulp it down like you did at Eagle Prep. We're not rushing."

And he laughed and said, "Is that how it's done?"

"Yes," she said, "that's how it's done. Take your time, Rev. Some day you may be with a really classy girl and you'll want to impress her with your table manners."

And he laughed again. "But I am with a classy girl right now." This six-foot-three blond Philadelphia Adonis in jeans, age thirty-four, with steel-blue eyes, a dimple in his chin, a perfect body, and rough hands—in other words, male enlightenment—he had laughed until the waiters and the guests looked at them and wondered who he was. Almost everyone knew who she was. She was Sylvia Lundholm, whose face had been on the cover of *Newsweek* as "beautiful poet and troubadour," who appeared everywhere in clothes made by Yves Saint Laurent, and who had once been the great love of her music partner Nick Dimani. She was a tall blond giant herself. And people loved her songs. And she? She loved Rev Cranwell. That's why she suddenly wanted to give up songs and have fun for as long as he would let her be with him. As long as the money held out. But she had money. A lot of it. And she couldn't think of a better way to spend it than to go wherever he wanted. In short: He was her new career. And it made her laugh too: a car salesman from the Bronx! A salesman on the speedway of her life.

They could go to the theater. They could go to "21." But Rev Cranwell had no desire to go to "21." And he didn't much like the theater. He preferred real life. The Daytona Five Hundred. On television, while he drank a beer. Lying down and watching the Indy. He thought that Sylvia's friends were using her. He thought her lifestyle was all bullshit. It seemed ridiculous that she took diet pills and went to so many doctors. "You don't need them," he said to her. "Stop taking pills. Just use your willpower."

"I'm afraid of weight," she said.

"Eat vegetables. And exercise." His solutions were simple. To the point. She loved to look at him. Hold his hand. Feel his strength. She tried to show him off to her friends.

"Who's that weird car salesman you brought to dinner?" Irwin Parma had asked in an outraged voice the day after meeting Rev. Parma owned a building materials company called Parma and Company. "Have you gone nuts?" he asked Sylvia. Usually Sylvia's escorts were someone Parma could discuss investments with. When asked the inevitable New York question did Rev say, "I sell cars on Jerome Avenue" to the Parmas just to shock them? Judy Parma, in her sable, almost dropped her newly capped teeth.

"Are you kidding?" she asked. Was he *really* a car salesman in the Bronx? Or was it a joke?

"You're not serious," Irwin Parma had said. Who was this guy? Parma wanted to know. And Irwin could get annoyed easily. Irwin Parma had changed neighborhoods when he was twelve. Then he had moved laterally like a hockey puck down from the Bronx to Park Avenue. His second wife (he called her his *good* wife) was a *shiksa* who loved children. All his kids now went to Spence. And Collegiate. His friends were impeccable. Not crowned heads, but business types or well-known artists. He owned stock in the upper middle class. He supported it. If the upper middle class went bankrupt, what would happen to Parma and Company? Sylvia was seeing a car salesman? If she wanted to fuck a car salesman, that was her business. But why did she have to bring him to The Palm for dinner and have Parma and Company paying the check?

"No, seriously, Rev, what do you do?" Parma had asked over his steak. He was nervously shifting his feet in the sawdust under the table.

"I'm into transportation." Rev smiled. It was a slap in the face to Irwin.

Rev Cranwell, who is that odd ball guy? Everyone that met him thought Sylvia was crazy. They didn't like him. He was spaced out. Weird. Oblivious, Sylvia followed him in a trance. She seemed to lose track of her ordinary routine. She forgot to show up at dinner parties, theater parties. The gentle evenings of her salon were things that slipped away. On Saturday afternoons she hired a limousine and filled a basket with the foods Rev liked—mostly fish—and went to visit him in the Bronx at the showroom. Her squid bill was enormous that month. The fishmongers at Rosedale Fish Market wondered what new diet she was on. She became queen of the squid, queen of the poached salmon and tile fish. Riding with a basket filled with beer and fish up to 177th Street in the Bronx, she stopped on Jerome Avenue in front of a battered window that said First Olds and went to see her love. He was selling Oldsmobiles, Cutlasses and Toronados.

She watched Rev stand in front of his desk in the showroom. A brand new brown Cutlass was on display. A black woman, quite round and strong, came and sat down. "My husband's a minister. And, lawdy, the church needs a car. I said, 'Honey, we don't want no Chevrolet—we want an *Olds*. Cutlass. Front-wheel drive. With a sweet sound.' Can you pick out a Cutlass with good speed control? My husband's been to see you, Mr. Cranwell. Says you're a first-rate gentleman. That's why we came to one hundred and seventy-seventh street and Jerome."

"Why? Where do you live?" Rev asked, smiling his blond-on-blond salesman's smile.

"One hundred and fifty-fifth. My husband said, 'Get Mr. Cranwell to sell you a Cutlass for God.' And here I am."

"What's your name?" Rev asked gently. He began writing in triplicate on the order form with a ballpoint pen.

"My name is Fiorella Bonwitt. I'm the wife of Reverend Bonwitt."

"Where do you bank, Mrs. Bonwitt?"

"Harlem International."

"Do you have a credit card?"

"Five."

"What terms do you want to buy this car on, Mrs. Bonwitt?"

"No terms. Daddy said pay cash."

Rev smiled. He took the order form, crushed it, and threw it in the wastebasket. "That will be six thousand nine hundred dollars. That includes the wheels and the tape deck." He looked straight into her eyes.

Sylvia listened. What followed was a little poem, a small lyric. He described the wonders of the car she was buying. How it didn't rust. How it drove. How it had a superior tape deck, the best power windows, finest automatic transmission. He told her how to maintain the car. All about the insurance. And the warranty. The love in his voice for the woman and the car was something so touching Sylvia wanted to cry.

"Thanks a lot," the black woman wanted to say. But for what? For giving her another vision about existence. She didn't even understand it herself. Revson Cranwell, when he sold a car, gave away a part of *himself*. His automatic soul.

12. Skiing Tahoe

"ECSTASY IS my frame of reference," Nick told Laurie. At the same time he was making love to her in the villa. "It is only my obsession that gives me pleasure and pain—and my only obsession is pleasure." The stereo in the villa was playing his first album. Nick felt good with Laurie. Felt young again and carefree. He had taken her to bed with him so many times, but each time he found her body more beautiful. He loved making love to her. Touching her. She was the most beautiful after she came. He would look down at her face and the innocence in her eyes, the soft white texture of her skin that always seemed moist, made him desire her. She would just take her blouse off and he would get excited. He still needed his wife, Lady Rita. But he was crazy about Laurie for the moment. He had them both. And that made him feel good.

Afterward, Nick dropped her at the casino. She was always on time to work. He went to buy some ski pants. Nick felt drained. He needed the mountains, to go up them and feel the ecstasy coming down—that was a joy for him, too. For Nick, to ski meant to gain back all his manhood. With the sun on his face, his goggles cocked, he was really able to forget everything and relax. To ski meant to edge his way into the earth the way he edged his cock into Laurie. The untracked snow made him feel powerful, the way he felt knowing that he, Nick Dimani, was the first great love of Laurie's life.

It was great to be back in the high world of Tahoe, where everything seemed better, even sex. It was still a pure world. A world where Indians, not so long ago, had worn snowshoes, grown maize and pine trees, and lived off the land. Lumber kept them warm in winter. They lived in a world of the cold lake and warm fire. Nick thought of how he loved Tahoe as he tried on the ski suit. Suddenly he heard a screaming voice and a giggle. Then more voices. His *fans.* Teenagers were all around him. "There he is! Nick Dimani!"

"Nick!"

"Hey man, that's him! The songwriter. The singer! Wow! In the flesh!"

Yes, even when Nick was trying on a ski suit at the Outdoorsman, they found him. He could never be private, especially in Tahoe. *Fans.* Those were his people. They loved him and wherever he went, he was still a star. As he tried on the stretchsuit, the young girls gathered around him. They were eager to be near their hero. He didn't mind them watching. They were people for whom he was a phenomenon, people who loved him and knew his songs. And he loved Tahoe people. The voices—the laid-back sense of how easy everything was. In Tahoe, there was no need to do much. Nature did it for you. The light, the air, the colors of green—that was the main event every day. He wished he always had lived in Tahoe. It was as if Tahoe was the bright side of the moon, the white side, and Brooklyn was the dark side. Brooklyn was the black world that he was escaping. Running from. Run, Nick, run. Ski, Nick, ski. Don't look back to the days of poverty and wanting to be somebody. You've made it now, baby. You can buy anything you want. Even love. Ski, boy, ski. Don't remember those acne days, those days of being fat and unwanted. They love you now. Look at them, the fans. You don't have just a family. You have fans. The suit looked good on him.

"There he goes! Is that him? That's him! He looks different in real life. Shorter. Younger. Is that really him? Get his autograph! Does he always wear ski clothes? Can you get me to him?" Such was the jive of celebrity and everyone wanted a piece of him that winter like every other winter for the past twenty years.

Later, in search of peace, Nick Dimani rode the ski lift eleven thousand feet up the highest peak in Heavenly Valley. Alone on the lift, pulled by the cables slowly up the mountain, Nick dangled his legs that sported shiny red plastic ski boots. Holding his ski poles as if they were great banners tucked under his arms, he felt as if he were a knight going to battle with the snow. A knight in shining ski suit, his warrior's mallet now made out of white nylon, his horse this incredible pulley. On the lift, looking down the mountains, he realized that the Tahoe Basin covered with powdered snow was the place he loved most in the world. He had skied Aspen, Sun Valley, Vail. He had skied Klosters, Saint Moritz, Portillo. And all of these places had been "good" to him. He loved to ski. But there was no place for Nick like Tahoe. It had everything. It had water and mountains and it was more than a home. It was a place where he could be who he really was. Not a famous composer. Or a singer. But a ski bum. Music and skiing were the two things he loved most in the world. Then came women. But really, it was skiing above all those things. The Sierras were so beautiful to him.

Nick had started skiing when he was about twenty, right before he and Sylvia Lundholm had their first golden record. The first place he had ever skied was right here in Heavenly Valley when they had one chair lift and rope tow and the tram had just been built. In those days, the mountains had been empty during the week. He had been insane with the sensation of flight, from the moment he had first put on skis. His own rhythms had told him what to do. He could almost dance down the Heavenly Valley ski runs. That first winter he had spent at least three hundred hours just going up and down the mountain, teaching himself, just as he taught himself music when he was young. Everything he knew in life he taught himself. He remembered suddenly what it first felt like to have control, to know that the skis on his feet responded to his thoughts, to fly down those ice mountains slowly or swiftly depending on what he, Nick Dimani, wanted. He remembered the first time, twenty-some years ago, when the skis disappeared until there was only his feet and the snow and he remembered those first winters when he couldn't get enough of skiing, skiing the mountain called Heavenly Valley. Heavenly, for Nick, was a woman he wanted to make love to again and again. He never tired of her, he wanted her skin, her flesh, he wanted to be in her always, that was how he felt about that mountain. He loved the Sierras. He loved the Nevada side and he loved the California side of Heavenly Valley. He loved the powdered snow. He would get up at sunrise, that first winter, too excited to even sleep. He would watch the sun in its redness light the sky and then fall on the blue of the lake and on the great sad black stones that jutted up out of the water like huge black petrified animals. He would watch the sun thunder its beginning on the white mountains, on the pine trees, on the entire basin, filling the water of the lake with its own energy. He remembered that first winter at Tahoe. Under the snow, the trees, shrubs, and flowers would lie still. And sleeping under the snow were the reptiles. The mornings of Tahoe would begin with a pure winter stillness. Nick remembered those days—he was playing Harrah's in the South Shore Room then. He, Nick Dimani, and his back-up musicians were the best act there was.

Now, slowly riding the ski lift to the top of the Nevada side of Heavenly Valley, he thought about those things. Now he was forty-three and powerful, and still king of the slopes. No one, not even the instructors who darted in and out of the mountain's curves in their shiny red ski suits, could ski faster than he could. Even those twenty-one-year-old brats who made love to the lonely wives as well as to their own girlfriends and wives, those young Adonises with bright blond hair and tiny buns, those heroes of youth for whom everything was easy with their new bones and supple legs, he didn't have to move over for them. He skied as well as they did.

"Really, Mr. Dimani," said Steve, Captain Courageous of the Heavenly Ski School. "Nobody skis better than you down this mountain."

"Who are you kidding?"

"Really, you're fast. When you rented that helicopter last week and we skied Kirkwood, I could hardly keep up with you, sir."

You bet your ass, Nick thought. He was pleased because Steve was the best there was in Heavenly Valley, at least in the ski school. It pleased Nick, riding in slow motion through the air, to reach the top of the mountain, looking down on the Jeffrey Pines, the lumber trees which made Lake Tahoe famous, looking down on the forest basin of great green pines tall and almost preening in the morning sun, pines covered in a white dust of snow, that he, Nick, was still one of the best skiers on the slopes. He still had power in his legs. He was supple. He was strong. And it made him feel good to know that he had that power over his body, that power to dig into the mountain and still make love to it. He thought about power and what it meant in his life. He, Nick Dimani, a short Jewish kid from Brooklyn with a name everyone thought was Italian, had grasped the power of the record industry. For twenty years, he had composed songs with Sylvia's lyrics that had sold as many records as any in the business. Of course, Sinatra, Billy Joel, Dylan—now Barry Manilow—Bruce Springsteen—these were the guys who had the killers on the charts. But he had been there, on top, and he was still there. What had that A & R guy at Mecca Records figured out? That everywhere in the world, Dimani/Lundholm songs played every half hour of the day. In Tokyo. In Guatemala. In Tangiers. In places you never heard of. He had been powerful in the business, and he could still stay on top if his new album wasn't a bummer. He had gotten the idea about writing some new lyric ballads about Tahoe and he knew that only Sylvia could find the right words for them. He had the power, all right, the power to stay in the business. But it wasn't easy. He thought of the black records, black discs made from acid, of sound etched into plastic as he looked down at the white snow.

As Nick rode the cable car slowly over the mountain, with no one sitting beside or behind him, no one in front of him, he thought of power and the fact that he was riding not in his kingdom but in Harrah's kingdom. Because whatever you could say about Tahoe, it was definitely Harrah's kingdom. Nick couldn't help thinking about Harrah. Maybe because he was living in his villa, once reserved only for the Harrah family. Or maybe because he had been thinking recently about money, and how much money he needed as the famous Nick Dimani, and how he loved having money and the things, the toys, and the girls that money could buy. One thing Nick knew: Money was power. It wasn't *how* you wrote, it was what you made. It wasn't what they said about you, it wasn't fame, not in the industry. It wasn't about music. It was about permission. And permission was money. That was what Harrah knew. "Money talks. Bullshit walks." And Harrah had made more money than anyone in Tahoe. His little bingo parlor had become the great gambling tables of Harrah's Reno and Harrah's Tahoe. This mountain country had belonged to one man—Bill Harrah. (Vegas was another kingdom. That once belonged to Howard Hughes, and now, to the boys, the syndicates. But Tahoe, Reno—that was Harrah country.) Harrah's Tahoe was the most luxurious hotel in the West, from the shows to the casino, from the swimming pool to the Summit Restaurant; there was action any hour of day or night in Harrah's world. But now Harrah was dead. His hotel, rumored to be sold for four hundred million dollars to Holiday Inn, stood as a monument to a man who was a mystery.

When Harrah was alive, nobody really knew him. Married five times, once to Bobbie Gentry, he was always an enigma. Those who hardly knew him described him as a tall, plain man who looked like a minister. A Mormon who never had scandal attached to his name, he started with a bingo parlor in the thirties and parlayed his brains and tact into a fortune. He had built the world's largest collection of antique automobiles, now a museum in Reno. He had created a hotel and two casinos that were called "tight as a ship" by everyone who worked there. He was a legend.

Once Harrah was driving toward Tahoe and was stalled in bumper-to-bumper traffic. Being an impatient man, he was digging his toes furiously into his Bugatti. Suddenly he turned to his wife of the moment and said, "Why should I be mad, honey? All these people are driving to leave their money in my casino!" And then Harrah's laugh, which came from the bottom of a big man, echoed through Heavenly Valley, echoed 8,300 feet to the top of the mountain, through the twenty-five lifts and the lodges and the twenty square miles of snowy terrain. His laugh echoed through the blackjack tables and the keno tables and the baccarat tables. That laugh, which had Tahoe as a backdrop yawning above the Carson Valley and the desert 4,500 feet below, echoed in the basin. Harrah laughed because in some new way he, alone, had *created* Tahoe: a place of Bingo parlors in the snow that became royal palaces, a place where natural beauty and natural greed and gamesmanship had combined or collided in the center of America, and America was exactly that—a natural place where the high stakes were always there to be won by some lonely sucker.

Nick Dimani missed Bill Harrah. No one could take his place to carve out another universe in the West. No one was the tactician, the gamesman, the gentleman that Bill Harrah had been. Nick Dimani jumped off the ski lift, still weaving in mind in and out of memory. As he skied for his life's sake, he thought of all these things.

13. **The Art of Being Nick Dimani**

WATCHING HIS own tracks against the bright sun, under pine, sun, and that air which hung above the lake, Nick Dimani remembered his early life. It seemed that he was back in Brooklyn in high school, in the courtyard where for so many years he spent his recesses daydreaming of being a hit songwriter, a composer. He was again on the dirty streets of Brooklyn, carrying *The Life of Mozart* home from school. He was in the "nowhere" of his old neighborhood. "Unheard of," his great-uncle had said. "A boy like you? A composer?" "Be a tailor," said his aunt. His mother bought him an accordion. He loved it and knew he would be a composer. Even in that time of distant march music in Brooklyn, when he was a young boy with acne, frightened by life and feeling like a zero in a world full of numbers, Nick had written music, even then (his own little blues).

Now, light-years later, as he skied, Nick remembered meeting Sylvia. She was a tall skinny rich kid then, who knew nothing. Spoiled by her parents, she had never known a Brooklyn school yard, she had never smelled piss in the high school toilets. She had been sent to boarding school, one run by Swedes, and had grown up celebrating Santa Lucia Day and Swedish Christmas and wearing an enameled blue and yellow Swedish flag, from Cartiers, around her neck. Her father rode in chauffeured cars; her mother wore sable capes and when Sylvia's father died her mother at least cried in champagne, which was better than beer. Sylvia, when he met her, was a tall gawky teen-ager. She must have been sixteen when he played that gig at Sarah Lawrence. He had his own band then and she had flirted outrageously with him. He wondered if she had been hot for him or hot for his music. He wore dark glasses. It was nineteen fifty-six and he was a beatnik. He had that peculiarly pleasing quality of being hip which drew girls to him whenever he played at college dances. Yeah, she dug him. And soon they were lovers, making it in his apartment in New York, not much larger than the Steinway his mother rented for him.

"How do you like my pad?" he asked, and it had been hard for her to be enthusiastic. He could tell from the look on her face that she found it dirty. "Well, I'm great in bed," he laughed. He began teaching her about music then, teaching her everything she knew about lyrics. How to write a stanza: *a b a b a b*. He taught her about bridges and repeats. He had shown her how to make a lyric simple, how to use new vocabularies. From his dreams he had pulled out all that he knew about feelings and rhythms and simplifying songs. He pulled out all the stops. He had taught her things he never even knew he had locked inside him about words and feelings. With her weird intelligence and zany head for vocabularies, she had written words for him that were little playlets, tiny little dramas of loneliness, desperation, and yearning. She caught on fast. She developed a talent for simplification, as if she could oxidize feelings into songs the way alchemists dreamed of making lead into gold. She could alter the words of lyrics, take a world and turn it into *a b a b a b.* He taught her everything. She would imitate him. Mimic him. Try to *be* him. He would say, "Pencil it in," and then all he ever heard from her over the phone was, "I'll pencil it in." At seventeen, she left college because of him.

"You're a nuisance," he told her. But he was glad she left.

"I don't care. I write better lyrics than anyone. I want to write songs with you."

He'd taught that bitch everything. How to make music and words go together easily. Now he *needed* her. She'd better come through, after what he did for her. She'd better get her ass out to Tahoe. She owed him that. Nick thought of Sylvia, skiing down the long empty slope which led to a secret place of pines in Heavenly Valley. *He needed her.* That little lost kid who wore an enameled yellow and blue Swedish flag around her neck, who laughed at everything and almost levitated from joy when she heard him play his compositions, who creamed in her pink underpants when he took her to Harlem to hear jazz for the first time, that beautiful young girl had disappeared. What had happened to her? He had handed her success on an enameled Swedish platter and now she wanted to destroy him by leaving.

"Yes," Nick thought, "I could kill her."

14. **Poinsettias**

THE YES-OR-NO game she played in her head was over. Whether Rev liked it or not, even if she had to leave him,

Sylvia knew she had to go to Tahoe. She *had* to write the last lyrics for Nick. It would only take a week or two. She'd do the album. Then disappear. With or without Rev. That night she picked up the black phone and called Nick.

"I'm coming to Tahoe."

She heard his silence and relief. "When?"

"Tomorrow."

"What time?"

"I don't know yet. It depends on Rev."

"Who's that?" Nick asked. He suddenly felt uneasy. He felt he was about to hear something he didn't want to hear.

"Rev's my new friend. I *told* you about him, Nick. He's coming."

"No he's not. Come *alone,* Sylvia. I can't work with any of your friends around."

"Either Rev comes or I don't come."

"All right. One person. Who is he?"

"Someone you've never met. I told you about him but you don't remember."

"A snide singer? A guy who's going to give us a hard time?"

"No. He'll just be with me. Until the album's finished."

"Fine. I'll arrange everything. Do you want to stay in the hotel? Good. I'll book the suite at Harrah's."

"Get two suites."

"How come?"

"Rev likes space."

"Is he your lover?"

"None of your business, Nick."

"Is he?"

"What's the difference?"

"I like to know the layout."

"Yes."

"Serious?"

"No."

"Anyone else coming?"

"Yes. One other person. A woman. An old buddy."

"Does she keep her mouth shut while you're working?"

"Yes, Nick. Don't be so nosey. My friends have nothing to do with you, do they?"

"What's her name?"

"Nancy."

"What does Nancy do?"

"She agitates."

"Great. But we don't need a revolution in Tahoe. We just need an album." He was very angry. *Fear* made him sound polite.

"She won't bother you. I want to spend some time with her."

"Will you tell these people you're coming here to work? Make it clear."

"I will."

"Just two weeks. That's all I ask."

"All right. That's fair. I've already written a lyric called 'Change.' "

"How does it go?"

She spoke into the phone quickly the lyric babble Nick understood. "Change/ I can see that you've changed/ I can see that you're not the person you used to be./ Change, I can see that you've changed/ I can see that you're someone who might be for me./ Change is like the snow/ It changes all that grows./ The moon can change, the sun can change/ And change is all we know."

"Sounds interesting. It's slow. I can use that in the first part of the album. I know just where to put it."

"Good. I'll see you later."

"When?"

"Tomorrow. I promise."

Before leaving for Tahoe, they made love. Rev lay in the oasis of her bedroom surrounded by wool blankets, tulips, carnations, baskets, red poinsettias. The two of them had undressed and lay silently, at first on her bed. He brought her to a climax twice and then entered her slowly. He kissed her body and she held onto him. She was drowning in his arms. She held him, her beautiful tall blond life raft. It was the first time she'd ever spent the whole night with him. That was the best part. Looking at him, waking and seeing him next to her in sleep. The next day they packed and left for Tahoe. She felt *safe* with him. And oddly peaceful.

15. Saint of the Soap Box

THE SAINT of the soap box, Nancy, read Mao Tse-tung. When she wasn't clipping newspapers, that's *all* she read. She said she really didn't need to read anything else. She was Chinese—born in Peking, family went to Hong Kong during the war, nine Chan sisters, all of them attractive, all of them now in America, spread across the country like Chinese porcelain flowers in the desert, but she was the radical. The revolutionary. She was the odd one who should have been a doctor. Instead, she had been an adventurer—had run a ballet company in Hong Kong, been a journalist, been the underwater photographer on a yacht (until she saw a shark and decided she was afraid of underwater worlds). She had written plays, run a bar in Cleveland, edited the *Report to America* in Saigon, worked on a book about computers, studied Fortran and Cobol, knew the computer languages, French, Spanish, Italian, been a scholar, a translator of Chinese agrarian dictionaries—she was a soldier of fortune and, in short, the legend of the Chan family. A cook. A nanny. She had had every job under the sun and she was sure Mao Tse-tung had been a friend of her grandfather's once, back in the wilderness, back in the days of the Long March. Why hadn't her family stayed in China? Damn it. At first she had been embarrassed to be living in America. Mao had shaped the pattern of revolution for poor peasants, and she? Nancy? Now she would concentrate on Africa. She wanted desperately for the magazine she was working on to be launched and succeed. It was called *Issues* and it was a monthly magazine bringing a radical new approach to the analysis of world events. Its starting point? The truth of the interdependence of the world system. *Issues* would provide, in her words, "a meeting ground for the best of journalistic reporting and academic analysis. *Issues* would investigate the underlying relations which connect apparently disparate events around the world. *Issues* would have a world-wide network of contributors and would offer an international perspective on world affairs." She had helped write the philosophy of *Issues* during her last trip to London. Just last week she had stood up on a soap box in Trafalgar Square along with all the other weirdos and had orated to the throng of thirty or forty drifters.

"Who cares?" a Cockney voice screamed at her, but she ignored this. She believed in issues. She believed in the Movement. "Everything else is bullshit," she said. She believed that finally what she was doing had meaning. She studied Islamic revivalism and the implications for class struggle. She researched American intervention in the Indian Ocean. She attended the socialist cinema and went as a delegate to the Cuban Film Festival. In Central America, Nancy Chan had buried herself into the Nicaraguan revolution. She reported to her own study group on the conflicts in Southeast Asia and the left's crisis of conscience. She was considered *brilliant*. She wrote about issues neglected by the established media—political repression and the opposition in Liberia, the development of black trade unions in South Africa, the problems of the socialist left in Israel. The Movement. That was her bag. Her life was debate. Her life was information. Her life was meetings. Reviews. Demonstrations. Surveys. All of this was her life, but it all took money. To overthrow imperialism she needed imperialist contributions. It was a paradox. But it was necessary.

One morning she woke up in her apartment on River-side Drive (unlisted phone number—phone tapped—you could see her walking by the Hudson, a fierce Chinese female figure in Mao Tse-tung clothes) and she suddenly thought of her old college buddy, Sylvia Lundholm. It was time that she paid Sylvia a visit and raised her conscious-ness. Sylvia had bread, and at least some political aware-ness, but Nancy thought she used her money for all the wrong things. Clothes. Cars. Guys. All the nonessentials. She, Nancy Chan, would have to pay her a visit. For the Movement's sake. And for Sylvia's. It was time that Sylvia Lundholm paid her dues. Became *involved*. Most of the single women who lived on Riverside Drive were into com-fort, into sex, into rollerskating, into psychotherapy, or into being divorced for the third time and loving it. But Nancy was into revolution. "The Movement thanks you," she would say after receiving even the smallest contribu-tion. Nancy wanted Sylvia's bread. It was time to get into the corrupt fortune of Sylvia Lundholm. Nancy would spend a few weeks hanging out with Sylvia. Not that she had the time, but funding was essential to the Movement. There weren't too many people inside the system who had any real bread and would part with it for anything except middle class bullshit. Sylvia could perform some radical acts by giving some nonradical bread to the Movement, via Nancy. The idea of getting into Sylvia's life didn't thrill her, but it was worth two weeks of her time, Nancy de-cided, for the bread. For *the movement*.

16. Product

"HAVE YOU heard the news? There's good rockin' to-night!" went the Elvis Presley-Roy Brown song in 1954. When you think of rockabilly, the purest of all rock and roll, you might think of Jerry Lee Lewis, who married his thirteen-year-old cousin Myra, or think of Elvis Presley, the colossus that encompassed its narrow world. You probably wouldn't think of Sylvia Lundholm, who spent her nights on top of a double decker in a boarding school secretly listening to her Motorola maroon portable radio at night under the covers so no one else heard. At fifteen, Sylvia was already in love with poetry, the poetry of rockabilly as well as the poetry of William Carlos Williams. "The pure products of America go crazy," Williams wrote, and those words, pasted above Sylvia's bed, would one day become the beginning lines of America's epic poem, *Howl*. Those words which would perfectly describe her future lover, Rev Cranwell.

Sylvia, a first-generation American of Swedish descent, was not a pure product of America, although a lot of people said *she* was crazy. But rockabilly was pure. It was at that time the only American thing Sylvia understood and loved. She was obsessed with that kind of music. She was also in love with Presley, whose sneer was almost the same as the sneer on James Dean, whose liquidy golden suits and pompadours and wiggling hips and thick lips and lidded sexy eyes filled her girlhood erotic dreams. At night she would often fall asleep and Presley would appear somewhere on a green lawn. She would walk with him to a hammock. She would lift up her dress and he would begin kissing her between her legs until she rocked back in the hammock in a magical way. She discovered Elvis Presley when she was twelve and he was twenty and she lived in boarding school and he lived in Tupelo, Mississippi; she discovered him with his voice in her ear from the Motorola; she discovered him in her dreams. And most of all, she thought about him during Geometry when Mrs. Bette Lee Haig, her favorite math teacher, stood at the blackboard explaining the particularities of pi equaling. But she never heard what pi equaled—pi equaled Elvis Presley.

When you love music the way Sylvia Lundholm did, you

want to write it. You don't sit passively back all your life as if in a math class. Unfortunately, Sylvia really couldn't write music. She had studied singing, piano, and violin and had sat through those endless hours of Music Appreciation where more Mozart was suffered by boarding school teenagers who would have rather been rubbing up against each other in social hour to the Everly Brothers on the phonograph. During social hour, when the teenagers of the co-ed boarding school were allowed to dance "to work off their sexual frustrations," according to Doctor Harris Gustavson, the school psychologist, Sylvia sat in the corner of a bay window in the Manor House with a large black notebook writing poems for songs. At that age she was too skinny, had short blond hair, thick lips, slanted blue eyes, large breasts, and she was too tall. She was a tomboy in love with words and she wrote them out to herself and imagined in some perverse way that she was writing songs for Elvis Aaron Presley. That was in boarding school. That was the beginning.

When Sylvia met Nick, she dropped out of Sarah Lawrence and began working with him. He gave her something she had dreamed of having—a way to make a living out of poetry, a way to live with music. The first time he had taken one of her lyrics and put it to music, it made her feel that she had come home, that she had found what pleased her most. It was a poem she had written in college. Nick had set it. Changed it. Shaved it. Pared it down. And found a melody for it. Sylvia and Nick worked well together. It was a *miracle* when she heard it become *music* instead of *just words on paper*. They worked a lot of different ways. Sometimes he worked off the hook that Sylvia wrote, a little catch phrase that Nick latched on to. Sometimes it became the title. A little grabber. Whatever she wrote, he'd grab on to it and use it. And expand from that. He usually wrote the melody. Then the hook would take him in a further direction. Then he'd play the song for her and if she liked it, they made a demo.

In the beginning, the love that she had for Nick was closer to awe. All of her teenage life, at boarding school and even at college, she had been an outsider. A gawky girl who read a great deal and had a difficult time talking, dating, or making friends. Then suddenly, her life began. Nick had pushed her into a world that had the highs of the music business—instant history. Making love with Nick was all mixed up with making records. Through Nick, she walked, by accident, into the world of the "big money," the world that controlled the music business. Sitting on top of the envying heap of "money" people was Joe Leslie, a building executive who started an entertaining business and film group. He "owned" many of the big stars. She would go to his office with Nick, an office which resembled a Dutch Colonial house.

"I want to make a record with both of you—what kinda material you got that's available that can also be a TV special?" Long before Mecca Records, there was Joe Leslie.

Nick spoke for the two of them. Joe sat behind his desk smoking a cigar. "Nothing at the moment. But we will get back to you." There was a silence. Outside the office Sylvia began questioning Nick.

"Why did you say we had nothing? We have so many songs!"

"Listen, I know these guys. The more hungry you make them, the more interested they are."

"But we have so much material. What harm does it do to let them hear it?"

"It's not ready. That's your trouble, Sylvia—you're in a rush. There is *no rush*. We have plenty of time. I want them to run after us."

"But Nick, it can't *hurt* us to have Joe listen to some of the songs."

"I said no. I'm not interested. I know these guys."

"Well, I can't let them hear the lyrics without the melody, can I?"

"You're welcome to. Let them hear the lyrics."

"Come on, Nick."

"Look, Sylvia—keep them waiting. Give them the whole package. Let them hear the whole demo. If they get really hungry enough, they will come after us with more money than you've ever dreamed of."

"It's not the money, Nick, it's a chance to have Joe Leslie do the recordings now."

They fought. It was the only time, she remembered, she disagreed with Nick. He thought she was impatient. She thought he was unreasonable. Following each other around New York, they argued on Fifty-seventh Street in front of the delicatessen. They argued in front of the Brill Building. In front of the Waldorf. You could have made a map of all the places they argued.

"Don't ever doubt yourself," he said.

"Why?"

"The name of the game is to be confident. Rock and roll? It's a con game. The whole industry is an industry of blue sky. The biggies give permission. The talent makes the product. But deep down in the toe of the shoe, it's something else. It's not being afraid. Everything you have to say is valuable." In the end, he was always right. Nick Dimani was smart. She knew this.

"You make me feel good," she said.

"I mean it, Sylvia, the poet is the person who tells the truth, a lot of truth, who suffers and confesses and lives life to capture it again one more time. The sanest female in the world is you, darlin', when you're most crazy. You're some kind of freak, a spiritual athlete who runs the distance. There's a savior in you, a wilderness girl that never got out of childhood. Out of the woods. Hold on to her. You write naturally. It doesn't come hard for you. It's not *how* you write, it's what you have to say. The agon. Your latent agon is always inside you. I don't know what put it there. I don't *want* to know. I just know that you have it. Hold on to it. Cherish the hurt. It's your future. Shit. Let *me* do the rest."

When she was young, so many years ago, there were moments when she loved him so much she almost forgot that she was a separate person. They would lie in bed and make love. He would tenderly put her under his arm as he lay on the bed with a black pen and music paper writing things he heard in his imagination. The old days. She loved the way he smelled. She loved to hold him. Often he would talk to her about music. He would tell her things. "I want to reconnect the music I write with the cosmic source," he said. She never stopped him from talking to her as if she wasn't there. He was her teacher. A large sagging double bed with white sheets and black ink stains was their university. She would look up at him.

"What does that mean?"

"Musical tones and planetary music move together. Music is a medium by which we discover ourselves. What occurs with single sounds in the micromusical region is enlarged every time music is written."

"Do you think of that when you're composing?"

"No. I think of *nothing* when I'm composing. But sometimes when I'm just waking up or taking a walk down the street, weird things come into my head. I *think* about sound. For example, yesterday I was thinking that a single sound which is nonperiodic is a wave structure which we call aleatoric. If I make a whole song similar to the ways the sound in my mind is organized, the individual components of the piece could also be exchanged or permutated without changing its basic quality. It's the relationship of one sound to another that matters to me. Every song has within it the compositional design of the process of change."

She held him. He knew secrets. He was bitter sometimes. Argumentative. It came from his poverty. But Nick was also so dynamic it was like being close to an event. He constantly gave off energy. Sometimes she had to get away from him. She would walk in the park. Think about him. Think about the *studio* where they were closer than they were in the bedroom. The studio *was* a bedroom; it was a large square padded place without any sound except the sound they made together, and with other musicians, which was engineered to travel back into their own heads. Making sounds in the studio was Nick's greatest high. She loved it, too. In some way, the studio was a womb away from the "reality" of life. There, swimming in the amniotic water of their words and music, she could float into memories. The frequencies, the pulses, the knobs, the musicians, the statistics, it was a mathematical trap in which they were caught. It was safe.

Walking by herself down a street, she would wonder about Nick. He was obsessed with "selling." Writing the music was part of the high, but actually "selling" the songs was what he enjoyed the most. He was a born con man and salesman. She would be embarrassed to empty her soul to so many of the sharks and biggies and moguls that Nick sat face to face with. A heat would come over him when he "sold," a "high." It was as if he were playing a chess game constantly and constantly winning. She didn't dig the con game. Nick did. He loved it. The combination of his "intellectual passion for music" and his salesmanship was what eventually made him a success. Before they won their Grammy, he had to push all the time. After the Grammy, it was different. People came to them. People in the industry and in the stores begged for songs. Their tongues hung out. They were dogs in heat. They panted for songs by Dimani and Lundholm. They were sniffing around constantly looking for material the way a dog in heat looks for a bowl of water. They were suddenly sought after by the panting dogs who snivel after success, dogs with fleas, with drooling lips, with wet eyes and drooping eyelids. They were sought after by the panting bloodhounds of the music business.

17. **Troubadours**

IN AMERICA, music is the chief meeting ground between black and white cultures. And Sylvia Lundholm at the age of nineteen, as a white girl, had virtually more going for her than any other young rookie in the music business. She was part of the successful Dimani/Lundholm team. She wrote all the words for their big hits. She was a girl who, although not a performer, had achieved the massive popular support of the black and white audiences. When Nick Dimani played the Apollo and Madison Square Garden, as well as Vegas, Sylvia Lundholm was recognized as his lyricist. She was one of the few white women who symbolized the essence of what used to be called *soul.* She and Nick were two of America's favorite troubadours. Their songs were on every jukebox, in every teenager's ear. At different studios, she and Nick had recorded records which went platinum and which went beyond the limits of rhythm and blues. Quite simply, from her very first recording session, she had songs whose words were on the lips of nearly every American. At the age of nineteen, Sylvia Lundholm, partner of Nick Dimani, was at the top of her profession. That year, "White Trash" broke every record for a single. Dimani/Lundholm were nominated that year for a Grammy for best arrangement, best lyric.

She remembered that Nick, looking like a disheveled madman, came into her bedroom and held out a round-trip ticket to California. She was going to Hollywood with him.

"We've done it, Sylvia."

"When did you find out?"

"This morning. I read it in the newspaper. In *The New York Times.* Not *Billboard,* sweetheart, but the *Times.*

Dimani/Lundholm, the name appears again and again. Look. We've been nominated."

"Tell me again what this means."

"It means that for the rest of your life, you'll be writing songs with me. Once you win a Grammy, baby, it's more than money. It's permission from the industry. It's the focus of world attention. We'll go from nowhere to somewhere big. And stay there. It means more than sales. Every performer, every studio, every motherfucker producer and record company will be at our doors to make an album with us."

After Nick went home that night, Sylvia sat and looked out the window. Left alone in her apartment she suddenly wondered what it would be like to be famous. Not just to have her songs sung, but to have her name known. A picture of her and Nick had been in the *Times* and in the *Post*. They were the youngest songwriting team nominated for the Grammies. "White Trash" and "Hello Again Happiness" had caught on to the point where big-time arrangers like Bob Mercey had set her songs for the leading singers; Sinatra had written her a fan letter; Ray Charles had asked to meet her; Otis Redding had kissed her hand and called her a "genius"—all of which created in her feelings of joy, bewilderment, confusion. She read about the "honesty of her approach" in *Cash Box*. And wondered, the night before the Grammies, if her songs, the songs she wrote with Nick, would win.

Flying to Los Angeles, she was numb on the plane. Photographers had taken pictures of both of them boarding. She had given an interview to *Look* and an interview to the *Times*. Most importantly, she was noticed. Welcomed. Everyone exaggerated the things they did for her. Crowds recognized her from the paper. A flashbulb illuminated her entrance to the airport. Her passage on the plane was filled with voices condescending and ingratiating. As she sat in First Class, a nun came out to meet her and Nick. She asked that they send a photograph to the Mother Superior, who listened day and night to "Hello Again Happiness." Sylvia whispered to Nick, "A *nun*. Can you believe this?"

The phones that rang at home rang again in Los Angeles. The evening of the Grammies, Sylvia sat with Nick in the Beverly Wilshire drinking rum and Coca-Cola and meeting moguls, agents, and singers who were in town for the awards. Her dress was glittery white sequins. Her pumps were high white satin. Around her neck was a gold chain with a diamond G clef which Nick had given her. Some of her songs about failed loves were sung at the ceremony by singers she had only years ago pasted on her wall. As she stood waiting for her name to be called, she knew she owed everything to Nick Dimani. He had given her the first *recognition* of herself. As a writer, as a lyricist, she was somebody. She wasn't that lost rich girl in boarding school, walking through the woods wanting to die because her parents were somewhere else; she wasn't that lost lonely girl with a Motorola to her ear. She was now a lyricist destined for *The Hit Factory* and airborne to immortality.

Sylvia heard her name being announced by the Master of Ceremonies, *"Best song lyric, Sylvia Lundholm,"* and she walked forward to take her award. Everyone in the audience looked at her. They were the old pros, the great names, the business sharks, the producers, the Richmond Schneiders, the people who sang showtunes to lowdown blues, the fantasy makers, the biggies from Dune and Columbia and Mecca, the boys from Cedar Communications, and suddenly as she walked down the aisle, there were hands clapping, hundreds of people reaching out to touch her, people screaming to her. She was in the maze of fame and she knew it. "Thank you," she said for her first award. Then she was receiving the second award with Nick standing next to her smiling to the cameras and holding her hand. How young they were! The youngest American songwriters to have made it big—a couple of brilliant kids right out there in fantasy land—golden record land, where golden records were better than halos. They were almost like sculptured angels in some Florentine frieze, both of them in white, embracing each other. She saw for the first time what fame was. She saw it with amazing clarity. She was someone everyone wanted to touch.

18. After the Grammies

LATER THAT night Nick disappeared. Was he coked out? Fucked? Frightened? She sat alone in her hotel room receiving calls while he was out vomiting Brooklyn out of his system somewhere in a bathroom in Los Angeles. He was taking sunshine—orange tablets. Acid. He was tripping out of his life because it had turned out all right. He entered the world where Grammies are not there, awards are not there. He had too much feeling in him. It was nineteen-fifty-nine. Bob Dylan was playing his harmonica in the village. The Beatles were tuning up in Liverpool. And Dimani and Lundholm's "White Trash" was everywhere. You heard it wherever you went. Sylvia's calls came from all over the world. From girls who had known her in boarding school. From housemothers. Invisible Swedish aunts. Incoherent cousins. Uppity librarians who had lent her books. Sick uncles. The next day she found Nick (he had fallen asleep in the lobby of the hotel) and the two of them went for a swim. Nick and Sylvia were no longer just lovers, no longer just friends or just composers of songs. They were celebrities.

Back in New York, Sylvia tried to convince herself that she was now "famous" as a lyricist, but when she awoke one morning a week after the Grammies and looked at the rain, she felt, "It's the same old me." She dressed in jeans and went down in the elevator, saying hello to the janitor. In some odd way, Sylvia found that nothing pleased her. She still went to the various doctors that held her body together. The muscle doctor was still the person to whom she confided her fears and angers. It was to him that she told her secrets about her childhood—the tears, rages, and years of loneliness. To her foot doctor, she offered her calluses and corns. To the sports doctor, she offered her stress. To the gym, she went like a good little girl, faithful to the rings; she went to the beauty parlor, to the diet doctor, to the different tailors and shoemakers. She spent her time "gilding the lily." The lily! Suddenly she was a hot-house flower in demand—no longer a dandelion but an orchid!

Who was Sylvia Lundholm anyway? The night before the Grammies she was someone whom a few people in the music business admired, an unknown name fixed on a label, an invisible person behind the success of Nick Di-mani. After the Grammies she received hundreds of telegrams from people she wasn't sure she even knew, invitations from composers to write musical scores for plays, invitations to give lectures at schools, invitations to political dinners, invitations to keep festivals alive, celebrations open, exhibitions going, cards inviting her to the Pen Club, the Designer's Award of the Year, tributes, painting exhibits, film previews, openings, demonstrations, corporation dinners—all of these things vied for her time, her attention. She was now a deductible target. It was as if she just sat in her apartment like a huge target and invitations like darts were thrown at her from every cause in the country. She was wanted. She was invited to give her money to everything from psoriasis to war protests. There was not a march or a dinner or an event in the arts, letters, or politics which would take place without her. She was mentioned, often, in the columns whenever she was seen at a restaurant; her dinner parties were quasi-newsworthy; she was interviewable. The celebrity circus with its acrobats performing the Hand-to-Hand Wrisley, reaching from one to the other, trying not to fall, to perform the difficult stunts, all of these above the air and space of other mortals —she was, in a way, *a nouveau freak,* which meant she was famous.

She was a harlequin. Someone people wanted to eat with, be seen with, sleep with, talk with, listen to, march with, vacation with. Her exodus from anonymity was accompanied by several events, a pillar of requests, the clouds of flashbulbs, the motors of other people's limousines. Unlike Nick, Sylvia was unchanged by the promised American land of celebrity. It was fun, sometimes, but it didn't mean that much. She regretted only that her parents were dead. Her mother would have been proud of her. Didn't she take her to museums when she was eight? Didn't she take her to concerts? And her father, a Swedish businessman who had a distaste for the limelight, would have at least respected the royalties. She was now a cash-box princess. With no one to applaud her royalty.

Nick and Sylvia were sought by those who give permissions. That was the time that Lionel Colesman entered their lives. He was one of the founders of rock and roll. He owned Mecca. He had the brains of Donald Pond, the taste of Arthur and Richmond, and more money than anyone. Lionel wanted Sylvia Lundholm. It was that easy. What Lionel wanted Lionel bought. His portfolio advisors advised him against spending so much money to own a songwriting team. Wouldn't he be better off with a racehorse? For once, Lionel didn't listen. Mecca was his toy. He played with artists as well as with municipal bonds and boats. He understood an artist's requirements: Money. The success of Lionel was simply that he got the best. He paid a little more. That's how the best is lured from one place to another. RCA offered one deal. Lionel found out. And went higher. He didn't care about tax requirements. He wanted, for some deep sexual reason, to *own* Sylvia Lundholm. He had seen a picture of her. She was sexy.

Too sexy. Almost vulgar. You could see the roots of her dyed blond hair. She was natural, but there was something trampish about her. Her smile turned him on. So he became an investor. He bought her talent. Unfortunately, Nick Dimani came with Lundholm. They were a team. Like Mr. Rolls and Mr. Royce. He got two for one. What Lionel Colesman wanted was Sylvia.

19. Zoo Time

AFTER THE Grammies, it was zoo time for Nick and Sylvia. The polar bears and zebras looked at them. They were a special breed of animal. They were stars. Rock and roll, after all, was always a circus. Celebrity was odd. Sylvia felt less comfortable with it than Nick. It was a monstrous thing. It made people hate you. It made them envy you. It made them up-tight. They would say, "Isn't that great?" In the world of the truly rich, people could invite you for dinner or lunch and still *loathe* you. If you made it, you were an insult to all the losers. It made them furious. But what was it to "make it"? Sylvia enjoyed money, but she noticed every month she was seeing more doctors than ever before. Was that fame? All the people that held her up with their expertise? The allergist for her hives? The gynecologist for her cystitis? The behavioral specialist for her weight problems? The dermatologist for her rashes? The trichologist for her scalp? The psychoanalyst for her stress? The kinesthesiologist for the kinks and knots deposited all over her body? She was famous. She was supporting all these doctors. Little bills arrived from them with columns of numbers. She looked at the bills. They came from money managers, cleaners, lawyers; they came from laboratories; they came from gyms; they came from

stores where she bought clothes and shoes she hardly enjoyed. Her wardrobe became more and more casual as she
became better known. Like Nick, she now wore jeans and
silk shirts that were custom-made. High heels from
Charles Jourdan. Hermes scarves from Paris. Watches and
jewelry from Cartier. And loneliness from the human condition. Things never took away the loneliness. Only in the
studio with Nick or in bed with him, did she feel whole.

The years Sylvia had spent at boarding school had made
Sylvia want her own home. In her own taste. She had
always had pictures of her ideal apartment. Now that she
had become famous, she decided to create her own apartment. She began buying paintings on her first trip to Paris
with Nick. While Nick would spend his time wandering
through Montparnasse, she would go in and out of galler-
ies picking up the paintings that she had dreamed about.
In Paris, they stayed at the Ritz. Her decorator, Oscar
Barshak, had given her a list of antique stores to visit, most
of them in mansions and in homes. She had bought Na-
poleonic chairs and small pieces of boiserie. It was the first
time she ever really had the sensation of being happy. She
would write to Oscar, this old fussy Russian gentleman,
about her adventures in the world of antique dealers, gal-
leries, French stores. Paris was a world of perfect objects.
Setting out from the Ritz one morning she bought Napo-
leonic end chairs with pink velvet fabric, a glass chandelier
that originally came from Venice, and a large rough
wooden table from the south of France that appeared by
its patina to have served peasants for centuries. The table
was made with pegs instead of nails. It was five hundred
years old and she loved it almost as much as a person.
Next she found French Provincial chairs with webbing that
was perfect, a set of white plain dishes from Provence,
Picasso plates. Out of the chaos of her life, she was now
going to furnish a perfect apartment. Rugs that were
made in Aubusson, glasses from Venice, tapestries from
the eighteenth century, golden candlesticks in vermeil

from Cartier, rare books—special editions of Baudelaire and Rimbaud. She bought all these things simply and with great pleasure, the way a fishwife buys cod. Each day she came back to the hotel with a different purchase, another antique. Most of the things she shipped to America special delivery, like a little girl who can't wait to build a doll house. Nick didn't appreciate her taste.

"So much money for a book?" he would ask, smoking a joint and examining one of her purchases as he walked around the suite at the Ritz in the white Sulka bathrobe she had ordered for him.

"It's a rare manuscript."

"All right. I can see that. But those paintings—why did you have to spend so much money on a picture of just a blue canvas?"

"That's Yves Klein."

"That guy has some racket."

"He just died. From overwork."

"Overwork? Spreading blue paint on a white canvas for a couple of thou?"

"Nick, I love you. You don't have to like rare books and Yves Klein."

"Man, I think you're crazy."

"Why?"

"Piling up all this shit."

"Who are you? Rebel without a cause?"

"I just don't want to own things."

"For how long?"

"I don't know. The titans, pigmies, has-beens, and never-weres of this world have to *own* things. Man, you're *making history*. Your words are like a lamp that goes on every time a record is played. What do you have to own all this stuff for? It's a lot of drek."

Nick was dissatisfied, ambitious, living on the fringe of Sylvia's dreams. They had to be together and yet they didn't quite connect. It was always as if there was a wire missing. Something was going wrong. When they flew back from Paris to New York, Nick moved out of Sylvia's apartment and rented a place of his own. His reason was he couldn't stand Sylvia's decorator. "The guy gives me the creeps. He always arrives with a little patch of rug, a small swatch of something. He is always carrying samples. And everything he orders for you costs twice as much as you'd pay for it in a store."

"He's a craftsman."

"He's a con man, you mean. That ladder—that ladder for your bookshelf. That's a fucking fortune. I know I come from what the media calls *humble* beginnings. I know I have a temper. I know I'm vain. I know about my so-called burning ambition and my so-called hatred of the highfalutin'—but I don't see what you *need* all this for!"

"Need what?"

"Need all these decorations. Need these peasant tables and chandeliers and candlesticks and candelabras and chairs and sofas and screens and tables and dishes and paintings."

"They're nice. I like a nice home. Is there anything wrong with that? Am I supposed to be the female equivalent of James Dean and rebel against a home? Which I never had? Most of those guys on motorcycles come from nice homes in Ohio. I never had a nice home. I can't help it. I like making love on clean white sheets. I don't like sand in my crotch. I like old things. I like to be in a nice apartment with white walls and paintings. Just because we write rock, do we have to live in the blackboard jungle?"

Nick and Sylvia fought about *things* a lot in those days. That was before Lady Rita arrived and turned Nick into a snob. They fought over Sylvia's decorator. They fought over Sylvia's freedom. She had a habit of only seeing Nick every *other* night now. She didn't want to be hemmed in. It wasn't that she was making love to anyone else. There was no room in her life for more than a few friends, her apartment, her writing, and Nick. She just needed time off.

"What are you doing when you're not with me?"

"None of your business," Sylvia said. But she said it lovingly. She always hugged Nick and made him feel how much she loved him. "What am I? An Italian-American housewife? Do I have to constantly tell you what I'm doing?"

"Yeah."

"Well, sometimes at night I cook. I like to cook alone. Sometimes I screen Elvis movies. I read Carl Sandburg. I love his poetry about the landscape. He seems to understand words and syllables."

"You're living out your teen dreams."

"That's right."

When her apartment was everything she wanted it to be, Sylvia turned to clothes. She had been described in *Esquire* by Gay Talese as the worst dressed woman in America based on her appearance at a party given by George Plimpton. ("Who cares!" Nick said.) She began to discover clothes. She found them in antique shops; she found them in army-navy stores; she found burlap pants and tied ribbons around them; she put heels and boots with mandarin jackets. She started the trend away from designer dresses. Suddenly in the stores there were mountains of Chinese shirts, peaked caps, old pink blouses from the forties, soft as rose petals, antique nightgowns washed and ironed. Wherever Nick and Sylvia appeared, there were photographers from *Newsweek* and *Women's Wear Daily*. The name of Sylvia Lundholm became a fashion catchword. Long corduroy skirts, mandarin jackets, old floppy hats, and boots were her trademarks. Closets filled with dungarees which she combined with silk shirts made in Paris. Clothes became costumes for Sylvia. Wherever she went, a style was born. Large white fur coats, capes made out of raccoon—jeans, silks, and furs were all mixed up. It was not clothes that she wore. It was a "look." She showed fashion that it could make fun of itself. But beneath it all, beneath the velvet caps and sable cuffs, beneath the sun-baked blue jeans, beneath the Yves St. Laurent bright pink shirts, the long scarves made in Italy, the Sorella Fontana coats and pea jackets, beneath the mesh stockings and hiking boots, was the old innocent Sylvia. Vulnerable. Sensitive. And natural in an oddball way. She was the "new" American girl: outspoken, generous, funny, and hilarious, without makeup. Stripping away the whalebone, under the corset, under the thread and rag and silk and camisole, was a Sylvia that people liked. Wherever she spoke, people listened.

She and Nick appeared on the Ed Sullivan show and he sang songs. Afterward, Ed Sullivan called Sylvia to the microphone. With his deep blue eyes and his odd neck that moved slowly toward her, he smiled and said to the whole world, "This is the great Sylvia Lundholm—the words behind the songs you've just heard." Everybody in the audience applauded.

"What is it like to be so talented?" he asked, "You were the youngest lyricist to ever win the Grammy, back in nineteen-fifty-nine. Tell us what it feels like."

Sylvia giggled in front of the millions of viewers, the great Out There who listened carefully for the truth. She was a saint that appeared in person, one of the holy ones of a world that was mushrooming, the yeah-yeah world of pop and passion. "It feels good," she said. "It's as if you have a voice. And you can make a difference. There are so many people who have a lot to say and yet can never reach out to anyone. I feel that I have the privilege to be the tongue for these people." She made *talent* seem effortless.

"What is it like for a young person to have so much to say?"

"It's like living with your senses wide open. Your eyes see a lot. Your ears hear a lot of things nobody else picks up. You have a way of feeling what goes on inside of people, almost as if you have X-ray vision into their feelings, the ones they don't show. You can sense humor and longing and anger. And then, when I put these thoughts into song, I simplify what I see. I take all these senses and try to put them into simple words." The questions were retarded. But she answered simply.

The audience loved her. Sylvia Lundholm was America's darling in the sixties. Everyone wanted to be able to write a song. The way Sylvia did. As naturally as they breathed. She and Nick were America's troubadours.

20. After All the Jacks Are in Their Boxes

"After all the Jacks are in their boxes,
And the clowns have all gone to bed,
You can hear happiness staggering on down the street,
Footprints dressed in red."
—*Jimi Hendrix,*
from "The Wind Cries Mary"

THE EARLY sixties were Sylvia's time. It was when music, because of Presley, because of the Beatles, crossed over and became the most important force in the country. Starting with The Beatles, the people who were articulating the pain and anger of the nation were the songwriters. The force of music was powerful, more powerful than the movies, more powerful than books, more powerful than the news. Music stopped being dumb music. The rock and roll of the fifties had often been the same chord pattern over and over. The same rhythms. The music of the early sixties—Dylan and The Beatles—made a transition for America. It gave America its poetry, its humor, its confession box. It was imitated. It was often put down by the intellectuals whose ears were castrated, but it was the new voice in America. Dimani and Lundholm were part of the new sound wave, the revolution of high art, pop, fantasy, religion, and nursery rhymes.

At the same time that Lenny Bruce came out of Hanson's Drugstore and resurrected the idea of pain, humiliation, and truth being the underbelly of comedy, at the same time that Lenny was standing up in clubs, cracking jokes, and showing the audience the stigmatas of being an original artist in America, music came into its own as an art form. The Beatles, Presley, Dimani and Lundholm, Neil Sedaka, were in the avant-garde soul of everyone, they were the new poets, articulating in their words and music the history and insanity of American feelings.

Sylvia and Nick were part of the new rock. Their songs were on every turntable, part of the hi-fi culture, inside the maze of the poetry now on stereo. And then, eventually, everyone got into it, even the intellectuals. The college professors were listening to it. They had to listen, because no one was listening to them. No one was listening to anything but music. The music stopped being rock and roll. It started becoming a way to live, a philosophy. America became a baby wrapped in the swaddling clothes of rock and roll.

Even when flames were bursting in the flametrees in Vietnam and the world was tortured by the news, the music industry was a world unto itself, a war unto itself. It was concerned not with student demonstrations and death in Vietnam but with students buying records and what kind of songs were selling. Bottom line was *their* message. Sylvia remembered all that. She was in Chicago making a tour for the latest Dimani album. She appeared at a record convention. The "biggies" from the record industry and some artists were locked in one of those grotesque sales pitches where everyone was selling everyone else, hype was all. And the company picked up the tab. Everyone was pushing The Byrds, The Jefferson Airplane, The Who, The Stones, The Beatles, Aretha Franklin, James Brown, the sound of Memphis, and Nick Dimani. Because she wrote the lyrics for Dimani, she was privileged to be one of the women considered privy to the entertainment. Usually women were the *interpreters,* not the *creators* in the sixties. She remembered it all too well.

After the ballroom, a few select artists, along with the biggies, were invited to the famous biggie, Donald Pond's, penthouse suite. Pond was the biggie at American Records. Later Pond would be fired in a world-publicized scandal, but in those days, he was a lawyer-turned-record-producer, riding high on discovering talent. Pond was having one of his famous private entertainments. Sylvia walked into his suite. The guests—disc jockeys, airmen, record pluggers, and retail salesmen—were already sitting and watching the show. On a huge bed a six-foot-tall blond German female body was being made love to by a tall black female body. At first she could hardly see the faces of the women. All that she saw were legs. It was almost like a boxing match. The men in the room sat breathlessly watching. Everyone was snorting coke at the expense of Pond and his record company. Marijuana was also being smoked. She was the only woman there as a spectator. So, that was how they really *sold* rock and roll.

She remembered, a man in a black suit who weighed over two hundred pounds stood behind her smoking a cigar and rubbing his cock against the edge of a table. "Yeah, yeah, yeah, do it, do it," a dwarf whom she recognized as a number-one salesman from the coast was saying. Indifferent waiters dressed in white linen suits, wearing white gloves, were serving champagne on ornate silver trays. The goblets and stems were grabbed by the spectators who spilled the champagne on the floor. The two women performing were exquisite. They were prostitutes, and when the show was over they were then made available to their guests. A famous liberal lawyer with a beard joined in the action. A fat record executive, whom everyone knew, laughed as he took white powder out of a small white paper cup. Music was playing. Ray Charles's record was playing, "Laughin' and Clownin'." And the "boys" laughed and clowned and didn't seem to notice Sylvia. She felt sick. *This* was the real music industry.

She remembered, that night, she stood there cemented in thick carpet. She couldn't get her feet to move. She was standing next to American Records' chief *artistic* representative, one of Donald Pond's henchmen. It was *his* job to scout convention locations before the boys arrived, round up the hookers, and make way for the lord of de coke.

Hallelujah! Save the Lord! For the meek shall inherit the earth! But the meek certainly didn't run the record industry. The billions of dollars' worth of records pushed to the blacks and the teenagers and the other markets were created not by artists but by these talent executives and account executives and dope pushers and businessmen who knew how to combine the hopelessness of the undiscovered artist with the dream of success. Donald Pond, American Records, payola—they were all part of the corruption of the country, hidden behind the ersatz word *freedom.* They were the herpes simplex virus behind the love masks. How to take the loneliness of the adolescent and feed him or her songs that were in a way a sort of drug. I want to hold your hand, my ass. The loving group was pushing sex exhibits, drugs, murder, anxiety, profits, and ripping off the artists. Sylvia wanted to write lyrics about it. She felt too deeply the pain of everyone, even of these record salesmen who needed to get boredom out of their veins, who lived this way as a normal part of their business life. She wrote:

Studio double O,
Where I need to go,
Sex exhibits, life's a joke,
Boozing, drugging, spooning coke;
Studio double O,
Where I need to go,
I'm in trouble,

There's no hope,
Dreams betrayed me,
I can't cope;
Studio double O,
Where I'm jailed
In their crime;
Studio double O
Where there's nothing
To find;
Studio double O
Where I spend all my time.

Nick wouldn't touch the song. She tried to give it to some other composers, but it was never published. The business didn't like the message. The company didn't dig the words. Nick never saw it as right for their image. It never got to be a song. Whenever she had a nightmare, she heard the lyrics. She saw what the lyrics were about. It was a repeated dream. What had once happened in reality appeared repeatedly in her mind. The cast of characters changed in each dream. In her nightmares, sometimes, she was at Donald Pond's party at the convention and saw the Isley Brothers or Jan and Dean or Dusty Springfield. Sometimes she saw Elvis or Jerry Leiber. Chuck Willis. Richmond Schneider, B.B. King. Mixed with them were Mozart, Karl Marx, Wallace Stevens, Allen Ginsberg, Ann-Margret, Chopin. The dream ended with her sitting in her large bed on Park Avenue and feeling cold sweat running slowly down her nightgown. Whenever she had dreams of that music convention, she decided to give up the business, to give up writing rock and disco. She was tired of being the fifty-hit wonder, the queen of stroll, the essence of smiles. She wanted to run away from what the rock sheets called the "democracy of talent" but what was really Sodom and Gomorrah redesigned to the corporate structure. She was tired, as Flo Kennedy, the Black activist and her heroine, had once said, of "stepping over a manure pile to pick a rose." She was tired of the shit-covered Toot-

sie Roll which was the record business. She was going berserk as an organ at half-time; she was living in the world
of teen angst—but what about her own angst?

Brill Building profits and Brill Building pop had driven
her to see an analyst, had driven her to vacations she didn't
want, men she didn't dig, clothes she didn't need. All of
that money she made couldn't cover up the hard edge of
every day's nervous unhappiness. She was now a Swedish
Alice in Wonderland, grinding her teeth, *having* to produce a record album every year.

Once, she wanted to be a poet. She wanted to live in the
world of odd colors and feelings. A world without wounds.
She slowly watched the biggies in the business picking the
bits of experience like tartar from their teeth with tooth-
picks. Into the nation's glass eye and deaf ear went all the
creations of black and white souls in trouble. But over at
American and Cedar and Dune and Casa Records, these
people were recycled into industrial poets—creating pain
for marketing reports, turning their hopes and humilia-
tions into profits that would be poured, drop by drop, like
warm oil, into America's ear. Sylvia felt ambivalent about
all this. She hadn't come up from the bottom. She had
been born rich. She hadn't needed to floss the teeth of
suffering. She was that alienated person who didn't have
to ask "What's happening, baby?", that poet-eyed person
who wrote songs easily, the way children sing about their
lives. With joy. And with innocence. She had gone to the
well of her own feelings and become, with Nick, a legend
walking around singing to herself all those early songs.
How had all that led to conventions in Detroit and Nash-
ville and Miami and Chicago? How had these simple tunes
about innocence led to desperation and coke and road
shows of dykes for the panting biggies? And who was she
to talk about whores anyway, when she had become a
whore herself? The industry smeared innocence in a
heartless way that took her blood away. Bottom line told
the only story. That was the conflict—all those songs about

pain, alienation, love-hunger, fear, discrimination, all those confessions that strove, like the maxims of Lenny Bruce, to open the scales of the eyes only, in the end, made some assholes in a public company profit. Baby, that was rock and roll. *The Talent* was tired.

21. Fame

FAME DID something to Sylvia sexually. It took away her softness. It took away the sweet joy of making love to a lover. Nick was once her lover. But fame brought her any-one she wanted. That was it. Sex became too easy. She had other lovers. They sprang up like dandelions on a green field. Many. Too many. She was young. And rich. And funny. And sexy. She was on top of it all. She learned to suck a man's cock. The girl of the sixties. Sweet sixties. She learned how to do it and enjoy it. The first cock she took in her mouth was Nick's. "Suck it," he said. "Just keep sucking on it until it feels natural." After that, there had been other cocks, other men. She wanted love. That's what she looked for. Instead, she was told that she was a good cocksucker. She gave good head. Not because she had to. Not as a whore. But for fun. She got off on it. Nick was into pot and pussy. She was into head. Those were the sixties. She sucked millionaires, boobs, sailors, laid-back lawyers, intense doctors, gymnasts, Olympic champions, record dealers, and feelers. She sucked and ate almost anyone. Then she got tired of that scene. She had "no heart for head," she told Nick after they had become *just* friends. She began to relax. Less *hot,* she calmed down. She went on a pilgrimage through the seventies. From promiscuous to not-too-interesting affairs. "My God, I'm becoming middle class," she said in the seventies. "I'm *fucking.* As well as sucking." Then she let ambition, hard work, and politics absorb her energies. She meditated and passed through a goofy crisis of spirit.

She was alone. That was all in the past. All in the past. Until she met the ultimate blond coolman-guru, Rev Cranwell. She forgot what sucking and fucking meant. With Rev, it was a different experience. She was no longer in the world of sex. It was pure pleasure. Rev was something else. Something good. He made up for the bad days. Now she wanted to give up fame. To get back to her authentic self. She wanted to love. Not fuck. You couldn't do that when you were famous. Rev was her god joke. He didn't care. Something was odd about him. He was kind but detached. Still, in his own detached way, he enjoyed her feelings. That was it. Rev gave her back feelings again, good feelings. He was so cool—he was either spaced out or burned out. Something was missing in Rev that she had to provide with her love. Her feelings made up for his lack of feelings. So she went back into who she was again. She "put out"—not sexually, but with kindness. He could do no wrong. That was her new attitude. Not "What can you do for me?"

"That's what I hate about fame," she told one of her old buddies who was bringing up two kids and studying law in California. "Fame and money. It becomes a What-can-you-do-for-me world. That's what the industry does to you. It takes your softness and your womanliness and your real crazy femininity and it eats it up. Just as it eats up a man's soul and masculinity, and castrates him; it eats up a woman's poetry and softness. So I say to you that fame sucks. And that's why I'm getting out."

It wasn't that she was afraid of *what* she became. It was what she *didn't* become. She needed time to think and just bop around.

22. *Lionel and Ron*

FLYING OUT to Tahoe, Lionel thought of Nick Dimani and Sylvia Lundholm. Once Nick and Sylvia had been at his mercy. Now it was the other way around. He owned the catalogue but he didn't want to lose Nick as a recording artist. The Dimani/Lundholm contract was almost up. Cedar had been making sounds about signing Dimani and Lundholm. He turned to Thimble on the plane.

"Should I shelve Dimani and Lundholm?"

"You have no taste, lovey," Thimble said.

"What do you mean?"

"What do you think? Of course you shouldn't shelve them. They've given you more hits than any other writing team in Mecca history. You're so used to being surrounded by yes-men who always give you the wrong answer."

"Let's stop quarreling like newlyweds," Lionel said to Thimble. Thimble as a yes-man hadn't been doing his job recently.

"Keep them," Thimble said. "Make nice. Don't close any doors." Lionel Colesman often felt that the music business wasn't worth the hassle.

"Why are we going to Tahoe?" Lionel asked Thimble. His voice was weary.

"Because you for some arcane reason care for Sylvia Lundholm. Because you can't stand to be thwarted in anything and you want to convince Dimani to stay with Mecca. And because you can't sit still."

"What do you think of Tahoe?"

"I think it's provincial. I think it's beautiful. Perhaps the most beautiful place in America. If you like snow. Which I do. And if you like gambling. Which I do. I'm very pleased about going there. We haven't been there in a long time."

"What is this sudden '*we*'? I don't think you should be addressing me quite so familiarly in public, Ron. My wife wouldn't like it. No one should ever guess we are lovers. We're just friends."

"How would anyone guess we are lovers? From the way you treat me?"

"I treat you the way I treat any employee."

"I'm not supposed to be an employee. Remember? I'm a buddy."

"You're a paid fag," Lionel said cruelly.

"To you I'm just a hunk of meat."

"Hardly. If you were really a hunk, I'd treat you better."

"I hate you when you treat me like this. A hunk of meat."

"Stop the soap opera. What are you supposed to be? My lawyer? My accountant? Jean Paul Sartre? You're not my intellectual equal, so why should I pretend you are? You service me and I service you. I like companionship when I want it. You want companionship plus cash and contacts. It's really the cash and contacts you want. Without the companionship. So you're bored with being nice to me."

"You're too possessive, Lionel. You're spoiled."

"If you had my money, wouldn't you be?"

"Your money? You mean, your wife's money."

"I increased it."

"You're demanding, Lionel. You take away my privacy."

"Really? Your privacy to do what?"

"None of your business."

"I tell you what. Why don't you get off at Reno and take a plane back to New York? Then you can have all the privacy you want. I never want to see you again."

They were nearing Reno. "Fasten your seat belt," Thimble said, as if the entire conversation had not taken place. "Look, Lionel, I'm your friend. The money you give me helps me out. I don't intend to spend the rest of my life with you."

"You'll be lucky if you spend the rest of the week with me," Lionel said. He looked out of the window. How he hated pretentious whores. He was beginning to despise Thimble. Thimble was good at repeating Lionel's ideas as if they were his own. He wished he hadn't brought him along. But it was too late. He'd have him as a shadow in Tahoe. The best thing to do when they got there was to give him a thousand dollars' worth of chips every morning and let him gamble. Lionel smiled. Thimble was a loser. It would probably last him half an hour. He shivered at the thought of seeing Sylvia, as the plane landed on the snowy runway. Tahoe! According to the Chamber of Commerce, it was the most beautiful airport in the world.

23. *Pentagon Landscape*

IN TAHOE, Sylvia Lundholm and Nancy Chan held all night rap sessions the way they had in college so many years ago. They sat talking in Sylvia's suite in Harrah's Hotel.

"Imagine, if you please, a world never forgotten, never away from my mind, a world of mace." It was Nancy speaking. The year was nineteen-sixty-five. It was the height of the Vietnamese war. Nancy, in those good old days, led many teach-ins and had become more radical since she was Sylvia's roommate at college. In her Chinese head the world was dangerous, and America was a place that needed a lot of fixing. Buddhist. Maoist. She often spoke about America as if it were a pipe that leaked. Nancy was studying Marxism. She tried to get Sylvia into it. For Nancy, Marxism was one of the answers. Depressed? Marxism. High? Try Marxism. Horny? Marxism. Nervous? Marxism. "Marxism saved my life," Nancy said. She had said that back in the flower generation.

"I didn't know your life was in danger," Sylvia had answered.

"We are all in danger." Nancy believed that then, as she did now.

Sitting in Tahoe they talked about the years that students and working people marched from the Berkeley campus to shut down the Oakland Army terminal, trying to stop the war material from being shipped to Vietnam. Nancy Chan had been one of the demonstrators on the march as well as one of the organizers. She was one of the women jailed. Sylvia had heard about it and had flown to California and bailed Nancy out. She had meetings with John Lennon, Jerry Rubin, Joan Baez, and Jane Fonda, but she was out there to bring Nancy back to New York. All night in Tahoe, Sylvia and Nancy talked out memories.

"Remember when you wanted me to take up Marxism?" Sylvia said. "Then you didn't like my songs."

"God it's good to talk," Sylvia said. Nancy was her all-time favorite pal. She loved Nancy. Quite simply, she would fly to the end of the world for her. She would demonstrate at the end of the world for her, too, but she didn't want to be a Marxist. She didn't know what she wanted to be. Sometimes she just wanted to be silent. She wanted to be good to humanity and belong to Rev. The first part was possible. The second part wasn't. Nancy was a partner from another part of life. Sylvia would never give her up. She loved her too much.

"If your songs don't really teach people how to undo all this misery they've gotten themselves into, what good are they?" That was the question of the sixties. Then, Nancy was in the center, in some odd sense, of her world. Nancy spoke straight. Sylvia remembered when she wrote "New Day Coming" for Nancy's peace march in San Mateo:

Hey Hey
The new day is coming
Hey Hey

Get rid of your sorrow
What drives you around
Won't be an Eldorado
Hey Hey

Nancy hated the song. For her it was too tame, too non-revolutionary, too Sarah Lawrence. "Can't you put in kick ass? The CIA sucks? Napalm blues? Something like that?" she asked angrily. When it came to napalm, she didn't have much sense of humor. But then, neither did anybody in those days. Sylvia had said calmly, "Why don't you write it?"

"Yes, I can write it, but I don't have a name. I'm in the Movement. Everyone in the Movement just talks to everyone else in the Movement. You and Nick will be heard! You have the power, sweetheart." Nancy was militant and often bitter. She lived in a world of private vilification and public suffering. She never forgot that she was *oriental* and part of the first world and the third world. "How about 'Pentagon Landscape'?" Nancy suggested. "I'll say it, you write it, *they'll* sell it."

That year, *Pentagon Landscape* was Sylvia's and Nick's hottest album. It hadn't been easy for Sylvia to persuade Nick to work on the music. He wasn't interested. He had just married Lady Rita, that snob with marbles in her mouth, the ultimate lady from England. He had switched from his spiel of "indifference to material things" to a new way of spending money that was vulgar and not in character. Houses. Cars. Apartments. Nick was buying up all the trophies for the *old* Nick who hated things. His wife was not a marital partner. She was a spending companion. But he wrote the album anyway. She had gotten him to do it with her. She had begged. And finally they had put the album together. It had an ironic jacket cover of the Pentagon upside down. And it hit! *Pentagon Landscape,* with its wit and its horror, was nineteen-sixty-seven. And as it always happened in the industry, Lionel Colesman, who owned Mecca Records and owned the songs, who couldn't care *less* about murder and Vietnam, made a lot of money.

Nancy and Sylvia remembered that year when the album hit. It was the year of the goat. It was the old times, raw seed times, the times before they flowered. The war was on. Rock music was hot. It seemed like a time when the country was going to change, when the raw seed was going to burst into something good. Clive Davis went to Woodstock and had a revelation, "These really *are* flower children," he said. Bombs broke Buddhas in Cambodia. Men tired of war blew up in the flametrees in Vietnam. Sylvia wrote her poems and marched in Washington next to Robert Lowell and Norman Mailer. She was right with them on the march, they were using the soles of their feet to impress America, walking against war. Poet soldiers. Nancy and Sylvia remembered.

"Remember 'If-you-have-a-lemon, make-lemonade' Hinkle?"

"Remember people turning on, tuning in, and dropping out?"

"Remember Dr. Leary and his swami shtick?"

"Remember the old days?"

"You've changed," Nancy said to Sylvia.

"Change is all we know. I've lived a thousand lifetimes since then." Nancy stared at her. Her beautiful Chinese face had no lines, just slight laugh lines around the eyes.

"You should be more political," Nancy said.

"I am political in my own way. I'm political as an artist. Art is the ultimate politics. Also, I don't have federal agents on my tail anymore. I can't say I miss them."

"*Art* is fine, but don't fool yourself. Be political with your body. Boycott. Demonstrate. You can't have art without bread."

"Why not? Bread gets stale. Art doesn't."

"Bread. Then guns. Then art," Nancy said. There was no convincing her otherwise.

God, Sylvia needed someone to talk to. She was glad Nancy had come out to Tahoe.

"There are some things that stand out from the sixties, Nancy. Nick's marriage. It was a shock that he married Lady Rita. I almost felt as if I lost him, but we still continued writing our songs. I watched Nick change. From Brooklyn desperado to Brill Building ambitious, to Star (that was with me), to Fifth Avenue and Paris and Monte Carlo *celebrity*, the perfectly tailored narcissist. He perfected the art of being an idol. He had caps glued on his teeth. Lifts glued in his shoes. His hands on the keyboards were now perfectly manicured. He had a hairdresser. Mr. Blue. He was the transplanted man, Nancy. He went from Brooklyn snot to international chic."

"Isn't it the same thing?" Nancy asked. "Snot and chic?"

"You make me laugh, Nancy. But even now, sitting here and laughing, I'm filled with secret anxiety," Sylvia said.

"Oh, Sylvia, that's so stupid. If you were political, you wouldn't have time for anxiety. It's a luxury. But I suppose we can only travel at our own speed."

"I married in the year of the goat. I married for a list of things."

"Tell me the list."

"One, I had no home life and wanted a home of my own."

"Already a mistake. A revolutionary has no home. Go on."

"Two, I was tired of digging around for a sex life."

"The price of getting laid is often too high. Besides, we put too much emphasis on sex. I like sex. But not as a narcotic. As a way that comrades communicate. Sex is a capitalist plot."

"I never found a comrade I wanted to fuck," Sylvia said.

"Too bad. The prick has no political conscience."

"I often think that 'Up the Revolution' is an excuse for not being up."

"And yet only a person who's turned on can really be a great lover."

"Oh God, Sylvia, let's not talk about sex."

"I love you, Nancy. A lot of people slept through the sixties. But you were awake."

Nancy looked at her. "I'd rather be awake and afraid, than sleeping."

"While you were awake, I was getting married. I married Rightman the wrong man. 'Nomen est omin'—that was my favorite expression. It means the name tells you about the person. The name is the omen. I married the right man. The wrong man, as it turned out, but in the year of the goat, it was the right man. He was the son of a millionaire, the heir to the Rightman Foundation and all its good works. He was handsome, a good cocksman. He was charismatic. Rich. A great lay. Everything. Except. He wanted a pussycat and he got a tiger. He wanted a sex kitten. He wanted a cupcake. Instead, he got a poet who threw a pie in his face. I put him into my songs. I made him famous. Remember, 'The Right Man Was the Wrong Man' from the album *Mister Right Is Wrong?*"

"Sure. That album made millions. Which I'm sure you squandered. Instead of putting the money toward the revolution." Nancy could never forget the Movement. Everything came back to that.

"Well, I know excess nauseates you. But I had an excess of Swedish normality, too. I wanted children. When I found out I couldn't have them, I was devastated. So I made up for everything with *songs*. All the Rightman songs were hits. Nick loved them. Everybody sang them. Remember the song called 'Snafu Your Marriage Rings':

Snafu your marriage rings,
Throw off your sandals;
Don't be a prisoner of
Cashmere and candles.
Snafu, be blue,
And wake all alone;
There's a life to lead
Once you snafu
Your happy happy home.

"That was in the album we wrote about leaving home called *Living on the Edge.*"

"That was the album I could relate to," Nancy said.

"I lived on the edge and the edge made me change. I knew loss, more than my own face in the mirror. Exterior life began happening. You were involved in revolution. I was involved in insight. It's the same thing. Mao was a poet. Castro is a poet. Neruda was a poet. Octavio Paz is a poet. Castro said that history will absolve him. Revolutionaries are yogas. But instead of sitting in the lotus position, they're cocking guns."

"I like that," Nancy said. "And now, how about a donation to the cause? It's nice to talk about poetry, but I need money."

"How much do you want?"

"I need five thousand immediately. Then another five for expenses for the concert in February. Postage, mailings—they're all expensive."

"No problem."

"I'm very grateful," Nancy said, "The Movement thanks you."

"Don't thank me. Remember me when you give the concert. I'd like to have Dollar Brand play some of the songs from the new album." The rap session ended. They hugged each other. They were the kamakaze survivors from the sixties. They lived apart. But close. There were only bonds of friendship. For Sylvia, Nancy could do no wrong. She had changed. She had in a way gone berserk. She had become an out and out berserk revolutionary. She dealt in guns. She was speeding on revolution. She had bought guns from Africa. She had advocated bombing the multinational corporations in South Africa. She was funding nuclear labs. She was boycotting banks that invested in *apartheid.* She was risking her life to track down collaborators with Rhodesia. She was not the Nancy she had been. Nobody was the person he had been. Nick was different. He was not the fast track to the future—he was the desperate straphanger trying to make an album that would not bomb. Nancy wanted to bomb South Africa. It was all insane. Absurd. Shake, rattle, and roll. Nick was on a fast train to more cash, more money, and more fame. And if the train crashed? He would take her with him. Nancy was berserk, but she would get her ten thousand dollars. Nancy and Sylvia were survivors. Nancy was a part of her.

24. The Casino

NICK WALKED through the casino. It was crowded. Nick lived for risk and action. Nick loved the action of roulette and poker. The poker game at Harrah's went on as usual. Of course the big stakes were played in Vegas, but it wasn't unusual for twenty thousand dollars to drop after a poker hand at Harrah's. Tiny was playing; so were Lonny Lunatic and Amarillo Slim. There were a group of fifty professional poker players who floated in and out of every game in Reno, Tahoe, and Vegas. They all knew each other and had secret nicknames.

Gamblers are hunters. The risk is more important than the winnings. Just as Tahoe Indian hunters once went out to capture jackals, otters, pelts, the Lake Tahoe gambler sets out for a night of killing with his adrenalin high, the juices in his mouth, in his thighs, in his genitals and brains pumping power—the hunt for Tahoe winnings. Fate and luck and brains have nothing to do with winning. For gamblers are more than men. They are hunters and they are obsessed with risk and the sport of the game. What has been called an addiction is no more or less than love, the chance to be more than a mere human, to hunt, to kill, and to become a *hero*. A hero with your own hands, the cards, symbolic animals inside the gambler's hands.

Nick listened to the chips on the tables, the roulette

wheels, the rakes of the dealers, the machines with their ironic mechanical tongues bobbing up and down spitting lemons, apples, plums, the vegetables and fruits of chance. This was the world that Bill Harrah had created in the Sierras. It was his kingdom and Nick loved it. Nick was a gambler with his own time, a gambler with songs. Each disc was a little chip. Walking around the casinos at Harrah's, the Sahara, and Harvey's, he thought of his album. Sylvia was working with him every day and it was as good a collaboration as it ever was. The creeps hanging around her—Nancy, whom he *never* cared for, and that quiet boyfriend of hers from New York—stayed out of the way.

That was all Nick Dimani wanted. To have everything out of the way so he could write the album with Sylvia. Modular microcassette tape recorders with their plug-in modules awaited his songs. Like a boxer, he couldn't wait to take on the industry.

25. *How Laurie Met Nick*

NICK REMEMBERED meeting Laurie a year ago. "Harrah's only promotes people from its organization," Laurie had said to him. She was relaxing during her twenty-minute break dealing blackjack in the pit. The entire lobby of Harrah's made up the casino. From one end of the glass door to the other end, there was nothing but roulette machines, crap tables, slot machines, keno, baccarat. Laurie was twenty-one and had grown up in Tahoe. Her mother owned the Blonde Factory, a beauty parlor in the town. From Vegas to Tahoe had been the one move Laurie ever made. Her dad had been a carpenter in Vegas who worked for Del Webb. He had drunk himself to death. Her mother, Billie, got on the Greyhound bus with Laurie in her arms when she was a widow of two weeks, puked through her first job as a waitress, then began working in a beauty parlor until she earned enough money to buy her own shop. "Put all my money in the bank for your education, honey," she told her daughter as she was growing up. They got along better than most moms and daughters at first.

"My mom bought a house in Mason Valley and that's what kept her sane," Laurie continued. "Every weekend we'd drive sixty-five miles down to Mason Valley where our house sits on the ten most arid acres in the valley. We had to irrigate it. There's no water there. And that cost a lot of money. But Mom said, 'Sanity is worth a lot to me, honey.' I grew up there in Mason Valley and here in South Lake Tahoe over the beauty shop. One of the things I remember from being a kid in Mason Valley was that our neighbor was a shepherd, a Basque who used to hang his meat up to dry in the sun. That was his dinner. One night our dog, Krepsie, came home with his dinner in his stomach and the poor shepherd came over to Mom's house and tried to tell us he was hungry and our dog ate the meat. But all he could speak was Basque and it was so sad because neither of us could understand him. A lot of people who work at the casinos bought houses down there because land was cheap. In those days it cost nothing. It's worth a lot now, though. Mom still goes there on weekends."

"Do you go with her?" Nick asked. He was getting excited about this girl, this strange beautiful local who had long black hair hanging over her large breasts, and whose thin shapely body fit perfectly into the tailored clothes she wore as a dealer. She was girlish but elegant in a simple skirt and blouse.

"No, I don't go any more. I'm too busy working at the club," she said. She noticed Nick looking at her clothes. "You have to be very careful about what you wear as a dealer. At Harrah's Dealer School, we were taught that as dealers, we have to be simple and elegant because the way we dress reflects the house. Also, Harrah didn't want the dealers to distract from the gambling tables. God, are there *strict* rules. You just wouldn't believe it, Nick." She was drinking her last Coke. Her rest period was almost over. He was trying to think of ways to make the moments left count. He was going to make it with her after her shift was over. That much was clear. He might even get her to come upstairs during her next twenty-minute rest period. He couldn't remember ever being turned on like this! He remembered saying, "Why don't you come up to my suite during your next break? I'll play you some records." God, he was hot. She was the best-looking woman he had ever seen in his life. Was she a woman? Or a girl? Something about her—her large blue eyes, her freckles—made her seem so naive and childlike. He wondered if he was losing his cool. This girl was no whore. She was bright. He could sense how sharp she was. If she wasn't bright, she certainly wouldn't be dealing at the age of twenty-one at Harrah's. They had the best dealers and croupiers in the world. Nick laughed. They could afford to! They made millions every day. Many millions. Nobody really knew how much. The exact amount of Harrah's fortune went with him to the grave. But Nick would guess that every day, twenty million was pushed at the tables, which meant a lot went to the house. Those were the odds. Harrah's cleaned up because it was the one casino in the world rumored to be legit. That is—clean. At least, it was the only casino in Tahoe where you could buy shares in the New York Stock Exchange. Why was Harrah's so profitable? He asked that question once of the manager, S.G. And S.G. had shot back, with a smile, "Because Harrah's is a class joint." And it was. There were more rules at Harrah's than in the army. Every employee, and there were hundreds of them, had a rulebook. Old man Harrah ran his casino the way Patton ran his troops. Nick had often reflected on what Harrah's secret was. How did he get so fucking rich? And he had come up with the answer: *controls*. He had designed a casino that was fucking foolproof. All his business secrets were his own. If you asked him, "How much did you make this year?" the old cowboy, who dressed like the Prince of Wales, just looked at you and laughed. Harrah was one of the old-time breed of Tahoe millionaires who kept their noses clean, their eyes on the till, and had every employee watching every other employee. There were no slip-ups at Harrah's. No money stolen. "The difference between people in the East and people in the West," Harrah once said to his buddy, Steve Govern, "is that the guys back East have forgotten how to be paranoid. They have too much education and culture to remember that someone is always trying to steal from you." Steve Govern had been one of Harrah's few friends. They were buddies, as many millionaires who are not competing for the same money can often be. Govern never wept a tear in his life except at Harrah's funeral. They were cut out of the same cowboy cookie mold. Both of them Mormons, both of them quiet men who kept a low profile. Both of them loved their kids. Both of them liked women and married a few times, although Harrah, who had married Bobbie Gentry after she wrote her song about jumping off the bridge, had married more times than Govern. Both of them kept quiet about their money. And that's what Nick thought about all the time: money. As he drank a frozen daiquiri, or fucked, or skied, or drove his car, or argued with lawyers, or talked to Govern at Tahoe T's, a local steak restaurant where he always ate lunch by himself because the meal was the best steak in town, he thought about money. How to make it, how to spend it. His mind was always on buying a new suit, car, boat, house. He loved money. He would have given his life to be as rich as Harrah. But right now, he wasn't thinking about money. He was thinking about sex. It was a sensation which Laurie brought out.

"I'll come see you during my next break. But don't tell anyone or I'll murder you. I could get fired."

"For seeing Harrah's greatest star? Come on, no one at Harrah's would fire you for making love to the show-room's greatest attraction! They wouldn't dare!"

"Don't kid yourself," Laurie said. "A friend of my mom's, who was a dealer and one of the best, worked at Harrah's for fifteen years. They finally let her work at the roulette tables, which is a great honor, believe me. You have to deal for years before they promote you. She left one day during her lunch hour to go upstairs to get the autograph of Engelbert Humperdinck for her kids, and it was all over. Her pit-boss found out and she was fired. She had to work at another club."

Nick ordered another drink. He liked the way she called him Nick right away. Most of the girls, the show girls and the dealers, were starfuckers. They called him *Mr. Dimani.* They couldn't wait to meet him. Laurie was almost shy, although she spoke her mind and everything she said seemed to have something genuine about it. Her voice was happy.

"How'd you get to be a dealer?" Nick asked. He wondered if she would really come across. The "townies" were funny: They considered themselves the aristocrats of Tahoe. No matter how much they might admire the stars, they stayed aloof. They stayed aloof from the gamblers, the skiers, forming their own clique. Even the bit players, the dancers and singers in the lounge, never met the town-ies. All at once, Nick realized how much Laurie attracted him and why. There was still an honesty about her. She was a dealer, which was the highest up you could go in Tahoe. It was almost like being an account executive in New York. It was the best job in town unless you owned your own business, were in real estate, or *fooled around,* which is what the rich tourists did, spending half the year in the mountain paradise and the other half of the year in other places. "How'd you get to be a dealer?" he asked.

"I was selling real estate and I heard that Harrah's was running its school for the summer. The dealer's school, as it's called, is run two times a year only, and there was one opening. I grabbed it. Real estate is iffy. When you close on a big house, you can make a good commission, but it's not regular work. I thought I'd do this for a while and then maybe go East. I'd like to go to law school or work in trading on the stock exchange. Deal in futures. Sugar, gold, coffee. Get to travel in Brazil. I think I'd like business. And I'd sure like to live in New York."

"Leave here?"

"Sure. I don't want to stay here all my life. I love it. I could never get the Sierras out of my system. Once you've lived right on the lake, you're spoiled. But I'd like to have a career and meet interesting people. There's no culture in Tahoe. People say they are going to start a symphony orchestra, but they never do. It's a nice place. It's a good place to get away *to*. I went to Harrah's because I thought being a dealer would be good money."

"Man, that's crazy. A dealer school. What was it like?"

"The school? It was the summer relief school and it was held in a back room behind the kitchen. Really, just a back room. They set up the different tables and each person studied to be a dealer in their particular game. There are the table games: craps, roulette, twenty-one, baccarat. They're all in the pit area of the club. And there are six pits at Harrah's. The floor men answer the phone, make sure every table has a dealer, make sure every table gets money. They replace the money whenever it runs out. Or carry it away. Every table starts with from three thousand to thirty thousand dollars. There are four schools. I went to blackjack school. They teach you how the player plays against the dealer. You learn how to shuffle the cards until you can do it perfectly. They watch you, making sure you learn and know what you're doing. It takes days to learn how to shuffle. They teach you the motor movements. It really takes about two weeks to learn how to deal, and then you're ready. You make fifty dollars a day in tips. You get a salary. Then you take your tips and everyone pools them. You get paid each day in cash. So you make from eighty to a hundred dollars a day for an eight-hour shift. Did I tell you about *the controls?* Someone is always watching you, checking on you. The floor man. And then there's a whole department upstairs: Mirrors looking down on you and the whole casino. You can't see them. But they can see you. Everything happening all day and all night is on film. You are continually being filmed no matter what shift you are on. There's the day shift. The swing shift— evenings. And the graveyard shift—that's the middle of the night. You get your tips from whoever wins while you're dealing. There are a hundred and thirty tables of blackjack. And every shift has three hundred dealers. You work eight hours and every hour you're off for twenty minutes. That's because you really can't *concentrate* on the game and dealing for more than an hour. The floor man is there to make sure no one cheats. Like that. If you see someone cheating, you're taught at the school the most important rule of all: Never talk to a customer. You call the floor man if you suspect someone of cheating and he calls observation. That's the mirror people upstairs. By the way, nobody ever *knows* who works in observation. Harrah's keeps this a firm secret. You only work up to observation from being a pit manager. Then a casino manager. Then one day, you may disappear and become part of observation, but no one is *sure.* You're never allowed to talk back to rude customers or crabby ones. You're not supposed to laugh. Or talk. You can't, too much. Or ever use any sarcasm. Or flirt, of course. You're there for one reason: to deal. You're not a woman or a man; you're *a dealer.* They write you up. And put you on file. If anything ever goes wrong, anything, even if you're late, that goes in your file. I did real well and they put me on summer relief. Then I had nothing in my file so I was the one dealer they promoted from summer relief to steady. You learn in school what to watch for: game protection. You are taught the second most important rule of a dealer: Always keep your eyes on the cards."

"Do you?"

"Yes."

"What else? This is interesting."

"This really isn't *that* interesting, Nick. You're kidding me," she smiled. He put his hand on her arm. Her skin was very tan. She had light brown hair on her arm and her legs were very long. She was skinny. Really pretty. And intelligent.

"How do you keep so skinny?" he asked. His hand moved over her hand to her leg. She drew her leg away.

"Don't. Even on your break, you have to be careful in public if you're a dealer. Harrah's has all these rules. One of them is you have to be thin. You have to have exactly the appearance they want. In fact, you won't believe this, but you have to sign a contract that if you get one pound overweight, you agree to give up your job. That way they keep very strict control of a dealer's appearance."

"What about the game?"

"Blackjack?"

"Yeah, tell me about it."

"The essence of the game is to get the blackjack hand. Oh come on, Nick, you play blackjack. I've seen you at the tables."

"I know. But it's a turn-on to hear it from you."

"Grammies turn me on. I saw you win the Grammy two years ago—you and Sylvia Lundholm—for that song you wrote that I love, 'Boldly Open Your Eyes.' Let's stop playing games. This is worse than blackjack. You want to make love to me and I want it, too. Where do I meet you and when?"

"After work. In my suite."

"Isn't your wife there?"

"I have a suite just for working. I'm staying at Harrah's villa. Come to the one I work in. Suite five-oh-nine. You don't need a key. I'll make sure I'm there. And I'll leave the door open." When she arrived, she found herself in a large mirrored suite with a black Steinway, the usual Harrah rattan and box furniture, and pictures of Nick's family around the room. There was a bar. He offered her a drink. "You turn me on," he said. He took off her clothes and noticed how perfect she was. She was wearing dark stockings and a garter belt. No underpants. And a black bra. Under her perfect dealer's clothes, she looked like a showgirl. "Wow," he said. He was holding his cock in the air. She knelt down. And began sucking him. Then she stopped, suddenly, and walked into the bedroom. Teasingly, she lay down on the bed. He began to climb on top of her.

"Wait."

She turned over. Her ass was the only part of her that wasn't tan. She was breathtakingly beautiful. He entered every hole in her body. She kept breathing heavily until she reached a climax that took several moments to end. "That was beautiful," she said, and looked at him. It was only then that he came inside of her. He had never remembered feeling so tenderly toward any woman. She had made him be the best lover he had ever been. He felt as if he could go on making love to her all night. He pressed his lips down on her and kissed her so hard he bit her. She pulled away.

"Still want to hear about blackjack?" she smiled.

"Yeah. Give me some strategies."

"You always have to know what to watch for."

She was turning him on again. Was it the way she spoke? When she talked, she moved her lips so slowly that he wanted to kiss them again and again. The more he looked at her, the more he wanted to look at her. She was the one woman he really ever wanted.

He remembered. The beginning was good. Whenever he thought about Laurie, he thought about the way he felt about her in the very beginning, when she made him feel he had someone, once more, to live for.

26. Cross-country Skiing

WHEN GOLD was found in Nevada, Laurie's great-grand folks panned for it in the mountains. She was a girl who only knew pines and the Sierras. She had plenty of time to play and always loved the mountains for the wildflowers in summer and skiing in winter. Since eighteen, she'd been putting money away by working as a dealer at Harrah's. Laurie usually skied Kirkwood. There were fewer crowds there than in Heavenly Valley. Today she was cross-country skiing and she had a date with Nick Dimani. She had to keep it from her Jesus Freak mother. Her mom would talk to Laurie every morning at breakfast.

"You know that life begins with God. Your sin has separated you from God. Jesus Christ paid the penalty for your sin," her mother said, fixing bacon and eggs, standing in a pink bathrobe and wearing curlers. The pink curlers formed a plastic halo around her head.

"Yeah, Mom," Laurie smiled.

"The only thing God asks you to do is to trust the Lord Jesus Christ and to ask him to forgive your sins so that you may begin a happy and meaningful life with God."

"That's cool, Mom. But I am happy," Laurie smiled. She turned on the stereo and listened to a Nick Dimani album. The fireplace was filled with Tahoe wood and the fire was filling the house with the good smell of lumber. She couldn't wait to be out of the house and in the snow with Nick. He turned her on just by looking at her. She hurried to finish breakfast. Thank God she didn't have to work today at the casino. It was her two-day break. She would ski all day with Nick. She would make love with him until her body hurt. Then he'd take her to the California Room at Harrah's. They could boogie until morning. Her mother never knew who gave her the diamond dancing girl that she wore around her neck. It came from the Jewelry Factory and it was Nick's Christmas present. She told her mom it was rhinestones and that she'd bought it in Reilly's. She loved her mom. But Laurie's mother hated Nick. And that was the problem. She told her friend Barbara, who was also a dealer at the casino, "Maybe I'm a starfucker. But he is somebody and he can take me from nowhere to somewhere. But my mom hates him because he doesn't believe in God."

"Sure," Barbara warned. "Don't put all your eggs in one basket." But Nick could do it. He had boats, cars, even a plane. He had everything, had been everywhere, had done everything. He was the best lover she had ever known. Really, what had she known before Nick? "He's so much *older,*" Barbara said.

"So he isn't young—so what? Sometimes money and sex can be exciting." That was something her girlfriend didn't understand. With an older man, you could let yourself be free. He wasn't into "relationships" and problems. He was into kicks and highs and he could take her higher than anyone else. The boy she hung out with before, John Saxe, was all right. He was a kid in the air force. But he offered her a "serious Christian life," and she wasn't ready for that. She would never be ready for that.

"Life begins with God," her mother said.

"I know, Mom," she said, and closed the door. Soon she was out of the house and in her Pinto driving to Fallen Leaf Lake. It was the largest of the smaller lakes surrounding Lake Tahoe, slightly below the east of Desolation Valley and at the foot of Mount Tellac. Laurie had her cross-country skis on the ski rack on top of the car. She stopped at Harrah's to pick Nick up and took his cross-country skis and poles from him.

"Thanks, Laurie," he said, "but I should be carrying the skis, not you."

"Don't be crazy, Nick, you're a star." She was happy. Together they drove to the lake. The car stopped at highway 89. They got out, put on their skis, and began skiing toward Fallen Leaf Lake. One step and a glide. One step and a glide. It was almost like jogging in slow motion. The cold weather slapped across their faces as they cross-countried into the woods. Into the snowy silence. Standing in the woods, they smoked some grass which Laurie kept in a stash box in her coat pocket. The snowy mountains spun around them. Slowly, Laurie reached into her back-pack and took out a red blanket and spread it on the snow. The marijuana was Mexico's best—Tijuana Gold. She felt mellow.

"You look good," Nick said. He smiled when he spoke to her. He began taking off his ski sweater. She took off her jacket and laughed. He put his hands into her ski pants. "You're wet," he said.

"I always am," she laughed. His fingers were cold. "Especially when I'm with you."

"I like it here," he said. "Ice on the snow. Icicles. Trees. The sky. And you, baby." He held her close to him. He felt her beautiful breasts under her ski sweater. He had his mouth on her breast, he didn't care if she was wearing a sweater.

"No one can see us," she said.

"I know."

"This is fun."

"That's the way life is supposed to be, but isn't," he said. She laughed. She always laughed with Nick. The trees covered them, a nest of trees and snow. They put their skis next to them and she slid over on her side. He opened the fly-front of her jeans. She felt him coming into her. He was built powerfully and his chest was enormous. She reached out and felt his strong arms. "How do you like it? In the snow, it's called a coolie."

"Are you serious?" She laughed. "It's fun, really." As they made love in the snow, Laurie remembered the first time they had made love. He had fucked her brains out. Ever since then, she had changed toward him. She was his woman. She had dropped all the little games that she, as the best-looking dealer at Harrah's, used to play. And now she was making love one more time in the snow. She could hear her mother's voice, "One more thing, Laurie, you can't thrive as a Christian alone. Meet with others who have trusted the Lord Jesus in a church where the Bible is taught."

This wasn't a church. But it was the earth, cold and pure and white. The earth was a temple, too. She turned over and looked up at Nick. Suddenly his face was tense. "Let's cool it and ski," he said. They put their clothes back on. Nick could be moody. Cross-country skiing, she listened to him talk. He told her everything, how he worked on composing, how he heard songs in his head, how he wanted this album to be about the Sierras and love. "Dig it? I want this album to be all about natural beauty and what it is like to groove in a world of pines and ice and high altitude. No one's ever done it."

"I hear you," Laurie said, and she understood when he talked about his music.

On Ski Wren Boulevard, near Heavenly, they stopped and rented hot tubs. It was in a private room within a restaurant. Nick called for cocktails. Piña Coladas. "Only in Tahoe," he laughed, "can you sit naked in a hot tub with a groovy chick, sit naked on top of the world and wait for a Piña Colada before you go back into the snow." He ran his hands over her body. Her naked body responded to his. The hot steaming tub made them feel good. They kissed each other and flapped in the water like two mad dolphins in captivity. The waiter arrived with more drinks. The waiter didn't seem fazed by their loveplay, by the tub, or even by the famous Nick Dimani.

"Only in Tahoe," Laurie said.

"Let's make love again and then ski," Nick said. Somewhere in his head, where he was cool, he was writing the music to *Playing Tahoe*. The music filled the chambers of his brains as he slid his hands over the tan skin of Laurie.

"You're the loveliest woman in the Sierras, maybe in the world," he said as they splashed in the tub. She was so lovely it made him want to weep with tenderness.

27. *Laurie and Nick*

DIMANI WOKE up early and looked at the sun coming through the villa's Thermopane windows and doors. Sun woke him. He loved morning skiing and he dressed quickly to ski the mountain. Nick loved to watch Laurie going down the mountain. He would watch her moving in her ski pants, her small backside moving like an oiled metronome, first to the left, then shifting to the right, and he would follow behind her. She knew Tahoe better than anyone, having lived there all her life. And she had always been too bright for the schools. School had been a joke. She'd gone out and gotten stoned in the woods. Listened to music. Liked to dance. And now, Nick Dimani had made her life different. He would talk to her some nights about his life in Brooklyn. They had been in two different time capsules. They would sit and smoke grass and he would tell her how music had come to him, how his longing to express himself had been a mystery even to him. "You know, Laurie, how some people are just mechanical, they can fix anything?"

"Yes."

"Well, I was just *musical.* It was like being mechanical. I had a talent. Music just *came* to me and I heard it. I could write almost any kind of sound or song. Classical. Popular. Just as some people can reach their hands inside a car and know where to fix something, I can do the same things with music. I was born knowing how to make sounds. It's a mystery to others. But not to me. I can wake up and just write music."

He could talk to her and she could talk to him. They would drive in the brilliant sunshine through the mountains right onto the Sierras. "I love Tahoe," Laurie would say, "but I'd like to leave. There's so much of the world I want to see, Nick. I promised myself for my twenty-third birthday I'd go around the world. I want to see what other countries look like. My mom's sort of angry with me. She'd like me to have some other profession, other than a dealer at the casino."

"What's wrong with that?" he asked.

"Nothing. It's good money. But it's not leading to anything more than what it is."

"Does everything have to lead to something?"

"For my mom."

"What would you do if you could do anything?" He didn't want her to change.

"Be a dancer."

Nick looked at her. "So do it. Go for it. If that's what you really want."

"It's too late for me. You have to start that when you're really young."

"You are really young, Laurie."

"No. I'm okay the way I am."

"All right. You can dance for me tonight at the Fantasy Inn."

"Wow. I heard about that place. It's supposed to be really nice."

"I'll meet you there at ten."

"Good. I'll be on my night off. If you want me to, I'll dance for you."

Nick dropped Laurie off at her house. He had a lot of thinking to do. He had to change his life in a few days. It wasn't that he was afraid of failure. Only people who had never succeeded were afraid of that. Suddenly he felt the energy to write the album. Everything was going to be fine. Seeing Laurie always made him feel young. He could relax with her, run with her, ski with her. No reason to fail. And if he did fail, he would at least fail with wit and grace. What was so terrible about failure, anyway? If you didn't risk, you didn't succeed. He would risk now. Risk if it killed him. Morris could take his music and make him, magically, talk to the world on cassettes and reel-to-reel. Suddenly, he felt inside of his bones the dreams that would become the songs of *Playing Tahoe.* Laurie made him feel alive, made him feel the *newness of life.*

28. Partners

IT WAS just like the old days. Sylvia and Nick stood all night near his Steinway, the one he had flown out to Harrah's villa, and watched the sun come up in the morning and spray the lake and snow with its brilliance. They argued and talked. It was good for them both to be alone, two silhouettes against the lake. And the songs started coming. The lyrics came out like fresh water. They had energy. And Nick brought them to life with music. The old Lundholm and Dimani team was cooking. It had worked in the sixties and now worked in Tahoe. Only Sylvia just wasn't that interested. Nick had days when he would play the chords in different sequences. He'd look at her lyrics and play with them. One chord led to another. He was still the innovative Nick. Polychords were his style now. Simple chords were pulled simultaneously together. It sounded good.

He'd take her lyric. Hear the rhythms. Pick out notes. He'd improvise on her words. The first eight bars of writing anything was fun for him. The first musical impulse was a turn-on. Then it became work. He took a lot of the stuff he wrote before she arrived and threw it out. When she was there, next to him, he invented in a different way. Her words were a turn-on. He'd improvise from them. He'd jump off of them as if they were little jumping boards. He needed nine songs for the album. The first four songs came easy. He played with them for her and she loved them. From old scraps of music paper with a few bars on them, he had made "Change." It was good. The next six songs were giving him trouble. She'd write a lyric. He wouldn't like it yet. And they kept working. Every night. Every afternoon. Rev skied. And Nancy gambled. And Sylvia was locked in the room with Nick at Harrah's villa. Slowly the songs came. She just wasn't as excited. The high was gone. She tried not to let him see it as she listened.

She wrote a lyric called "Ice Harvest":

I burst out of myself;
I am who I am;
The evergreen opens
in ear, eye, and spine—
You're mine for this winter.
Ice Baby, you're mine.

Rev was her ice baby. Ice baby eyes. Bored eyes. Tahoe blues. She wanted to be with him forever. He was smart and funny. Fun to be with. Being with him made her high. She kept writing. Just as she had written each decade of her life into her old songs, she wrote now about Rev:

CRYSTAL MAN

I see through your glass;
You are mostly the cold;
I see through your soul;
You make me whole.
Crystal man—I find I love you best.
Are you life? Or are you death?
Crystal man—I love you best.

The album was coming along. Nick airfreighted the tapes to Morris. He called and his enthusiasm was contagious. "Hang in there! This is terrific!" All was well. It was a long time coming, but they'd have a big album. Sylvia wrote a song called "Lovingly" and played it for Nick:

Lovers, when at last from sweet content,
You are caught in dreaming argument,
You will drowse in grass
Under sea where swans are bound at last,
Lovingly, lovingly.

"That's great! That's the best!" Nick said. "I love you." It was the first time Nick Dimani had said that in the twenty-three years that she had known him.

The album was going well, but Sylvia was nervous. She wanted to leave Tahoe and be with Rev, alone. Rev was getting bored with just hanging around while she worked with Nick. Her greatest fear was that he would split. Just disappear. She fantasized with anxiety that one day she'd come back to their suite and he would be gone. No address. No phone. Off on some other adventure. Windsurfing somewhere beyond her reach. She would die if he did that. But she suspected that one day he would say, "It's too much responsibility, babe" and he'd just get up from a table where they were eating lunch and split without even looking back at her.

29. Melon's

AFTER LOVEMAKING in the suite, Sylvia would lie in bed and think about Rev. Melon's, she remembered, was where they used to go. "Want a beer?" she had asked him that first night at Melon's.

"Umm hummm."

"What did you do before you sold cars?"

"A steam fitter."

"And before that?"

"A tuna fisherman."

"Out of where?"

"California."

"And before that?"

"A logger. A foreman on a Clyde skitter. Ran a big restaurant. Dug for oil."

"How old are you really?" She had known him a week then and wasn't sure of his age. He looked younger and yet older than someone in his thirties. He was boyish and battered at the same time. He could be fifty or he could be sixteen. He had no age.

"Thirty-four."

"You're younger than your buddy John."

"John's a kid."

"And you're not?"

"No. I'm a man." He laughed. "I've been around."

"Where did you meet John?"

"In school. Harvard. We were both studying business."

"What happened?"

"I worked on Wall Street for a while. In a suit. In an office. I didn't like it. I decided I wouldn't ever do anything that I didn't like again. Anything that wasn't fun."

That was the beginning. Looking back at the nights at Melon's, Sylvia never thought this conversation would ever lead to anything more than a casual friendship. What a mistake! The tall blond stranger whose smile was instantly a part of her life became the center of fantasies. She became obsessed by him. She would sit and think about his smile. His casual nature. She remembered in New York when he would pick her up in a car from the lot that was marked with chalk on the window and take her to a movie. They would drive around the city at night; he would puff on a joint and turn up the radio to listen to rock music from the fifties. It was the feeling that he brought out of her that was new. She had grown so tired of the *business.*

Of copyrights. He looked like James Dean as he drove
around in the darkness, speeding through the night
streets.

Sylvia wrote a lyric about Rev when she met him. It was
less like a song, more like a letter to herself, a memo about
where she was at:

You who only
Speak through motors, speak to me.
In dreams I drive
With you
In Andalusian colors,
In strange boats called
Rivas
Over the blue
To arrive in that place
Where speed becomes
Innocence.

A reckless driver
Waits inside your mind,
To perform odd stunts
Such as driving
A bike into an ocean
Or racing
Through dirt roads
Where the motor
Sounds like hearts
Revved up to explode.

I live close to you,
At heartbeat;
Driving with you
To a beach
Where nothing is lost
And love is faster
Than the speed of light.
                    Speak to me.

She knew he would leave her.

30. **Treatments**

IN TAHOE, Rev opened up to Sylvia. Away from First Olds, he spoke to her more often, made love more often. But to him, opening up meant insulting Nick. "I hate the little creep," Rev said.

"Why?"

"No reason. I just do."

"He's my partner."

"He's a pain in the ass. I don't trust him."

"Don't be mean, Rev. That's not like you."

"I'm not mean. I'm practical. What are you going to get out of *Playing Tahoe* besides another album? And money that may or may not happen, depending on how good the album is. Meanwhile, you're writing on spec. Aren't you tired of spec?"

"Everything in life is on spec. Besides, Arthur Morris is going to produce the album."

"Make Nick pay you at least. Up front."

"That's not how it works. Don't worry about the money."

"Why do you have to be so charitable?"

"I can't change."

"You can try," he said.

"For you, I will."

He laughed. He always laughed at her. In some way, they came from two different countries. Rev spoke slowly but his mind was quick. He saw things as they were. Not as they might be or should be. She listened carefully to each word he said. Hungry for his truth. He was a truth drug to her. Whatever he said made sense. It had *logic*. The king of common sense. The car salesman with the truth in his tank. But he didn't know how much she loved him. She tried to seem *casual*. Perhaps he did know. But it made no sense. So it never "came up."

"How did you get to be the way you are? No feelings. And total practicality."

"I don't know. It must have been the shock treatments."

"Why did they give them to you?"

"My parents thought I was too wild. Too angry. They thought they would calm me down."

"Did it change you?"

"I think so. I don't remember. The shock made me see things in a practical way. Nothing's a big deal." It made Sylvia angry to think that his parents did that to him. She would *atone* for their mistakes. She loved him.

"Why did they give them to you?"

"I dunno. Someone told them it would straighten me out."

"Do you think about the treatments ever?"

"No. I never think about them. They gave me dough-nuts afterward. That's what I think about."

"Do you miss the self you lost and don't remember?"

"It's no big deal."

"It is to me."

"Why?"

"Because I love you."

"No you don't. Don't say that."

"Why not?"

"I don't want the responsibility."

"What was it like afterward?"

"I wrote some poetry."

"About what?"

"I don't remember."

"Aren't you *mad* they took out your memories like an appendix?"

"What good would it do to be mad?"

"Don't you have emotions?"

"No."

"When was the last time you were interested in a woman?" she asked him.

"Before you?"

"Yes."

Rev took a drag of the joint he was smoking. "I was driving to New York from Phoenix and I had a car accident. They put me in a hospital. When they checked me in, the nurse was horny."

"How could you tell?"

"You can always tell. The way they look at you. She had large breasts and she wasn't wearing a bra and she turned me on, too. They put me in a private room and the doctors came to look at me. They called my parents. It wasn't anything really serious and they said I'd be out in a few days. They wanted to do X-rays and I had hurt my leg. That night the hospital was really quiet. I knew that she was sitting outside waiting for that little light to go on. So I pressed the night light and she came in. I asked her if she could give me a massage. She said she could. She took off my top and started rubbing oil on my chest. Needless to say, my cock got hard and I watched her slowly take off her underpants. She reached up to get something out of the closet and I saw her naked ass. I was struck with how round it was and she had a suntan. As she came to the bed she massaged me again and I felt how wet she was. I lifted her up on top of me. I'll never forget how sweet she smelled. It was some sort of perfume that smelled like lilies, the kind my mother had, calla lilies. She gave me a thrill, riding on top of me. I felt her squeezing my cock with her cunt and riding on top of me until we both came. Anyway, that was the last time I was laid before I came to New York."

"Did you ever see her again?"

"No. I checked out of the hospital the next day."

"And?"

"There was no 'and.' In retrospect, it was nice. That's all."

"Do you ever feel anything?"

"No, not really. I don't like emotion. I'm a casual guy."

"I'm the opposite."

"I know."

"Want to hear about my last affair?"

"Sure. If you want to tell me."

"You have time?"

"Well, how long is this going to take? Is it an epic?"

"All right. I'll tell you another time."

He laughed. It was an odd laugh. Sort of a giggle. The laugh of a prince who was born with everything. And, she thought, he did have *everything*. Impossibly good looks. A wealthy and social background. Youth. No problems. *Everything*. A sense of humor. *Everything* except emotions or pain. Or ambition.

31. *Antistress*

"WHAT DO you want in life, Rev?" Sylvia asked. They were lying in bed taking it easy. Rev watched color TV. He paused. He always took his time answering her questions.

"I dunno. An Excalibur, a Trans Am, and a cigarette would do it. A Riva. A new Harley-Davidson."

"What about people?"

He ignored this question. He didn't need people. He lived a life similar to the book she read by Stirling Moss, *In the Track of Speed*. All through the book, Moss talked about cars, formulas, roads, miles per hour, maximum speed, emergencies, tow ropes, first place, second place, revolutions, autodomes, races, round and round, faster and faster. There was nothing *personal* in a Stirling Moss book. It was the mechanized mind of an auto-artist. The human being was totally replaced by the engine. He wasn't born: His gates crashed open. He didn't have an adolescence: He was learning the *tricks of the trade*. He didn't feel: He had car wrecks. He didn't have problems: He had racing demons. She wondered where Stirling Moss was now. Selling wax, she had heard. His life had been slippery. Rev was the Stirling Moss of her life. His ambition? A machine. His desire? Speed. His friend John once said, "He'd rather fuck a car than a girl." And she had laughed. Now *she* was the girl and it wasn't so funny.

"Oh yes," Rev said, "I think I'd like a trailer. Furnished in trailer modern. I could put it somewhere, maybe Marina del Rey. Then I could walk out to my boat." She looked at him. She couldn't believe how opposite they were. Was this what she had survived for? So she could love a man whose dream it was to live in a trailer? (She wondered if this was really mid-life crisis.)

"If I wore very high heels," Sylvia said, "pink plastic curlers in my hair (I'd let the roots grow out so it wouldn't look too natural), if I wore high heels and an Olga padded bra, if I chewed gum and cooked greasy pork chops and kept the Mickey Mouse radio going with Puerto Rican music while the color TV blared in the background—could I come and cook for you? You'd come home to the trailer and I'd have the pork chops ready."

"Sounds good." (*What* was happening to her?)

How downwardly mobile could she be? Rev was the antiexecutive, the Lenny Bruce of the gentile world, the slap in the face to morality and success, the anti-Horatio Alger. This blond giant, her sun god, her muse, this incredibly well-built blond male *machine,* perfect face, perfect body, perfect coordination, perfect sight, a slip-streaming expert who could respond to any wheel, whose greatest "lift" came from driving mile after mile without resting his engine, this king of double clutch, whose dream was to travel downshift on the least amount of power so as to save his engine while maintaining a better than standard speed— this hulk of blond aerodynamics wanted *nothing* from her but to "kid around" and to laugh. "Can you imagine?" she said to him, "that I used to be the most aesthetic person alive? I couldn't live in a house if I didn't hear Bach playing somewhere in the background, if I didn't have two hundred dollars' worth of fresh flowers throughout my living room or on the terrace? I, who loved expensive clothes, whose ambitions made me so sick I had to see five analysts, this odd person who is me, now wants to live in a trailer? Now would be happy to just plant flowers and do nothing but 'hang out'? It's mad. It's a slap in the face to my analysis. And yet I have this odd Homeric vision, looking back on my life and the history of my female bachelorhood, that the American Way leads you to an insane asylum, and the un-American way leads you to a trailer. Can you imagine all those people dealing with stress? Coping with stress? Who could come and see you, Rev, and learn *to take it easy*? I remember reading a brochure from the Brookdale Center for Continuous Education that said, 'Stress can be controlled through a variety of simple techniques that you can master.' Rev, you are the master of antistress. That's what you are. The relaxation king. You're a slap in the face to my ambitions."

Rev laughed. "I guess so."

"I've got a great idea."

"What?"

"Let's go on a tour of Europe. Fast food restaurants of Europe. From Wimpy to Wimpy in Europe. And let's combine it with a tour of automobile factories. The Ferrari factory in Rome. The Lancia factory in Milano. The Porsche factory in Buchenwald or wherever it is."

"Sounds good."

She had a vision of driving throughout the world with Rev. And steering with him out of the planet, into the galaxy. He could drive over the snow-covered mountains of the moon, struggle through light-years past the dwarf stars and large stars into the sun. He could give hand signals and drive into the sun, her god, her Greek god in his chariot. She would drive into the galaxies with him and nothing would matter. There would be no stress. After twenty years of rock and roll, a world of no stress seemed

like paradise. He was her antimogul. Her anti-kill-yourself
ethic. And for a Swedish workaholic like Sylvia, who
couldn't forgive herself two minutes of "not doing something productive," he was her hero. He didn't buy all that.
He didn't buy the product. He didn't buy the wrapping.
He was so American he was anti-American. He didn't want
to land up on top. He didn't want to conquer any worlds.
He would be happy in a trailer. Stop the music. Stop the
money. Stop the bullshit. Stop impressing people. Stop
buying things. *Stop being who you are not,* he was teaching
her. And she understood, through Rev, how absurd the
whole past twenty years had been. Her fame was a useless
thing. No room for that in a trailer.

The next morning Rev bought a black Trans Am and
paid for it with the cash she gave him. He seemed happy,
for a while.

32. *Lionel and Ron*

"MY REAL father died six months before I was born," Lionel said. Tears were in his eyes. He was telling Ron Thimble the story of his life, but Ron Thimble wasn't listening.
Lionel thought to himself, I might as well be singing "God
Bless America." He wondered if Ron was good for his
mental health. Lionel thought only a lunatic could spend
time with Ron Thimble.

White bathrobe over white shirt—Lionel was dressed
for lounging. He was an untouched, unathletic man. As
he stopped his reminiscence and spoke into the phone, a
telephonaholic, his eyes looked out the window at the panorama of the Sierras and the perfect winter day. The lake,
a huge splash of purple surrounded by the ice mountains,
seemed calm. Lionel switched easily from traumatic mem-

ories to corporate orders. In his mind they were both the same thing. Now he was discussing his business programming ideas with one of the officers of his corporation. Lionel spoke like a master of computers should speak, in his deep controlled voice which had authority and arrogance well under control. It was the submissive voice of authority which can suddenly drop into anger. Lionel, for the moment, looked to Ron Thimble like a trumpeter swan. It seemed that Lionel was the bird and Ron the birdwatcher, Ron's telescopic eyes always fixed on Lionel's movements; seeing his prey and noting the details was enough for him. Like a birdwatcher, he didn't care to shoot, only to observe and talk about it afterward. Thimble was always sharpening his pencil, checking lists, and watching Lionel in whatever habitat he happened to be. His eyes never left the trumpeter swan.

Lionel turned to Ron after he hung up the phone. He lit a cigarette and placed it in his immaculate art deco cigarette holder. Everything that Lionel touched was expensive. His cufflinks were Fabergé eggs, miniature ones. His shirt was designed by Ted Lapidus especially for him. His bathrobe, white silk by Sulka, created for only one other individual, the Duke of Windsor. And so the Duke of Tahoe sat in his tower, nervous inside, calm outside. Ron the birder spoke quickly, "What the hell are you so nervous about, Lionel?"

"I don't know what she sees in him." He hung up the phone.

"Rev?"

"Yes. It's interesting. Years ago she was in love with Nick. Can you imagine any two men as different from each other as Rev Cranwell and Nick Dimani? Nick is from the ghetto. Ambition brought him from the garbage and nightmare of Brooklyn into the social world where he is at the top of his profession: He's on every most-wanted-entertainer list. He skis with the Kennedys, eats with the greatest social families of Palm Beach and Los Angeles, travels with celebrities, and his upwardly mobile little ass has sat on every dais in the world. Rev, on the other hand, started at the top where Nick wanted to be: an old Philadelphia social family. Cousins to the Mayflower snobs, Boston Brahmins with marbles in their mouths, the social set of the fading Wasp gentility. He devoted much of his life to lacking ambition, his only criterion in life is how much hassle is involved and if there's a hassle, he avoids work. A man who has never had to claw for survival; he has a motor instead of a heart. I've never seen anyone more dedicated to cars. And Sylvia? She's the least mechanical person I've ever met. She couldn't even change a light-bulb, let alone a tire. And now she's with that gentile grease monkey. I don't understand it."

"Take a look at him and you'll understand it."

"All right, he's attractive."

"You've got to be joking. He's the best-looking man either of us has ever seen."

"Sylvia likes talent."

"He has talent."

"For what?"

"He can con anyone into anything."

"And she goes for that?"

"After twenty years of the rock business, she goes for gentile understatement. Wouldn't you?"

"She can change her life so easily?"

"She told me, my darling, that she has a Homeric vision. She envisions history as it's been reflected in music to show that the apocalypse is here. And she says her contribution is to live quietly without any of the *trappings* of success. And write. She has a vision that she wants to write."

"She just wants to get laid more often."

"No. She told me she's going to write *her* story. She wants to live near the ocean. The vanity of rock and roll no longer interests her. She finds the music business sinister. That shit doesn't go down with me. But that's what she told me."

Lionel looked out the window. "Emmies and Cash Box trophies and golden records may no longer interest her, but give her two weeks near the ocean with that two-bit Fangio, with that mechanical baboon, and she will long to come running back to her own legend. I know talent."

"You should stop thinking of her as *talent*. She's a frustrated woman."

"I made her exist. Now she's running after some patrician fuck-up who's into *seed*. The seedier the better. He thinks it's amusing to drive a Trans Am with an eagle on it. All these upper-class washed-out Wasps want to be street people. Gentile guilt. All of them want to escape— escape what? The dark? Their mothers' houses? The embarrassment of manor houses and horses and coffins and privilege, the unfriendly gods of Philadelphia? I pity those people. The juice went out of them so long ago. They need to speed to escape the monotony of manners and good schools and inherited money."

"And you?" Ron asked Lionel.

"For me, life is always exciting. I'll be sorry not to see Sylvia. In so many ways, she's a genius. She seems too warm and talented to be elbowed out of her own world."

"Rev's mad, you know."

"I know. That's what she loves. He brings out her compassion. Sylvia must *love* deeply. Once she loved Nick. And she loved music. Now she loves—the freedom of Rev's life. He's an idiot, but a good-looking idiot."

"Don't kid yourself," Thimble said. "He's not the fool you think he is. He's pretty fucking smart if you ask me. He's out for all he can get. And Sylvia's at that age when she doesn't mind giving it to him because she has nobody else. He'd sell her into white slavery if he could. I find all this very funny."

"What?"

"The acrobatics of your feelings."

"Why do I hunger for what I can't have?"

Ron looked again at him carefully, the birdwatcher observing Lionel through telescope eyes.

"Let's get out of here."

"Tahoe?"

"No. Just this hotel. I need some air."

Lionel couldn't stand these catty conversations. That seemed to be all they had left. He wondered if Ron was jealous of Sylvia.

33. Sylvia's Homeric Vision

WALKING IN the snowy fields, Sylvia thought of life versus history. When she walked in the fields behind Harrah's Hotel, walked up the snow paths that led higher and higher to the mountains, she could think of who she was and what her feelings were for Rev. She thought of her electric typewriter with its cold and hungry plug and how she had spent the night writing love poems for Rev in Swedish, poems she would never dare to show him. Sometimes when she wrote about Rev, she wrote in Swedish, her father's language, the Swedish coming so easily.

"Why do you write in Swedish?" Rev asked.

"It's the language I never suffered in."

At night when the constellations would emerge, she would sit needing to pour out her feelings for Rev. Waves of light would cross the ceiling. In her mind, she could express the feelings for her sunlight, her muse. With Rev, she felt like writing again. But why poetry? Why confession? With him, she knew that she no longer needed the false form of the lyric. She was in love with a man who had, quite simply, made her change her genre. Before Rev, the lyric had been enough for her. She could twist the rhythms, the rhymes, the mathematical patterns to fit an original thought. A lyric joined with music made her feel good inside. But since Rev, the lyric had become a technical thing. She wanted now to change professions, change genres, change what she had to say. Music was no longer necessary for her life, except in some abstract way. She wanted now the original language; she wanted to push aside the music, to make the music invisible, to create with silence as her partner, pushing her own thoughts to the wall's darkness. She wanted to fish for herself.

She walked higher and higher up toward Heavenly Valley, climbing the snow paths along the rocky hills of the State Line. She wanted not to be tied to present or past. She wanted to write something new. Soon her commitment to Nick would be over and she could start again to write the way she wanted to. She felt as if she had been living in a Homeric tale. The rock business was like a war in which Nick had been Hector fighting in a bloody battle, she had been Helen of Troy, Richmond Schneider had been Zeus, Lionel had been Achilles. They had all fought in the blood and mud to win. But to win what? An Emmy? A golden record? What was the point of the battle? The battle of the record industry, millions of innocent singers, writers, lyricists, A & R men, agents, lawyers, managers, guitarists, millions of innocent people lay slaughtered in that battle. Every day another battle. Every day more blood. The slaughter of the men and women going to battle for what? Money? Fame? Wearing their mikes, electronically prepared for battle, their mike their shield, drowning in the studios, bandaged by tape, communicated into death. She had lived through those battles. And she was tired. She now wanted to be the seer, the blind poet with eyesight scratched out to make way for insight, the poet with eyeballs turned inward who recorded those battles. She had a Homeric vision of her life, and she wanted to put it down quickly before it escaped her. Rev had taught her to do that. She wanted to write the life she had lived while she was still bloodied. Inside her was the knowledge that she was mortal, that death would come, that before it was too late, she had to warn the others.

That was it. She had to write as a warning. As a confession. She had to question and feel and then to write what she knew. Rev had inspired her to do that. He had looked as a friend on the vision of her life and found it absurd. Empty. A bunch of users. He had taught her to get down off her throne and become the Sylvia she really was. She was close to writing now. Was that what loving was? A new way of writing? She wondered. She had to start again.

34. Sartori

SARTORI WAS Harrah's chief in command of maintenance. Sartori was a gardener who rose to the top. He could be seen every day vacuuming the pine needles in front of Harrah's villa. A secret intellectual as well as a gardener, he had once written a book called *Instant Community* which he published with a vanity press. Nobody knew why he wrote this book. In it, he had written:

The Instant Community must only deploy new transportation systems. This means no cars, buses, trucks, or subways. Streets are obsolete. Only modular automated transportation: people movers. Monocabs, monorails. Hovercrafts. Helicopters.

The management of Harrah's believed Sartori was crazy. Nonetheless his book, once it had been self-published in Nevada, had sold a thousand copies. Now that he was reaching an age of reflection, he considered writing another book. To be truthful, it would be a book about Tahoe. Sartori had kept this project in his mind and thought about it every day on his maintenance rounds. "Yes. For all my life I've lived in Tahoe. I was born here. I came here before it was ruined by the tourists. I came here when the splendor and majesty of bright blue lakes, white-covered mountains, and the smell of timber still was silent. The snowy fields could be walked through during the winter. Tahoe was a silent place of bristle cone pine, sego lily blossoms, desert pupfish, and wild horses down in the valley. Lake Tahoe was formed as the basin of the mountains when they sank. The basin filled with water to form the lake which now flows down to the Truckee River at Tahoe City and out to Reno and Pyramid Lake, Nevada. When I was a child, the winters were severe. I can remember snowshoes and my daddy putting me on skis. There were coyotes loping through the forest at dusk, mule deer in the meadows looking for beddings and grass under the snow; there were golden-mantled ground squirrels, chipmunks, raccoons that came with their masks at night to peer at you, and the beavers who chewed the fallen aspens along the streams and made their homes of aspen trunks and branches.

"There still are these mammals, but you could see more of them than when I was a child. You could hear the birds, and see them migrate and come back again. The bright blue stellar jay could pick at your bacon as you camped in the Sierras in the summer, the tree swallow darted in and out of holes in snags near the rivers, the red-shafted flicker dug for insects in the bark of trees with its strong beak, and I remember listening to the woodpecker and the mountain chickadee scanning the pine firs for insects. The Sierra birds in those days flocked into the meadows, the rocky cliffs, and the marshes and lakes, and there were even some year-round residents that added song to the white winters. As I grew up, I remember swimming naked in the marshes with only the leopard frog to keep me company and the carpenter ants and even the garter snakes kept me company."

Sartori talked to Nick beneath the towering pines. "It was the pines that I loved most, the pines that made Tahoe what it is, the white mountains of winter with the pines jutting out together in their tall majesty covered by the snow. The pines gave summer and spring the odor of heaven. And whatever heaven is, it must look in some way like Tahoe was. The Jeffrey Pine, which grows quickly in the open sun, and the sugar pine, these tough godly trees with scaly needles and long cones, these trees became my only friends. And slowly, I watched the changes in Lake Tahoe. I saw the middle-aged comedians, the professional hookers and dealers, the gambling aristocracy taking over the landscape, these newcomers to the pine world. Celebrities replaced blue jays. Gamblers replaced the raccoons. And the mountains were now filled with the smell of gasoline; the buttercups bloomed bright yellow but so did the green carpets in the casinos, the game machines. What started out to be the most secretive country of the Indians, filled with pine trees, became—a troupe of gamblers.

"I didn't always work for Harrah's. I studied. I got many degrees, but slowly I realized that if I wanted to live in Tahoe, I had to have a job with good benefits. So I went to work for Harrah's. I met him because one of my girlfriends was the daughter of his gardener. I saw her picking up the pine needles in front of her home one day. We used to court and she told me that Bill Harrah was always a gentleman and very nice to her. He paid for her college education and treated her family with dignity. That was the kind of man Bill Harrah was.

"You see, Harrah was the kind of man that America doesn't make anymore. A western Horatio Alger, you could say; his grandparents, the Fisks and Meyers, came from Iowa. His grandfather was a minister and some of their clothes and pictures are now behind glass frames in his antique automobile museum. Bill Harrah always liked Tahoe. Maybe he liked it because it's such a pretty camping ground or hunting area. Maybe he liked it because there wasn't much here but sawmills. Big timber came from Tahoe for all the mines, but Bill Harrah also saw the possibility of people coming to the Nevada side and gambling. And he knew people would rather gamble behind open doors in Nevada than closed doors in California. He had run bingo games in churches in California, and he came to Reno to open a bingo parlor in the back end of a restaurant. He bought land from Eddy Sahadi, who was a hophead, never worked a day in his life or even collected a paycheck. And he opened up Harrah's. That was in the early fifties. Harrah's in Tahoe was where Harvey's is now.

"Harrah was a six-foot-one-and-a-half-inch-tall man. He weighed a hundred and sixty-five pounds, was in good shape; he wore glasses. A quiet man and always wore the finest clothes. At the end of his life his hair was gray. He was a generous person; he showed everyone courtesy and respect. And he could get anything he wanted out of people because he always said please. But there was another side to him, a side people never saw. He would drink and just live to hunt ducks. Drinking and chasing ducks and chasing women were his favorite occupations when he was a young man. Till he married Sherry. She straightened him out. You see Bill Harrah always liked women who were reasonably smart, smarter even than him. Smart women with class. And that's what Sherry had. She got him to work, stop drinking, and pay attention to what he could do to develop gaming in Reno and Tahoe. She was so smart, she would read *The Wall Street Journal* and go with him to all his lawyers' meetings. And there wasn't any detail of business where she didn't know twice as much as Harrah or any of those lawyers. She pushed him. She got him to cut down on his duck hunting and drinking; she got him to cut down on his cigarettes, though there she wasn't so successful and he smoked five packs of cigarettes a day until he died. Which is probably why he died. And Harrah—he respected women. He liked a woman if she could teach him something; he loved a talented woman. He was always learning and growing, and the people he learned from the most and spent the most time with were very smart women. That's why the woman's powder room is one of the nicest parts of the villa. He tried to please women and he was always a person who would ask his wife's opinion, whichever wife it happened to be. You know he had five wives, each one taught him something. He cared for his wife Sherry the most. Married her and divorced her and then remarried her; she's the one he has the two adopted sons with. She lives down in Reno now and runs her own restaurant. Said to be very fancy. And she has lots of real estate on her own.

"His pride and joy was this villa. His hobby, outside of automobiles, was fine furniture. Antiques. He loved anything beautifully made. Anything with class. Anything that came out of the past. And so he built this villa. It's thirty-three thousand square feet. It's a twelve-million-dollar home. It's on five lots of Lake Tahoe. There's carpet everywhere. Mirror everywhere. It's got big furniture; you see Harrah was creating a kingdom—a world—and he wanted everything in it to be the biggest and the best. Even the furniture. He told his fancy decorator from San Francisco who came up and did the house for him, 'I want the best and the biggest of everything.' Of course, he had the ranch house in Sun Valley which has very tight security. The house near the Crummer Estate, also tight security. His widow, Verna, she's about thirty-two, she's living now in the Sun Valley home. You see, *Sherry* taught Harrah everything. Nobody will tell you this but me, but I know a lot of things other people don't know. I know how she showed him how to tack property. To acquire it. To use it as collateral. The corporation sold just last week to Holiday Inn for four hundred million. I'm sure you read about it. Harrah was working on that merger before he died. But that's nothing. The secret is, there are a lot of things that aren't in that corporation. Harrah was like Howard Hughes in the sense that he was a very secretive man. Secretive as a pine cone. He had this deal cooking in Australia. No one knew why. But he had some idea that Australia could be a big gambling center and he traveled there all the time. Something about taking money out and putting money back. Like Hughes, Harrah always went for the best executives. He surrounded himself with a tight circle of his friends from boyhood and then he went out and raided the best management from all the gambling casinos in the world. Sherry showed him how brains could make money. And Harrah had one quality that no one else I ever knew had: He could always tell who was smart and who wasn't. He could always tell if a man or a woman was smart. And if they were, he hired them. He knew how to delegate his work. He gave a lot of his burdens to his lawyer, Meade Dickenson, who Harrah thought was smarter than anyone even though a lot of the others were jealous of Mister Dickensen. But to get along with Harrah, you had to be smart and work hard and respect his privacy. Harrah cared a lot about his privacy. And of course about security. The day he died I moved a lot of the arms out of the Harrah villa. He had guns and bombs and all sorts of thing here. He had a secret gun placed over the liquor cabinet, too, to give you an idea of the kind of man Bill Harrah was. Lots of arms in his house. You see, it wasn't only a kingdom. It was Harrah's kingdom, and he had to protect it. The house is filled with paintings, of course, and Perma Placque pictures of entertainers who played Tahoe. And of course, everyone at one time or another has played Tahoe. Sinatra, Jack Benny, Wayne Newton, Sammy Davis, Jr., Bill Cosby, you, Mr. Dimani, Ann-whats-her-name-Margret, everybody. And they all had to come and have dinner with Harrah and have their picture taken. That was always a part of the deal. Harrah treated every celebrity like they were just that—a celebrity. If they were in New York, he'd send one of his private jets for them so they wouldn't have to be bothered flying a commercial airline. Of course, he wanted them to get here on time, which was part of the reason he sent the jet. And then he not only sent his plane (he had many planes and boats, besides the hundred-million-dollar car collection), but he took two whole floors of his hotel and he had that just set aside for whoever was playing Tahoe and you got treated like the star you were. He knew it was the stars that brought the gamblers into this place and he not only paid big money, but he made the stars feel right. He always signed a contract with the stars. That was part of his way of doing business. And that, like everything else Harrah did, paid off. I'm sure Sammy Davis is worth much more today than he was when he first signed the contract. The one thing about Harrah is, he got whatever he wanted. Whatever he wanted.

"For example, when Neil Armstrong took that first step for mankind and put the American flag on the moon. That was the biggest moment in the history of the earth. Harrah thought so and so did everybody, I'm sure. Really! And so, Harrah wanted that flag. Not just a flag that was in the ship. No sir. That flag that got put on the moon. And he got it. He got Wayne Newton to get that flag from John Glenn. And it sits there right now. In the dining room. In a glass case. All documented and everything. You see, whatever Mister Harrah wanted, he got. It's all there in that house, Mr. Dimani.

"I have to go now. You see, I have a secret. I have my own power. It's this little black book here. I have a document. On everything Harrah did. And on everything his friends, all the celebrities, did. It's all here in my little black book. Some day, I'm going to write a book. But that's a long way from now. Right now, I'm just happy to weed the garden and care for the villa."

Nick liked Sartori. He was a character.

35. *Kicks*

NICK AT night writing music: He could lose himself in it. Music was his great hero. His great love. He would sit alone at night and think that he loved to ski, he loved sex, he loved drugs. But most of all, he needed all that other *stuff* because nothing else could take him as high as music. He liked to do it. To make it. Even more than hearing music, he liked to create it, sing it, play it. He was in love with keyboards and his fingers on them.

At night when the cosmos played around in the sky, he looked at the stars and remembered the good old days when he was a kid in love with other people's songs. In love with the make-believe ballroom, Al Jolson's records, Frank Sinatra, and Sammy Kaye. The freaky sense of wonder that came over him when he first heard Frankie sing in person. The magical quality of his eyes and voice, his life force and energy. He was some primitive beast who had to have a beat. Without music, life was dull. It was the pits. Take away music and you take away life, he thought. For him a day without music was a day without breath. Music was his life rays. Each day he fought a hypothetical battle against silence. Music was his beam of heat. His invisible light. When he sat in a chair composing, he didn't need tits or coke or skis or cigarettes. He was airborne. He was creating in his own way the cosmos all over again. Music was his weapon against boredom.

"When it comes, it's fantastic," was the way he once described writing music to Laurie.

"What's it really like?" she asked.

"What's it like?" he laughed. Civilians could never understand. "You create a real-life counterpart to ecstasy. You go through the galaxies stopping at light-years and chewing on stars. You're eating up the universe. Music is always like a laser beam. It's a highly concentrated particle of light that comes out of the gut like a germ. Music is an incision. Like lasers, it cuts and burns through anything. It's as if, Laurie, I live in a vacuum of space. And with music I heat up and I can do anything. I become like some sort of intergalactic shootout. Music is a beam. It comes out of me. Like blood. Like light. Only intuition tells me when I hit a target."

He rapped like that with Laurie. But often, alone, composing *Tahoe,* he knew that music was more. It was a smoke screen he threw up between himself and the world. Little Jewish Nick could hide behind the screen, a refuge from others. Behind the screen, he didn't have to be afraid. Afraid of what? Of himself. Of his feelings. Of his needs. Of his need to drink. Of his need to drug. Music had no guilt. It was his defense against being merely human. It was his immortality pill. It had no time span. It moved him in and out of past and present and future. It was his revolving screen. He needed it. To hide behind. And become the giant he needed to be. Other times? He was just a midget in Gucci loafers. A pigmy in the world of giants. A lot of people in the entertainment industry thought they knew Nick Dimani. He was more than a "guy who loved to talk." He was driven. And that drive led him to money, discoveries, art, wall-to-wall carpets, domesticity, and philosophy. Finally, he had to cut back on everything but music. "It's where I live," he said. But music lit him up. It was the only time he could forget who he was.

Composing—it didn't matter to Nick. He became Tahoe and his music.

36. Bonnet to Bonnet

REV AND Sylvia drove around Heavenly Valley in his Trans Am. "It may be crazy, baby, but I'm in love with you. I want to drive your car, near and far, that's all I want to do."

"What's that?" Rev asked. His voice, as always, was slightly bored.

"A lyric. I wrote it when I was fifteen."

"Oh yeah?"

"If you'll slow down, I'll sing you the whole song."

"Don't bother. I don't have to love your lyrics, do I?"

"Of course not."

"Are you hurt?"

"No."

"Good."

He brought the car to a jolt. He stopped the engine and grabbed her. "Ummm. That tastes good," he said after biting her lips.

"You're not car-broken," she said.

"I want to kiss you again."

"Go ahead."

Suddenly they weren't speeding anymore. Rev was. In his head. He had smoked a joint and he was racing in front of a crowd in his head. He was driving a Maserati; the great crowd swarming around the pit watched him. He was driving fast, past Fangio; he overtook Fangio and started some real dicing. He was driving at 92.77 mph, which wasn't very fast but bore out his theory that the best way to win a race is at the slowest possible speed at which you can keep the competition at bay. In his head he was driving at Brand's Hatch. What a contrast the little kidney-shaped circuit provided to the winding reality of the Sierras. There, in his head, a big crowd, estimated at 50,000 had gathered to see him drive. The big event was the International Challenge Trophy for Formula 3 cars run in three eight-lap heats and a twelve-lap final. He was the back row of the heat. Yes, he was at Brand's Hatch with the Maserati. He was coming home for the Gold Cup in over thirty-six laps. He was running beautifully and soon overtook the field led by Reg Parnell in a Ferrari. Suddenly he was able to establish a commanding lead. The Maserati was running well and in the later stage of the race he was able to beat the record for the course. He was driving with daring and control—

"Rev?"

"Yes."

"Do you want to make me happy?"

"Yes—I guess so."

"Let's go back to the hotel."

And later, much later, when he was imagining he was in a silver Mercedes disappearing at the Italian Grand Prix at Monza, he held Sylvia in his arms and touched her hair so softly, holding her so gently, that he forgot almost who she was. He was entering her body but he was thinking of Grand Prix racing. He was with the engine and touching her flesh. She was his car, his speed; he loved the distance he could place in his mind between the both of them. He saw her getting excited like a motor slowly revving up. He made her come. He made her come again. She lay back on the bed and smiled at him. He disappeared into the dream world where he lived, a world of speed and exhaust pipes and engines, a world he could only imagine as he raced bonnet to bonnet from his dream world into another dream which was faster than speed.

37. Lady Rita

RITA DIMANI was not upset that Nick was running around with a young girl in Tahoe. She had spent so many years being his attendant there was something predicated about the way she was accustomed to adjusting to his affairs. Patience was her game, and her devotion to Nick's career was a legend. In the beginning of their marriage she had gone on the road with him and marveled at the world he opened to her in London, Tokyo, Paris, Philadelphia, Boston. She had been a glorified groupie herself, a winner-wanter, and Nick had provided her with the excitement she didn't have in her own life. A fine English girl whose parents came to America during the war, she was slightly high-strung and intellectual. She graduated from Teacher's College in Oswego, New York, was overwhelmed by the privileges, the "perks" of being joined to a celebrity. Now she was concerned with youth and health. She missed Nick truly. They were friends; it didn't matter if she saw him or not. She was concerned with the hysteria of aging and spent all her time revisiting the fountain of youth. She prayed at the plastic surgeon's office the way others prayed at Lourdes. The day that Nick confronted Sylvia with his plans, Rita had consulted a certain Dr. Berg in New York City. Waiting in the office, she thought of how much she loathed the pacifying nature of plastic surgeons' offices. This was her second "consultation." The receptionist had called to confirm the appointment in the morning. It had been made two months in advance. Dr. Berg was the most popular "eye" surgeon in the city, who had been recommended by Dr. Love, her cosmetic dentist (an eye for an eye, a tooth for a tooth, a recommendation for a recommendation). Arriving exactly on time at Dr. Berg's office on East Thirtieth Street, Rita Dimani looked in the mirror. She was holding a round silver helium balloon from a bank and it floated up to the ceiling. It mocked the serious nature of the office. The receptionist had obviously had her face done a thousand times. Her eyes were almost lifted to the roots of her hair. She wore a diamond on a gold chain around her neck. That was the status symbol which told the world she worked but she didn't *have* to. The coffeemaker was broken. Muzak played in the background to soothe nerves. Rita sat there alone on the couch. At forty-three, she felt old. Her eyes sagged. Her breasts sagged. So did her behind. It was as if she suddenly went from being an adoring frail teenager to being a thinning aging wife. She had spent the morning with Armando LaChina at the Town Tennis Club. Bowing her head in humility she now sat in Dr. Berg's office filling out the twenty pages of forms. Last period? Any health problems? Nervous breakdown? Of course she had a ner-

vous breakdown. Who didn't? But she wasn't going to tell
that to the receptionist or Dr. Berg. What did a nervous
breakdown have to do with having your face fixed? She
wanted a lift, not a psychological testing service. Soon she
was called into Dr. Berg's office. He was a pleasant man in
his forties with a double chin. His office was obviously
decorated by an amateur, probably his wife. Huge pictures
of movie stars were on his desk. Probably satisfied the
patients.

"What do you want done?" he asked. She sat there, the
proper English intellectual beauty afraid to speak. The
Muzak even played in his office. It was hard to talk about
skin to "Deep in the Heart of Texas," but she would try.

"I want cosmetic surgery," she said. Her English accent
surfaced when she was nervous. She wondered if she
should tell him that her lovers were all in their twenties.

"Why?" he asked. Who was he kidding? That was his
bread and butter. He lived, as they said in the Bible, by the
sword. Was he going to pretend he didn't really want to
give her cosmetic surgery? What was his schtick? She wondered if he only operated on atom bomb survivors from
Nagasaki. And if so, how come he had such a fancy office
with pictures of silver screws in silver frames on silver
wallpaper in the ladies' powder room. How come all these
famous women smiling out of Tiffany silver frames? How
come the receptionist with the diamond as big as a moth-
ball around her neck? Come on, now. Should she tell him
she ran after young cock?

"I feel old," Mrs. Dimani said, trying to sound like Rita,
a person with her own mind, not Mrs. Nick Dimani. Her
hands were shaking.

"You have beautiful skin. You don't need a face lift. I
can just look at you and tell you that even before I examine
you." It was as if he had kicked her in the stomach. Did he
know what it was like to be Nick's wife? Every little starlet
and fag in the world wanted a piece of Nick's ass. Didn't
he see she was aging?

"Dr. Berg, I have skin around my eyes. My breasts sag."

Dr. Berg looked at her under a mirror, felt her small perfect breasts. "Nonsense." (May be nonsense to you, doctor, but not to a guy nineteen.) "You do need your eyes done. We'll take away the extra skin and fatty tissue. As for your breasts, one inch at the most. But why do it? You're trading scars for uplift. The nipple and the skin under the breast will be scarred." He took a rubber breast down from the closet and showed her the scar.

"When can you do this?" she asked nervously. She didn't care for the rubber breast.

"Come back into my office and I will look at my book." The dance of the knife. Sitting in his office, she decided not to tell Nick about the breast surgery. He wouldn't like it.

"The fee is three thousand five hundred for breasts. Two thousand five hundred for eyes. Five thousand for the two. The breast operation isn't painful. For some reason, that area is almost immune to pain. The fee is payable two months in advance."

As she looked at Dr. Berg, thoughts poured through her mind of how, as a younger woman, she spent her money on jewelry. Then furs. Then coats. Now she was down to the skin. "Very good," she said, smiling. "Money is no problem. I am consulting another surgeon and then I will get back to you." Back at you. Where had all the youth gone? To Nick. To Nick in a delicate package of her life. Lionel Colesman had called Nick all morning, wanting to talk with him. She had given her entire life to Nick Dimani—was it worth it? She thought of the children as she got into a cab. "You don't walk out on four children," Nick always said. No, he was a lifer. She took the cab to her friend Julia's apartment building. Unlocked the front door. Climbed the two flights and unlocked the doors to the apartment. It was empty. Julia had gone to work. Almost automatically she put up a pot of coffee and began making the bed. A key in the locked door made the door open. With a small excitement in her body, she ran to the door, propelled by juices that she otherwise never felt. Steve walked in. He kissed her on the lips.

"I've only got an hour, Rita," he said, putting his newspaper on Julia's floor. He began taking off Rita's clothes. He was gentle. Suddenly they were naked and on Julia's bed. She looked at him without love. "Sit on my face," he said with a smile. He began making love to her with a passion she had never felt with Nick. He was almost hurting her.

"Stop. Please." After he made love to her, she went out to the kitchen. Now, finally, she wanted to make love again, but he didn't have time. She poured him some coffee. She would take him in her mouth, she would kiss him, hold him another time. Always "another time."

"Nick's in Tahoe," she said to him.

"For how long?"

"For a while."

"Good. I have to babysit with my son who's down from Boston. My wife's on a goodwill tour again. But maybe we can go to a show one evening. Does Julia mind that we use the apartment so often?"

"No. I'm going to send her a case of champagne," Rita said. Upper-class English voice. She let him hold her closely. She smelled his breath. It was always clean.

"I want to fuck you again," he said. She looked at him with her wide and sad eyes. It occurred to her, as if on a computer, that if Nick ever found out that her lover was the engineer who designed the stereo system for their Fifth Avenue apartment, he would kill him. The bill had been twenty thousand dollars, and now Steve was fucking her. Having him so close, she often thought of how useless it was to be angry with Nick Dimani. He had never been the lover that Steve was.

"I'm thinking of having my face fixed. Just the eyes," she whispered.

"Are you crazy, bitch?" He was almost screaming.

"You're a beautiful woman, Rita. Don't destroy what you are. You have a few wrinkles. So what? They make you interesting."

"Thanks. I don't want to be interesting. I want to be sexy." She laughed. He grabbed a hold of her face. She was crying. "You are, baby. You are. And I like you just the way you are now."

"Nick doesn't." The English accent became a whisper.

"Well, tell him to go fuck himself. Tell him Steve said so." They laughed. Again, the computer went on in her mind. She hadn't laughed with Nick like that for a long, long time.

38. Rock Dream

SYLVIA AWOKE in Rev's arms. They had been making love all morning. She felt the warm sperm in her hands. The milky sperm that she loved to smell. Lying with Rev in the liquidy bed, she realized again how much making love meant to her. Having one more cock inside her meant nothing. When she was young, sex had been experimental, a high, a way of doing something new to your mind. Now, at this age, it was meaningless until it was an exchange of pleasure. She knew she gave Rev great joy and pleasure. Making love was almost the only way to really *know* him, and she loved the unconscious strength that came from his arms. The snow was falling in Tahoe. Rev was getting restless. He wanted to go somewhere—he wasn't sure where. At night he sat listening to The Beach Boys in the room, reading, waiting for her to come "home" from working with Nick. He didn't gamble. Didn't like seeing the characters in the lobby. He kept a notebook and wrote down some of his thoughts. Sylvia would lie next to him and tell him it wouldn't be long. She'd be finished writing the material with Nick in a week or so.

"I hope so," he said. She loved his handwriting. It was the handwriting of a boy. What was he writing? Like him, it was secretive. She never knew.

39. *Playing Tahoe*

THE HUGE club-room in Harrah's Hotel was filled to capacity. Lorin, the headwaiter, had to put in extra chairs. A lot of celebrities flew up from Los Angeles to watch the act. "Catch" the act, they said. The velvet walls and the gold chandeliers of the big club room faded out of sight. The waitresses brought the customers their three drinks. In all the club rooms in Tahoe, you got three drinks for the minimum, and the drinks arrived before the show started. Sinatra was in the audience. The band came forward on pulleys. The neon sign with the names of some of the Dimani songs dropped from the ceiling. Neon titles glowed in the dark. "White Trash" flashed on and off in red neon. The huge Steinway floated on stage as if by magic. Sylvia had cajoled Rev into watching the act with her. They sat holding hands in one of the front booths.

Nick walked on stage in his tuxedo. Everyone stood and applauded him. The piano was turned toward him. It had a mirrored top so the audience could see his fingers. He played "Hello Again Happiness," their big hit from the late sixties:

Hello again happiness,
You made me feel so good;
Hello again happiness,
Suddenly I was understood.

The audience went wild. After Nick played "White Trash," about two hundred people stood up and applauded with such energy Nick had to play the song all over again. It was their favorite Dimani/Lundholm song of all time. Nick rapped, played, sang, joked. Everyone cheered him on after each song.

"I've been lucky in this business," Nick said confidentially to his audience. "And it's been you, my fans, who have made me lucky."

Lionel sat next to Ron Thimble. Thimble had been into his drug bag, taking coke. He felt invincible.

"I'd like to kill Dimani," Lionel said.

"What else is new?" Ron said in a loud voice. He laughed hysterically, then added, "At least let him finish his patter." Lionel sat in the dark. His killer's face was seen by no one but Ron Thimble. And Thimble was having too good a time to take it all seriously. He just "loved" watching Dimani perform. Dimani was so nineteen-fifties. Ron was into nostalgia and into seed. "He's seedy in a way no one is seedy today. He's really the essence of seed. He's an original crazy. I just love him."

"Forget what I told you," Lionel said. And sipped his scotch. The amps were too loud. He made a note to tell Dimani. Nick Dimani did big business in Tahoe. The bouffant hairdos, polyester suits, pointed shoes, sequin dresses were all there. Avon cosmetics glowed in the dark. You could breathe garlic from the big rollers. The little pussycats who wore ski parkas created by some schlock firm that used Pierre Cardin's name were sitting up front holding on to the arms of their husbands, who all looked like aging Dion Dimuccis.

Rev fumed in the darkness. He hated this kind of show and he had not wanted to come. He had ended up promising Sylvia that he would go, but now he was fuming. He hated the comedians and he hated Nick. Sylvia had pleaded with him to come and they had fought about it. "I love you, Rev," she pleaded.

"No, you don't," he smiled. "You just keep putting me on."

"I want to buy you a plane, a boat."

"I'm not a whore."

"Why do you say that? I'd just like to see you happy."

"Well, I don't come cheap. And I don't fuck on command."

"What do you mean?"

"Well, if you bought me a car, I wouldn't want a Trans Am. I'd want a 1909 Thomas Flyabout Model One. Price when new: three thousand. Price now: a hundred thou."

"Why so expensive?"

"These things are maintained better than new cars."

"Stop it. Rev, just come with me."

"Shut up. You don't have an option on me."

"Just come. This is the last time I'm going to Nick's show. He wants to try out some of the new material we've been working on. This is my last album, and Nick is singing one of the songs tonight for the first time. I get so nervous. It would be easier if I had you with me. I'll never ask you again."

"Yes, you will." He laughed.

She went over and hugged him. "We can make love after the show. I promise I'll make you come three times."

"Sounds good," he said in his bored way. She was getting bad vibes. He was not the Revson of her dreams, the Revson of the sea. He was the annoyed Rev who was about to cut out. The Rev who found every woman a cunt. He was the passive macho stereotype of the Wasp; he was the real Rev she didn't want to know. She only wanted the fantasy. The Rev who was available and game and up for everything, the way he was when she first met him. Now he was just a mixed-up piece of Wonderbread from Philadelphia who had the attention span of a slug. He was the up-tight gentile dial-tone she once accused him of being when she had smoked too much grass and drunk too much wine. He was the difficult spoiled brat who wanted everything his own way. The Duke of Earl who was really a monster. He was the bad Rev, not the prince. He was the frog. She would unfrog him.

"I'll never ask again," she promised.

"All right," he said, without changing his mind about Nick. He got dressed in the bathroom, locking the door as usual. He didn't like her or anyone watching him. And so it happened that they sat there in the dark watching Nick sing all the oldies.

"I'm going to split," Rev whispered.

"Please, sweetheart," Sylvia begged, holding his hand.

"All right," he said, and smiled at her. The prince was back. The frog disappeared. The Rev who was the stuntman, the Rev who drilled for steam, the Rev who was the tuna fisherman, the Rev of the car deals, and the Rev of the surfboard, the Trans Am boy with blue eyes who was a soldier of fortune, the Rev she loved was back. The club room was now a boiler room.

"And now, may I introduce a piece of my soul?" Nick was saying to the two thousand hushed fans. A spotlight went on Sylvia.

"Shit," Rev said to himself in a whisper. "Everyone's always a piece of his soul. If I hear that expression one more time——"

Nick talked to the audience as if they were his family. In the background, drums were playing. "You've been a wonderful audience. And now I'm going to give you a special treat: a sneak preview of my new album, *Playing Tahoe*. But first, here she is, my partner for over twenty years, the woman who wrote all the lyrics for my big hits, the person who believes in me more than my own mother—my better half, Sylvia Lundholm." Drums. Spotlight on Sylvia. And, by mistake, on Rev. Sylvia stood up and took a bow. She tried to pull Rev up with her, but he could not be moved. He sat there in the dark and felt icy cold. The spotlight was acid. He felt as if he had had acid thrown all over his body. He could feel it on the golden hairs of his chest, on his face. Acid. He hated Nick. It was as if Nick was now

exposing him, Revson Cranwell, to the world of trash and
curiosity seekers. The world of staring eyes, the world of
perspiration, exhibition. Nick was searing away his privacy. He'd like to kill the friggin' little bastard, he thought
as the spotlight hit him in the eyes like a bully. It blinded
him.

Sylvia loved the light. It was like the sun. It made her
feel good. Two thousand customers applauded. Sylvia
moved away from the table and, followed by the spotlight,
began running up onto the stage. She was now playing
Miranda to Nick's Prospero. Everything was being created
by her mentor, her weary mentor who was so proud of
her accomplishments. *Bully-monster. Honest Lord. Dingdong
Bell. Damned sprite. The master. The swabbler. The boatswain
and I. The gunner and his mate loved Moll, Meg, and Margery;
but none of them cared for Kate.* Why were these words rushing through her head? Where was Rev? Suffering a sea-
change? *Those were pearls that were his eyes.* It was all a snurvy
world. Nick the boatswain. Rev suffering his sea light. And
all those people rocked in the sea of Nick Dimani's voice.

While running on stage, Sylvia thought of all the different possible scenes in her life which contained the possibility of human happiness. She thought of bobbing up and
down on the waves with Rev. She thought of sitting on the
ski run, climbing higher and higher into the Sierras. She
thought of holding Nancy's hand and walking with her off
a boat in Cuba where they would be met by people who
knew and loved them. She thought of entering the temple
of her work, sitting at a typewriter and trying to bring out
of her soul everything that she knew was true, writing her
bones out, and feeling the peace that comes from that.
None of these scenes involved Nick. A scene holding Rev's
hand, Nancy's hand, her own hand in between words on
the typewriter. Where was Nick? Why was she herself on
the stage at Harrah's?

"This, folks, is Sylvia Lundholm. This little girl with her
great mind has written something totally new."

"Thank you all," Sylvia said breathlessly, "for being behind us all these years. We hope you'll like a few of the new songs we've been working on here in Tahoe. We want you to know, this is our last album." A hush. Then she ran off stage laughing. Followed by the spotlight, she slid into her seat next to Rev.

Nick followed her speech by saying, "She always says that, folks, after every album." He laughed. Everyone applauded. "You'll be hearing Dimani and Lundholm for the next decade." He sat down carefully and began playing a song from *Playing Tahoe*. Rev looked at Sylvia in the dark. He hated her. She felt it. Waves of ice. Radar.

"Why did you let him make a fool out of you?" he asked.

"What do you mean?"

"Never mind. Let's get out of here." He stood up and moved his huge body quickly out of Harrah's show room. Nick was still sitting at the piano singing under the spotlight. Rev pushed past the red velvet ropes, past the maitre d' in his black and elegant tuxedo, past the black and white baby pictures of the stars in the lobby, walking swiftly out of Harrah's into the snow. Sylvia followed behind him. "I thought *this* was your last album," he turned on her.

"It is." He was screaming at her. Tears ran down her face. Streaks of mascara formed on her cheeks. It was frightening to see him lose control. It was like a powerful car that was going berserk.

"You're a liar," he screamed, "I don't like people who lie. You're not leaving Nick. I don't care, but you don't have to lie to me, Sylvia. He's a creep and you're a creep." She was weeping. The few gamblers who were now fed up with Harrah's and going home were waiting for the car jockeys to get their cars. They stared.

"Never mind," he screamed, and began running.

"Where are you going?" she cried. She ran and caught up with him. He grabbed her by the arms.

"I love you, Sylvia," he screamed. "Don't you understand? Why are you hurting me? Don't you see how evil that creep is? What he's doing to your life? He has control of you, the way people who are mindfuckers have control of their victims. What are you—the Swedish moonie you once called yourself? Is that what you want?"

She stared at him. He was berserk now, totally, engine racing, steam coming out. She didn't know what to say to calm him down. "Nick is a beautiful person. He gave me something to do with my life. I can't hate anyone who has done that for me."

Rev's voice became cold. "Stop hating yourself, Sylvia. You're somebody. Even without Nick Dimani, hard as it may seem to believe. When are you going to believe it yourself? Try it. He's ruining you. If you can't see that, I can't teach it to you. You have to see it for yourself."

They stood there screaming under the falling snow. Pissed off, Rev jumped in the car, turned on the motor, and fishtailed away in the snow. He didn't like anyone to see him angry. And he was angry. He wondered what the world would be like if he could magically erase Nick Dimani; just the way a magician waved a rabbit out of a hat and then made it disappear, he would like to make Nick Dimani disappear. Dimani's a pain in the ass, he thought. Even if he got Sylvia to leave Nick, Nick would still just be a phone call away.

Sylvia didn't need that creep, but Rev needed her, and it really was a pain in the ass that Nick was trying to control her. What he loved about Sylvia and hated at the same time was how she was a pushover for being controlled. She seemed, because she was beautiful and talented, to be tough. But this creep was taking advantage of her loyalty. She was afraid to break Nick's heart. Rev knew wherever Sylvia went, Nick would always be on the other end of her life, like an angry parent who wouldn't give up a child. Not that it was his business, but if he was to keep seeing Sylvia, he would have to see Nick. It would give him satisfaction to wipe Nick off the blackboard, to see him disappear like a number that was no longer on the blackboard. Rev began daydreaming, the kind of daydreams he had

had when he wanted to kill his ex-wife. He could push
Nick off a chair lift. He could drop him in the lake. He
knew that the lake was so cold, a body wouldn't bloat and
float to the surface. Maybe the easiest way would be to do
something with a car, an area that Rev knew well, a death
stunt. It was pleasant to think of wasting Nick.

40. Nancy's Tahoe

SYLVIA AND Nancy were having a drink in the lobby of
Harrah's. The world revolved around them unnoticed.
Cowboys in boots with huge Stetsons and buckles on their
belts walked around, drinks in hand, waiting to bet with
the next roll of dice. Women in pink curlers and wash-
and-wear dresses collected quarters out of the gambling
machines when everything came up lemons. Tall skinny
waitresses walked around in their mesh stockings looking
for suckers to give away drinks to. Serious men who studied gambling the way professors study archeology watched
the wheels turning around and around and tried to figure
the odds. No clocks ticked. In the gambling world there is
only win and lose. No time. No age. The quarters made a
jingling sound. High-heeled hookers mixed with tourists.
Guys on uppers, hookers turning forty, pit bosses, waitresses on the graveyard shift—all stood as if petrified
while the gambling continued as usual.

"When the revolution comes, all this will be over,"
Nancy said.

"Christ, Nancy, am I glad you are here," Sylvia said. "At
least I have a friend I can talk to. Sometimes when I'm
working with Nick, I feel so lonely. He's surrounded by
lawyers and dressers and managers and old cronies, but
they all speak *his* language."

"I know what you mean," Nancy said, "rich talk." Nancy had been overtly underwhelmed by the majesty of the hotel, the gamblers in the casino, the action at the lounge bars. She hadn't come to Tahoe to be a tourist. In fact, Tahoe was to her just another example of corruption. She was all business. "That ten thousand dollars is really important," Nancy reminded Sylvia. "You sure you can manage it?"

"I think I can manage it."

"Good. Part of it will be used for a telethon against the seven sister oil companies—Exxon, Gulf, Mobil, Standard Oil of California, Texaco, British Petroleum, and Royal Dutch Shell—who have grounded, impoverished and defrauded the consumer with gobbledygook about their OPEC bedfellows 'topping off' tanks and an almost deadly silence about Alaskan oil, tax credits on their OPEC rip-offs, and their multinational cartel violations of antitrust proscription against horizontal and vertical integration—in producing, transporting, refining, and retailing oil products."

Nancy was a fanatic. All this in front of the keno machines.

41. *Rev's Grand Funk*

"I DON'T need to be here for fresh air," Rev said. They were sitting in the lounge of Harrah's. It was about six o'clock. Rev had just smoked a joint in the men's room. In the lounge, some dude no one had ever heard of was playing guitar. He was an imitation of Dion Dimucci. He was backed up by some singers who were imitation Fordham Baldies, imitation Belmonts. At lounge acts in Harrah's you never see a real anything. You get imitation nineteen-fifties. Dion Dimucci was the best of the street-corner singers. He came from a candy store in the Bronx and each of the Belmonts, his back up, came out of other candy stores. He was so fucking cool and crazy he captured America, which was looking for cool guys in leather jackets who hid their scary feelings. He sang "The Wanderer" and "Ruby Baby." He was the Brooklyn Bridge. The guy in the lounge act wore a leather jacket and held the mike up to his acned face. He had a pompadour and he was the shadow of Dion. He wasn't as good. He was just an act.

"I just wish you'd finish with this album and we could get out of here."

"Let's not talk about the album. Let's talk—Rev—about future plans. Let's talk about us. I thought you would be *happy* with your Trans Am."

"It's okay. But I'm getting tired of Tahoe. I can take just so much of Nick and his warmth."

"How about a trip? We can sail around the Caribbean. We can go to St. Martin. There's a place there called La Semana. Sand. Air. Sea."

"I wouldn't like La Semana. It's too up-tight. All the people there are square, if you know what I mean."

He looked bored. That was his natural look.

"*Where* should we go?"

"Anyplace else. How about *Detroit*? It doesn't have to be a place where you run into all these obnoxious people who give their résumés."

"What do you mean?"

Rev's voice was gentle. "Look, Sylvia, I like you the way you are. I'm not interested in *contacts*. All the people around you are just coming on all the time. They're on *all the time*. You know what I mean? They're not cool. Nick Dimani walks around with a briefcase filled with his own clippings. I mean, don't you think that's pathetic?

"Well, there's a certain kind of poor guy who has to do that. Who is always insecure. When he walks into a hotel or restaurant, he always says, 'I'm Nick Dimani.' A lot of

actors are like that. Self-loathers. If they're Jewish, they
have to marry a Swedish girl. If they're high-class goys,
they have to run around with Puerto Ricans. If they're
poor or high Wasp, they try to act black. If they're black,
they try to act poor or high Wasp. My whole world is filled
with middle-class black guys trying to act like the Mellons
or the Whitneys or middle-class Jewish guys dying to be
celebrities and goyish—the Jewish John Lindsays of the
world. Or funky guys trying to be classy: Salesmen trying
to be the coked-up jet set. And comedians telling you how
famous they are. Always unauthentic people trying to give
you their credits. Well, that's what I want to take you away
from. I don't mind Heavenly Valley for a week, but it's
now been two weeks and I'm tired of snow, if you know
what I mean. I like when you're relaxed, which is hard to
be in a place like this. I mean, Tahoe is all right, but it's all
being rotted away by show biz and developments. The
environment's going to be ruined by all these tacky little
houses. Nick Dimani is partly responsible. When I was
skiing last week, I heard that Dimani is going to go in
partners with one of the locals and buy up the virgin ter-
ritory. There's a guy called Mr. Tahoe. Ever heard of
him?"

"No."

"Well, he's powerful. And he's one of the boys. He
doesn't break your leg directly. He gets one of the mob to
do it. Sylvia, I hate both of those guys. Mr. Tahoe and
Dimani."

"I think you're making a mistake about Nick."

"You think so? Who do you think backed Dimani? Who
do you think carried him during the time he was in a so-
called slump? Who do you think bought him his house in
the Bahamas? Or his duplex on Fifth Avenue? Who used
their payola to buy him air time? Your business happens
not to be as clean as you'd like to think it is. Who is Dimani
really? An entertainer for the mob. And you're his silent
partner."

"You've been checking him out."

"Yeah. And I found out he's not a good guy. You should get rid of him. He needs you. But you don't need him. He can sing to the Red Cross without you."

"Look, Rev, I know you don't like responsibility. I was always the opposite. I wanted to make a name for myself. I wanted fame. I dug it. It was a kind of dope. When Nick sang on television, in the clubs, I got off on the fact that we were a team. I was somebody. The money coming in didn't hurt either. I signed a contract and everything was fine. Then, a couple of years ago, the shit hit the fan. I realized that everything about my life was wrong. Fine for my twenties. But not so great for my forties. Being a lyricist was fine. Working with Nick was fun, writing songs. Sometimes they were recorded. Sometimes they were just lyrics that never got on. Then I started writing for myself. Poetry. A novel. I found out that the real voice inside me didn't care about *marketing*. Didn't give a flying fuck about who sang and who didn't sing my words, about 'out there.' There was no *out there*. So I decided to get out of this whole mess slowly. That's when I met you."

"So, let's split."

"I have to finish writing this material."

"I'm splitting," Rev said.

"Wait a week."

"Till the album is done?" Rev puffed on a joint.

"Yes."

"When will that be?"

"Next week. I promise."

"All right. Forget it. I'll wait."

42. *Harvey's Wagon Wheel*

HARVEY'S, ONE of the four large casinos, stands in the middle of Tahoe. A golden skull of a steer is lit in neon.

Harvey, once a butcher, opened a bingo parlor. Now his restaurant and hotel and gambling casino *is* Tahoe. The Wagon Wheel, the restaurant on top of Harvey's, is where the action is. Lionel knew this, rode in the elevator, and found himself sitting at the cocktail bar next to a Eurasian. She had long black hair and an incredible face that was smooth and unlined. Even though she was dressed in just jeans, a sweater, and heels, he could tell her body was the kind he was attracted to: thin and lean. She turned him on. She was drinking a Bloody Mary. The lights were dark in Harvey's. He couldn't see how old she was. But she looked good to him. He wondered how much she would cost.

Something deep inside his brain told him to offer a thousand dollars. Wouldn't that blow her mind? Whores in Tahoe make fifty dollars a night and a tip, the best ones, the gentile girls with pony tails who look as if they'd rather be kneeling on a ski slope. The whores with pony tails. A new breed of hooker. Sadly, Lionel wasn't into broads. He wasn't into pony tails. He liked to be beaten up. He liked hookers who looked mean. Now this Eurasian, she looked good. She probably would go for handcuffs, amyl nitrate, musk, kink. He approached her slowly. Money always did the trick. Money was a portable prick. It was the substitute for virility. Wasn't that why success was so important to so many people? Money, the portable cock, the portable cunt.

"Can I buy you a drink?" he asked in his low voice, sitting next to her and purring. He was quite sure that his five-hundred-dollar sweater, his Pierre Cardin ski pants, and his seven-hundred-dollar boots would impress her.

"I already have one," she said. She didn't look at him. Her voice was low and hostile. He was turned on.

"Have a second one on me," he said in his charming voice, prince toad at the cocktail lounge. Too bad his wife didn't turn him on like this.

"Too late. This is my fourth one."

"Are you one of those feminists who don't allow men to buy you a drink?"

"That's right. I always buy my own drinks."

"I'm sorry," Lionel said.

It was a case of mistaken identity. She wasn't interested in him. He felt angry. Lionel was like a child. When he was angry, he stamped his foot, he pouted. At his office, he was able to scream at his secretary, insult her. Once he threw something at his wife (that was when the special code and separate bedrooms were instituted). Who the fuck was this Chink? He could have any hooker in the world. In his business, women were a liability. He could get a blow job any time of day or night. Wasn't that obvious?

"I'm sorry. I thought you were available," he said in his upper-class voice.

"I'm not," she said.

"Well, you shouldn't be seated at this bar," he smiled at her.

"Why? Is it reserved for hookers?"

"I don't know who you are. But you'd look a lot better in my bed than sitting on a plastic stool in a crummy bar."

"And so you thought you'd offer me a thousand dollars, Lionel?"

"How do you know who I am?"

"Your initials are on your sweater. And I figured LC stands for Lionel Colesman of Mecca Records. I've heard Sylvia talk about you."

"My God," he said, smiling his Mecca smile.

"I'm her friend," Nancy said, lighting a cigarette. "Who do you have to fuck to get out of this place?"

Lionel was not amused. Who did she think she was? It shot through his head that Sylvia might have told her something about him. *Keep cool,* he thought. "Well, I'm sorry. I hope you're flattered."

"It's all right, Lionel," Nancy said. She kept looking at the mirror in front of her as if she was looking beyond her own eyes. A band was now playing disco music. Some teenagers were beginning to sit down. The soap-box radical crossed her legs. "I've heard a lot about you, Mr. Coles-man," she said. "You own Mecca Records." Her voice was cold.

"Among other holdings."

"How's the record business?"

"It's doing very well." Suddenly he smiled. He turned to her. "Aren't you that crazy revolutionary friend of Sylvia's? I've heard mention of you."

"Crazy? Is that how she describes me? I think I'm more sane than crazy."

Revolutionaries bored Lionel. He hated radical chic. He hated *activists* of any kind. He paid the bar bill, not paying for Nancy, and got up to leave. As he rode down in the elevator, he thought of Nancy. Well, she could have fooled him. He would have thought she was a hooker. He was angry. But she was cute. Now he felt really horny. As he left Harvey's and walked into the snowy night, he began walking toward the Sahara. He'd look for Ron Thimble. Thimble was probably gambling at the roulette table. Ron was a loser. Every day he took out five hundred dollars and dropped it on the tables. He always lost. He seemed to enjoy it. Well, the night was just getting started in Tahoe. The acts were about to start. There was always the cocktail act, a supper show, and the late act starting at midnight. Ann-Margret was playing the Sahara. He had seen her show the night before. She was talented and at-tracted to him. He thought of sending her flowers. No. He wanted a piece of ass instead. He changed his mind about the Sahara.

He walked into the lobby of Harrah's. Down the green-carpeted casino which was the lobby of the hotel, past the dudes in cowboy shirts and hats and boots at the crap tables, past the dozens of women who leaned over the gambling tables, he walked past the young and the old and the lost and the fat and all the young men with bad skin and all the women with acrylic dresses and the lovely young girls who were dealers looking lovingly at him with their love eyes which cost fifty dollars a shot if you wanted them. He looked at the cocktail waitresses and the pit bosses and listened to the sound of the dealers and the crap tables and realized that he enjoyed Tahoe. Tahoe was in his blood. It was the action that he loved against the high Sierras, those huge mysterious mountains in the back of it all which glistened in the moonlight. It was the rock that he loved, the Nevada rock; behind all that action and evergreen and poker and cocksucking was heavy Nevada rock. The nickel state. He rang up the manager and spoke to him in his most charming voice. S. G. was his buddy. He *owned* him.

"Where've you been?" he asked S. G.

"Around," S.G. shot back, wondering what Lionel wanted.

"S.G., can you send me up a girl? Do you have any Eurasians, not too old? You do? Good. That's what I'm in the mood for." He hung up the phone. And waited for pleasure to ring his room bell. He needed a piece of cunt to hold on to. He needed something to hold on to. He was feeling shaky. Dimani was really beginning to annoy him. Who the fuck did he think he was, taking his new material to Cedar? And Nancy annoyed him, too. She would have been goddamn lucky to get her ass in his ringer. Who would want her once she opened her mouth and began her commie rap? He would fuck anything but a liberal. He wished they'd all go drown in Siberia. Two days in Moscow would cure their commie bullshit ideas. He lay back on the bedspread, took a sip of scotch, and waited. The bell rang. He was delivered.

43. Lionel and Nick

THE SUITE that Harrah's kept for Lionel was his own suite. It was also the presidential suite, on the top floor. It had

an indoor swimming pool, a brass double bed, quadraphonic Dolby systems in every room, a Jacuzzi, hot tubs,
and a view of the golden-nugget panorama of Tahoe.
From his suite Lionel could look out and see Emerald Bay,
Desolation Valley, Rubicon Bay, Mount Tellac, and Lake
Tahoe. Both the California and Nevada sides were covered in snow and Mount Tellac showed its crystal peak
against a clear greenish-blue sky. Lionel kept his skis at
Harrah's and they were neatly waiting for him against the
wall in their blue canvas cover.

The chambermaid had prepared Lionel's bed with the
blue satin sheets and blue satin covers he liked to sleep on
and kept, permanently, at the hotel. She laid out his blue
silk bathrobe and pajamas. The walls were covered with
Lionel's personal paintings, sketches, and watercolors by
Larry Rivers. Fruit was arranged in white porcelain bowls
which Lionel had designed himself. Champagne and caviar waited on the glass table for Lionel. The icebox was
stocked with Lionel's favorite chocolates, fruits, and patés.
White peonies, Lionel's favorite flower, had been flown up
daily to perfume the suite. When Lionel entered, he was
pleased. He sat down for a moment by himself. Just for a
moment. Lionel hated to be alone. An evening alone was
an evening of despair. And he had arranged for Nick to
meet him privately before he went out for the evening.

Nick arrived. Lionel was furious at him. He loved and
hated him. Nick Dimani had been a thorn in the side of
Mecca Records for the past few years. Years ago, Nick had
been into him for six hundred thousand. After his comeback, with Elton John's help, all the money had been returned. But this time, Nick had gone too far. Lionel
opened the door in his usual formal way. He was wearing
a tuxedo. Nick was wearing jeans, gold chains, boots, and
a silk shirt which showed his chest, the obligatory form of
the industry.

"Won't you come in?" Lionel said in his deep friendly
voice. Nick Dimani was a necessary object that Lionel
could not afford to lose. Especially not to old rival Arthur

Morris. Morris was everything Lionel was not: funky, warm, brilliant about jazz, daring. Lionel was smooth, up-tight. And he knew it. But Morris was not going to take Dimani away from him. Lionel offered Nick champagne. He sat down and Nick sat down next to him.

"How are you?" Nick asked.

"Let me tell you about the legend of the paper plate," Lionel replied.

"Anything you say."

"They trace their ancestry back to the forest; they come from trees that are proud and strong."

"Go on." Nick held on to his glass and tried not to squeeze too hard. He didn't see the point of one of these Lionelesque lectures.

"During hard times, the trees were cut down. They were sold to the mills. Their very treeness was corrupted by colored acids; they were bleached and burned and their fibers dispersed as sawdust. They were taken from the forest and crushed so that they were made into paper plates. You could see them at any picnic. Thin. Pliable. They were made to be replaced. They are thrown away."

"So?" Nick tried to be casual. He was sweating under his arms. The silk shirt had huge perspiration holes.

"That is your business. The artists? They are paper plates. They can be thrown away at any time. Do you un-derstand?" Lionel sipped from his crystal goblet and smiled. "As a friend, I love you. But as a performer, Nick, you are a paper plate. No more, no less."

"Why are you here in Tahoe?"

"Because I'm not sure I want you to make *Playing Tahoe* with Morris."

"In my contract, I have the right to make an outside album."

"I'm not talking about your contract. Your last album didn't sell, Nick. To put it bluntly, it wasn't your best work. Now I hear that you and Sylvia are writing some interesting songs. I'd like you to record that album on Mecca. Not for Morris and his company."

"It's just special material."

"Playing Tahoe?"

"How did you know the concept?"

Lionel sipped his champagne. "I'll make a deal with you, Dimani. Do the album for Morris. Go to Muscle Shoals. Record it with him. But make sure that the next few years you record with no one but me. And one other thing— this may seem petty to you, Dimani. But I'd like to take up your offer of a piece of the action. Half of whatever you get."

"Fuck you!"

"Wouldn't you like to." Lionel smiled.

"Listen, Lionel, you're not getting one cent of *Playing Tahoe.* I've got the right to make an independent if I want to. That's part of our deal."

"If you have my permission."

"Says who?"

"Says this." Lionel held up a silver handgun. He turned up the stereo so loud that a shot could not possibly be heard. The music blared the Dimani/Lundholm hit: *"Roll me, Roll on, Roll me, roll me, roll me, honey, roll me down, roll me down honey."*

"I get the message," Nick said.

"Good. I thought you would."

Nick hadn't forgotten the slap of Lionel's ridiculous demands in the past. But no point in arguing with a gun.

"How are you and Sylvia getting along?" Lionel asked.

"Fine. Why do you ask?" Nick said.

"She just seemed to be tired of the business. Sometimes a writer just doesn't feel like writing. It's an occupational hazard of being too rich. What's her lover like?"

"A pretty box. I don't like him. He says he's a fisherman. A black sheep of the family. His parents are very social and live in Philadelphia."

"Is he after Sylvia's money?"

"Of course."

"What else does he want?"

"A human fish on his hook, I guess. How do I know what he wants?"

"How long are you staying in Tahoe?"

"A while. Long enough."

As Nick rose to go, he realized that he still loved Lionel. That was the name of the game. The industry!

44. Bugs in Heat

DIMANI WAS having a breakfast meeting with Kenny. He was the big man at Squire Records and was personally responsible for the success of The Ramones, Secret Places, and The Talking Heads. His finest moment came when he was asked at a loft party, "What do you *do* for the Ramones?" And he said, "I love them so much, I can't begin to tell you what I *do* for them." And that was his answer to her. Kenny was a music mystic for whom money was everything in life. "I'm as altruistic as a cobra," he told Nick when they first met. That's why Nick liked him. He was twenty-seven years old. Nick was a golden oldie to Kenny.

There were two people in the business whom Nick respected. His hero was Arthur Morris, a beautiful guy, a real person, responsible for everything. And Kenny. At twenty-seven, Kenny had the insight to take punk rock and develop it with a sense of humor that turned into money. He was making history, and that was what his attitude toward Nick Dimani was. Kenny was the kind of boychild who had worshiped Presley, had bought Presley's Stutz, and for whom working in the record business was like working in a museum. "The business is ugly," he told his shrink. "But if I wanted to just be interested in music,

if I wanted to play guitar in a pure way, I'd go to a mon-
astery."

"That's interesting," the shrink said. The shrink also
had fantasies of living a life of rock and roll. Nouveau
movie star dreams. Even shrinks live by the media. The
reason Kenny was meeting Nick for breakfast was really
just for informational purposes. He wanted to know what
the deal was between him and Morris so he could be cool.
To be cool, you had to be one step ahead of everyone else
in the business. You had to know about something before
it happened, not afterward. That was the scene according
to Kenny. They both went up to the steambath together.
Tahoe was filled with gamblers, thugs, dealers, and little
roaches from the industry who sucked up to Nick. Dimani
was up to something. The word was out.

45. *Nick and Sylvia*

"I want songs about Tahoe," Nick said. "Songs about the
water, the Truckee River, hang-gliding above Peavine
Mountain, the west which was made from ponytrails and
railroad cars, the West Coast, the Sierras, the outdoors.
You can't find another place with desert, hills and trees,
snow and ocean—Carson Valley, Lake Tahoe. The view
from the top of Heavenly Valley, the smell of the lumber,
the solitude of the Sierras. I love this place. Because it's
still pure."

"How about a song called 'Snow Plant'? It's the plant
that comes up first after the snow melts." Sylvia impro-
vised. That was how she always worked.

There's a plant that comes
After the snowfall,
And it's red and it's very small,

It's the love that comes after a lover's fight
Which nobody wanted at all—
Lovers quarrel,
Lovers quarrel,
Nobody wanted at all.

"I hear you." Nick began improvising on the keyboard. "Yeah, I like it. It's about making up after a quarrel."

"Maybe we should call it that."

"Making up?"

"No, 'Snow Plant.' It's perfect for the album. It goes with 'Ice Harvest' and 'Crystal Man.' "

"All right, I'll work on it."

"And I want something else. You'll know what I mean. I want a song about water. A song about the Indians and what they thought of the lake."

"A boogie song?"

"No. A ballad."

"How about a song about the Black Rock Desert in Nevada? The desert which you're even afraid to enter. Or the dunes of Pyramid Lake?"

"No. A song about the lake. According to Paiute legend, the lake was formed by the tears of a great Indian mother. I want something in the song that says why Tahoe is so distinctive. I want a song about the snow, the rugged mountains, the dry valleys. About people who don't want to be in cities."

"An earth song."

"Oh God, Sylvia, the whole album has to be that. Love of the earth and water and sun. That feeling. *Playing Tahoe* has to be about the one thing we have—fertility. An album about people who are anxious and about the end of all that anxiety. About how a life lived in nature is never dull. Something changes. Something happens all the time."

"I'm with you."

"People saying: 'Who could live there? It's so boring.' Well, I want an album that tells the romance of the outdoor lifestyle. About the unpretentious way that people live in Tahoe. About how the lack of distractions creates a modesty in people. Look, I've been playing out here for years now. Every time I come back, I swear, I wonder why I ever leave Tahoe. Why leave the place? Every day I'm out here, I walk in the open country. I look at the Sierras with snow blinding my eyes. I listen to the directness of the people. There's something in this place that's so un-pretentious—a heritage—the purity of the Indians still exists here."

"The songs are taking shape."

"Good. I think *Playing Tahoe* is going to be our best."

"I hope so. Because it's going to be our last."

"Don't say that."

"Look, sweetheart, I'm really very fond of you and I would do anything for you, but I have my own life to live and I want to live it. It's a life with happiness in it."

"What kind of happiness?"

"The happiness of just being left alone and not doing anything."

For the next few days, Sylvia worked hard. She wrote seven lyrics and Nick fooled around with them. The album was taking shape. Nick played "Snow Plant" for Sylvia.

"I like it," she said. "It's a different sound. No one's written anything like it. I know Morris will like it."

Sylvia showed him a lyric. He didn't like it. An argument began. "Listen, I've had enough," she said.

"Why are you making all these problems for me?" He banged his hands on the piano.

"I'm not making problems for you. It's just that I'm tired of hearing you be an asshole. There's something frenzied about you, Nick. And it's boring."

"In what way?"

"Whenever you want something, you're manipulative and you usually get it. You wanted me out here. In Tahoe. You have an album idea and you want it so badly to be a hit. Still another hit. So you get Sylvia. You send for your soul. That's it, Nick."

"You know, Sylvia, our friendship aside, I don't like working with you anymore. I think you're really a cunt."

Sylvia picked up the lyrics. She tore them in half, throwing the paper in the air, and walked out. Sylvia walked out of the elevator and into the gambling pit of the hotel. The wheels were turning around. The dealers dressed in tuxedos or short skirts were standing like robots over the cards. A man came up to her. It was Thimble.

"Hello, Lady Sylvia."

"Nick and I have had a disagreement."

"Since you've been here, he's been in a lousy mood. I thought you were partners."

"We were."

"Oh, sweetheart, Nick loves you. He does. He wouldn't be where he is today without you, and he knows it. It's just love."

"We aren't lovers."

"All right. You're more than lovers. You're tied together in the bondage of working. You're doing the Tahoe album. You're collaborators. Stay cool. Don't let Nick upset you. He gets mad at everyone."

Sylvia stood stiffly while he embraced her. She wondered if he was doing this for Mecca Records. In this business, there was no such thing as friendship. Sylvia walked through the casinos and thought of Dante's Inferno. Here were the misplaced, the unwanted, the condemned, in the lobbies of greed. There was nothing in this casino but sadness and hope for the right lemon. Everyone gambling. Everyone losing. Suddenly, she realized with compassion that Nick was a loser. She had to help him.

Nick found Sylvia sitting at the lounge bar. "I'm sorry," he said.

"Look, I don't want to hassle you. I told you I'd come out here to write the album with you, and I'm not leaving until we have eight or ten songs," she said.

"Good."

"I have some dummy lyrics for a song called 'Green

Tree Horizon.' I've used a work tune similar to 'You Don't Have Any Problems.' "

"Let's see."

She took out of her bag an envelope on which she had written some words. He looked at the lyrics. He smiled. He ran the lyric through his mind, editing, changing, tapping. Finally he looked at Sylvia. "That's going to be a song and a half. I have to push a pencil around and work on the lead sheet."

Sylvia finished her drink. She missed Rev. She had to go up to her room. To find him.

46. *Loving Rev*

SYLVIA WENT upstairs to the suite to find Rev. He was watching television. He looked at her when she stepped into the room with a look that meant he was feeling aroused. His blue eyes shone like lights. He liked to make love to her in front of the television. He liked the vulgarity of the noise.

Afterward he smoked a joint and she brushed her hair. With a joint, it was easier for him to open up. She didn't need drugs for that, but he did.

"I was born in Philadelphia," Rev laughed. "My father was an architect at that time. My folks have retired in Palm Beach. My mother used to try to get me interested in museums and cultural things, but it really didn't rub off on me. I have two sisters. Both of them do charity work. My parents sent me to the Eagle Prep School in Switzerland and I ran away. Then they sent me to Le Rose and I ran away. They didn't know what to do with me. That's when they gave me shock treatments."

"That's ghastly. For running away from school? That's the most horrible thing I ever heard."

"My parents didn't know how to cope with me. Later, I went to New York to study acting. My father gave me an allowance and I lived in Manhattan. I went to the Actor's Studio and I worked as a maintenance man for Cable TV to make some money. I liked the maintenance work more than acting. I got bored with the study classes. I was too stiff, I guess. I just didn't emote. I couldn't loosen up. And I decided I didn't like acting. I kept working for Cable TV and then went to Harvard. My father stopped sending me money. When I went home at the holidays for family dinners, my parents looked at me as if I was speeding on mescaline. They couldn't understand why I didn't want to work on Wall Street or take over the business. I'd sit in the big house they have in Philadelphia and drink beer and play blackjack with a computer, and they figured I was a wasted life. I played darts.

"According to my mother, if you're not 'successful,' there's no point in being alive. My father would take me in the library and offer me a cigar. He would give me port. And it would be a scene out of a television show. Father and son. Talking heavy talk. It was very intense, because my father wanted me on Wall Street. Married. Monied. It was all right for his daughters to help sick people, but he wanted my face on *Fortune* Magazine. Why couldn't he have had a son that would have had his values? Most of all, why wasn't I a jock? He couldn't discuss anything with me. Not football. Not sports. I couldn't even play tennis, for God's sake. He asked me what I wanted to do with my life. It was a Christmas weekend. The sun was setting over the ocean and I was watching it. I wanted so badly to hug my father and explain to him that I wasn't him. I was someone else. I didn't know who I was, but I knew who I wasn't. I wanted to live a relaxed cheerful life. I didn't want responsibilities. I didn't want a family. I wanted to live simply. To read. To listen to music. To play cards. And to be left to myself. He kept asking me what I wanted to do with my life and when I said 'fish,' I thought he was going to smack me."

"Fish what?"

"Fish tuna," I said.

"Behind my father stood the social register, years of Calvinistic prosperity, years of doing the right thing, the right club, the right friends, the right schools, the right diseases, the right way of spending time. He lives in a world of spinnakers and plaid jackets and clubs and class reunions, a world of matching baggage. I was out to destroy all that with my duffel bag. I didn't want to get into a yacht and race his colors. I wanted to get on a fishing boat with a bunch of grubby guys who worked for shares."

"Fish?" he asked.

"Fish," I said.

"And I left wondering why I had wounded him. I didn't mean to wound him, but it was almost as if the blood came spurting out of his nose, his eyes, his mouth."

Sylvia listened and held him close.

Rev driving the Trans Am. Midnight aristocrat. Sylvia next to him. Staring into night sky. Rev smoking a joint. Thin white cigarette to lips. Deep breath. Smoking. Suddenly the desert out of whack. Pine trees dancing into deep rock. Night lights blinking on and off like out-of-sync angels—bright lights of Tahoe illuminating the black desert sky. Highway. And silence. Sound of tires on snow.

On the highway Rev guns the motor of the Trans Am. Deep breath. Car on Highway 395—driving—driving to Spooner Grade. Then into Carson City. State Capital named after old frontiersman Kit Carson. Today, Wayne Newton, legend. Yesterday, Kit Carson, legend. Pine trees bending under moon. Down from mountain to desert flatland. Trans Am gliding like black shark swiftly toward Steamboat Springs. White moon, disc, rolling in sky stereo. White moon shines down on old Spa at Steamboat Springs.

Light on steam rising from the ground. Moonlit jets of steam out of desert earth. Then suddenly, the feathers of light of Reno lighting the desert sky.

Rev to Sylvia, "Who's playing Harrah's?"

"Jim Nabors."

"How come Wayne Newton doesn't play Reno?" Rev asks.

"Couldn't afford him. Room isn't big enough. Wayne Newton's the king of Nevada. Just as big a draw as Frank Sinatra or Sammy Davis, Jr. When he packs them in, they need the showroom at Harrah's Tahoe, which holds about two thousand people."

Rev lights another joint. Night. Stars. The smell of marijuana curls through the car like sweet fog. The car moves through the desert, smelling of old sweet leaves.

"He's a big shot around here, isn't he?"

Sylvia laughs. Car goes slowly now.

"He sure is. He's a legend. He used to be a pear-shaped country boy with a pompadour, a fat boy with slicked-back blond hair playing the lounge at the Freemont in Vegas. Then some dude manager took him on. Helped him develop an act. Told him to change his outfit. Fix up his songs. Write them himself. Drop sixty pounds. Now he wears sequins. He's six foot three, broad shoulders and narrow hips, small waist and handsome as any movie star. He spends a lot of his time playing the Stardust Hotel in Vegas. Which he owns fifty percent of, I'm told. Probably more."

"How much is that worth?"

"Nick told me they offered us a six-percent share of the Stardust last year for five million dollars. That means Wayne Newton's share is worth close to fifty million. But that's not all he owns. He's got the largest antique automobile collection in America, next to Harrah's, a ranch where he raises purebred horses, Arabian horses. He's not hurting for cash."

"Not bad," Rev said, unimpressed.

"Wouldn't you *like* all that?" Sylvia laughed.

"I'd take the cars, anyway."

"The album's almost finished, Rev."

"That's good."

"I'm happy that I came through for Nick. He's excited about the tapes."

"Good."

"I think we will be out of here in another week."

"Sooner the better."

The car glides into the city. Breathtaking speed again. The car speeds toward the bones of the city. White bony houses. Huge white whales in darkness. Buildings of glass are huge mammals in the sky. Crustacean car floats into Reno's darkness. Over Virginia Street shines Reno trademark sign, "The biggest little city in the world." They could be underwater. Sylvia giddy. Happy to be with Rev. Feels as if she's scuba diving. Floating in the coral reef of Reno.

"Never been to Reno," Rev says.

"I have. Fifteen years ago, Nick played Reno. I came on the road to watch his act. I remember Pick Hobson's Horseshoe Club was the place to go. Small-time gambling casino. Then, Reno was the divorce capital of the world. You could get a divorce in six weeks' time. No questions asked. Bill Harrah changed Reno the way he changed Tahoe. All the little women getting their freedom papers would stay at the dude ranches, dance square dances with the local cowboys. Now the women filing for divorce come with their Vuiton luggage and stay at a five-hundred-and-forty-room monster hotel. They sit in their suites making long distance calls to their kids, drink Bloody Marys and Piña Coladas, go downstairs and play craps, sit in the club room and dream of the future—everything's changed."

"Guess so."

Rev switches on the radio. Blast of sound. Wayne Newton's voice on airwaves of desert. Shining voice curling with smoke through the window pane. "He did pretty good for a fat country boy," Sylvia says.

Rev smiles. Aristocratic smile. Drives to parking lot.

Takes last drag of joint. Two people sitting in car. Wayne Newton. Sounds of voice curling around car. Rev stares out of the car window. Holds Sylvia's hand. Sweet smell in their hair. They sit for a moment in darkness. Listen to Reno sounds.

Cowboys. Virginia Street. Divorce. Wayne Newton. Biggest little city. Square dance. Del Webb's Sahara Tahoe. Laughing. Club rooms. Carved out of desert. Golden Hotel burns down. Harrah builds hotel. All of Nevada merges as they hold hands. Rev, in darkness, thinking about Wayne Newton.

"Want a joint before the show?"

"No thanks. You know I'm not into drugs. I'm high anyway."

Sylvia in her own high. Her Trans Am high. Rev, her drug. Her under-sea-level drug. Rev, her legend.

47. *The Ski Lodge*

LIONEL BELIEVED in defensive fucking the way some people believe in defensive driving. What did that mean? It meant that in the very beginning you watched out for what the other person did. He couldn't afford to be in any kind of scandal—he might lose Karen. So in the very beginning, before any sex got underway, he laid down the ground rules. Especially when it came to men. Years ago, when he first met Ron Thimble, Lionel was aware of the fact that it was best for his image that his public persona be kept pure. That meant his bisexuality was a personal matter. He wasn't "in love" with Thimble. He found Thimble convenient as a combination servant-companion-lover. He was always "available," and that was important. His life was being ready to keep Lionel company on his many personal and business ventures. Nothing about Thimble would give away the fact that he was gay. A smoothie from the South, Thimble had come from a wealthy family, had a small income, and excelled at sports. In the beginning of their relationship, Lionel had laid down the rules, never in public should they appear more than buddies. In the event that Thimble wanted to leave Lionel's side at any time, there would be a ten thousand dollar bonus waiting for him at the lawyer's office. It meant that Thimble wasn't working for Lionel, just entitled to gifts. And small gifts had been provided. A cooperative apartment in the Bay area and one in New York, a car, a wardrobe. And Lionel relied on Thimble, since he was younger than most of his friends; Thimble understood music, the new music, something that Lionel was never sure of.

It was in Tahoe that Thimble was most useful. Together they skied Mount Tellac, went to the shows. Thimble and Lionel were seen at the Sahara, watching Vic Damone. At the Park Tahoe, they sat in the huge new clubroom listening to the Four Seasons. And at Harrah's they went to see Nick. But it was at the State Line, a club and ski place, that they had the most fun. It was four o'clock and a new small group, led by a guy with long hair called Steve, were playing. Young California boys and girls, mostly in their twenties, were dancing to the music. "Who is this guy?" Lionel asked Thimble. They were sitting in front of a fireplace. After-ski dancers were dancing in their ski clothes.

"I think he's a local," Ron said. "He's very good."

"He's more than good," Lionel said. He watched Steve the way an eagle watches his prey. Steve, who called himself "A legend in my own mind," played his own songs and was the local celebrity at Tahoe.

"He is more than good," Thimble said. "I think he's a real talent. He's hot. I think you should sign him."

Lionel sat drinking his screwdriver. The dancers kept moving back and forth on the floor, young men in tight ski pants and suspenders holding girls in boots and ski pants.

"I love your taste," Lionel said to Thimble. But Thimble wasn't hearing him. He was deep in the music, wandering in his own daydream of Steve and no one but Steve playing music to him. Everything about him turned Thimble on. The fact that he had his shirt open, his body, his smile— but who was that young girl sitting next to Lionel? A young girl with a Heavenly Valley ski cap was jumping up and down.

"That's my song, my song," she screamed to Thimble. "He wrote it for me."

"He did?"

"Yeah, we live together. He's my baby. He wrote that song for me." Steve was playing a song that made everyone want to dance. He was moving like a jellybean. Ron felt something hot passing over his body. It was the anger that came when someone was out of his reach. It frustrated him. There was nothing like the thrill of "turning" a straight guy, but that meant a relationship: dinners, help in the person's life, being friends, playing big brother, all of which meant time, energy, and that was actually what he didn't have with Lionel. Lionel kept his eye on Thimble. He "owned" him for the moment.

"Actually, he's not as good as I thought," Thimble said after another set. "Let's get out of here and take a drive. I'm feeling claustrophobic." Climbing over the skiers while the set was still going on, they left the lodge. Down the steps. And into Lionel's Porsche.

"I thought you were impressed with that group," Lionel said.

"I was and I wasn't," Thimble said, taking the curve around the mountain. He was speeding and he seemed angry. Lionel started to laugh.

"Didn't you turn him on?" Lionel asked.

"Cut it out," Thimble said. He often behaved like a spoiled brat. He was beautiful and he was used to getting any man he wanted. A rejection was a slap in the face to him. He hadn't worked all those years, turning his body into an art form, to be rejected by some clod who played the guitar and was living a soap opera with a young girl in a peaked hat.

"Takes two to tango," Lionel said. "That's all I know of life. That it takes two to tango. That's my philosophy. Haven't you found it to be true?" Thimble was speeding. "That's all right," Lionel said. "I'll give you the night off tomorrow and you can go back to the State Line and pick up one of those ski instructors. They're not as straight as they pretend to be."

"I know what you mean," Thimble said, and smiled.

48. *Nancy and the Cowboy*

"YOU LIVE in these parts?" he asked.

Nancy stood at the craps table. A tall country-western cowboy stood next to her. He wore a ten-gallon hat and silver spurs.

"No. I'm here visiting," she said in her Oxford accent. It intrigued him. He had never met a Chinese person before. At least one who spoke so elegantly.

"You sure got a purty voice," he said.

"Thank you."

"You like it here in Tahoe?"

"It's not a question of liking it or not liking it. I'm here on business," she snapped.

"Like to gamble?"

"Yes. It runs in my blood."

"Mind if I buy a young purty lady like you some chips?"

"Yes, I do."

"Reckon I don't understand why."

"I like to pay my own way."

"Then can I buy a purty lady like you a drink?"

"All right. If you insist."

They moved over to the lounge bar at Harrah's.

"What kinda business you in?" he asked, as they clinked glasses.

"The revolution business. I'm here to collect some money from a friend of mine who's working on an album. A record album with her partner, Nick Dimani."

"Never heard of him."

"He's playing Harrah's. In the big room."

"Oh yes. He's the feller with all them big records. Folks say he's got a lotta money. And a lotta talent. Reckon you have to have a lotta talent to be in show biz. I'm a country boy myself."

"From where?"

"Houston. Where else? Got a ranch outside Houston. Houston's a great little place. We got the tallest buildings and the biggest swimming pools. But we ain't no fools. We gotta ballet company that's just as good as any dance company up in New York."

Nancy looked at him. He wasn't bad. He obviously wanted to make it. Why not, she thought. As if catching her intentions, the cowboy paid the bill and walked to the desk.

"I'll take a room fer two," he said quietly to the desk manager. For some reason he didn't want to go to his own room. Nancy didn't ask any questions.

He was a good lover. Her body was lean and he knew how to make her feel good immediately. She relaxed in his arms after she had her pleasure and he made love to her again. Later he said to her, "What kind of revolution you into, purty lady?"

"Guerilla warfare. Africa. The Caribbean."

"You must be kiddin' me."

"No. I'm serious. I'm raising money for a socialist magazine called *Issues,* an alternative to the lies of the establishment press."

"Can I make a contribution?"

"Of course. If you feel politically moved to do so."

He got up and walked naked to his pants. Out of a lizard wallet he took two five-hundred-dollar bills. He gave them to her by pressing them in her hands. She looked at them. She had never seen five-hundred-dollar bills. She laughed. To think a cowboy could fund guerilla warfare. And a cowboy with a real cowboy hat and real boots and real spurs. Sometimes America was a great place.

49. Nerves

WHITE AND magical, white and phosphorescent as geometry, white and perfect, it snowed in Tahoe. The snow came down and Nick felt like a boy. He loved working with Sylvia. Despite Rev, despite all the problems, it was almost like it used to be. Just like the old days. She had the words and he had the music and they were able to fit together perfectly. He felt good for the first time in a long time. But something was wrong; he knew it.

Arthur Morris was worried. He called Nick in Tahoe. It made Nick nervous. He didn't want to ever disappoint Morris.

"How's the album going?" The rich jocular voice through the black telephone sounded good to Nick. He loved Morris. He was the only person in the whole industry Nick trusted. Trusted and respected. He had the soul, man. Everyone said that. Toothless black singers and rock stars and whores and sax players, survivors and superstars, funkies and talking heads, punk babies and drummers— all the acrobats of the jazz world and the rock circus—they all loved Arthur Morris. And why not? He had taste. He was never out for a quick buck. He was above all that: the priest of soul. He was the pontiff of good music. Everyone loved him. He had that mystical effect on people. Morris was the one guy in the business without enemies. But Morris was worried. He called every day.

Nick heard his voice through the network of Harrah's switchboard which linked the hotel and the casino and the villa up to the rest of the world. The Harrah switchboard was the aorta and ventricle of communication. The plugs reached out and connected the voices and rhythms of the world beyond the Sierras. Nick looked forward to Arthur Morris's warm hello every day. But today he sounded worried.

"Don't worry. The songs sound great," Nick said. He meant it.

"I know. I've been listening to the tapes. But when will you have them ready to go?"

"Another week?"

"You said that last week."

"I want these songs to be really beautiful."

"How many do you have left?"

"Sylvia's working on some new lyrics. I played them back to her last night and she freaked."

"That's good. Then the album will be ready in a week?"

"Absolutely."

"Good. I've been worried. You know I booked the studio in Muscle Shoals. I have to work on a whole different backup. I want you to have the right sound this time."

"I know."

"Then I'll call you tomorrow."

"Good."

"Take it easy."

Nick was worried. Six songs were written. But that wasn't enough. They had to complete at least twelve songs to have an album. All the pieces of his mind were in a puzzle. He'd go out and listen to the sun. The sun sang, as of old, its song to him. Sun music. Snow music. He wished he was a bareback rider riding into the rays of the sun. He wished he could ride beyond the Sierras into a place where the sun set. He had to tell Sylvia about that. She had to get that into the lyrics. If they got that into the lyrics, everything would be all right. He felt like a child. He felt young and like he was living in a dream, with all the old fears like ladies-in-waiting bowing down to him, the fears. He would live in the joy of writing music, forget the fears. Nick Dimani had waited to be as inspired as he was now with the concept of *Playing Tahoe* for all his life. Morris could wait another week. Writing these songs, Nick felt like a boy living in a new pumpkin under an old star. He felt happy. No one could take that away from him. He wished the time when he worked with Sylvia would never end. With her, he felt like a poet living in his own sealed-off world. He dreaded the end of the collaboration. He felt happy, at least for now, despite Morris's anxiety.

50. *Sylvia's and Nick's Bebop*

"MAN, I don't dig what you're doing." They sat together, Nick and Sylvia, in their suite in Harrah's villa, facing each other as collaborators for the last time. With her, Nick could shed his pretensions, his accumulation of new habits and new wardrobes. She knew him *when*. Together they embodied the good old days. She had written songs with Nick Dimani when he lived in a *pad*—not a co-op or a chateau. She had once been his "girl," his "old lady," and he had called her Our Lady of the Sounds. She had seen him licking his jazz lips. She had watched him pay his dues. She had seen him as a performer get his show on the road. They had been *tight* and things once were no big deal. Slowly, he had gotten hip to society and money. He had gone from being a white black man to a white man without the blues. He had known her too when she was a

middle-class *gal* (before the Women's Movement, everyone was a gal), and he had known that sweet Swedish side
of her personality, when she walked around without
make-up and cooked meatballs. He had seen her change
too from loving things that smelled like wood, from being
scared of the biggies and the smart alecks, to becoming
this person she now was. And that was what was annoying
him in Tahoe. Who was she? Why had she started to let
him down? "You don't have to shit me. You can level.
What do you see in him?" Nick asked.

"In who?"

"Shit man, in him. In that zombie you brought to Tahoe.
Don't you see he's out for all he can get? Your new sidekick
is just a creep, as far as I'm concerned."

"Well, you're not concerned."

"Don't shit me, Sylvia. I'm hip to what you feel. I just
don't get it. Tell me what has mesmerized you about this
car salesman."

"He's quiet."

"All right, so you like white bread instead of pumper-
nickel. I can see that his goyish manners could attract
someone's attention for a few minutes. But to hang out
with him? Man, what do you see in him?"

"What do you see in Rita?"

"That's a good point. I once thought she was classy.
Before she nailed me for almost all my bread and began
acting like a *meshugana*. But we have kids. She's my *wife*.
What the hell—that's my screwed up life. I'm talking
about yours. What is it with you?" He was almost weeping.
She flashed on how much she had once loved him. Suddenly she saw him as Nick, the victor of a thousand keyboards and trumpets, the Hector who had won the battle
of nightbulbs and dressing rooms, who had gone to battle
with all the mediocrity of run-of-the-hall sidemen and
A & R men; he was the genius who could hurt inside, and
she felt her resentments toward him melting. He had
gorged himself on Erroll Garner sounds and Bird and Diz.

He had checked out of Brooklyn and moved into grimy pads; his life had been playing up a storm; he had super-imposed his life on the keys until he had made himself into a gentleman. And there he sat, trying to *talk* to her, drinking a Fresca instead of the Cuba Libre he drank in the old days. He was coming on strong and wanted, of all things, not "Beat me Daddy to the bar," but enlighten-ment. Hi de ho, he wanted to know her as she was now, not as she was then. But wasn't it too late?

"Look, Nick, I don't want to hurt you, it's just that Rev is a vagabond. He's an adventurer. He needs very little to survive. Sometimes I wonder how he can *endure* boredom the way he does, but in other ways I see him as an existen-tial person. The action, not the word, is important to him. Sartre said, 'Hell is other people,' and I think this has been engraved on his soul. I think he eventually wants to live in a trailer, ride a speedboat, drive a fast car. Those are things that make him happy."

"You mean he's a Stepford husband? The mechanical man?"

"For me, I guess he's a magician. He performs tricks. And I don't want to know *how*—he does it, and that's enough for me."

"What else does he do? Besides his vaudeville magic act?"

"He likes me."

"What else?"

"He can drive well."

"The girl with the drive meets the man who can drive. A soap opera. I'm touched to hear it. I'm glad he can shift and handle the wheel. What does that have to do with you?"

"I respect all that. Once when I was a little girl, my father took me to Sweden. We drove through the grass country. It was summer. All the flowers were blooming along the roadside. We stopped and had Swedish goats' cheese at a small inn and I remembered that drive all the rest of my life. I felt so happy. You know, whatever Rev does, he does well. You know Rev is a weird person. I think the happiest time in his life was when his parents let him go to the Skip Barber Racing School. He had just run away from prep school for the second time. And he wanted so badly not to go to school anymore, not to go to Yale where his father had gone, not to have to disappear into the world of debutantes and boring people. And once, once only, his family understood him. They let him attend racing school. He studied on the three-day competition course and he practiced on a good car all of the racing skills. And he was so happy for a while."

"So? You like goats' cheese and he likes cars. So what? Do you mean to tell me you're throwing over a career, a career at the top of the record business, for a schmuck who learned how to drive a car at the Skip Barber Racing School? You mean to tell me that you are throwing over a career as one of the great lyricists to be a homemaker in a trailer? Don't give me that jive. Please, you're bending my head. Don't tell me that you're going to drive away into the sunset in a Formula Ford with someone who might have made a major commitment to racing if he hadn't found it such a frustrating experience to make a commitment to anything. He's a little slow on the uptake."

"You understand the core of jazz. Why can't you understand the core of other things?"

"What core? That you've gone temporarily insane? That guy has the brain of a baboon."

"Why is it that when I try to pierce gravity you call it insanity? Why can't you allow me to change, Nick? You've changed."

"In what way?"

"In every way. You were different twenty years ago. You traveled by bus. You drank beer. You ate hot dogs. You were a survivor. But what have you survived for? Have you ever asked yourself that question? Do you ever ask yourself when you wake up and look in the mirror and

see how tired your eyes are, why your face has so much
pain? Why your rent on all your houses amounts to thousands of dollars a day? Why you need young girls around
you constantly in order to be the Don Juan you want us to
believe you are? Why do you need all those things? Why
do you spend your time with tailors and accountants and
lawyers and money managers when in the old days you
had vitality and used to hang out with drummers and people who had nitty-gritty in their soul—not gravel—but
nitty-gritty. Do you ask yourself why you stopped jamming
with artists? Why you stopped seeing artists? And spend
half your time with all the miniartists, the ersatz artists, the
interior decorators and designers and bullshit artists who
only want to laugh at you because to them, you're still
vulgar? What happened to your life gig?"

Sylvia spoke in a whisper. Her face was almost expres-
sionless.

"Man, I don't get you," he said to her.

"I'm just a different kind of hipster than you are, Nick.
I can't collaborate anymore. I am not able to work with
anyone. If I write, I want to write alone. I want the loneliness that I gave up when I worked with you. I want the
pain back. I'm tired of the easy way. And I don't think I
should be writing lyrics. I think I can't get what I really
want to say into *a b a b* and a bridge. I'm tired of rhyming.
I'm tired of my formulas. Once they made me happy: To
hear my poems set to music by you made me feel as if
something great were exploding inside my mind. I traded
loneliness for rhythms made by someone else. But now, I
want to write poems that don't reach the masses. I want to
write for myself and perhaps a few other people. I don't
have to come into people's living rooms or be a household
word or have my thoughts inside of transistors and playing
in fourteen different languages. I'm out to be anonymous,
not famous. I think the whole package that I bought, the
money and fame package, was the wrong package. At least
for me, dig?"

"I dig," he said.

51. *Teatime*

LADY RITA hated Revson Cranwell. "Did you talk to her about getting rid of him?" Rita asked. Trying to look girl-ish and erotic, she was wearing a navy blue and white sailor suit. To Nick she only managed to look like an aging girl.

"I did."

Silently a butler arrived and served tea. They might have been sitting in Wales or Devon or Sussex. The silver was Harrah's finest Queen Anne silver. The porcelain belonged to Rita. She always traveled with her own porce-lain. It was part of the ritual of their marriage that whenever they were together they have tea using her por-celain. At exactly four o'clock, they had met in the living room of Harrah's villa. As Rita took the English muffins out of the porcelain dish, Nick remarked, "Bill Harrah was an Anglophile. He would have approved of us having high tea in his living room. His suits were sewn by the finest English tailors. He traveled often to the English motor factories and met with royalty in England. He was a com-bination of a lord and a cowboy. His Mormon background gave him discipline and manners, but his travels in Great Britain civilized him."

Rita wasn't listening. To her, Bill Harrah had been a fool. Besides, she rarely listened to anything her husband said. She was deep in her own thoughts about Rev Cran-well. Everything about him disturbed her. He was *too* handsome.

"Are you thinking of something else?" Nick asked.

"No. I'm thinking of Rev and Sylvia. What an absurd couple they are."

"And?"

Rita knew the one lesson of history: that common ene-

mies make common friends. She had become closer to
Nick recently since their bond of hatred toward Sylvia's
boyfriend united them. It was now all they had to talk
about. "He's a borderline fag," she said.

"Why?" he asked, absentmindedly.

"Because he doesn't want to fuck me," she said.

That makes two of us, he thought, but he didn't say so.

The Tahoe sunset was rising in the mirror, pushing
against the walls' darkness. They sat there stiffly, like a
little king and queen, lit up by the arching light of the sun.

"When are you having your surgery?" Nick asked. He
had found out about it from the doctor, who always
checked with the husband to make sure the bills would be
paid. He never drew a knife without a certified check. No
tickie, no washie. No checkie, no knifey. It was the law of
the surgeon's jungle.

"I'd rather not talk about it," Rita said. To discuss eyelids and cosmetic surgery upset her. She'd rather think of
a plastic surgeon as someone with a magic wand who could
pass her back to the youth she so desperately wanted to
find. The word *knife* made her ill.

"I'd rather talk about the baboon. Is he staying in
Tahoe?"

"As long as Sylvia stays, he stays," Nick said.

"And how long is that, may I ask?"

"You may. But I have no answer. Another two weeks.
Until the album is written."

"Is it going well, in a creative sense?" she asked, pouring
another cup of tea.

"Yeah. I guess so."

"Are you pleased?"

"Yes. Sylvia is writing lyrics which evoke the inner world
of Tahoe. There is nothing abstruse, nothing clumsy
about the songs." Nick wondered why he disguised himself
in a certain armor when he was with his wife. Once they
had been lovers. Centuries ago. Then she had believed
that he had wisdom and great power. He had taken off

her clothes with tenderness, kissed her thin white body, brought his lips upon her thighs and her belly as if he were kissing a bouquet of white lilies. He had loved the gleaming white skin, the fragrance of her body. But that was long ago.

"My God, Nick. It must be hell to have to *relate* to him. He is so removed from everything. When he speaks, he's so slow. It's almost as if there's something retarded about him."

"I don't like him."

"Can you persuade Sylvia to make him leave Tahoe?"

"Of course not."

"Why not?"

"I can't afford to hurt her feelings."

"Why not? You hurt mine."

"I don't mean to. But remember, she's my bread and butter."

"You've shut me out of your life," Lady Rita complained. She was almost crying. Question mark: Why did she feel so sorry for herself? She had enough shoes to found a shoe museum. He often thought if he lined up her suede high heels heel to toe they'd be able to stretch across the Atlantic Ocean. Like Christ, she could walk across the water. But unlike Christ, she relied on Charles Jourdan and Botticelli for her every move. Lady Rita was nothing if not extravagant.

"We used to laugh together."

"It's hard to laugh with you. Your sense of humor is so different from mine." More tea. More accusations. More domesticity. He wondered suddenly why he ever married, ever had children, ever loaded himself down with all the ties of a family man. He longed to be free. To be rid of this woman and all of the ties and familiarities that went with being married to her. Then why did he telephone her every night wherever he was? Why did he need her? Rita would have sacrificed her life for him in the old days. But was that what he wanted? A sacrificial lamb? Was he so ashamed of being a Yid that he needed this champion

of manners, this phony Duchess of Windsor from nowhere to tell him how to behave? Was he the Jewish Prince
of Wales? Why had he needed her values? Somehow he
had lost the warmth and energy he used to have in the old
days. She had performed surgery on his lifestyle and soul.
She had cut away the old buddies, the old jazz lips and
hipsters who once hung around him, gotten rid of the
greasers with pomade in their hair and dirty fingernails
and rhythm in their fingertips; cut out of his life for good
the arrangers and saxophonists and junkies and bebop
boys, the buddies from *nowhere* that he had played gigs
with and loved so deeply in the days of his first bursting
on the scene. Rita had whited out the black guys, replaced
his buddies, the loonies and funkies, with her *quality* people until he had felt like a prisoner in her upper-class
dungeon of house and home, kinder and kitchen. He
would have to sneak out to a jam session like a prisoner
climbing out of his jail. And now she sat across from him,
sipping English tea. "Cream? Milk?" He wanted to scream.
He missed his balls; he was pussy-whipped. He missed the
old jazz days. He missed the days before he became a
prisoner. Before he knew the possessive quality of Rita's
domesticity. By giving him plenty of rope, she had choked
him to death.

"What are you thinking, my love?" she asked.

"Nothing. And you?"

"I was thinking of a joke that made me laugh when I
was a young girl in Sussex."

"Let's hear it."

"I'm afraid you wouldn't think it terribly funny."

"Try me."

"In Lancashire they have something called Silver Bands.
A man was going around collecting money for the Lancashire Silver Band and he came upon an old country
woman who was deaf. She opened the gate and the man
said, 'I'm here to collect money for the Lancashire Silver
Band.' 'What did you say?' she asked. She held up a hearing horn. He yelled into the horn, "*I'm here to collect money*

for the Lancashire Silver Band.' 'Speak up, young man, I can't hear you,' she said. And so he screamed into her hearing horn, *'I'm here to collect money for the Lancashire Silver Band.'* And once more she said, 'Eh? You're what? Could you repeat that?' Finally, he screamed at the top of his lungs, *'I'm here to collect money for the Lancashire Silver Band.'* The old woman tilted her head and said, 'What?' He started to leave and grumbled to himself, 'Fuck you.' At which point the old woman screamed back at him, *'Fuck the Lancashire Silver Band.'* "

As Rita told this her eyes filled with tears of merriment. She was a little girl again. She had literally made herself laugh. Nick didn't think the joke was exactly funny. He preferred Borscht belt comedy. She was no Lenny Bruce, but he didn't dare offend her. "You should be a comedienne," he said drily. He took his linen napkin and wiped his lips. He decided to see less and less of Rita when he got back to New York. Once the album was over, he was going to devote himself more to music. As if she could read his thoughts, she said, "You plan to see less of me, don't you?"

"Why do you ask that?"

"I can read your mind."

"Fuck your mind reading."

"Fuck the Lancashire Silver Band." They laughed. Yes, sometimes they laughed together. This was one of those rare times. He wished Rita would just relax and not be so up-tight about very nearly everything. He vowed to be consistently nice to her until the album was finished. And to try to laugh more.

52. Shopping

LAURIE WALKED into the Outdoorsman. As a kid, she had needed ski clothes and her mother had never been able to afford them. She had been a blue angel, on the ski teams in high school, but she couldn't be on the Heavenly Valley Ski Team without the equipment. She had been thirteen then and her mom had not been able to put enough money together to buy her what she needed.

"God loves you, very much," Laurie's mother said. "He showed his love for you by bringing you into this world with all your beauty and gifts. It is not necessary to pile up gifts for show to find favor with God."

"But it isn't for show."

"Never mind. God loves you, Laurie. With or without skis." And that had been the end of it. She had worked as a waitress through high school and now had the best job a girl could have in Tahoe, dealing at Harrah's. But even with her money saved, the clothes at the Outdoorsman were expensive. Magically, she could now have anything she wanted. Her hunger for clothes was more than just a hunger. She had been denied the best of everything and now it was hers. She walked over to the ski jackets and picked out two outfits that she tried on. With her small behind, high breasts, and thin body, they fit her perfectly. One outfit was a downhill racer's outfit, a hotdogger's suit, exactly the kind Suzy Chaffee had worn when she skied Tahoe. The other was a tight red ski suit, the kind that the top entertainers who walked casually through the casino in their ski outfits wore. She bought a turtleneck and then looked at the skis and boots. Rossignols were the best. The skis were two hundred and fifty dollars and so were the boots. Now she bought two of each. After-ski boots, goggles, silk long underwear, Scandinavian sweaters, thick leather gloves, glove warmers and tights, tight angora sweaters, ski glasses—she piled them all up. They looked good on her and she knew it. It all came to two thousand dollars. The salesgirl, who had gone to South Tahoe with Laurie and had known her all her life, now stared curiously at her. As she piled up sweater after sweater without thought of price, the salesgirl wondered how Laurie was going to pay for all the clothes.

"Did you break the bank, Laurie?" she asked.

Laurie smiled. "I won at keno," she giggled, and took out over two thousand dollars in hundred dollar bills that Nick had given her. She couldn't wait to go on the slopes. In her mind she saw herself skiing down the slopes of Squaw Valley, skiing Alpine Meadows, Homewood, Mt. Rose, Kirkwood, and Northstar. She'd have a different outfit for every day, thanks to Nick. She couldn't wait to have Nick see her in her new clothes. Happily, she jumped in her car and gunned the motor. The clothes, piled up in the back of the car in boxes, made her feel giddy. She slowed down at the Jewelry Factory.

"I want to buy you some presents," Nick had said the last time they were at Fantasy Inn. If anyone would have told her that presents could turn her on, she wouldn't have believed it. But the thought of having anything she wanted had excited her and made her want to make love again and again. And now Nick wanted to buy her a ring. It made her almost frightened. What had she done to deserve all of this extravagance? She wasn't any better looking than many of the cocktail waitresses who walked around Harrah's in black stockings and short dresses, with creamy white breasts that everyone looked at. Nick could have any of the Sahara girls, any of the dancers at Harrah's. There was a new group called The Dance Machine that had played the Sahara for weeks. One of the dancers came back stage and hung around Nick's dressing room. She was six feet tall and had enormous breasts. Why hadn't he been interested in her? Why had she lucked out?

"Speak to God often about your needs," Laurie's mother had said. And she had spoken to God. She wanted to look rich. She was tired of not having anything beautiful or luxurious. And God—had he sent her Nick Dimani? Someone had sent him to her. And she walked into the Jewelry Factory. Nick was looking at the diamond bracelets. As Laurie came into the store in her new white ski outfit, Nick turned and looked at her. He seemed appreciative of the way she looked.

"How do you like your diamonds? With or without emeralds, my love?" It was a dream that was going to end the moment she woke up. Shyly, she walked over to the counter. The man who waited on them wore a cowboy hat. He was used to selling diamonds to Sammy Davis, Jr., Wayne Newton, all the entertainers who brought business to the Jewelry Factory. Pictures of the celebrities and the man in the hat were right behind the counter. She had been there once before. When she first met Nick and he had bought her the diamond dancer she wore around her neck. Now a bracelet. Nick held in his hand a bracelet with huge emeralds and diamonds.

"Try this on," he said. She put it on her wrist. Her hand was shaking. "I'll take it!" he said, almost like a little boy. He grabbed Laurie's hand. "While they're wrapping that up, you know what I want for you?"

"What?"

"A ruby ring. Which is a surprise. I'll have it wrapped. And a barrette. I want a beautiful gold barrette for your hair." He took his hands and ran them through her hair. "You make me happy," he said.

"Why?" she asked.

"I don't know. Your energy. Your youth. Your excitement about things. Everything I give Rita, she has twenty of. With you—it's really like experiencing giving someone a gift."

"I don't have anything," Laurie said.

"Yes, you do. You have me."

Later, at the Fantasy Inn, they lay on the water bed and watched a porno movie. They were advertised as "adult movies" and they played on cable TV. Nick lay with Laurie next to him. She was wearing nothing but the bracelet. Rita, his family, Sylvia—all of this was a million miles away.

"You know what?" he asked, running his hand over her body. "When this album is finished, I'm going to send Rita back to England. She needs a year with her family and is always saying how she wants to see her mom. They live in Sussex. The girls are in boarding school and Rita will be only too happy to see her folks. Then I'm going to give all this up and take you around the world."

Laurie felt herself getting wet. It was as if he touched her most sensitive parts. It excited her, but she was also afraid to believe Nick.

"Are you for real?" she asked, licking his neck and letting him touch her gently.

"I mean it. I'm going to take all the money from *Playing Tahoe,* and I'm going to buy a boat. I'll get Sinatra or someone who knows all about boats to help pick one out in Newport or Fort Lauderdale. That's where they sell the best boats. And I'll buy a boat for about five hundred thousand dollars and we'll sail around the world. Just me and you. And you can bring your mom if you want."

The thought of Laurie's mom on a boat with Nick Dimani was hilarious. "It's pretty hard to leave Tahoe," Laurie lied. Her mother wanted Laurie to lead a good Christian life. But, wasn't making love to Nick a Christian act? If God hadn't wanted people to make love, would he have given them beautiful bodies and genitals? Wasn't making love a holy thing to do? Just another way to praise God? When she made love to Nick, she felt happiness and even holiness pulsing through her blood. How many times had she thought after making love, "Thank you, dear God, for this beautiful pleasure." Now she knew that people who taught that sex was evil were people who were trying to destroy the joyfulness of life. Love wasn't a sin. Jesus wanted everyone to feel love. No. What she felt for Nick was good. It had made her a better Christian.

"What do you think of the idea?"

"I think it's what I always wanted to do with my life," she said.

"Nobody has to know you," Nick said. "I'll call the boat the *Rita* and that will make everybody happy."

"Don't call it the *Rita*," Laurie said.

"All right, I'll call it the *Miss Tahoe*, after you."

"I like that."

"And we'll find a captain and a cook and a second mate and we'll sail everywhere. We'll go to the deep blue waters of Alaska. We'll sail down from the inland waters of Seattle and up to the North and across the gulf to Cordova. We'll sail into the last great wilderness world. And then, we'll fly to Europe and meet the boat in Monaco. And there, we can sail down to Sicily. I've always wanted to sail to Sicily on my own boat. And when we get there, I'll buy a Riva. That's the greatest powerboat made. The Italians can make great powerboats. We'll water ski and spend a summer in the sun. And then go on to Hong Kong and Bali."

"Bali," Laurie sighed.

"Don't you like Bali?"

"Are you kidding? To go to Bali with you? On our own boat?"

Nick lay back. If he could make his record, he could do all this. The record. The record. It wasn't always this easy. Once an album was music. It was cowbells, whistles, and vibra slaps. It was drums and tom-toms, porto-seats and music stands. It was musicians and studios and the fun of working. It was the music he wrote. But that had changed as he had gotten older. Now an album was money, the money to have Laurie next to him for a year. He had no illusions about Laurie. She'd want someone her own age. She'd want a young body and a young head and she'd grow tired of him. Even tired of traveling. That was the way things were. But he could be with her for a year. Show her the world, make love with her, and drink into his own body all the excitement that she had in her. Laurie was life. And he needed her. For a year. And that's what the album had become. A new chance to live. Money for boats, cars, necklaces, Laurie. He was buying her love. So what? He was giving her something: a chance to expand. To be more than a dealer. A local yokel and young girl without any joy in her life. After a year with him, they would both be richer. The price he paid was knowing that if he didn't have money, she wouldn't want him. It was a small price to pay for the happiness he had. He held her close to him. The water bed at the Fantasy Inn was like a boat. She held on to him.

"You've given me a chance to live out what I've always wanted. Do you mean it? Will this really come true?"

"If we want it badly enough. We have to want to make it come true. We have to work on it. Everything becomes real if you begin with a dream. The dream is the light you have to turn on. Artists and mystics know that. It's like music. You have to hear it in your mind first, because if you don't hear it there, it won't ever come out. Same thing with the boat. With us. With the future. With the beautiful year we can spend together." Laurie held him. He was her life-line.

53. *Existentialist Acts*

REV REMEMBERED the boredom of his childhood. He wanted to speed. He wanted to go faster. The car was the only erotic thing in his life in Philadelphia. None of the girls looked like Jayne Mansfield. They all looked like school teachers. No one had big tits. They all had tweed coats. The inside of the car was as erotic as the inside of a woman. Everything was so dull. The women were so frumpy. They never wore eye makeup. His mother was like that. Her world consisted of public works. There was no sex. There was only the laundry, and the cocktail parties, and the little girls of Northeast Harbor who always looked as if they wanted to go somewhere. They never went anywhere. The ballparks, the sandlots, the supermarkets, they were all so immobile and staid. The red interior of his car was vulgar. Rob needed vulgarity. Vulgarity was absurd. But vulgarity was life. Vulgarity was the trompe l'oeil interior of his life. Vulgarity was sex and tits and lipstick and steamy fast cars. He wondered what it had been like before the shock treatments, when he had had strong feelings about things. He thought of these things as he lay back in Tahoe and made love to Sylvia Lundholm. He liked Nancy, too. Not her war resister crap. Or all her talk about building South African armaments. He was bored by political visionaries. But there was an excitement in her, the same quality of energy as Sylvia had. She was a fusion of sex, energy, and high spirits. She was an original, and she was fun if you could just get her off her political soap box. He wished she would stop wearing those T-shirts that said, "A woman needs a man like a fish needs a bicycle." They were so nineteen-sixties. She was like a china teapot that had been smashed, another smashed person. That's why he understood her. The smashed people of the world came to Tahoe. It was getting on his nerves. He wished that Nancy would come with him when he went fishing. He liked her when she talked about the sea. She understood it. But then he'd have to put up with all that Mao Tse-tung crap. He didn't know what he felt about Sylvia. He couldn't feel. But then, she had enough feeling for both of them. People who had hearts as big as Sylvia's, were often the most fragile people. Why were they together? They were both poets and both whores. But mostly they were poets.

54. *Young Cock*

"I DON'T know how this happened to me," Rita said to herself. Quirky, nervous, high-strung, Rita Dimani, who had been born in another world, a world of books and tea and museums and English politeness, the quiet, once mousy English girl who married Nick and instructed herself in trendiness, suddenly realized with a terrible pang, a pang as sharp as a bugle call, that she was aging. She would be old. She was old. This resulted in a sort of nymphomania as curative. Her friend from London, Peter Eyre, had taken her to lunch on his last visit to America.

"Pedophilia," he said over his Bloody Mary.

"What on earth is that?" asked Rita.

"It's what's happening to you. And to Nick. I'm quite sure. And certainly to me. We've all become pedophiliacs. We like younger people. People with enthusiasm."

"How did it happen to you?"

"Well," Peter remarked in his bored way, "I suddenly found myself quite bored by society. All those people in my set were—so old. So used up. It was as if I looked at them and they were all wearing faces that were as scratched as phonograph records. I mean quite literally I couldn't stand them. When I was young, thirty years ago, I wanted to be one of them. But now, I want to be with very young people. And you, too, no doubt."

After that conversation with Peter, she was aware how she was drawn to every young man. In Tahoe, her ski instructor, a young man named Steve, aged eighteen, rode with her on the rope tow. She tried not to look at his face, which was unlined, or hold his hand. Sitting close to him in the middle of the air, going slowly toward the top of Heavenly Valley, she asked him about his life and if he had ever been to New York. She searched out feeling in his face and felt that in every way he was comfortable talking to her. She longed to touch him, to hold him, to find a way to switch the dreadful conversation to something more intimate, and suddenly she knew of a way. When they reached the top of the hill, she suggested they ski off to the side, down a trail where there were no other skiers. Suddenly she fell down. The instructor bent over her. "Are you all right, m'am?"

"No, not really."

He bent over her. The word *pedophilia* had not left her skull. Suddenly she pulled him down to her and kissed him on the mouth. Kissed him very hard. This had happened to him before. He didn't act too surprised. He responded with a classless California remark such as, "You turn me on." Rita Dimani was after young cock. Everyone knew where she was coming from.

55. *Looking-for-Action Blues*

LIONEL WAS not having the good time he expected to have in Tahoe. It snowed again and again. Young Lionel Colesman had been a playboy. Old Lionel Colesman found himself out of the action. Was he passing through a phase? Karen was spending Christmas at a Chess Tournament in Reno with the children. She would be up to Tahoe for New Year's. Meanwhile, there was Ron Thimble to pal around with. There was Sylvia. Emptiness came into his stomach. Lionel was used to summoning people on command: buying modern dance companies, purchasing the love of orchestras. If he was "lonely," he could always finance company. People didn't love Lionel. They were bought by him. He gave out his favors generously. And still, there was the nagging feeling inside of Lionel that despite his nose being fixed, his accent being perfectly Harvard and gentile (he loved to quote T. S. Eliot in his deep low voice, and the way he said *c'est la vie* was absolute perfection), despite all that, deep down in his gut he feared that his children laughed at him. One of his daughters made fun of him.

"You're old," she said. He had been eating breakfast. Karen was still sleeping. His daughter looked at him and said, "And you're bald." He remembered this bitterly. He had swallowed his toast.

"I'm the best-looking fifty-three-year-old you'll ever know," he had shot back. But under his tan, under the perfectly tailored clothes, he had a pain in his soul. He had missed out on being a husband. He had never been a good father. How could he? Despite the obligatory baseball games and trips to Africa and France and Sundays with the children, he didn't like children. They made him feel uncomfortable. Only in the world of ballet, music, and finance did Lionel feel powerful. He wondered as he sipped his scotch on the rocks what he could do now to make himself feel more—at home. The thought occurred to him to give a party. A party at Tahoe!

To show his power, he would give a party. He thought of the food first. Lionel fancied himself a gourmet. The fact was, he did know about food. He would have Frazer and Morris fly in caviar. Not the three hundred dollar a pound caviar but the new American caviar which they sold at Frazer and Morris for only a hundred dollars a pound, and tasted just as good. No one could tell the difference. He would fly in pounds and pounds of fresh caviar and already he felt as if he was saving money. He had a billionaire's sense of savings. He also thought about the menu. He'd have the Rosedale Market pack fresh salmon and bass. And he'd serve squid and fresh shrimp. Pounds of asparagus. He loved asparagus and mushrooms. And of course, champagne. He'd order from his own private collection at Sherry's, some decent champagnes. Several cases of Moët et Chandon. And the music—that came second. He'd have The B-52s and The Talking Heads flown out at once. Neither of these groups had ever played Tahoe. They were too hip. Punk groups with their minimal high-tech sounds had never been to Tahoe. He'd show Nick Dimani a different side of music today. He'd show him what was really hot. He'd fly them out on his own airplane. He'd show Nick he could still get the best of everything.

Barry Manilow! He'd have Miles, his manager, and Barry Manilow. He'd take care of Nick. And John Denver. He'd call Jerry Weintraub at Management Three and take care of Nick's ass. With The Talking Heads and The B-52s and Manilow and Denver, and Ann-Margret, Nick would be outclassed. He'd invite a lot of the local ski instructors and their girls. Nothing like beautiful young bodies to make a party fun. And where?

At Harrah's. Not the hotel. That wasn't private. He'd talk to S. G. and get Harrah's mansion. It was a huge black stone house about a mile long overlooking the lake at the point in Skyland. It was soundproof. And had a feeling of its own. That's where he'd throw a party. The night before New Year's. He didn't mind dropping twenty grand. It would be worth it. And it was deductible.

Ron Thimble made the calls to send telegrams to those out of town. Good old Ron. He was awfully good at social things. He rode around in Lionel's black Porsche, delivering the invitations in town by hand. He printed them himself. A man who spends his whole life being a rich person's friend has to have odd talents. Ron had studied calligraphy in New York. He could handprint invitations perfectly. He could ski. He could laugh at Lionel's jokes. And he "did" something. Director of children's documentaries? No one was ever quite sure of what it was Ron did, other than be Lionel's friend, but it was enough for him. Happily, he set out to draw into Lionel's net all of the "in" people of Tahoe that winter of nineteen-seventy-nine.

Sylvia received her invitation with an odd premonition. Was she really ready for those Blakean punks, The Talking Heads? Was she ready for John Denver? Could she stand "old times" and the faces as well as reputations that had aged? Surely, somewhere in the souls of all those invited, was the memory of the great parties in the sixties thrown by Lionel at his townhouse, thrown by Lionel at "21," thrown by Lionel so often that the columns were filled every day with another Lionel Colesman event. It had been years since Lionel had given his old big parties. They were like huge permissions. You received your invitation and you knew you had permission to be famous.

Sylvia was hesitant about how to mention to Rev that this party was taking place. They were sitting in the seventeenth-floor suite at Harrah's and Rev was watching television. Sylvia had just taken a shower and was wrapped up in one of the huge white Harrah towels. She sat down next to Rev on the couch. "Rev, I know you. You hate parties." She put her arms around him. Somewhere in his life, Revson had been so hurt, so badly hurt, that it was hard to cuddle him, to hold him. Winters his parents had lived in a white manor house in Boca Raton with three houses on the estate. In order to communicate, his mother wrote notes:

"Welcome, Rev. The food is downstairs."

The notes would instruct, cajole, implore, praise. Sylvia wondered if that world of the dead Wasp, that Philadelphia world had been responsible for the odd infliction of ice that ran up and down the spine of Rev Cranwell. It was as if his whole life had been lived in a world of notes, cane chairs, martinis before dinner, people who spoke with marbles in their mouths. It was a world of seventy for dinner, servants, placecards, sterling cigarette cases. A world where his grandmother thrived. All the grandmothers drove old Buicks and did exercises and were chipper. All the grandchildren had shock treatments, ran away to Austria to study singing, or looked into the distance with eyes that never seemed alive. Somewhere the stuffing got lost in the sofa. Somewhere the manners became ossified. The privileges turned into odd rituals practiced by people who resembled stuffed animals. As an aging gentile, Rev wandered in and out of jobs, lives, places. With Puerto Ricans, black people, Jews, he felt assimilated. But he was always an outsider. Like the Hiroshima survivors who lived by psychic numbing, he wandered around the spaces of America as if dead. The identity went like this: I should have died, I would have died, but I didn't die. If I am alive, it is impure of me to be so. It is an insult to the dead, who alone are pure. As a survivor from the worlds of Philadelphia and NE Harbor and upper Wasp social values, he was the one who had a great deal of difficulty coming to terms with the experience of "lower class" people, who to him seemed to be so much more "alive" than he was. He had trouble coming to terms with their experiences, their passions, their needs. He had trouble giving it some acceptable inner form or meaning and placing it within what he could call a life or a formulation. Rev walked with infinite insecurity; with guilt, and responsibility for some catastrophe that he was in some way to blame for, he walked in a world of Sylvias, Nancys, and Nicks. It was only the character of Nick Dimani that changed insecurity in Rev to hatred. He hated Nick.

He wondered why, quite often, as he sat in his tower suite at Harrah's, why he disliked Nick so much. Why wasn't Nick his type of guy? Smoking grass, rolling a joint, he would let the thought of Nick Dimani cross his mind. Sylvia would be working with him, and Rev would think of them both and become agitated. He was a little fuck. That was how Rev described Nick to himself. He had a hard time dealing with Nick's authenticity. Nick wasn't pretending to be someone else the way he was. Nick wasn't searching for himself. He was a Jewish guy from Brooklyn with a name that could be Italian, whose boundaries were clear. He needed to be Somebody in the same way that Rev, from the genealogy of the Saltonstalls, needed to be Nobody. Whereas Rev, with his perfect body and perfect chiseled white skin and face that resembled Michelangelo's David, needed to blend in with the background. In order to survive, Rev thought it was funny to sell used cars in the Bronx, to leave on the spur of the moment to drill for oil, to work on a construction team, to fish in the deep tuna seas of California, stopping for highballs at night with the other fishermen, none of whom came from his background and none of whom grew up with all the symbols of privilege. Nick needed to exhibit himself in the same way that Rev needed to fade out of view. He had *found* himself. Rev had not. Nick had courted the bitch goddess of success and won. Rev had been indifferent. Nick knew how to deal with the demands of fame, money, sex; how to dangle money and how to "fuck on command." Rev was never able to handle all that—he was neither consumed by power nor by its absence. There was no precedent for his life. Nick the star, the great person seen in the night, the composer, the performer, was a violation of everything Rev's family had been. He was the vulgar American, and he was filled with juice and energy and anger and power that was missing in Rev. It was almost as if he had been slapped in the face by Nick. Rev was an adventurer. He adventured "down into slumsville" and found it exciting. Nick adventured "up." Rev wore a number of masks. He was the "good guy" at work. When he sold cars in the Bronx, he could be the good salesman and say, "How ya doin'?" to the mechanics and blacks and Puerto Ricans who came in off the streets.

"Who do you actually sell those cars to?" his mother had asked. She sat very straight.

"Spics. Blacks."

"Don't say 'black.' Say 'Afro-American,' " his mother said. She leaned forward to whisper. But with "spics" and "blacks" he could get along. He could laugh. With Sylvia, he could get along. He could laugh. She tended to become too much a part of him and he was already thinking that he truly loved her and would want to take her with him, anywhere, away from Tahoe. But now, as he was locked in the Winter of Tahoe and he had to face Dimani, what was it Sylvia was asking him?

". . . the party?"

"What party!" He sucked on a Carlton.

"You weren't listening. Nick Dimani is going to Lionel's party and he wants me to go with him. It's a party that Lionel is giving at Harrah's old mansion in Skyland."

"The house that looks like a mausoleum?"

"Yeah."

"I'll go with you."

There was a certain belligerence in his voice. He surprised Sylvia. Sometimes, out of nowhere, he would be
very definite, very insistent. Usually he was sweet and went
along with things and was not willing to hassle. He didn't
play tricks or have emotional weapons. He was what he
was—honest, pure, kind. A gentleman. And then, suddenly, there was a childlike insistence in something he
said. It was as if you could see the old Rev, the sadistic,
wild Rev who drove motorcycles too fast, boats too fast,
who was wild and ran away from school, the wild unman-
ageable boy they tamed with shock treatments. These en-
counters were rare. Because he was so handsome, because
he was so perfect to look at, because he was a tall blond
giant with perfect manners and a sweet boyish smile, it was
rare for Rev to ever have to lose his temper or insist on
anything. But suddenly, it was the other Rev whom she
saw.

"I'm going to the party. I hate Nick's guts. But I want to
go." Sudden anger: the purring gentile prince from Philadelphia, then the huge Bronx good-guy high-train smile.

"Why do you hate him?"

"I don't know why. No reason." Rev looked indifferent.

"Well, if it causes you a problem, you don't have to go."

"I said I'm going," Rev replied. The television was blar-
ing its commercial. Sylvia walked over to the grayish-gold
bureau and helped herself to some ice and scotch.

"It's going to be one of Lionel Colesman's punky parties.
Punk. And public relations. To show the world how powerful he is. A mixture of punk rockers, some young girls,
and some ski instructors. When Lionel gives a party, all of
the melancholy bones of his face light up. He lays out a
party as evidence of his wealth and power."

"I'm going," Rev said. When he became definite, he also
began to pout. Like a little boy, his blue eyes became focused. His lip stood out. His voice, which was low, got even

lower. You had the feeling that he could easily stamp his foot, throw a scene.

"If you want to. I'm surprised," Sylvia said. She held his hand. It was a rough warm hand. It was a hand that had such strength in it.

"I'd like to see those people in action." He laughed.

"No, you wouldn't. You'll hate it. You don't like parties. At least the ones I've taken you to. You never seemed to like them."

"It's lonely at the top," Rev said, and smiled. He was thinking of the man in the tiny powder blue suit with the sequins on it at the circus, the little acrobat under the spotlight who sits on the top of a pole that almost touches the ceiling, a tiny freak in sequins under the Big Top of Madison Square Garden, trying to stay balanced on a pole. Everyone, all the kids in the audience, looking up. And Rev, smoking a joint and laughing, hoping the little freak would topple off the pole and fall.

"What's that supposed to mean?"

"I don't know." How could he tell her about the image of the little man on his pole at the circus? He didn't understand it himself.

"Sometimes your handsomeness creates anxiety in me," Sylvia said.

"I'm not handsome."

"You are."

"I don't think so."

"Why not? What do you think is wrong with you?"

"I don't like my hair. I don't like blond hair. And my eyes. I don't like not having eyelashes."

"You can dye them."

"I've done that."

"So?"

"I don't like my nose."

"What's wrong with it?"

"It's too large."

"You know, Rev, you're nuts. You're the handsomest man in the world, and you don't like yourself."

"It's a question of taste."

"Well, are we going to the party?"

"I guess so."

"It's not until next week."

"Good," said Rev.

"That gives us a week to ski. I only am working with Nick part of the day now. The songs are going better. So we can ski Heavenly half the day."

"Want a joint?" Rev asked.

"No thanks."

"A screwdriver?"

"A screwdriver."

56. *Invitations*

NICK RECEIVED his invitation at Harrah's villa. The word got around in Tahoe that a lot of heavies were invited to the party. That meant that Lionel had asked Barry Manilow, whom he was trying to woo. The word was that Lionel had also offered to fly in Sinatra and Leiber and Stoller. Of all the songwriting teams, Leiber and Stoller were Dimani's only heroes. Jerry Leiber was one of his idols. Leiber had written the words to "Hound Dog" for Willie Mae Thornton in 1953. Three years later it became Elvis's biggest hit. Leiber was his idea of "class," a word Nick used over and over when he described the people he envied. Both Leiber and Stoller came from poverty. Stoller, like most white composers who specialized in the black idiom, had studied classical music. Leiber, his lyricist, was a natural poet and mime and dancer, a raconteur who took the joke of a lifestyle and added its own authenticity and put it all into a lyric that resembled a short movie with a beginning, middle, and end. It was Leiber's "playlets" and Stoller's energy and harmonies, which could capture every kind of riff there was, that created such classics as "Kansas City," "Yakety-Yak," "Love Potion No. 9," "Poison Ivy," "I'm a Woman," and "Charley Brown." They had taken black sound and grafted it to white, raucous funk, creating at the same time a rock and roll sound that was synonymous with Presley and with all the anger that poured itself out in the greaser-outsider mentality. They were writing existentialist blues when nobody else was, and Nick admired their guts and humor and style. He wanted in many ways to be like Jerry Leiber—cool, a collector of art, but Leiber moved in a world of intellectuals, a world that Nick felt out of place in. That crowd at Elaine's was not his. Still, he could get together and have a drink and a cigar with Jerry Leiber and remember the old days of rock and roll: The Clovers, The Drifters, The Coasters singing "Poison Ivy," The Dixie Cups, The Cheers, Ray Charles and Little Richard and Little Esther and Big Joe Turner, The Isley Brothers, The Shangri-Las, John Hammond—all the magical names out of rock and roll history. The Jellybeans! The last time he had seen Leiber, they had been at Elaine's. He was with Sylvia for her birthday. Leiber had been there with his wife Barbara and some film director who was going to make a movie out of Leiber's and Stoller's lives.

"Hey Jerry, how you doin'?"

And Jerry, a little grayer but still with his impish face that resembled a bobby-sox hero, with those expressive eyes, one blue and one brown, smiled, clownlike. He got up. "I don't know where I am, man. I got your phone call and I meant to return it, but I'm just moving and I can't ever find any phone numbers. Anyway, I got the nice invitation to come to a party from your wife, but I never go to parties."

That meant that even if Lionel flew Stoller in, Leiber wouldn't come. Nick Dimani's reaction to the party was, "Fuck him." If he wants to show off his connections in Tahoe to get some more publicity, let him. He's not going to get my album even if he invites the Pope to his party! The whole joy of his career had come down to a power play. Once he had loved sitting at a piano with a cog inside his head turning around and around, fitting exactly into the right sound. Once it was music. Now it was power. What he had loved so much as a kid—sounds and tunes —now was paranoia. As Nick showered, as Nick combed his hair, as Nick received his daily massage, as Nick looked into the mirror and talked into the phone, all that he could think of was that he didn't want Lionel to get his greasy little ambitious hands on *Playing Tahoe*. He was now driven to finish the album, but it didn't depend on him. It depended on Sylvia. He had to drive Sylvia into working harder, into more sessions, more profitable sessions. There were a few sessions that had been just like the old days, except in the old days nobody would have interrupted. And now this fucking Revson, the James Dean of Tahoe, kept walking in and out of sessions with his black leather jacket and his monosyllabic instructions. Jesus Christ, Sylvia was lost in the movie *The Wild Ones!* Why was she living out this adolescent crush? Rev was the kind of guy you fell for in high school on a dry fuck in the back of a Chevrolet. But this maniac and Sylvia were actually planning to dump the music business and take off in some kind of boat. Well, let them anchor both of their lives off the Canary Islands. Let Rev go and be a carpenter or a garage mechanic or whatever it was he wanted to be as he climbed down the ladder of success, running away from his upper-class Wasp background. (What on earth was he running away from? Everyone in the music business was trying to be exactly what he was running from! Didn't every Donald Pond and Richmond Schneider want to be a blond tall *sheygetz* from a Wasp social family?) This Revson moron wanted to be an imitation of Elvis Presley in *Jailhouse Rock*. He wanted to be a greaser instead of a refined gentile. Well, to each his own shtick! The only thing that pissed him off was when Rev and Sylvia bopped into writing sessions looking as if they were high on Quaaludes (which Rev probably was—Sylvia never touched drugs, she was too nervous and neurotic) and looking as if they had just finished making love.

"I can't take my eyes off him," Sylvia would say. Was she camping around? Was she for real? Was this the Sylvia Lundholm he had met twenty-five years ago and started teaching "the ropes" to, so that they had become closer than Siamese twins? He had saved that fucking broad's life. If it hadn't been for him, Nick Dimani, she'd be just another rich girl with a college degree and an army of masseurs and hairdressers and facial specialists and young models licking her ass. He had given her a reason to live, had pulled her out of those depressions she used to sink into, had gotten her out of that middle-class lifestyle that could kill anyone. He had seen that her head was fixed. He had taken the trouble to bring her into a world that was energetic. Hadn't she gotten off on the energy of music and being a legend rather than just being a misplaced Swede under a hair dryer wearing Bulgari jewelry and making dinner parties and worrying about the chiropodist and the gynecologist? If it wasn't for him, she'd still be taking tranquilizers and shopping at Bergdorf Goodman and talking about her broken home. Or she would have freaked out and been one of those middle-aged women who become fanatic about politics, fanatic about a guru; she would have been an aging moonie. That's what she was anyway. Scratch the surface of her cowboy boots and jogging pants and trendy hairdo and that's what she was, an aging Swedish moonie. Famous! Freaking over a Philadelphia gigolo imitating black lifestyle and running around Tahoe on a motorcycle. And Nancy! There were no words to describe that Third World cunt! Wasn't she a little old to be a commie? That's what trendy Sarah Lawrence girls did in their twenties, not their forties. *She's ruining Sylvia's head,* was all he could think. Sylvia had once been perfectly happy writing lyrics like "Oh Dorothy." Did

she have to write the "Pentagon Blues"? It didn't matter
what they did, as long as she finished the album. Thank
God for the fucking contract!

Sometimes Sylvia would surprise him. She'd arrive to
work with him just like in the old days and she'd start
improvising on a lyric and dancing around and scat singing, and he would be the old genius from Brighton Beach,
sitting at the piano playing whatever he felt like, and it
would all mesh until spontaneously he found the music
and she found the words and their improvisation would
turn into a song. That's how they had written "Sierra
Cool," which was the best song so far:

There's a place in the Sierras,
A place that we can dream,
A place where the air is magical,
Life's not what it seems.
A place of pine cones and snow,
Where anything goes.

And now, she was never really able to keep her mind on
her work. For all he knew, she was probably thinking of a
million other things. This was her last album. The promise
of rock aestheticism had dried up, leaving Dimani and
Lundholm the same place as it left Leiber and Stoller:
nowhere. Unless they came up with a new sound. And the
new sound was *Playing Tahoe*. It was in the exploitation of
the concept of Tahoe, in the Tahoe jewelry, in the Tahoe
clothes. Back in the fifties you didn't write songs, you
wrote records. That's what Jerry Leiber said. But today
you didn't write records, you wrote *spin-offs*. You weren't
writing "Shine on Harvest Moon," you were selling lip-
shine and nail polish and dolls. The Tahoe concept had
infinite promotion possibilities. Look at Ralph Lauren and
Western clothes. With the concept, you could sell black
boots, studded jeans, everything Western. That was the
power of the album! Tahoe was America. It was the health

message of a new kind of love. Since there was too much physical love in the world, substitute being free, being high on health, being a physical, outdoor person for love. Sylvia had to write the right lyric. She was the only person who understood what *sold* today. Wherever her head was, it was commercial. She was the heroine of The Talking Heads and Blondie and Brian Eno. Nobody in the business was as hip as Sylvia. That was the problem. That was why he, Nick Dimani, was a desperado. He needed her to add her poet's vision to the album. He looked again at the "Evergreen" lyrics:

It's no lie
That you're mean—
All your fruits
Are evergreen;

Yeah! He would have one more shot at being a winner. Wasn't it like a game of craps? The whole music business was no different than a gamble. The basic strategy was to be ahead of the game. That was the only way to win. To invent trends. The way Leiber and Stoller had written "Hound Dog," when everyone else was just laughing at hillbilly. They had written their playlets about jail and convicts and the whole black ethic while everyone was into ponytails and white bread. It was more than crossing over. It was—there was no other word for it, Sylvia said it all— corporate poetry. And he had it with the new concept of the album. He'd go to the fucking party. He hated Lionel's balls. He knew how bullshit the party would be. Everyone trying to be cool, to be unfamous. But he'd go for one reason: He would die to finish *Playing Tahoe*. He looked at the words for "Snow":

Snow, the white snow,
I need her love so;
But it melted,
Where did all the love go?

Often I wonder
why you hurt me so?
I saw your face before me
in the snow.

There is something secret
that I have to do,
I want to spend my life
helping you.

57.   *Lionel's Agony*

LIONEL DIDN'T LIKE NICK. BAD VIBES.
HE WAS A SHARP GUY FROM BROOKLYN PRETENDING TO BE THE
REINCARNATION OF BACH.
HE WAS A SMALL COMBO MAN AT HEART.

LIONEL IDEALIZED SYLVIA.

THIMBLE WAS A NECESSITY. AN ANNOYING NECESSITY.
LIKE AN AFTERNOON NEWSPAPER. OR AN ALARM CLOCK.
LIONEL NEEDED ADORATION.
THIMBLE PROVIDED IT. GOOD OLD RON.
INSTANT LOVE,
LIKE FAST FOOD, COULD BE BOUGHT EASILY.
BUT LOVE
WAS FOOD, WASN'T IT?
SYLVIA LIVED IN A FANTASY.
THAT FANTASY WAS HER LOVE FOR REV.
REV DIDN'T CARE ABOUT HER.
BUT PEOPLE NEEDED FANTASY.
SHOULD LIONEL TAKE HERS AWAY BY
POINTING OUT THAT REV DIDN'T HATE HER—
HE MOCKED HER?

REV WAS WHAT KEPT SYLVIA GOING. HE WAS HER STICK.
SHE NEEDED HIM TO LEAN ON. WAS IT GOOD TO LEAN ON
FANTASY? THAT WAS HIS QUESTION.

JUST AS one animal sniffs out another, Lionel saw Revson
Cranwell, the man that he could never be. He knew, without even knowing how he knew, that Rev deeply liked
Sylvia. He admired her talent—without any desire to have
talent himself. He was beyond talent. He admired her feelings—which he did not have. And he enjoyed with humor
the warmth and the strength that she offered him. He
liked her precisely because she had remained innocent—
childlike—and because she did love him. Their comrade-
ship was a slap in the face to Lionel. Lionel knew that he
needed to degrade women, to feel superior to them, to
have them want him so he could buy them. Their attention
was important to him only so he could reject them. He
couldn't reject Sylvia because she didn't want him. This
annoyed him.

And so, early one morning, Lionel arranged to ski
Heavenly Valley with Sylvia. "I don't like your friend,"
Lionel said. He was determined to belittle Rev and under-
mine Sylvia's affection for him.

"Which one?" Sylvia asked. "Rev or Nancy?" They were
drinking hot cider at the Snowbird, a small bar on top of
one of the lifts. Sitting at a table outside amid a crowd of
other skiers, the sun coming down on their faces. Lionel
stirred his cider with a cinnamon stick.

"Rev." He looked at her. She had expected this little
outburst of jealousy. She knew about his frustrated passion. She knew that she was the one person he wanted and
couldn't *have,* not with all his money and his dark good
looks and his low voice and his power—even though he
had a magnificent body and skin that seemed polished by
a jeweler, dark skin that looked almost like light cinnamon.

Even though he was good company and sometimes witty, he couldn't have her. And it burned a cigarette hole in his soul. It made him cranky, mean, sarcastic; it even made him feel suicidal. It made him drink too much, the frustration of wanting Sylvia. Everything else he could buy, seduce, manipulate. But she was tantalizing. She was *there* for him—and not there. She would answer his calls, be civil to him, talk to him for hours. She would claim to be his friend. Indeed, tell people how generous and funny and what a good friend he was. But never could he believe in her friendship. If she was such a friend, why did she make him suffer?

Sylvia knew he thought these things. She knew, with her highly developed sense of intuition, that he loved her passionately, and it was a love that she could never return. Often she had thought, perhaps—someday—but now that she met Rev, there would never be a someday. And Lionel suffered. She could sense this and so she was even kinder to him than before, which made it even more unbearable for him. She sensed with a second sense that the *beloved* often feels, that he dreamed about her. She knew from intuition and from her experience with unrequited love that in dreams he saw her naked, that she stood in a shower with her body bare and that he dared not touch her. In dreams, he could reach out to her nakedness but never really put his hands on what he wanted—her flesh, her soul. Sylvia called him sweetheart, made appointments with him, and then, frightened that she was teasing him or leading him on, would break them at the last minute. She was confused by his passion. Why didn't he just *like* her the way she liked him? Why couldn't they be pals? But the more she hinted at a wonderful and prolonged pal-dom between them, the more it tormented him. She saw it in his eyes. So recently, even in Tahoe, she avoided him. And now he was furious about Rev. It was almost as if she was hurting *him* by seeing Rev. So she tactfully kept the two of them in different spaces. But it didn't matter. She was *hunted* by Lionel and just as a hunter has extrasensory knowledge of where the prey can be found, he knew where she was, and where Rev was. There was no fooling Lionel. He was too clever. So she gave up and appeared with Rev everywhere, to add to the agony of Lionel. And now she had to listen to him *insult* Rev. She drank the cider and pretended she didn't know what he was talking about.

"Please—I can't hear anything bad about him. You're entitled to think what you want, but you can hardly expect me to sit here and listen to you say one word against the person I adore. If you talk against him, Lionel, I'm going to get up and leave."

She felt like leaving anyway. The snow was powdery and the sun was up. It was a shame to be wasting the morning talking.

"You're just jealous," she laughed, trying not to sound serious. It was important that she save his face and not give Lionel the slightest idea that she knew about his passion, knew what he was feeling. She felt so sorry for this man. She sensed how he needed love, how empty his kingdom was, and how lonely it was for him to be married to the wrong woman. In so many ways, Lionel was a unique man, a man whose toys were music and ballet and theater, whose dreams were interwoven with creating beauty and using his fortune to create architectures of sound and movement and light. But his married life was a dubious boat, a boat that was sinking. And his need for dogs, children, country houses—all this was frustrated by a wife with thick ankles and a passion for chess. And so he turned to Sylvia again and again in his dreams and in life. His passion for her was like an infection. No one in the widespread galaxies of his fortunes and conglomerates and business networks could satisfy his hunger for love. No one could Telex him the love he lacked or compute the love he needed. So he turned to Sylvia. Considering he owned Mecca Records, she could hardly deny him companionship. But his craving made her uncomfortable, as if she were a gingerbread cookie and he could break off a piece of her to eat. A finger or an arm or a head. And so she listened to him.

"I feel this man is wrong for you," Lionel repeated.

"What do you mean?"

Lionel looked at her.

"He's a sick man. He's not cut off. He's selfish and thinks only of himself."

Sylvia was so innocent in the sunlight. Sitting in her white ski suit she seemed to belong to the Sierras, a part of them that had become animate.

"I'm just warning you because I care for you, sweetheart." It was nice when he called her sweetheart.

"Oh, Lionel, don't be so protective of me."

"To you, Sylvia, Rev is interesting. He fascinates you because he has no ties, no commitments, no job, no real center. You've worked your ass off writing songs and putting up with the record business for twenty years, and you're tired. I understand that. You want to be free, to be young, to be able to just go—to divest yourself of all your ties. He is, after all, handsome. And perhaps even amusing, although his wit has never been apparent to me. But he's cold. There's a cruelty there that I sense. He could slit your throat. And I think he will."

A shiver passed over her. "Don't be ridiculous," she said.

"I've heard him talk to you, Sylvia, and I'm not being as absurd and foolish as you think I am."

"What did you hear him say that was so disturbing?"

"I heard you talking about going to Europe. And I heard him turn you down. When you asked him why, I heard him say in that cold ice-voice of his, 'Well, that's life in the big city,' and I heard him tell you that he didn't like to be committed to any plans, or some kind of shit like that. I also heard you crying when he left the room."

"Is my suite bugged?" She was outraged.

"As a matter of fact, it isn't. I was walking on your floor

on the way to pay you both a visit. I thought I would drop in on you. When I heard this little lovers' quarrel, I left as discreetly as I came. You never knew I was outside the door—which was open, by the way—and I've been meaning to talk to you. To warn you."

"About what?"

"Warn you about your destiny. Why do you seek pain?"

"I don't."

"You do. Otherwise you wouldn't be with Rev. Don't you see he hates women because he hates himself? His body is a dead giveaway. He's so stiff. He has no flexibility. Did you ever watch him dance? I've watched him in a discotheque. He's almost like a robot. He's like a machine. There's something sadistic about him. As if he could enjoy hurting people."

Sylvia didn't want to hear these things. She felt confused.

"Please, Lionel, stop."

But he continued. It was a need to get out of his system all the venom he felt about his rival. "And his need to travel. To get up and go. His need to keep moving. It's not childish, it's demented. It's his escape from himself."

"Don't be such a judgmental person. What did Keats say? 'It's better to be an imprudent moveable than a prudent fixture.' He wrote that in a letter to Fanny Brawne."

Lionel sucked in his cheeks and looked away. "Maybe Fanny Brawne bought that shit. But I don't."

"Come, let's ski," she said. And tugged at his hand. She wished she could make him happy instead of miserable. If she could only end his suffering.

Later, she told Rev about the conversation. He laughed. "Lionel's jealous of me," he said with a smile.

"I'm afraid so."

Rev saw how upset she was. "Don't worry. You won't let him or his fag friend influence you. You're a big girl. You can make up your own mind."

She looked at him. The important thing in their relationship, she thought, was love. She was bound to him by deep affection, sexual attraction, and by feeling that they were one flesh. Every other attraction seemed draining, even dreary. With him she felt alive. Willing to serve him, to be with him, or when the time came, to be without him. It was as if every moment with him she was saying a little prayer and the prayer was, "Thank you." No one understood how much he meant to her. He was her secret. Even he had no idea of how much she loved him. So much for Lionel's fears. Lionel was wrong. It was his unrequited love talking.

58. Getting Out

"THIS LIFE is a crock," Rev said.

"I know."

"When are we getting out of here?"

"A week."

"Is that how long it's going to take you to finish the album?"

"Yeah. I promise it won't be longer."

"Better not be. I can't stand this joint." He was combing his hair at the mirror. Towel around his waist.

"Isn't there something you can do to keep yourself occupied?" she asked. Rev was a child who had to be amused. His attention span wasn't very long. He didn't read. That was a problem. Most of Sylvia's life had been reading. Hardy. Auden. Lowell. Celine. Bellow. Colette. These were her life-lines. Rev only read *Road and Track*. "How about gambling?" she asked.

"Two nights in the casino are about enough for me. I played poker at the Sahara. And I dropped five hundred dollars here. That's enough. There's no percentage. I mean—I can't win."

"There must be something to keep you occupied."

"What?" He was running the electric shaver around his face. The radio was on. It played rhythm and blues. Wherever Rev went, there was a radio playing.

"What is bothering you, Rev?" she asked.

"I'm not having any fun," he said in that toneless voice she knew.

"What would be fun?"

"To get away from people I don't like. I don't like Nick."

"Why don't we take the day off today? I'll tell Nick I'll work with him tonight."

"Sounds good."

"What would you like to do?"

"I've never seen Harrah's automobile collection. Down in Reno. Let's go there."

She dressed carefully. Jeans. Boots. A heavy sweater. Rev liked her to wear eye makeup. He was an anxious child. Eager to go see the toys. "Lookin' good," he said when she was dressed.

"That's the first compliment you ever gave me."

"I like your beehive haircomb. You look like one of the Shangri-Las."

"I like your zoot suit. You look street smart."

"I am," he said.

"I know," she answered.

Rev felt good behind the wheel of his Trans Am. The large black car had a yellow eagle painted on its front chest and eagle's fire on the tail. It was Rev's favorite American car. He liked the engine. They drove noiselessly to Reno. The windows were open and Sylvia felt the air in her lungs, the pure Tahoe air that always felt good. She looked up at the snow peaks and felt happy. Driving with Rev.

"A penny for your thoughts," she said to Rev.

"I'm thinking about pennies," he said, and then added, "I don't like that question."

"I'm sorry."

"Forget it. I don't like to be asked what I'm thinking

because often I'm not thinking anything. I don't think a lot of the time. It's very relaxing."

"I wish I were like you."

"You could be."

"How?"

"Stop being so emotional. It gets in the way. Don't be so nice to everybody. Stop helping. Stop being charitable."

"I've never wanted to be selfish."

"Why not?"

"I felt it wasn't the correct way to be. There's an emotional sweetness in giving to others."

"Could be. A lot of nice guys are rats in sheeps' clothing."

"Don't you trust anyone?"

"No. Not really. I have a few buddies. But I'm not attached to anyone."

"Were you to your wife?"

"No."

"Why did you marry her?"

"I don't know. It seemed like a good idea at the time." The car was speeding. Under tunnels. In the flat land of the Carson Valley. Past road signs. Billboards. Rev loved driving. He was feeling good. She could tell.

"How did you meet her?"

"My buddy, John, introduced me to her. He was going out with her. We used to hang out together. One day he said to me, 'Rev, I can't handle Arlene anymore,' and I asked him why. He said, 'She's too possessive. She doesn't like me fooling around with other women. And you know, I'm not a one-woman man the way you are. She told me she'd cut my balls off if she found me screwing another woman. That's heavy. Why don't you take her out?' And I did. I mean, she was very attractive."

"What did she look like?"

"Arlene? She was tall. Had long red hair. She had street smarts. She ran all the best cha-cha studios in New York City. She was a businesswoman."

"Did you work for her?"

"Sort of. After we were married. I used to collect the money. I'd go around from one studio to another picking up the cash."

"What else did you do?"

"Nothing. Slept a lot. She gave me an Excalibur. I spent a lot of time in the shop. When you have a car like that, you spend most of your time in the shop. I had a motor-cycle. That was in the shop, too. I used to race. She never liked it. She didn't like the waiting around. And that's what racing is. Waiting around."

"Grand Prix racing?"

"No. I don't like that. The little cars are too nervous. They're like mosquitoes. I like the dirt races, the bang-ing of cars against each other. We broke up. Then I went back to her. But you can't go back. You know what I mean?"

"Why did you leave her?"

"Arlene?"

"Yes."

"Because she stopped wearing eye makeup. When I first met her, she wore high heels. She used eye makeup. I sort of fantasized that I was Dion Dimucci and she was Jane Russell. But she didn't wear eye makeup. She stopped giv-ing me spending money. She took back the motorcycle. Made me take out the garbage. Wanted me to be what I wasn't. So I split."

"What did she want you to be?"

"Humphrey Bogart. And I wanted to be Dion Dimucci. Know what I mean? She wanted a husband. Someone strong she could count on. It's hard to explain. She be-came too possessive."

"Did you have another woman?"

"Of course not. I was into cars. Not women. It was just that Arlene got on my nerves."

"Her difference in class? Lack of education?"

"Not that. She was classy. In her own way. Arlene had

good taste. And she had studied at some university. Spanish literature. She was very intelligent. No sense of
humor."

"Is that important to you?"

"Yes."

You see, I'm the perfect woman for him, Sylvia said in her
head to her masseur. *I wear eye makeup and I'm funny.*

"What an awful business marriage is," she heard herself
saying to Rev.

"Yeah. It is."

"Do you think you'll ever get married again?"

"I don't think about it. I don't plan to. I don't want
children."

"Why not?"

"It's the ultimate ego trip. I'm not good with children."

"Wouldn't you like to settle down?"

"No."

"Never?"

"No."

"Why not?"

"I like my life this way."

"Which way?"

"This way. Being free. Being able to pick up and go
wherever I want. When I want to. I don't ever want to own
anything."

"Not even a boat?"

"Sure. That's different. If you bought me a Riva, I'd
play with it. Then sell it. That's different."

"Why don't you want to live anywhere?"

"Movement. That's where I live. I don't want to tie myself down to any one-to-one relationship. Or house. I live
everywhere." Sylvia remembered the black man in the studio, Jimi Hendrix. His philosophy. It was Rev's. The existentialist hero. With a wheel in his hand. The wheel of the
Trans Am. The gentleman bum. The high-class cowboy.
The classy hard-hat. The upper-class lowlife. The toney
street smarts of Dion Dimucci. The rebel without a cause.

The aging hipster. The groovie gentleman. The stranger. The new Elvis.

Treat me like a fool,
Treat me mean and cruel.

The words of "Love Me" went through her mind:

If you ever go, darling,
I'll be oh, so lonely.
I'll be sad and blue,
Crying over you dear, only.

Rev would leave her. It was just a matter of time. The question was how long, how long could she hang out with him? It didn't matter. *That's the funny thing, doc,* she continued in her mind to her masseur. *It doesn't matter. I've gotten to the point where one man is as good as another. Any person is as good as any other person.* And she could hear him answer:

"That's good. That's what you should feel. Independent. Don't depend on anyone. Especially not a person like Rev Cranwell."

Why? What's wrong with him, doc?

"What's wrong with him? What are you? Crazy? Everything's wrong with him. To begin with, he sounds like a psychopath."

Why? Just because he had shock treatments? A lot of people had shock treatments.

"No. Not the treatments. Who am I to judge that? Although, between you and me, it would be good to know why he had them. But because he doesn't seem able to attach himself to anyone. To feel. To relate."

But no one can today. This is nineteen-eighty! The days of responsibility and feeling for one person are over. Life has become a wilderness of people who don't want to feel anything. Rev is just more honest than most people. Everyone is out for himself. It's dog-eat-dog. But it goes under another name. Existentialist.

Cosmic. Every bastard has a philosophy. It's shit on everyone or be shat on. But that passes as "Take care of yourself and the world will take care of you." "Dump on everyone," doc, has become, "To thine own self be true." Look at this guy. Driving toward Reno in the Trans Am I bought him. Wearing a ski suit I bought him. Look at this guy in his new down vest. You say he's a prick. I say he's beautiful. Maybe a guy out for himself and a guy who wants freedom is the new American hero. Nobody wants to be a doctor or lawyer anymore, doc. They want to be free. No responsibilities. Fun. The Playboy *mentality carried into a philosophy. Every knave is a king. Every king is a jack. Every ace a heart. Every heart a club. It's a new game. I haven't learned the rules yet. But I'm trying. It's erotic. And ironic. I'm looking for insights. Perceptions. That's what I'm doing, doc. Looking for perceptions. I haven't really understood what the rules are. And maybe there are no rules. It's hard to find the roadmap when there's no road.*

"Stop talking to yourself," Rev said. He was still speeding toward Reno.

"What do you mean?" she asked.

"Sometimes you talk to yourself."

"I'll try not to."

"Who were you talking to?"

"My masseur."

"I told you to get rid of him. Those guys are charlatans."

"I can't just get rid of him. I've been seeing him for years."

"Well, wean yourself away. When you go back to New York, instead of seeing him five times a week, see him four. Then three. Then two. It's the way I stopped smoking. First I smoked a pack of Luckies a day. Then I switched to Carltons. Now I combine Carltons with Velamints. One day—maybe next week—I'll stop smoking. It's bad for the lungs. Too bad. Because I like to smoke. Same thing with your doctor. It's fun. But it's bad for you."

"Why?"

"He's bad for your lungs."

"What do you mean?"

"It's hard to breathe when someone is pushing on your body and telling you it's helping you solve your problems. Life is problems. Life isn't meant to be solved."

"I'll take it under advisement."

"Sounds good."

"Sometimes I wonder what it would be like to spend a month with you. Would you always be saying 'Have a nice day' or 'Sounds good' or 'How ya doin?' I think it would drive me crazy."

"It would."

"But I'd still like to spend some time with you. You're my buddy."

"Sounds good."

59. *Harrah's Automobile Collection*

REV TOOK a joint out of his silver case and puffed on it. He parked the Trans Am in front of the Automobile Collection, a huge warehouse with a sign in front of it that said, "HARRAH'S AUTOMOBILE COLLECTION."

"Where the hell are we?" Sylvia asked.

"We're at Harrah's ersatz museum. To err is human. You know the saying."

"To err is human. To ersatz is divine."

"Yeah."

"This is the industrial revolution's answer to the Metropolitan Museum of Art."

"Yeah."

"Instead of Tintorettos, Mercer Raceabouts."

"That's right," Rev said.

"Instead of Cézannes, the Pope Hartford Seven-Passenger Touring."

"You get the picture."

"Instead of Rembrandt, the 1930 Packard Speedster."

"American Art: The Auto. You got it."

"Harrah's world."

"Let's go for it." They got out of the Trans Am and walked slowly toward Harrah's Automobile Collection. Sylvia knew in her bones this was the closest she would ever get to walking down the aisle with Rev Cranwell. They proceeded slowly toward the museum. Two blond giants. To see the powerful cars. As they entered the museum, Sylvia realized that she was in an equivalent of the child's Disney World. It was a Disney World of cars with a few Harrah touches thrown in. There were slot machines everywhere. And souvenirs sold at the entrance. A barker came up to them. It was one of the guides. You paid him to give you the Harrah spiel. Rev gave him a dollar. He was a midget, a clown. A prankster, a freak.

"Welcome to Harrah's world," the freak said, playing the fool. "On July 3, 1977, Harrah's automobile collection had the distinct pleasure of welcoming its three-millionth visitor."

"Tell him to go away," Rev whispered to Sylvia.

The freak continued. He smiled at them both, acting deaf to what had been said, though of course, he had heard Rev's annoyance. It didn't stop him. If anything, the freak became more insistent, more factual.

"Nearly everyone discovers a special car, one they picture themselves driving. Children like fire trucks, young people enjoy the motorcycles and race cars. And almost everyone hesitates a few extra minutes near the twenty Dusenbergs or the Rolls-Royces or the Packards or the Pierce Arrows. They're all here, from the one-horsepower 1892 Phillion steam to the 500 GHP Ford GT Le Mans Race Car."

"Fuck off," Rev said.

The freak continued, only now he addressed his spiel to Sylvia. "The collection began in 1948 with the acquisition of two cars: a 1911 Maxwell and a 1911 Ford. Presently the ten-acre thirteen-building complex had three large showrooms, restoration shops, Pony Express museum, saloon, cafeteria, administrative offices, the best automotive research library of its kind, and a souvenir and reception area."

"That's enough," Rev said to the freak. Something in Rev's voice, the icy-killer voice he used when he was truly annoyed, stopped the freak from continuing. He walked away, sulking. A courtier banished. As he looked back, he suddenly whirled around and bowed. He then found others who were receptive to his act.

"Little asshole," Rev said. They passed through the souvenir shop and moved into the front part of the museum. Silent men in white garage-mechanic pants bent over machines.

"This must be the restoration room."

"Yeah, only it's not this glamorous. This is just part of the show."

"No grease monkeys. These guys look like movie stars."

"Part of the showmanship of Harrah. The real restoration takes place somewhere else. To restore a car is a filthy and long process."

"They say he spent millions every year on this."

"He could afford to. It was a tax write-off."

They walked toward the first showroom. They entered it the way you enter a church. Rev was stunned. "This is something," he said.

"All these cars—they look like Faberge jewel boxes."

"I never saw anything like this!"

"Not in the Bronx, anyway!" They both laughed. They began walking silently down the corridors of cars. There were hundreds of them. It was the only time in the months she knew Rev Cranwell that he ever sounded enthusiastic.

"This is a classic," he said, standing in front of a perfectly polished bright yellow gleaming Mercer Raceabout. There were endless corridors of brilliantly painted cars, the colors as vivid as bird feathers: bright red, bright yellow, bright blue. The collection was staggering. It was almost as if the cars were marbles that had been thrown out on the floor. They walked through the first showroom of five hundred cars to the next showroom. In all, Harrah had over a thousand antique cars, which constituted a journey into the past. They looked silently at the machines. Rev was in awe. At one moment, the way a good Catholic stops to genuflect at the altar, he stopped in front of a car that touched him deeply. Antique music played in the background on hidden speakers. Elements of the past hung on the walls. There were photographs of the era that each car came from. There were costumes from the era mounted in glass boxes. The museum was a collection that began in 1948 and covered the whole history of the automobile, from Phaetons to Bugattis, from custom thoroughbreds to modern racers, from front-wheel drive to rotary engines to safety bumpers to steam-powered vehicles. There they were, all in a row, gleaming, restored, like brilliant jewels that shone under the lamps: the treasures of America.

Walking down the corridors of the showroom, Sylvia thought how surreal the event was. Machines that nobody wanted were collected here by Harrah and became works of art. How like the mind of Marcel Duchamp with his *found objects,* pieces of junk that he labeled art until they actually became art. Harrah had envisioned the junk yards of America filled with unwanted engines, blown-out tires, ripped roofs, broken rumble seats, punctured fenders, and twisted fins. He had saved the automobile in its history the way paleontologists saved bones from endangered species. Old airmobiles, like old dinosaurs, were pieced together, shined until the complete history of the automatic transportation business, America itself, was there on display. Old cars were America's heritage. Antiques of motors.

Rev stopped in front of a 1932 Aston Martin Tourer. He breathed deeply. "This car was made to do three things well," he said. "To go fast on the straight, to go fast around corners, and to keep on going." The car was brilliant green. They stopped at Cases, Fords, Rolls-Royces, Napiers. The 1903 Napier Grand Prix held Rev's attention for an hour. He stared at it, as if praying. Leaving the showroom, Rev held Sylvia's hand. "That was powerful," he said.

"So many classics," she said.

"That Thomas Flyer, winner of the race in 1907—perfect condition. That was something else."

"That 1946 Lincoln Zephyr four-door sedan," she said. "My father came to visit me in boarding school in that car. Then he came in a 1947 Cadillac. Then in a 1948 Packard convertible with a swan. Then in a 1949 chauffeur-driven Bentley. The history of his life was in his cars. As he got older, his cars got larger and larger. As he shrank into illness, his cars got stronger. When he died, he had an enormous Rolls Royce Sedan. His life had been spanned by cars, from a Pierce Arrow to a Rolls Royce."

"I know what you mean," Rev said. They went to Howard Johnson's outside of Reno and had lunch. He hardly said anything. He was lost in a car dream. But he looked good. Sylvia saw him look truly happy for the first time.

60. White Trash

Driving with Rev back to Tahoe, Sylvia thought about how she had paid her dues. About her hit record, the one she and Nick had won the Grammy for, "White Trash." But the pain in the song had been her pain. *Cash Box,* in their Rhythm n' Blues column, had first announced "White Trash" to the world. It was 1959. She remembered the column had been titled "Sleeper of the Week." In memory she saw it yet, that column which had put them over the top. "White Trash" had sold as many singles as "Hound Dog," which Leiber and Stoller had written. *Cash Box* said:

Nick Dimani gives a frenzied rendition on the top deck, titled "White Trash," and the result is a waxing that will excite and catch itself playing time. The tune is a rhythmic Latin tempo middle and Dimani wails it dramatically, easy when he should be easy, and dramatic when he has to drive it home. The rhythmic handclapper has just enough of the erotic to stir the emotions and raise the blood pressure. Flip is a mood piece the Dimani/Lundholm team wrote. . . .

"White Trash" had been the first time Sylvia put herself into a song, had taken her own life experience and used it to expel the demons that choked her and kept her from sleeping. She had been through her first painful experience with a hustler. The first winner-wanter had come into her life and out of that, she and Nick and Mecca Records had made a fortune. She had turned pain into money. She thought of Bee-Bee Handrell and how she had met him:

WHITE TRASH

You slept and wept and whined like an ass,
So I loaned you a bedspread
And some sheets and some cash;
And I helped your career,
But you were too low class;
You ain't no gentleman,
You're just bad white trash.
Bee-Bee,
Don't you see?
You're low class
White trash.

At first you smiled and acted polite
And you needed some money to feel all right;

So I gave you a wardrobe
And wrote you some checks;
And you gave me some of your
Down and dirty sex.
But now I know you're stupid and crass,
You ain't got no manners,
You're just bad white trash.
Bee-Bee,
You're not for me,
You're low class,
White trash.

Bee-Bee
Baby
I don't owe you a thing.
You stole
My baby's candy,
And my daddy's black ring.
And now
You're in trouble,
Cause you're hurting for bread,
But I ain't your mama
And I hope you drop dead.
Cause Bee-Bee
You're crude,
And you're just a bad dude.
White Trash,
White Trash,
Get off your ass,
Too bad your real mama
Didn't teach you class.

"White Trash" had been a playlet about Bee-Bee the country boy from Dallas she had met at a gym. He had been a teacher at Orshevsky's, the gymnastic parlor where she had gone to work out. He wore cowboy boots and a cowboy hat even at the gym. When he helped lift the would-be acrobats on the swing, his hands would become familiar. He taught them to do the Wrisley and to reach higher for the rings. One evening when she was taking a night class, he asked her where she was from. She said, "Another planet," and that was the beginning of their affair. They were both young then, but he never had any cash. He wanted so badly to be a model or an actor, to be somebody famous. He had bought the movie screen version of life and saw himself as the James Dean of Orshevsky's. They had made love and he had confessed with his puppy-dog eyes and his whining southern voice that he had always wanted to really travel. She had taken him to Acapulco for the weekend, where she had gone so many times before, and with Bee-Bee she had stayed in the Villa Vera. But he had made use of his time to flirty-flirt with other women in front of her, to windsurf with some blond person, to water ski with some brunettes, to ignore her on the beach and make up hostile speeches about how just because she had money, she didn't "own" him, and how she shouldn't be possessive. She considered leaving him in Acapulco where he could be just another beach boy with acne and a southern drawl. But in the end they flew back to New York. He was the type of person who would ask her for money, clothes, photographs for his modeling career. (What career? He had a jutting chin, psychopathic eyes.) He lied. He became a parasite that had eaten its way into her life. She had gone from respecting him and his ability as a gymnast ("My body is a work of art," he would say, oblivious of modesty) to loathing him; he was a peacock. And she had found things missing in her apartment. She suspected he had taken them. Later she found out that every time he went home "early" to a flat he shared with a roommate, he was screwing the janitor's wife in the building and she was giving him grits. "I'm into comfort," he would say. "I love spending other people's money." Not bad for a country boy. The pain she felt when she discovered his lies was almost unbearable. She had lain in bed, under a comforter, unable to move for weeks. She had mothered herself, written him letters which she tore up, and finally written "White Trash" as a way of relieving herself of the anxiety she felt when she discovered he was a thief and a liar. That was the medicine of the lyric. It could cure her of whatever really hurt deep down inside. She had paid her dues. Nick had seen the lyric and set it to a haunting melody. Recorded it. And Mecca brought it out. Everyone sang it. With Bee-Bee, Sylvia had paid her dues.

She thought of all that riding back to Tahoe and she wondered if Bee-Bee foreshadowed Rev. Rev was a gigolo, too, but he was different. Bee-Bee was a cheap hustler. Rev was the Maharishi of Gigolos. He had a philosophy to offer. For every penny she laid out, she received a wealth of philosophy back. Rev was the Yogananda of Hustlers. The real difference was that he had a sense of humor, which made him less of a hustler and more of a buddy. Besides, she knew what she was paying for this time. And at least Rev wasn't trash. On the contrary, he was a great gentleman, and that made all the difference. He knew when to say, "Thank you," and to him, it was all a joke. He was upperclass, which put him in the same category as Lionel Colesman and everybody else in the business. In some way, he was perverse. He never asked for anything. Which meant that she would give him everything. The ultimate hustler never asked. He was so undemanding, the Yogananda of the "I Want! I Want!" philosophy. Besides, he could take care of himself. And he could take care of her, too, if he had to. That was the difference. It pained her to think of how much she loved him. So she didn't think about it and neither did he. That made everything all right. He didn't want a hundred percent of her fame. He just wanted ten percent of her earnings, which made him no different from any other agent. Bee-Bee, Rev, they were all playing James Dean, the George Washington of macho. But Rev had succeeded. He was truly carrying on the James Dean legacy. Bee-Bee secretly had a cause: He wanted to be famous. Rev had no cause whatsoever, which made him a guru. His true philosophy was speeding. And it didn't matter where he was speeding to. He was born wanting to risk his life, but he hadn't found anything worth risking it for. Except speeding. The Trans Am sped through the desert toward Tahoe.

61. *Laurie*

"Do you love me?" Laurie asked Nick.
   "I do. Yes. Of course. I do with all my heart."
   "Well, make love to me."
   "I just did."
   "I want to again. I can't get enough of you, Nick."
He put his hand on her breasts. They were perfect. He entered her again slowly. A ship coming home. In the sea of Laurie he could float for hours, lose track of time. He thought about the album. He was obsessed. He thought about it even while making love. For Nick, it was taking too long. A few of the songs were good. Arthur Morris liked them. He had booked the studio. Was Laurie taking too much from him? Sometimes he wanted to leave her flesh and just make love to the piano. That was his love. The keyboard. The silence of working. She was getting to be a pain in the ass.

62. *American Empire*

IT WAS exhausting to think of writing this book. Nancy got up, paid her check, and carried her tote bag close to her as she sought out the sauna. In the sauna, she read her copy of Mao. How relaxing. Naked. Sweat. Mao Tse Tung. Sweating on the cedar bench, she felt as though she were living in a dream. What was she doing in Tahoe? Was she really accomplishing anything for the Movement? Sylvia had promised her the ten thousand dollars. She hoped that Rev wouldn't do anything to get in the way of that. Rev had said little to her. She wondered if he was politicized. She made a note to check that out. The rest of the people were grinning at her constantly. Nick Dimani, what an ass! And that group of people around him—his wife, his girlfriend, the entourage of a star. She had visited him in the South Shore Room. The acts were absurd. The West was corrupted by these absurd shows. The restaurants were terrible. They advertised, "From English Muffins to Chow Mein and Escargots." She had gotten food poisoning on the chow mein. She could sue if she wanted to call attention to herself. And the stars—Sammy Davis, Jr., Wayne Newton, Eddy Arnold, Ben Vereen—they passed in and out nightly in the casinos. That was enough sweat.

Opening the sauna door, she breathed in the cool air of the locker room. After the swim which she took every day in Harrah's pool, she walked into the hotel lobby. *Hopefully this book can be dynamite. Readable. Poetic. Humorous. Historic. Have insight into the man behind the myth. The poet inside the revolutionary.* Would they give her enough money to go to Cuba and talk with Castro, or even give her enough money so she could first go to Zimbabwe or to the elections? "That's dangerous," Sylvia said.

"So what?" As if Sylvia knew about danger. *I promise to create a book,* Nancy thought to herself, *that will excite the reader on every page and still make a major contribution to our understanding of Castro's leadership and world events.*

Nancy stood in front of the machines. They were tempting. The Chinese in her loved to gamble. As a child in Hong Kong, she would ride the ferry to Macao with her aunts and they would all gamble in the Macao fan-tan

tables. As a teenager, she played Mah-Jongg with her sisters. She could still recall the sound of the Mah-Jongg
tablets on the table. She had a yen to gamble. It was an old
addiction. Why not? Putting a dollar in the slot machine,
she pulled the lever. Suddenly, the machine began spitting
out silver dollars. One, two, three, four—a hundred silver
dollars and they were still coming. The machine was vomiting silver dollars. She had hit the jackpot. The prunes
and lemons and apples were spinning around. Everyone
was staring at her. Everyone had forgotten his own luck
and was looking at the silver dollars being regurgitated
from the machine. She had put one over on Harrah's, all
right. The hundreds of gamblers watched in silence.
Someone was lucky, someone was actually a winner! She
kneeled down and scooped up the money as it came gush-
ing from the machine. There were hundreds and
hundreds of silver dollars and they simply wouldn't stop
being belched onto the floor. "The Movement thanks
you," she said humbly to the machine. Luck!

"Brunch," the sign said in Harrah's seafood restaurant,
"The Perfect End to a Friday, Saturday, or Sunday
Night." Nancy ignored the sign. She sat alone at a table
eating a bowl of rice. In front of her was a proposal she
was writing. She always carried with her a portable study
stand, the equipment of the true loner. She propped it in
front of her whenever she ate alone, which was most of
the time. Around her in Harrah's restaurant swirled the
families, the cowboys, the pregnant women, the women
who still wore beehive hairdos, the boys in jeans, the girls
wearing their down vests, the children in their sweaters.
Everyone carried a tray. Nancy was oblivious to the mob
of people. With her rice, which she had put into a cereal
bowl, she was alone. She read the proposal:

Why this book? Whatever happens in Cuba will continue to
affect the psyche of every American.

She took a yellow pencil out of her canvas bag, a white tote bag that was now gray from being carried around the world. She erased what she had written. She started again. She wanted this book on Castro to bring her some money, and she knew she had to word the proposal in such a way that someone would buy it.

"Why a book on Castro?" Sylvia had asked.

"Why not?" she replied.

"Are you a Cuban expert?" Rev asked.

"I have access to the mission at the U.N.," she replied. What the hell did they know? She began the proposal again.

CASTRO
AN INTIMATE PORTRAIT OF A REVOLUTIONARY
by Nancy Chan

When Castro burst on the world scene in the late fifties, he became the first hero of the left in America. The world followed his revolution via television and in this country for many he was then canonized into the outrageous antihero.

That sounded good, she thought. American. Hero, anti-hero. It was all bullshit. But everything was bullshit. Why not a proposal? How much money could she get? Enough to go to Zimbabwe? She would love to cover the elections for the free press. If this book on Castro didn't sell, she would be totally dependent on Sylvia Lundholm. Who wasn't coming across until her album made it big. Ten thousand dollars. Really! The Movement couldn't move on ten thousand dollars. The Movement needed at least twenty. That would pay for stamps. For a brochure. Cover the printing of tickets for the Zimbabwe Emergency Concert in February. But not much else. She shouldn't be mad at Sylvia. She had agreed to use her influence to get The Dire Straits to play at the concert. Dollar Brand, Machito, Jimmy Owens, and the New York Jazz Quartet were already committed. Maybe Sylvia would fork up another ten grand. If she stayed in Tahoe. But the Castro book would help.

"During the Baby of Pigs—" (she crossed out "Baby" and wrote "Bay") "—he again emerged as the triumphant leader who outwitted the Kennedys. Throughout his public life he has excited feelings of political outrage, envy, and admiration." *To say the least,* Nancy thought, putting rice in her mouth and wondering if anyone would really want another biography of Castro. "In the next three years, as the president of the nonaligned movement, we will watch him and be affected by his decisions." *I'll say.* "In order to understand our foreign policy toward Cuba and our relationship to South America, the Caribbean, and the developing countries, here in this country there is a hunger to know about this man. A history of Castro is really a history of our country's adolescence."

63. Rev and Nancy

HEAVENLY VALLEY is the largest ski area in the world. At an elevation of 6,200 feet above sea level, the Sierra Nevada weather can get bitter cold so that the coyote howls and stalks small animals for food, the deer blend into the bush, and Lake Tahoe itself becomes a magic attraction for skiers all over the world. Although the action goes on night and day in the casinos, at Harvey's, at the Sahara, at Harrah's, at all the resorts, thousands of people come to Tahoe to gamble at night and ski by day. The peaks of the mountains are dotted with woolen caps. Clear. Crisp. Clean. The sun shines on the snow. And the winter of eighty was the best winter for skiing in many years.

Rev had run down the mountains five times. He was

always happiest out of doors, and the skiing, especially in the morning, had been perfect. He had ridden the cable car. He thought he saw Nancy walking without skis through the snow. He called down to her, "Nancy—wait! I'm coming down to join you," and she looked up. "Don't move," he screamed, "I'm coming right down!" She looked up at him and laughed.

"Good," she called, "because I'm not coming up. Because I hate skiing. I'm just going for a drink."

In a moment, he had jumped off the cable car at the next level and had skied parallel down like lightning, turning left and right over the snowy hills until he was next to her. He put his arm around her and almost knocked her over.

"Care for a drink?" she asked. She took a silver flask out of her Chinese worker's jacket.

"Where'd you get that jacket?" he asked.

"Mao Tse-tung lent it to me," she said with disdain, taking a long swig.

"What are you drinking?"

"Dewar's on snow."

"I think I'll have a swig."

"Can I make you some ice cubes?"

"Nancy, all these months I've known you, I've never talked to you alone."

"It's hard to talk to a person when he has a motor running."

"What do you mean by that remark?"

"I thought the only thing that interested you was cars. And motorcycles. Planes and powerboats. Toys. That's all you ever talk about."

"I know what you mean," he said, laughing, showing his sense of humor. He was beginning to like her.

"The other day I heard you talking to Sylvia about Harrah's Automobile Collection and I thought I would die of boredom. You practically had an erection over the 1929 Ford Town Car."

"Actually, it was over the 1930 Mercer Raceabout."

"I'd take a 1915 Franklin Roadster. Competing against all the other six-cylinder cars at New Haven in May 1916, a Franklin set an economy record by traveling fifty-five miles on one gallon of gasoline. The company stressed the fact that the two most important principles of Franklin construction were the light weight of their air-cooled engines and the resiliency of their wooden chassis frame."

"Where'd you learn that from?"

"From the Harrah's Automobile Collection Special Edition. Where else?"

"I don't meet too many women who know anything about antique cars."

"You don't meet too many women stuck in Lake Tahoe with nothing to do. The book about Harrah's Automobile Collection came with the suite. Along with the Bible."

"I thought you'd be out there organizing the workers of Tahoe. What about those poor busboys? They look as if they could use a raise. Or how about those exploited women—those cocktail waitresses who have to walk around like bunnies in mourning, in their tight little black dresses. Isn't that sexism? Or reverse discrimination?"

"I didn't realize you were so observant."

Rev looked down at her. "Come on, sweetheart, I'm taking you for a drink. A real one at the lodge."

"I'll race you down hill."

He started laughing. "Sure—with no skis."

"I can always slide."

He suddenly lifted her up. "Come on, I'll ski you down." And he took off for the bar holding her around the waist. She laughed all the way down. At the bar, she was amused. She ordered a double scotch and started talking about boats.

"Don't pamper me," he said. "I know you'd much rather talk about *Das Kapital,* which I happen to have read, by the way, at school."

"Fuck Marx. This is my R & R time. I haven't spoken to

anyone about boats in years. All my concerns are about organizing rallies and demonstrations, study groups, teach-ins, bulletins, newsletters, economic boycotts—in fact, making myself into a royal pain in the ass to all of you blond uncommitted Americans."

"I'm committed. To different things. *Excaliburs.* Cigarettes. Trans Ams. Piper Cubs. Roadrules. The Bible."

"The Bible?"

"That's the little blue book for trade-ins. It tells what a car is worth."

"I don't know about speedboats. I only know about sailboats."

"Oh. One of the purists."

"Yes. I started sailing a junk. In Hong Kong. My father never wanted to be radical. He toyed around with boats. He contributed—without knowing it—to the economic growth of the colony. Look at all those junks and sampans that now bump each other in the South China Seas."

"How old were you when you first started sailing?"

"Before I could waddle. Always without a motor. That was a long time ago. The last time I was on a sailboat, I signed up on a ten-month expedition from Australia to the Aleutian Islands."

"I'm impressed. What were you? In the galley?"

"It didn't start out that way." She laughed. "It ended up that way. But that's a long story. I was supposed to be the underwater photographer and historian of the journey. But it turned out that I was the only female crew member. The boat, called the *Naughty Marietta,* was ridiculously plush. It belonged to an Australian millionaire."

"What was the boat like?"

"Seventy-two feet of luxury. You won't believe it. Four different refrigerators for four different temperatures. One for champagne and chilled wine. One for dairy products. One for frozen meat. And one for vegetables. The galley was all pushbuttons. One push on the button and the table lowers to cocktail height. Another push on the button and the chairs are lowered to lounging position. The trouble was, the oven was not gimballed!"

"Not gimballed! What kind of tub was it?" They both laughed heartily, two seasoned sailors exchanging knowledgeable tidbits. "You know," Rev said, "you are fun to be with! You are more womanly than I'd ever expected you to be. You're even very attractive. . . ."

"Cut it out, Rev. Do you think all activists are asexual?"

"No. But I've never met one quite as funny and sexy as you are."

She looked at him and then said what was on her mind. "I want another drink."

"Come on. There's a better lodge just a mile down. The Norwegian. You'd like it. They have a fireplace."

"They also have rooms. With nice double beds."

He took her hand. It was soft. He found himself ready to make love to her that minute. She obviously wanted him also. In a few moments, he pulled up in front of the lodge. He checked them in and ordered drinks in the room. The room had a fireplace. She took off her ski clothes and began warming herself in front of the fire. Suddenly he was naked in back of her. She felt how excited he had become. They fell on the bed and he was kissing her. Nancy was surprised at how gentle he was; she felt the surprise of being close to someone. She thought how different people are when they make love. He was almost passive. She held on to him with her strong arms and kissed him all over his body, discovering how beautifully he was made. He was almost perfect. She had never seen such a magnificent body. And she wanted him. Quickly she drew him into her. They made love again. Then again. Afterward he lit a joint and they began talking in bed.

"I think we've done something we shouldn't have," Nancy said.

"Is this guilt speaking?"

"Friendship. I know you just met Sylvia. And I know you really care for her and she cares for you."

"What we've done has nothing to do with Sylvia. Or my relationship with her. Or your relationship with her. I just felt that you were my comrade. And then I felt that you were more than my comrade. And I just acted on it. I was attracted to you. I'm not married, am I? It's not hurting anyone."

"Good. Let's just be buddies."

"Buddies."

"Now I can count on you as another body I can count for my demonstration."

"Do you always get to look at the bodies so closely?"

"Every one of them."

"Well, you can count on me any time."

"Good." She got up and dressed quickly.

"Where are you going?"

"Back to Harrah's. I have a feeling I want some air."

"Mind if I join you?"

"Thanks, Rev. Just this moment, I want to be alone." She walked down the wooden steps quietly and out into the snowy fields.

64. Rita's Mid-life Crisis

RITA AND her mid-life crisis annoyed the hell out of Nick. Nick was always nervous when Rita and the children joined him. They had worked out a perfect arrangement: She stayed in Sussex or in their apartment on Fifth Avenue and he wandered in and out of the rock scene, free to do as he pleased, free to be bisexual, asexual, or nonsexual. Rita preferred to be faithful. Not because Nick would care what she did with her body, but because she played so much tennis, she was often too tired for affairs *and* the children *and* a social life. That was how things were supposed to be in England. The men were supposed to get their rocks off. And the women were supposed to play tennis. Tennis was the fucking replacement. An occasional flirt with a tennis instructor was allowed, but even the instructor had too many clients to service all of them. Rita was a function-a-holic. The Germans have a word for it: *functionlust.* She got off on functioning like a machine. The house was perfectly cared for by maids, the kids had all their cavities filled and were hugged and chauffeured. Nick's career was publicly handled by Rita, who was his hostess and public wife, appearing on mandatory talk shows. And it seemed to suit both of them. Rita adored Nick. To her, he was the most charming and intelligent man she had ever met. She had spent two years trying to marry him and had been determined to get him away from Sylvia Lundholm and every other groupie who threw herself at him. She simply looked the other way. She found out early in the game that Nick's weakness was a sweet personality and no hassle. And so she never hassled him. She took more shit from Nick Dimani than any woman in her right mind would accept. But then, Rita Dimani was never in her right mind when it came to Nick. She was crazy about him. She was not only crazy about him, but about what he represented to her. Rita was a small-time English girl from Sussex with rich parents and a certain nervous fragility. She had, as a young woman, heard Nick Dimani entertain; when he had actually taken her out, she determined to get him at any cost. She watched him practically make love to Sylvia Lundholm, whom she knew she could ease out. Sylvia had moods. Nick didn't like moods. Also, Sylvia had a mind of her own. And often didn't listen to Nick. Rita had learned, and her motto with Nick was, "Give him plenty of rope. To hang himself." She had never complained. Never asked for attention, never tried to have a career of her own. Her career was keeping her body in good condition and dressing well and running a house and being there to listen to Nick. Nick came first. The children second. Her looks third. And tennis fourth. After all that, there was Nick's business partners. Her job was to jolly along Nick on whatever ego trip he was on. And to understand him. And understanding Nick Dimani was a job. A job and a half, she used to tell her shrink. Silently, Rita had her own breakdowns. Silently, holidays would pass which reminded Rita of her life in England, and she would falter and fall apart. Crying jags in solitude, while he was away, were never reported back to Nick, for when he was home, she was always cheerful. Always merry. And in return for the career status of being a nobody, she became a somebody. She became Mrs. Nick Dimani. Oddly enough, that was all she wanted. To get laid by Nick Dimani was not her only dream. Her dream was to use the power of being his wife for other ends. And her ends were subtle. She was secretly involved in a conspiracy to turn all of New York and possibly the world into a needlepoint mosaic. Rita attacked her needlepoint the way Joan of Arc went to battle. Her camping ground was Mrs. Larson on Madison Avenue. There she made her battle plans. She plotted which pillows to cover with flowers, which pillows to cover with little banal sayings, and which pillows to cover with kittens. She was content with putting little things such as, "Nobody loves a smartass," and "My ass is mine." Rita, Rita, pumpkin eater, lived very well with a man who could keep her. And he did keep her. The usual doctors (facials, surgeries, breast lifts, vacuuming of the thighs, silicone for wrinkles, all thanks to a Dr. Berg) and then of course, there were hair packs for her bleached blond hair, thanks to a tricologist called John Wilkenson, and of course, the usual dentists and cosmetic surgeons that bored women frequent. In addition, there were decorators, oh God, were there decorators. Masseurs and tailors and shoemakers and antique dealers and chauffeurs and Rita's little Rolodex read like a Who's Who of Manhattan classified pages. She knew exactly the right exterminator if she had to get rid of water bugs. And exactly the right chiropodist if she had a corn.

Exactly the right doctor if her child needed soft contact lenses. She was a directory, a guru of facts about everything. Nick was both grateful and tired of her at the same time. He was guilty about not being with her and fearful of having her drop him. He was excited by the stability she afforded him. He could always look at the losers that gathered at the watering holes and casinos and benefits and say, "When I go home, I have my kids and a beautiful home and people who dig me and want me—I have substance." Rita was Nick's substance. And yet, he wished she'd keep her substance in England instead of cramping his style in Tahoe. He couldn't risk her leaving him. And at Christmas, Rita liked to be near Nick. Chanukah, Christmas, Passover, Easter—she was his holiday wife. And she arrived with her entourage of Vuitton bags, children, nannies, and needlepoint needles. He wanted to be with Laurie. And Rita was going to be around. It might get difficult.

"Keep her occupied," he said to his dresser. "That's part of your job, baby."

"I don't like to do this kind of work. I don't know what to do with your wife, sweetheart. I'm a dresser, not a babysitter."

"You're whatever I say you are, if you want to keep rubbing two nickels together. Pimp, hairdresser, dresser, wifesitter, what the fuck difference does it make to you?" Nick took a bill out of his pocket. "Take her gambling," he said, putting the hundred dollar bill in his hand. "Just don't let her get near Laurie."

65. *Rita and the Hot Box*

"Am I mad? Because I love young boys?" Rita asked herself. "No you're not." She wore old-fashioned English clothes which concealed her beautiful body. She couldn't get enough of young boys. And Rita outwitted Nick. He always thought of his wife as the "perfect lady." He never suspected her betrayals. And that's what she came to Tahoe for. To be turned on by young bodies. To find young boys. Secretly, she attended the "swingers" parties with ski instructors at Kirkwood. Slyly, she managed to make a rendezvous with the maitre d' from Harrah's. She met her lovers in places that would never be suspected. She met them, for example, at the roulette table. There was one admirer of Rita Dimani, a fifteen-year-old son of one of the wealthy families from Squaw Valley, who followed her to the swimming pool at Harrah's. His young cock became erect as he watched her dive into the pool wearing only a shiny bikini. Her breasts were large and he imagined sucking them. He got hot watching her. When she came out of the pool, her breasts were completely visible inside the shiny suit. He could see her nipples.

"Can I offer you a towel, Mrs. Dimani?" the boy said.

"Thank you very much," she said noticing him. One rarely saw such perfect teeth; they were white and smiling at her. She looked down his perfect body and noticed the erection. She walked to the sauna. He followed her. He kept his bathing suit on and looked down at her. Inside the sauna, her clitoris grew larger. Silently, he slipped inside the sauna. He began licking her, eating her cunt, until she began to moan. The sweat poured down both of their bodies. "My God, you're good," she said.

"For a child?"

"Take your suit off," she said breathlessly.

"I have an eight-inch cock," he said.

"Put it inside me," she said quietly. And he did. They rocked back and forth slowly. She told him she felt his cock in her stomach. He moved up and down on her, sweat pouring down both of them. In the hot box, he made her come quickly, then slowly. "I've never felt anything like this," she said. "Your cock stays hard for me so long."

"That's because I'm young," he said. He flipped her over and entered her from the back. "I've never felt any cock like this," she said.

"Good. It feels good to me, too."

"Are you sure?" she asked.

"Yes."

"I'm not too old for you?"

"I like older women. With tight pussies. They're better lovers." She came again. She stood up with the sweat streaming down her beautiful body.

"Have you ever made love to a woman my age?" she asked.

"How old are you?"

"Forty-three," she said. She expected him to be shocked.

"Sure. Many times. I dig older ladies. It's the new thing. Didn't you know?"

"No. I didn't."

"Can I see you again?" she asked. She tried not to sound desperate, but she wanted that hard cock inside her one more time. She would pay for it if she had to. But she wouldn't have to. He wanted her too. She took his cock in her mouth. It was still large and hard. She began to suck him, kneeling down. He looked at her.

"Be careful of your teeth. It's so large you could hurt me." He came in her mouth. She swallowed his sperm. She put a towel around her and slipped out of the sauna. He followed her in a moment. Later, in the lobby, he whispered to her, "Lady, I love fucking you. Let's do the same thing again at five o'clock."

It was the most exciting moment of Rita Dimani's life. She would have him again. This child-man who made her feel so alive. She was elated, flying; she could still feel his hard young cock in her mouth, in her stomach, between her breasts. "I'll do anything to have you inside of me again," she whispered.

"Your accent turns me on, lady. I can't wait to fuck you again. I'm going to fuck your brains out."

"When?"

They were standing in front of the keno table. They might have been talking about gambling. She might have been a woman with her son. She was almost three times his age. "I love fucking you. Older women are the greatest," he said in her ear. "I'll see you at five." She stood there listening to him. A stranger would think a son was saying good-bye to his mother. She felt herself become moist as he whispered to her. She wanted him again. His young body, his young beautiful torso, his young beautiful face. She had never felt anything like it. As she stood there, she couldn't believe her luck. She would have his cock again. She wanted him.

"Lady, you're the greatest. Your tits really turned me on," he whispered.

"Shhhhh," she said. "Someone will hear you."

"So what?" he smiled. "I dig you."

She couldn't believe her luck.

66. *Fantasy Inn*

LAURIE WAS dealing. She had been taught the English version at Harrah's school, where the players' cards are dealt face up and the dealer only holds one face up card, no down card. While she was shuffling, she felt her body rush with an excitement that she hadn't really known before. The best-looking man she had ever seen in her life was standing at the table. It was Revson Cranwell. She had seen him with Sylvia Lundholm. Carefully, she kept her eyes on the cards. The pit boss was watching her as he usually did. Rev was staring at her. He had an odd, distracted look; his eyelids hung just slightly down so that he looked either bored or sleepy. But when she looked up from the cards, he was smiling at her. It was three in the morning and he looked brushed by the sun and vibrantly alive. He had a windburn on his face except for around the eyes where his goggles must have been. As he bought some chips, she noticed how perfect his hands were. They were rough, masculine hands. He wore an expensive Cartier watch that was made out of white gold and inlaid with brilliant gold. She noticed it was hinged with golden screws, each leaf of the watch. The face of the watch was square and she could tell the Cartier design. Being a dealer, you became a connoisseur of jewelry. You could tell a person's background and taste without even looking at his face. Laurie had never seen a watch as thick and beautiful as the one he wore. The golden inlay and screws matched perfectly the tiny golden hairs on his arms. He seemed all golden in the darkness of the casino, as if the sun god had come into the gambling pits and lit the room with an incandescence. Sylvia Lundholm was lucky to have him. As he stood and took his chances, he didn't have the air of sweating out the game like so many other desperadoes on the graveyard shift. He had the hands of a con man; he was even more deft than she was in handling the cards. He picked them up with the hands of an artist who had been playing for a long time. As he exposed his cards, every movement of his hand was graceful. She tried not to watch him too steadily. She wanted to hold on to her job. When her break came, she walked toward the door. She had twenty minutes to relax and she felt she needed some of the night air. She felt her pulse quicken and she sensed that he was following her. There was a sense of excitement and disbelief. He was mysteriously after her. She was being hunted. As she walked into the parking lot, she heard his steps. He didn't say a word but caught up with her. He just smiled. Then he said something that surprised her.

"I like watching you deal."

"Thanks."

"I used to deal, too." They walked toward the center of

town, talking. Laurie was heading for Tahoe T's to see her friend, Denise, who was flipping steaks. Denise and Laurie had studied biorhythms together for the past week. It was a very California thing to do, but they were having fun. She began to tell Rev a little bit about it and he wanted to know more.

"Really?" she said. "You want to know more? It's not boring?"

"No."

The gates of her enthusiasm were opened. She had been working like an automaton for eight hours, dealing, and it was tiring. Often she wished she had someone to talk to. Usually the people who showed interest in her were hustlers or horny drunks. The energy of her silence was broken: "Imagine," she said excitedly, "that your body has three clocks that keep perfect time, never losing a second. One clock controls your strength, another your mood, and the third your intelligence."

"Sounds good," he said.

"It's been really interesting to work at Harrah's and watch the different moods that gamblers go through. I used to be very moody myself. That's why I thought this would be fun. They cast your chart and the chart tells you when it's a good time for your body to lose weight and so on. It's a combination of astrology, hormonal information, and bullshit. But it's interesting. It's almost as if your body were a large ocean filled with the secrets of the sea. All these waves of perpetual darkness and energy going on at the same time. Denise and I get off on it."

"I used to be a fisherman."

"What else did you do besides being a croupier and a fisherman?" The snow was coming down in a light flurry. The casinos had their lights flickering. Sylvia had taken a phenobarbitol and gone to bed. He had taken a " 'lude" and gone out to drop money on the tables. Rev was relieved to be walking through the snowy night with Laurie. He liked Laurie's physical type. Laurie was almost like a mechanical doll, the way she dealt, the way she smiled, the way she said predictable things. He liked her because there was something of the gambler in him, because every time you fucked someone, there was something of a gamble involved: a gamble if you get it up, a gamble because you were constantly faced with decisions: how to make your first move, how to play your hunches. He didn't need a hand signal to know that Laurie was attracted to him, too. What the hell was a beautiful girl like that doing with Nick Dimani? As soon as he thought that, she looked at him.

"Look," she said, "my break is over. But I'm going to call in sick. Would you like to make love with me at the Fantasy Inn?"

"Sure," he said smiling.

With Rev, it was always easy. He just had to think something and a woman did it for him. That's the way it was all his life. "What's the Fantasy Inn?"

"You'll see," she said. "It just opened. They have Jacuzzi baths, whirlpool baths, adult movies. It's a turn-on. It's a fuck place. They just started here in Tahoe and the guy who built it is already opening another one. It's going to be as big as fast foods. You'll see. You'll like it."

"I'll go for it," he said. They were standing in front of a brown shingled building with a motel sign announcing adult movies. He was suddenly hot.

67. Sylvia and Rev

WALKING BACK to Harrah's in the morning, Rev thought of all the women in his life suddenly taking on a whole new aura in Tahoe. There was Laurie, sleeping in the Fantasy Inn, turning in her dreams of love. He had been passionate with her in the way he had often been with strangers. He had no desire to make love to her again. Sometimes fucking was just a relief for him, something he did out of boredom. Then there was Nancy, who was turned on too. But all of her politics were crazy. She would probably kill herself some day in a demonstration, climbing over a fence. That's what those people always got themselves into: made-up tragedies. It was always South African Day or Hiroshima Day. She would always have a banner: changing the letters for every demonstration. She probably traveled with a huge black banner with felt letters that were pinned or unpinned depending on the event. Sylvia was the one who most aroused him. Her body was the only body that made him feel good. Her breasts excited him. Her thin hips, the way she smelled, the vulnerable way she trusted him, he liked all that and he liked her toughness. She had been through a lot. She had gone into the rock wars and come out stronger than the others. She had broken down and been made whole. It was as if she had forged her personality out of some kind of molten steel that had made her tough. Under the facade of the hip, Sylvia Lundholm was a woman who was so hip she didn't have to prove anything. Under that passion, she was as cool as he was; she was someone who was trying to change her life. He liked that.

His whole life was one change after another. She was trying to get out of the marble, to expose herself to something new. She had written the words to some of America's history. The sixties and seventies had, from time to time, been summed up in her bitter ballads, her gospel wondersongs, her wounding words which had the ring of truth, which told America where it was. Had she been a musician, too, the way Laura Nyro was, or Carly Simon, she could have sat on a boat somewhere in the Greek sea and taken her tape recorder and recorded her visions. But she needed the music half: She was yoked to Nick Dimani. Nick had hooked her into a world in which she would always be an alien. Forever, she'd be tied to the pathology of the music business, to the pathology of the Donald Pond mentality which needed her words to grease the corporation machine. Just as the corporate biggies raided each other's list of artists, he was going to raid Sylvia Lundholm and take her away from Nick Dimani. If he was ever going to get her to be herself, he was going to have to get her away from all that. Suddenly he felt tenderly toward her. He walked away from the diner in the early morning snow to Harrah's. The graveyard shift was still going strong in the hotel. He walked through the glass doors and took the elevator up to her suite. He opened the black mahogany doors that led to her bedroom. She was up. Naked and sleepy, her skin milky and warm. Her hair was braided and she looked almost like a beautiful sea maiden.

"I've become middle-aged since you were gone," she said reaching up to him to put her arms around him. That was the weird thing about her. She didn't care if he was with other women. Or where he went. She was the only woman he knew who never reproached him or asked him what he was doing. Jealousy wasn't a part of her personality. She was too loving for that, too fair for that.

"Welcome back. I love you, Rev. I was thinking about the things you said last night. And you were right. You know what? You're the best friend I've ever had. No one in this bullshit business would ever tell me the truth about anything. One of the things about being on top, so to speak, is that you're surrounded by bourgeois sycophants, liars, people who live off you and make a living from flattery. You're the only person who has the strength to be straight with me. I hope that no matter what happens, we'll be lifelong friends. I want to know you forever."

"I don't see why not," he said in a cool way. He couldn't handle emotion. He was determined not to let her cry. He turned the shower on. As he came out of the shower he stood in front of her drying himself. "I can't stand it anymore," he said.

"I know."

"When are we getting out of here?"

"One more song. I'll just write it and it will be over. I won't go with Nick to Muscle Shoals. I'll let him do all the arrangements without me. He knows what's up. As soon as the party is over, we'll cut out."

"Sounds good."

"Meanwhile, how about Heavenly Valley? Just the two of us? Let's ski this morning. Tomorrow's the party. Then we leave."

"Sounds real good. Just count me out for the party."

"You changed your mind? I want you to come with me."

"All right. I'll let you talk me into it. But then we split."

"We sure as hell do." She looked happier than she had looked in a long time.

They skied together from the top of Heavenly Valley. It was a cold morning and a lot of the locals were skiing. Rev had been one of the best skiers. Athletics came easy to him. Sylvia was good, too. The powdered snow felt good to both of them. The afternoon sun came out. It was a day of white snow and sunshine. At noon they met at the bottom of the lift, stuck their skis in the snow, and sat out in the sunshine drinking apple cider and eating sandwiches. They joined the other skiers in sunbathing and snoozing. Somewhere a car raced in Rev's mind. Things seemed to be going right for a change. All that he knew was that he was going to be leaving Tahoe. He breathed into his lungs the fresh air. It was a good place to ski, but he wouldn't want to stay here. "Move along, move along," something was saying to him. It was the restless, wild feeling that he had always known. He opened his eyes and looked at Sylvia. She had her eyes closed in the sun. There was something heroic about her.

68. *The Sayings of Nancy Chan*

The sayings of Nancy Chan as carefully written out for Sylvia

THERE'S NO REAL LIFE FOR THE POET
IN AMERICA—ONLY LIVING DEATH.

IN THIS WORLD, THE MILITANT
IS AN ANATHEMA,
THE POET A FOOL,
THE ARTIST AN ESCAPIST,
THE WOMAN OF VISION A CRIMINAL.

OUR FIGHT IS TO GET OUT OF THE
MAID AND MADAME MENTALITY;
IF WE WERE TO MAKE THE LEAST EFFORT
IN THAT DIRECTION,
WE WOULD INSPIRE THE WORLD.

SEX WILL HAVE NOTHING TO DO
WITH THE ART OF THE FUTURE.

THE DREAMER WHOSE DREAMS ARE ONLY
UTILITARIAN,
HAS NO PLACE IN THIS WORLD.

69. *Nancy's Departure*

IT WAS snowing lightly. Powdered snow on the Sierras. As Nancy skied, she thought only of the struggle of liberation of Zimbabwe women. She was daydreaming of their black hungry faces while she looked at the powdered snow. "Dear God, Tahoe's beginning to get on my nerves," she said. Nancy was standing with Rev and Sylvia at the foot of Heavenly Valley where the first cable lift begins. It was late Saturday morning and hundreds of skiers in their waterproof ski suits and their knit caps carrying skis over their shoulders stood waiting to get on the tram which would lift them up the mountain. It all seemed to Nancy to be like one of those great panoramas by Hieronymus Bosch—the peasants with their flushed faces, the pointed red caps, the jolly people waiting for nothing in particular, for Icarus to fall from the sky. "As much as I like to ski, I'm tired of Squaw Valley and Alpine Meadows and Kirkwood. I've skied Northstar and Mt. Rose and I'm getting ready to split. I've too much work to do. The ski resort world seems so stupid," Nancy said.

"Stay another day," Sylvia begged. She felt suddenly lost. Being with Nancy made everything else bearable.

"There's no reason why I should stay," Nancy said. "You're all right without me."

The two women watched Rev as he walked to the car. He was going to ski Incline Village. He waved good-bye to both of them. "Why don't we go to Christianna's?" Sylvia asked. It was a lodge nearby.

"Very good."

Sylvia went to the bar and ordered each of them an Irish coffee. There was a fire in the main lodge. Sylvia sat at the bar and waited for Nancy, who was warming her feet and reading *Southern Africa,* a magazine published by the South Africa Collective. She had had all her mail forwarded to Sylvia and through her magazines Sylvia was keeping up with some of the events in the Third World. She had written out a check for five thousand dollars for Nancy to use in any way she found necessary. It was to come out of the *Playing Tahoe* advance—which she hadn't received yet—but it was needed immediately—Nancy made that clear. And the check was written.

"I'll miss you," Sylvia said.

"There's so much for me to do," Nancy laughed. "First, I'm going back to New York to work on the apartheid situation. They have an insatiable need for cheap labor in order to fuel their economy and ensure continued high profits. The apartheid policies have diminished women's economic productivity. Most of the women work as domestics for whites. Many work illegally. If a domestic worker is living with her children in a township, she will have to leave them at a very early hour, only returning home very late at night. After she has spent the day cleaning the large house of her 'madam,' cooking for the children, generally attending to their needs, doing laundry, she will return home to her tiny impoverished quarters to find food, often unsuccessfully, for her own children, feed them out of her own pathetic salary, and fall asleep exhausted. Her energies are directed to the home of her employer. She has no home of her own. If she is a 'sleep in' domestic, she will only have more restrictions placed on her life. She will never be able to have a husband or lover stay in her room for even one night; neither can her children ever live with her. A woman who breaks the rules runs the risk of being caught in one of the regular police raids on domestic workers' quarters and jeopardizing her job. But this oppression has not been accepted passively. Shortly before the twentieth anniversary of the Pretoria Women's March another march took place in South Africa. This time it was Soweto women—among them were the children and grandchildren of the Pretoria protestors. The police responded with guns and an uprising spread throughout the country. Over a thousand women and students were killed on the streets before the resistance was subdued by the white police. The only possibility for real change, Sylvia, lies in the complete abolition of apartheid. That I, as a Third World woman, and as a militant, have a special role in this process should be obvious. I understand how black women have to face not only repressive laws but grave cultural difficulties. The struggle, I believe, can be won. It's my struggle too."

"When did you first become a militant?" Sylvia asked, "When you left Sarah Lawrence?"

"No. I think it was when I was a child. My family was a wealthy Chinese family in Hong Kong living in the colonial society that still exists there. I saw how women were treated, how they existed to serve the men. The women also served the 'madams.' It was 'amah' and 'madam'—the Chinese were loathed. 'Dogs and Chinese Keep Out.' I saw signs like that. It's only been in the past fifteen years, however, that I've become aware of what was needed from me. I must say that as a Third World woman, I understand how the Africans have been made into nonpersons. I want to devote the next part of my life to resistance of apartheid —especially to helping South African women. That—and my work on *Issues* and the Committee on South African War Resistance—is just part of my work. You see, that's why I have to leave."

"Do you ever feel lonely?"

"Never," Nancy laughed. "All of the people who work with me in the collective are like my sisters and brothers. I've put away all thoughts of a personal life and I don't miss it at all. It's the Chinese in me. I come from a big family."

"I hope I can help you with more than funds."

"We need everything. People. Stamps. People to work in boycotts. Investigative reporters. There's a case against the Space Research Corporation which has been building for a few months which shows that the corporation may be partially a subsidiary of the South African government as well as an arms supplier to the apartheid regime. Space Research is the American-Canadian defense contractor located on the Vermont-Quebec border that has been discovered smuggling long-range Howitzer shells and a sophisticated artillery system to South Africa in violation of the U.N. arms embargo against Pretoria. It's as if we were sending gas to the gas chambers of Auschwitz and the gas factory transaction was being orchestrated by the First Pennsylvania Bank. It's all madness. The first thing I'm doing when I get back to New York is to work on a sit-in at Princeton University, a nonviolent sit-in at Firestone Library. To get them to take their funds out of Citibank. Citibank invests in South Africa despite the embargos."

"And then?"

"London and work on the next copy of *Issues.*"

"And then?"

"I'm off to Namibia. Amsterdam. The Washington Office on Africa. Collaboration with other organizations, speaking, writing, sit-ins, and so forth. There's much to be done."

"I wish I was going with you," Sylvia said.

"Why don't you come? You're an adventurer."

"I have some things to finish first."

"Such as?"

"The Revson question. He has something to teach me that I haven't yet learned. And I feel that if I stay with him it will help me."

"Do you really think it will be fruitful?"

"Yes."

"How? He's not political."

"He's probably where people will be at one day when they're free. I think of him as being *liberated*—your word —in almost every way."

"But if he's not involved in the struggle, what good is that?"

"He is. In his own way."

"Suit yourself. I think you're wasting your time with him. Part of the reason I came with you, besides the need for funding, was to talk to you about the struggle. How I think you have to pledge yourself to something more than your own personal creativity."

"I will."

Nancy ordered another drink.

"I know you sense that I slept with Rev. I didn't mean to hurt or offend you. I hope you understand that," Nancy said impassively.

"You haven't hurt me. I love you both very much. And his body is his own. And his life is his own. He's never tried to be dishonest with me. Whatever we have, it goes beyond the personal. We are friends."

"That's good. By the way, I do care for you, Sylvia."

She looked at the Chinese woman whose face seemed to have all of the marks of intelligence, humanity, and suffering. She wanted to tell her how much she loved her back. But it was hard to find the words. They had known each other for so long. Sylvia ordered another Irish coffee and they drank to the revolution.

70. *Lounge Act*

I told her I was a flop with chicks,
I been this way since 1956,
She looked at my palm and she made a magic sign,
She said, 'What you need is
Love Potion Number Nine.'

SOME DUDE, a country-western boy imitating Elvis, was singing "Love Potion Number Nine" in the lounge. No one was really listening. Still, the song was putting people out of their sexual misery. Whoever I am, he was thinking, and you're going to know someday, I'm going to make it. Nostalgia—I don't remember anything. I'm too young, but I'm hip. High on grass, amyl nitrate, Spanish fly, girls, drive-in movies. Ski Kirkwood, ski down Heavenly Valley, doing everyone a favor. Feel embarrassed, standing here, nobody listening, everyone talking. Hate the smoke, the dirty little cigarettes and smoke. You don't know who I am, but I have private dreams of glory. This uncontrollable frenzy I learned from the movies. Grew up on them movies, they taught me magic and how to be famous. All I ever wanted was to get out of South Dakota and be free. Someday I'm going to be a movie star, maybe make my mother proud. Then everyone will have to admit that I was quite a performer. Watching television, going to church, pop music, rock and roll. Locked with girls in back seats, rode dirt bikes, got high. And one day learned to play guitar, watched Elvis, quite a fable. Want to be kinetic and outrageous, want to be someone famous. Not just a greaser, teased into performing, some one real. No zero. Sometimes frightened I won't make it. All these rich guys watch me nightly. Some agent one day. Packed my clothes and left one morning. Mama crying, the old man wanted me to study something. Be a professional, a dentist or something. Fuck that. I'm going to be famous.

Lionel was pouting. And drinking Perrier. Brooding about Sylvia. And the party.

"You are definitely too high cock," Thimble said. They were having a drink at Harrah's lounge bar. The hotel swarmed with gamblers; the two men sat outside the lounge. The lounge act stinks, thought Thimble. Thimble was getting high. After three vodka martinis, Thimble could forget that Lionel was square.

"What does that mean?" Lionel asked.

"High cock?" (Lionel thought, The boy's not bad. Bad voice. Good body.)

"It means someone who is too classy. For example, at Harvard, I'm sure they taught you to love chamber music. Cultural things. Chamber music is very high cock."

"What else?" Lionel thought sitting with Thimble was amusing. It was much better than trying to pick up hookers. Thimble was vaguely a hooker, but at least his voice was intelligent. Thimble had a deep, strong voice, the voice of an aristocrat. "High cock is all those cultural things you do in New York, Lionel. Funding the American Dance Theater. José Limón is very high cock. Or contributing to the 'Wilderness Foundation.' Very high cock, indeed. And off-off Broadway, those plays you drag me to where people pause between speeches because they really don't remember the lines, those small drafty theaters where everyone studied at one point with Marcel Marceau. Very high cock. Anything boring is high cock. Culturally boring. That's your life, Lionel. Very high cock." Thimble laughed his special laugh. Half laugh, half giggle.

"What else?" (Lionel wondered if the boy was straight.)

"Well, if you're a writer and you say, 'I don't care if this sells,' that's high cock. Or if you only watch Channel Thirteen, that's high cock. People who constantly refer to the *New York Review of Books,* that's high cock."

A fat woman sitting next to them drinking a Tequila Sunrise interrupted them. She was fat. Lionel loathed fat people. God was she fat! "Excuse me," she said. Thimble wondered if he had offended her. He was prepared to offer his apologies. Lionel was repulsed by her. Trying desperately to be seductive, she turned toward Lionel. Her breasts were enormous powder kegs. "High cock in Los Angeles means something else," she said. "It means smartass. Just the opposite. You know? Los Angeles people say 'high cock' when they mean some ass who is just trying to impress you." Crossing one fat leg over the other, she returned to her drink. Lionel could barely look at her.

"Well, you see how semantics differ from coast to coast?" Thimble giggled, and ordered another vodka martini. He at least was having fun. "A mink coat is not high cock. A mink lining is. Having lunch at Lutece is high cock. Lunch at Le Cirque is low cock." What made Lionel so square, he wondered.

"What's low cock?" Lionel asked.

"Oh God, I'm low cock. Low cock is stud. Low cock is

vulgar. Low cock is Passaic, New Jersey, and a Cadillac convertible. Rev Cranwell is high cock trying to be low cock. Nick Dimani is low cock trying to be high cock. Harrah's is low cock. Tahoe is high cock. The rock industry is low cock. Goddard Lieberson was high cock. *People* Magazine is low cock. That book you're reading, *Nim: A Chimpanzee Who Learned Sign Language,* that's high cock. The Skip Barber Racing School is low cock. Squaw Valley is high cock. Kirkwood is low cock." What was the use? Lionel had no sense of humor. None. Thimble sipped his drink. The bartender was low cock, he thought.

"Sylvia? Is she high cock?"

"Definitely. Sylvia loves all those intellectual things you do. *The Collected Poems of W. H. Auden,* isn't that the book she reads at the ski lodge while everyone else is drinking Irish coffee and trying to get laid? She worships Thomas Mann. Very high cock. She goes on walking tours. She plays racquet ball and squash. Very high cock sports. She told me she spent a year writing a play called 'The Sabbath of Witches.' She believes in laissez-faire. And serves tea in her celebrity suite. She's always praising such things as 'the life of fantasy'—Sylvia, my darling, is very high cock. She must have learned all that in that fancy Swedish school she told me she went to. The boarding school where they taught her to speak English with that slight accent so peculiar to high cock people. They always speak as if they were from a foreign country even though they are American."

"You speak that way, Ron."

"I'm just trying."

"Would you like another drink?" (Who was that boy? The one imitating Presley? Lionel wondered.)

"No thanks. I'm dreading this party you've put me in charge of."

"Why?" (Nice ass. Lionel always looked at a small ass.)

"I can't decide whether the party should be high cock or low cock. It's a terrible decision."

"High cock," Lionel said. (Was the boy a borderline homosexual?)

"Smoked salmon? The best wines? The A list?"

"Exactly. Let's invite the Dollar family, Dollar Steamships."

"High cock means no photographer."

"That's going too far."

"Okay, we'll have Lady Jean, The Cushings, Mick Jagger, The Smiths, Dodson. Betty. Patti Smith. Balanchine. William Styron. All very high cock. Argyle tablecloths. Leiber and Stoller. Donald Pond—high cock."

"Do me a favor—surprise me," Lionel said.

"That," said Thimble, "is very high cock." Thimble knew he was too high. But he was proud that he had actually made up a game. He could play High Cock, Low Cock forever. Slowly he slid from his seat and walked to the men's room. Lionel sat alone at the bar watching the lounge act. The boy sure could sing and wiggle his ass. Lionel made a note to send for the boy when he got to his room. The boy looked like someone who needed help. It was amazing how helping someone's career could get you anything. That. And cash. Lionel listened to the lyrics. *Poor Elvis is turning in his grave,* he thought to himself, and paid the check.

71. *Chopper*

THE SNOW falls. The gamblers gamble. Harrah's stands in the dark. More than a hotel, it juts out of the wilderness like a snowbound immigrant that is made out of something other than flesh. Made out of lights. *It is a mountain in itself,* Lionel thought whenever he returned. Yes, Harrah's at Lake Tahoe is a castle amalgamated by lights, casinos, tourists, restaurants, pools, gift stores, boutiques, dealers, bellboys, waiters, entertainers, a huge square box rising in the snow, rising out of the mountains. Its logo (thought up by some clever PR firm hired by Harrah) is "Come to life." Its publicity, which reaches out to the world, announces, "This time really get away. Put yourself in the most luxurious hotel in the West. There are incredible shows to see and colorful places to visit. Harrah's is alive with activity."

However, Lionel Colesman got tired of Harrah's easily. It wasn't a bad place at night, he thought, but during the day it was deadly. Lionel needed action during the daytime. It was bad enough that Sylvia Lundholm was avoiding him. He saw her from time to time when he visited her for brief moments of business, but she was always shadowed by the Bronx car salesman and at night she always went to sleep early. At night in his dreams he could possess and love her. Love for him was essential, and even though she avoided contact with him, he imagined kissing her breasts, being in a room with her as she walked naked in her fishnet stockings and black bra and high heels. He imagined her making love to him. But the more he desired her, the more he lived in a dream world and the more he felt alone. It was a loneliness that no deal, no other man or woman, no lover could extinguish. And it centered upon a vast self-love. He was an emperor seeking pleasure and never really finding it.

One day he woke up and decided to ski. He had watched like a boy enchanted with winter, the snow falling during the night. He had seen the snowflakes come out of the black Tahoe sky, the night sky filled with stars as white and distant as snowflakes that were beyond reach. And that morning he telephoned Sylvia Lundholm in her suite in Harrah's Hotel and asked her to ski with him. She agreed. And he felt elated.

"I don't feel like skiing today," she said in her soft voice, which seemed almost always to be on the verge of affection. "But if it pleases you, Lionel, I'd like to very much."

Suddenly, Lionel felt joy, the way he felt when he made

a fortune. Sylvia! He would be spending a whole day with her. Immediately he put together a ski party.

The very rich when they ski Tahoe don't bother with ski lifts or rope tows or the common lot of skiers in red knit caps and mittens. No. Lionel could afford a helicopter. Which is a different way to ski. The mountain is packed. The helicopter drops you into a fragrance of winter that has no footprints, no ski tracks, but a mountain of powdered snow. It's a nice way to ski and one that few people can afford. But Lionel could afford anything.

And so, Lionel Colesman spent an hour on the phone, lying in his enormous bed, arranging the details. A helicopter was rented for two thousand dollars, a chopper with a pilot who was an old friend. A private instructor was also rented, and carefully Lionel chose the best instructor, Steve, from Heavenly Valley. He had been a downhill racer and a hot-dog champion. A local photographer was rented to capture the day in pictures. And to promote his image, a picnic basket filled with Beluga caviar (which Sylvia liked) and Dom Perignon champagne. He made sure a brook trout, a salmon, a sea bass, and some tile fish were included as he heard that the car salesman liked fish and so did Sylvia. He prepared the activity for the day—powder skiing, then lunch, then another hour-long ski, then back to the hotel. No point in making it too long a day.

The party of six entered the chopper. The photographer took pictures of everything: the captain, Lionel, Sylvia, Rev, and Nick. He had to invite Nick. And indeed, the ski party was as much for Nick as it was for Sylvia. He had made up his mind to announce to the press that the party he was giving at Harrah's was *for* Nick Dimani. "Why the hell are you doing that?" Thimble had asked.

"You really are getting on my nerves," Lionel shot back. That was the night before. No wonder he had a hangover.

"Because let me remind you, Lionel, that you hate Nick Dimani. So why make a party for *him?*"

"Because I own his catalogue. Is that enough of a reason?"

"Not for me."

"Because I want to show the world that I'm pleased, really pleased, that Arthur Morris is producing the album independently. What do I care? I have the catalogue. I have the next album. It's only money."

"I see your point," Thimble said.

"That's good," Lionel said with his catlike smile. Behind the smile was an angry question. Why was Thimble so stupid? Lionel had promised himself to avoid dumb people. And yet, Thimble was dumb. Really dumb. He had taste, but he was dumb about business. All this crap about high cock and low cock. He had nurtured Thimble with cash and affection and what was the point? He was dumb. And annoying.

"What are you doing tomorrow?" he remembered asking Thimble.

"Driving to Squaw," Thimble had said, "with Steve McQueen."

Bullshit, just bullshit, Lionel thought to himself. Steve McQueen wouldn't be caught dead with Ron Thimble. That left him free, though, to pursue Sylvia. Thimble's grotesque show of affection in public would upset everything. Lionel thought of all this as he entered the chopper. It was going to be a wonderful day. Karen was playing chess. Thimble was in Squaw Valley. He would be exiled on a mountaintop with Sylvia. As the chopper descended on the mountain he found time to be alone with her.

"I love you, Sylvia," he wanted to say. He wanted to tell her how she was the only person who attracted him. How his wife bored him. How his family ignored him. How tired he was of money. And fags. Especially Ron Thimble. He wanted to be the Lionel he used to be with her, to talk to her about W.H. Auden, to quote his poetry to her as he once had done, to tell her that in dreams she was a vision who touched his legs, his thighs, who made his whole body come to life. The mountain was like a glacier.

It was cold. Even the ski instructor admitted that it was a raw day. Lionel watched sadly as Rev and Nick skied down the mountain, competing against each other. Lionel was amused. Sylvia looked at her book and stayed in the chopper.

"What are you reading now?" Lionel asked. As he came close to her, he could smell her breath, her perfume.

"Auden. As in the old days. 'Law Like Love' is still my favorite poem."

"Read it to me."

"All of it?" She laughed.

"Just the beginning."

She read:

"Law, say the gardeners, is the sun,
Law is the one
All gardeners obey
To-morrow, yesterday, to-day.

Law is the wisdom of the old,
The impotent grandfathers shrilly scold;
The grandchildren put out a treble tongue,
Law is the senses of the young."

She skipped the middle verses and continued reading to him, dutifully, in her soft voice:

"Like love we don't know where or why
Like love we can't compel or fly
Like love we often weep
Like love we seldom keep."

"Why does that poem mean so much to you?"

"I read it at college. At Sarah Lawrence. I think it was the first poem I read in my life that I responded to. It made me realize that poems could have periods in the middle of lines. And it made me realize that poems could be as real as real speech."

"Didn't you meet Auden?"

"Yes."

"When was that?"

"After I met Nick and left college, I was at a party in the Village. There I met Auden's lover. He liked me. And invited me to visit both of them in their apartment on St. Mark's Place. I was afraid to go. I was so awed. I called the night before to cancel my appointment, hoping to speak to my friend. Instead, Auden answered the phone. He said, with his English accent in a very gruff voice, 'Whoever you are, young lady, you are calling too late at night and you have disturbed me.' The next day I showed up at the exact time I had promised to come. His lover was in the kitchen. I was admitted to the house by Auden himself. I was amazed that the house was so dirty. And poor. For some reason, I had imagined that Auden was very neat and rich. I tried not to show how disappointed I was that he lived in a mess.

" 'Don't mind the flat,' he said. 'Our house in Vienna is so much nicer.' And he led me into the living room. I was almost able to forget the dirt by looking around and reminding myself that within those walls, amid the dirt, dust, books, rags, and broken furniture, lived the world's greatest poet. His face was very lined. It was almost as if it were a piece of ripe fruit that had shriveled up and was completely dry. He had wrinkles everywhere, bags hung over his eyes. He was the best-looking person I had ever seen. He was King Lear. He was the gardener. How nice his welcome really was. He brought some flowers over to me. He sat me down across from him. 'Now tell me, young woman, whoever you are, who is your favorite writer?'

"I looked at him, afraid to say the truth."

"What were you afraid of?" Lionel asked.

"Saying the wrong person."

"What happened?"

"I said shyly, 'Colette.' "

"And?"

"Then a strange thing happened. He came over to me and kissed me lightly on the forehead. 'That's my favorite writer too,' he said. After that we became great friends. I worshiped him until the day he died. Know a lot of his work by heart. In many ways, he had more of an influence on my lyrics than anyone else. He rhymed beautifully, you know."

"I know."

Oh Rev, get me out of here, Sylvia thought at once. Lionel looked from the chopper down the mountain. It was a perfect afternoon and he wished it could stretch into endless time. Even though it was cold, the sun was out. He sat on the top of the mountain with Sylvia. They ate lunch together and shared a timid similarity. Only with sadness did he see the skiers return. There was too much ambiguity in Sylvia for him to feel that she cared for him. But for the first time he felt happy with her. That happiness was worth the trip to Tahoe.

72. *Laurie's Breakaway*

LAURIE WAS leaving Harrah's. She dreaded telling her mother. Right before the holidays, the snow came down. The two women, mother and daughter, faced each other across the dining room table in the log cabin. A fire was crackling red and orange and blue, warming the house.

"Whosoever committeth sin transgresseth also the law: for sin is the transgression of the law. And ye know that he was manifested to take away our sins, and in him is no sin. Whoever abideth in him, sinneth not."

"Mother, stop that."

"Don't tell me to stop saying God's word. This is the Soul-Winner's New Testament. Praise be to God. *Little children, let no man deceive you.*" Laurie looked out the window. She saw the snow falling. She would miss Tahoe. She would always come back. Her mind wandered to Paris, where she and Nick would live. Not all the time. "One can't always be on a boat. One has to have roots," Nick said. And Nick had promised her an apartment in Paris. He had promised to buy her a beautiful apartment on the Île Saint-Louis. She had never been to Paris, but he had played there and performed there so many times that he knew Paris as well as a Parisian, he had told her. Looking at the snow, Laurie imagined going with Nick on the Bateau Mouche. He had told her so many times how he loved that boat, leaving from the Pont de l'Alma and eating French food while one sailed around the city down the Seine. She was secretly decorating her apartment in her mind. She would have only antiques. What fun it would be to walk down the tiny streets on the Left Bank and go with Nick to buy chandeliers with delicate crystal, desks with pegs instead of nails, billowy French fabrics to cover delicate chairs; she would make Nick a home filled with plants, antiques, Mozart, paintings by Picasso. She would spend her time making herself beautiful and arranging candlelit parties for his friends. She would give him all the attention and love he no longer found with his wife. She would construct a world of such joy and beauty that he would stay with her forever, even if they were not married. She would be the mistress of Nick Dimani and wear high-heeled shoes and low-cut dresses of the finest velvet and she would study French with a tutor. She knew that she would make him very happy. She would be his mistress in bed, his hostess in the salon, and his closest friend. She imagined herself typing letters for him on a small Olivetti portable typewriter that looked out on the Seine from their window on the Île Saint Louis. The happiness she felt inside her body was almost too much to be contained.

To be twenty-one and live in Paris with a great composer —to have all the money in the world to spend on objects of art—what more could any woman want?

"What are you thinking, Laurie?"

"I'm thinking of Nick. Our future."

"Child, there is no future with Nick. It's a sin for you to see him. He's a man with a family, don't you understand?"

"No. I don't understand, Mother."

"Stand free. 'Adultery, fornication, uncleanness, lasciviousness, idolatry, witchcraft, hatred, variance, emulations . . . drunkenness, revellings, and such like: of that which I tell you before, as I have also told you in time past, that they which do such things shall not inherit the kingdom of God.' Galatians. Think. Read your Bible."

"Mother, I love him."

"Don't give to him what you should give to God, Laurie. The fruit of the spirit is love, joy, peace. Long-suffering gentleness, goodness, faith."

"I love him."

"Don't run wild, I beg of you. You are all I have. I raised you to be a good Christian woman, Laurie. I gave up my life for you."

"I know, Mom. And I appreciate it."

"Do you, Laurie? Do you appreciate the years when I worked at night with you in a carriage next to me? When I worked during the day in the shop and as a cashier at night to keep you with me? After your daddy died, I could have sent you to a foster home. Or to live with my folks, who wanted you so badly. But I said, 'No—she's my baby. If I have to scrub floors, I'm keeping her with me.' And I raised you to love God, to be a good girl, and look at you now, how beautiful you are, and how honest you are. The pit boss at Harrah's told me you're the finest dealer they have. Neatly dressed. Always punctual. Smart. You're going to go places, Laurie."

"I'm no different than the other girls there. Everyone is neatly dressed. Everyone is punctual. You have to be or you lose your job. And that's what I have to tell you, Mom. I'm leaving. I'm leaving Harrah's."

"Your job? You're leaving your job?" Suddenly the older woman stood up from the table and threw up her hands. "Why me, God? Why me, God?" She began to cry.

"Sit down, Mother," Laurie said. "Let me tell you without your being hysterical."

Laurie pulled her mother's arm. The older woman sat down. She was holding her small Bible, holding it as if it would *change* what her daughter had just said. She carried the King James Bible with her everywhere. It was her home. Her protection. Her armor. God was her armor. She knew He would not let her down. Laurie would change her ways.

"Mother, you live in a stained-glass world. Every little piece of your world is sealed in lead. Just like the beautiful stained-glass windows in the cathedral. You live in the world of yellow and orange and blue glass. With sun streaming through the glass. A world of prisms and light."

"I live with God," she said.

"I live in another world, Mom. It's not a stained-glass world, but it's a world where things happen to me that I am so grateful for. I'm grateful to God for Nick. He's going to take me away from the casino."

Laurie's mother rose to her feet like a majestic oracle. She opened her Soul-Winner's New Testament. And she began to quote, although she knew the phrases by heart, her favorite passages. She was puffed up as a priest fattened by the words of God: " 'For every high priest taken from among men is ordained for men in things pertaining to God, that he may offer both gifts and sacrifices for sins. Who can have compassion on the innocent and them that are out of the way, for that he himself also is compassed with infirmity and being made perfect, he became the author of eternal salvation unto all them that obey him. Praise the Lord to bring eternal life.' Amen. Oh help me, God," she added and sat down. Tears came down her face.

"Mother, Harrah's is an honest casino. I've loved working there. But there's a secrecy I can't stand. I'm always being watched. It's just like the FBI. Everything you do is always on film. Nobody knows who is watching you, but a pit administrator reports to a manager and a manager reports to a casino manager who reports to a hotel manager. I'm watched constantly. And something else—it's good money, Mom, but there's no future for me there. You've always wanted something better for me."

"That's true."

"I'm tired of being a dealer. Nick offers me so much, Mother. I'm crazy about him."

"I know."

"Being a dealer can be so boring. It's good money. But where is it leading?"

"Yes, child. But Nick, it's a sin what you're doing. Couldn't you find some nice Christian man?"

"No nice Christian man plays blackjack. Where am I going to meet someone I like in Tahoe?"

"Your friends have. Look at Margie. And Laura. They're married."

"Margie's married to a *shoe salesman,* Mother."

"What's wrong with selling shoes? It's honest."

"Mother, if I promise to go to church, will you stop nagging me about Nick? You're ruining my happiness."

"What is happiness now is heartbreak later on." And then she lifted her head and whispered, "Oh God, save my child."

"Don't aggravate yourself, Mom, life is too short."

Laurie went to her room. It was cold, but she was excited about shopping. The next day was her day off. Nick had given her three thousand dollars to buy herself something —anything she wanted—for Christmas. She had already gone to all the boutiques and she now knew exactly what she wanted. In Harrah's, in the gift shop, there was a white marabou coat. All feathery and soft. She had tried it on. It made her look like a swan. She had picked out beautiful golden sandals and white mesh stockings, a long white angora strapless dress with silvery straps. She was prepared to spend her money all at once. The clothes would cost two thousand dollars. She was putting one thousand in the bank. She was excited by the idea of looking beautiful. The next time she saw Nick, she was going to go out with him in public for the first time. He was taking her to see the show at the Sahara. They would be joined by two of Nick's friends, and she knew she was supposed to look as if she belonged with them. It didn't matter. She loved Nick. He was her new family, her lover, her friend, and her brother. The love she had once imagined she would find suddenly was there inside of her, for Nick. She would devote her life to him. All the time she had Nick on her mind. She thought about him constantly. She loved him for his weaknesses as well as for his strengths. She knew he had been *through* everything. That was why she loved him so much. He was the essence of the troubadour. He was seeking out sounds from the wilderness. He was a genius. He had been through the drug culture; he had suffered pain; he had survived. That was what she wanted to be: one of the great survivors of her own time. The thing that was so important to her about Nick was that he was musically innovative. He had written melodies that were sung by every big band in America. From acid rock to hard rock to punk rock. His ballads had sounds nobody else had. He was a classical artist. With Sylvia, he had created music which could define people's lives. She loved making love with him. She just loved him.

Nick was not in a good mood. Sylvia was having trouble writing that last song. Morris was getting anxious. If Nick didn't have all the tracks laid down in a week, he could forget it. Morris was calling him every day. He had booked the studio at Muscle Shoals. Morris was a pussycat if you didn't cross him, but if you didn't have every song perfect when you walked in that studio, you could just forget having Morris produce them. That last song had to be as good as all the rest. Sylvia had written a song called "Ice Days" about making love in the snow, but it hadn't worked. The song was now about death. It could be the best song they had ever written together, but it needed more work. Her song about the lake, about how people who drowned in the lake were never found because it was so cold, was a little morbid. Did he really want two songs about death on the album? With her talent, she could write a lyric in two minutes. She just didn't feel like writing now. "I'm having a difficult moment," she said the day before.

"Fuck you! I'm having a difficult moment too," he had screamed. "If I don't give Morris twelve fucking great songs, there's no album." Nick was not in a good mood.

Laurie's mother fell on her knees before bed and prayed to Jesus. But Laurie? She lay covered by a feathery quilt, as excited as she had ever been in her life. Laurie could see the hundred dollar bills lying in her drawer, the fresh green bills that Nick had given her. They almost seemed to have a special unreal quality, like little green passports to every place she had ever dreamed of going, to everything she ever wanted. In her mind, before sleep, she spent the dollars over and over again. Shoes, stockings, garter straps, lacy underwear made out of imported lace, all these things were sold at the boutiques in the large hotels. She had never been able to afford them before and they turned over and over in her mind as if they had a life of their own. It seemed that in her dreams she could hear her mother telling her to be a good Christian, speaking from behind the stained glass. *"Be not deceived; God is not mocked: for whatsoever a man soweth, that shall he also reap."* The strangeness of things stirred in her night soul, and she tossed her blond hair from side to side, knowing that even if Nick was without a cent, even if she never lived in Paris, even if she was to spend her whole life just holding him close to her at the Fantasy Inn, she would love him anyway.

"What is it about sex that binds people so closely to-gether?" she had once asked him, and he had stroked her hair.

"You're so young," he had said with such tenderness that she had wept on his shoulder.

"Sex is such a bond," she had said then, not ever guess-ing that the unity that she would feel with Nick would be the strongest emotion of her life, one that would guide her to leave home, the familiar surroundings of the casino where she was liked, even to leave the wrinkled earth and ice-capped mountains of Lake Tahoe, where she had been born. Her zone of feeling had a depth that she had not ever known before she made love with Nick Dimani. It was as if he had taken her from the top of the ocean, which was her life, and dropped her into that secret place of perpetual darkness where only mysterious things hap-pened that were beyond a woman's control. Certainly all the crushes she had in high school, the Tahoe boys who drove old cars, wore jeans and cowboy boots, and screamed "Yippeee!" out of the windows of their fathers' scratched and banged and mud-splashed Fords and Toy-otas, those boys with baby faces and unshaven chins, those boys as intellectual as young cows—certainly those expe-riences with the other townies were nothing compared to what she felt, now, for Nick Dimani. Although she was often frustrated by despair, knowing he would never leave his wife officially, she had constructed a structure in her mind in which she could be with him always. And in some graceful way, as she lay in her bed, she knew that although she now lived in a log cabin that resembled a shack, on the wrong side of the tracks, with her life poisoned by her mother's Christianity and hate, soon she would erase all this, the way an artist erases a line of charcoal with his thumb. Soon she would live in a world of music and privi-leges as the love of Nick Dimani. For she knew he loved her. She knew he loved her with all his soul. She thanked God that he was not like the other, lesser men. The prob-lems that she had with Nick Dimani—Rita, the children, the marriage, his drug problem, the demands on his time, other women, his temper—these became as disregarded as the snow falling gently on the path to her mother's house. She knew she would have to shovel away the snow in the morning. But it didn't matter. She had built her life. It was to be, she knew this, bone to bone, lip to lip with Nick.

Like any narcissist, Nick stood in front of the huge mirror of his bathroom in Harrah's villa as if it were an altar. Holding his black electric razor, he shaved carefully, knowing that this was an important evening. He wondered, vaguely, where Rita was. He had gone into her bedroom that afternoon and she had been sleeping. The separateness of their lives had once pleased him. Now it depressed him. She was probably at the State Line Bar drinking beer with all the town kids and ski instructors. He couldn't be angry that she hung out with these kids. He didn't really blame her for preferring to be with the beautiful and young people in Tahoe. Look at Laurie. She was only twenty-one. What's good for the goose is good for the— as he shaved, he remembered her saying that. "What's good for the goose is good for the gander." Was this the life that he had planned? Luckily, the children knew nothing about all of this. They had no idea their parents were swingers. They had been brought up in England and America knowing manners. They were young ladies. "Whatever happens, the children must never know," was the first and last commandment of his life. "Protect the children," was the old Hebrew belief, the love of family, sewn into his brain with a suture that could never be broken. Rita was challenging him. He had only one choice. To leave her. Or to protect her from herself. He could help her. She needed his help. Perhaps after the *Playing Tahoe* album was finished, they could take a vacation together. Make love again. Once he had loved making love to her. When she was undressed, she was so very lovely. He remembered her as a young girl and suddenly he felt frozen in the sadness of things. He would not let himself think about the past. He would take the present and control it.

Nick did not like picking Laurie up at her house. To begin with, his Porsche often got stuck in the snow. He refused to put snow chains on his cars. But that wasn't the real reason. He had once picked up Laurie in his brown Rolls-Royce and her mother had come out of the house and thrown a cabbage at the car. It had been humiliating. A cabbage. He had never gone there again. Instead, he met Laurie at the bar in the Sahara. She was sitting there waiting for him drinking a gin fizz. When he saw her he got hot. As simply as that. He was still very attracted to her. Just looking at how innocent she was, she was more attractive, damn it, she was the best-looking piece of ass he had ever had in his life. She looked more like a showgirl than a dealer, although all of the dealers at Harrah's were turn-ons or they wouldn't have the job, would they? Suddenly, he felt another attack of guilt. How was he going to tell her? He had rehearsed in front of the mirror, holding his black shaver as if it were a microphone, the way he was going to tell her. He had to tell her. It wouldn't be kind to lead her on, and he was a kind person. He knew it was important to be *good*. Would he have so many fans if he wasn't *good*? He didn't want to hurt anyone. He didn't want to hurt her. He wanted to be kind. She was young and vulnerable. He knew that. Now, when he looked in her eyes, he saw so much affection, so much love. He felt the way a butcher felt looking at an animal before slaughter. He knew he had to tell her his plans. The question was, how? The best thing to do was to be loving. Above all, *no hassle.* That was the other commandment after, Protect the Children. The other commandment was, Thou Shalt Not Be Hassled. He would find a way. He had unloaded plenty of broads before. This would not be easy. But he could do it. He had to. For her sake. But he wanted to fuck her first. Before the hassle. She might not be such a great lay after he'd told her. They never were.

73. *Laurie's Bebop*

I HATE *you, Mother,* Laurie wanted to say. But did she hate her? Not really. She needed her and loved her. Ever since childhood, she had lived under the unhappy idea that her mother belonged to Jesus and the beauty parlor. And not to her. More than that, when she was growing up she wanted what she had called a mommy-mommy. A mommy like the other mommies. "And what is that?"

"Someone who stays home and cooks."

"Child, that's not what a mother is. A father is water. A mother is blood. A mother is someone who loves her child. God blessed me with a beautiful baby girl and when your father died, I decided I would bring you up and give you what I never had, a home filled with joy. All the tools to go out and fight the world, the shield of knowledge, the great armor of an education. I would instruct you and give you guidance. And all of this costs money. So honey, you know your mommy has to work for a living. God decides and woman provides." And so her mother polished nails, put on hair cream to straighten curls, smiled as she applied permanents that stunk to high heaven; her mother was Queen of the Curlers, the Duchess of Hairdryers, the Catherine the Great of Sets and Blow-Drys, the Empress of Hairdos. Laurie had grown up in the shadow of an enormous hairpin. She had remembered when she was four, "b.p."—before parlor. Those were the days of cuddles and kisses and perambulators. Later, her mother worked so hard she seemed to see her only at dinnertime or when she knelt in church. And then? She had grown up loving freedom. Her values were so different from her mom's values.

"Why do you need Nick?" her mother asked. "It's a sin to commit adultery, darling, and God doesn't smile on cheats and liars."

"God doesn't smile on me," Laurie answered.

"What do you mean, darling?"

"You think God intended me to stay home at night? You think God intended me to be jailed in this shack with you as my keeper? Do you think God wanted me to be imprisoned in the misery of your stupid life?"

"Take that back, child."

"Damn you! I won't. I'm tired of being treated like a child, Mother. I'm not a retard. I'm twenty-one and old enough to be allowed to have my own life."

"With a Philistine?"

"Does everyone have to be Jesus Christ? Does everyone have to be Saint Paul? Do I have to get laid by the angel Gabriel, Mother? Can't you see that sex isn't a sin?"

"Do you think I believe that? That's the devil talking."

"Well, I don't want to have to lie in bed clutching the New Testament to my navel every night. I'm young, Mother. If you wanted to spend your life giving permanents and bobs, as you call them, to idiot fat women who spend their lives under hairdryers, that's your business. But I'm through. I have my own life. I'm tired of being the daughter of a hairdresser in Tahoe. There's nothing beautiful about the beauty business."

"God forgives you."

"You keep God. I'll keep Nick."

"That's the devil talking." Her mother crossed herself.

She hated her fights with her mother. She wished she and her mother could communicate the way mothers and daughters did on television. She wished. "Daddy's girls and Mommy's boys"—Laurie was a Daddy's girl, but her Daddy had died many years ago. Her mother got only crumbs of affection. For her mother, she was a precious stone, but her mother had ceased being precious to her a long time ago. Nick was in many ways the father she never had. When he bought her shoes, he was buying her more than shoes. He was giving her the attention that she craved, the attention her mother gave only to clients as she combed out their hair. Somewhere she was envious of the attention that her mother gave to the strands of strangers' hair. "I feel like all I am to you is a dandruff speck," Laurie said.

"No, no, child, you are my life. Without you, God's world would not be as perfect as it is to me. You've brought God's word into the flesh and I'll always love you. Some day you'll understand. Meanwhile, you should be reading the New Testament. It's just as great as Zola or Shakespeare. Try reading it aloud."

Laurie hated being in the same house with her and wanted to get away. Someday she would slam the door on Jesus.

74. *The Prick Scene*

OH GOD, yes. Nick dreaded what he had come to call The Prick Scene. Every relationship of his life, since he had been married to Rita, had to end in a prick scene. There was no other way. If you didn't *marry* them, you were a prick. The tiredness of it all, the repetition of it all, was a burden. A burden married swingers had to bear. It was better to get it over with. It never worked. First they wanted fame. Then money. Then a hundred percent of your ass. They all wanted security. That's the way women were. He, Nick Dimani, was not going to change anything. Only this woman, this lovely young girl, was different. She had obeyed him. Anything he had wanted, she had done. That was the trouble. She controlled him with kindness. Just as his mother had. His mother had been so fucking sweet he hated her. Overbearing. Well, at least Laurie was not overbearing. She was just the opposite of his mother, at least in that direction. Had he run away from his fat, vulgar overbearing mother only to find that even a thin *shiksa* from nowheresville could control him? Was he afraid to hurt her? Why? Was it really because he feared violence? Somewhere deep inside, did he think that she would be so furious she would hurt him?

"Hello, my love."

She turned on the bar stool. Her large breasts could be seen coming out of the top of the white angora strapless. They were so white and juicy that he could hardly resist touching them, even in public. He was standing in front of her with an erection. Just looking at her made him feel as if the old Nick Dimani, the futile guilty man, had to be erased. It wasn't Laurie he wanted to get rid of. It was his guilt. Why would he want to unload this beautiful young girl?

"Are you going to stand there, or join me for a drink?" she asked. She had laughter in her voice. That was what he loved. Her voice was a happy voice, a musical voice. It wasn't the nasal nyah-nyah-nyah voice that Rita had developed. Her phoney English upper-class accent was a pain in the ass. Really!

"I love you, my sweet," Laurie said.

Please God. Help me.

75. *Nick and Laurie*

EVERYONE MOBBED Nick Dimani arriving at the Sahara, as he stepped out of his Rolls with Laurie on his arm. "Quickly, into the hotel," he said. She had never been *seen* with him and it was frightening to have people running after them. Once inside the hotel, a guard escorted them to the Sahara Show Room. Hanging on the walls were bizarre baby pictures, oil paintings of the stars, obviously taken from baby photographs. It was odd to see pictures of Helen Reddy, Sammy Davis, Jr., Frank Sinatra, Diana Ross, Ann-Margret, all as children. Somewhere there was a great moral in this Rogues Gallery of Babies—even *stars* began as babies. They were human. Even though money might buy them the largest cars, five-hundred-dollar boots, expensive shades, glittering chains, and opulent rings, they—the stars—were once brats who wore diapers, made doo-doo, sat on a pottie. Was that what the pictures lining the walls were promising? Ducking from the curious onlookers, just before they entered the showroom, Laurie rushed into the ladies' room to look at herself in the mirror. Her blond hair was clean and thick and fresh. She had put it all on top of her head and it looked *hot* that way, she thought. Her makeup was almost nonexistent. She liked the natural look. The dress she had picked out suited her perfectly. She knew how to make herself look good. "Lookin' good," she said to herself in the mirror. She had never felt so good, so happy, so eager for life. She was awake and ready for the joy of the night, sitting next to Nick Dimani; she could see that her face was flushed, that the slight veins in her neck were showing. She was even slightly nervous, the way she had once been in a high school play before going on stage, nervous that she would forget her lines or trip on her costume. She took one moment to breathe in and out, a little yoga that she knew would calm her. Then she walked out of the ladies' room at the Sahara Hotel. Nick was waiting for her. No. She had never felt happier, more eager for an evening. Excitement pulsed in her. She was determined to have Nick to herself at least for a few hours. As they walked into the showroom at the Sahara, led by Norman, the most attractive captain who took them to the best seat, a lounge made out of leather which accommodated four, she saw that Nick's friends were already there. They were introduced to her by Nick as "Mr. Colesman and Mr. Thimble"—two of his friends from the record business. They were both not only attractive but extremely polite. Mr. Colesman kissed her hand. Both of them stood up when she was presented by Nick. *So this is the high life,* Laurie thought. She had read "Town & Country" where Lionel Colesman's picture often appeared as he sailed through Acapulco on his yacht, flew through Rio in his plane, or windsurfed off the coast of Chile where he owned a huge oceanside ranch. He was handsomer in person, she thought, and looked the way a tycoon should look.

The show began. First there was a comic. She had been to many shows at the Sahara, as everyone who lived in Lake Tahoe had, and was used to the routines. First a waitress comes out and brings you three drinks. The cover includes three drinks, whether you want them or not. The three drinks arrive at once, before the show. Then a photographer, a miniskirted woman, asks to take your picture. Nick didn't want any pictures. And then the lights dim, the waiters bow and move back from the tables, the noise stops as the clanging of spoons and forks is hushed by the captain whose business it is to keep the room quiet for the performers, and the opening act begins. The comic is usually some clown whose claim to fame is that he knows the performer, the headliner. In this evening's show, there were to be two headliners: Abbe Lane and Vic Damone. After the comic, Abbe Lane came out and made a lot of Xavier Cugat jokes. Abbe Lane was sexy and charming and could sing better than most singers. Her Xavier Cugat jokes were lost on Laurie, who was too young to know who he was. This annoyed Nick. At least with Rita he had common reference. With Laurie, it was impossible to talk about most celebrities since she had never heard of them, she didn't watch TV. She had never seen any of the movies he grew up with and this was the kind of thing that separated them, her generation referred to other things than those he knew about. The health generation. They were all *into* grass, health, and granola. Into Looking Good,

Feeling Good, and Go For It. None of them had ever had a martini in their lives. None of them *suffered* or went into analysis. Shampoo was important to them. So was cream rinse. So were vitamins and earth shoes and zinger tea. When he wanted a zinger, it wasn't a tea bag! Laurie was innocent. She watched the show. Oh God! He wondered what it was like to see Vic Damone for the first time!

Vic Damone appeared in the spotlight. He was wearing a velvet jacket. He crooned the songs that he had crooned in the late fifties and the early sixties. Dimani had known him forever, from the same clubs; they had played golf together. "He's gorgeous," Laurie said. For Nick, the whole act was one of nostalgia. But for Laurie, she was hearing Vic for the first time. He didn't look like a leftover from hunger. He looked mature, and she dug him. "God, he's fabulous, really!" she whispered to Nick. She was getting off on Vic Damone. He could have been her father. "He's so sexy and greasy. I just love him." None of the songs were repeats. She was hearing them for the first time. God, she was young.

"Some tits," Thimble whispered to Lionel.

"Who?"

"Who do you think, asshole? Nick's girl."

"Yes. She's plausible."

"Very low cock."

"Everything about this evening is low cock," Lionel said with his catlike smile. "Especially Vic Damone. I think he's so low cock, he's high cock."

"Whatever he is, you should sign him for Mecca. I think he's fabulous."

"He's too expensive. Does the Michelob commercial, you know, 'When you're out of beer, you're out of life'—or something. He's a millionaire. He certainly isn't hurting for cash."

"Yeah. I heard that. That's what they say about all those guys. But when it comes right down to it, when push comes to shove, they are all broke. Totally busted."

"Speak for yourself," Lionel said drily.

"Look at the suit. The suit alone, shoulder pads, must have cost a thousand dollars."

"What's a thousand dollars for a suit?" Lionel asked. It was the kind of question that was *very* Lionel. Nobody but nobody paid less than a thousand dollars for a suit in Lionel's world unless they were really rich. Then they shopped at Barney's or could be as eccentric as they damn pleased.

"And that suntan. He looks like a million bucks," Thimble said. He was obviously attracted to the singer. "That guy's a star. He's a big, big talent. He always is. And he always will be."

"He's getting a pretty penny for playing Tahoe. But even if he's a millionaire, so what? What's a few million today? Spending money."

"Shhhh," said Ron. "Not so loud."

"Why? Am I saying anything wrong?"

"No. But I want to tell you something. Don't repeat this. This whole evening is the ultimate in low cock. That girl. The outfit. Did you see the outfit? She's dressed like Anna Maria Alberghetti used to dress in her movies. And those *shoes.*"

"Oh, you're just jealous," Lionel said.

Thimble shut up.

Nick was holding Laurie's hand. He wanted to make love with her. As he sat listening to the show, he thought of leaving right after it was over and driving to the Fantasy Inn. Laurie looked at him. She was thinking the same thing. He could tell from the way she looked into his eyes. Her eyes were lovely, just a touch of mascara on those long lashes. Her eyes, her body, she was so lovely. Maybe he could straighten her out another evening.

As they turned right out of the Sahara garage onto the highway, toward the motel, Laurie held Nick's hand. "Are you hungry?" he asked.

"Very. We didn't have dinner. And those drinks really made me nervous. Do you want to stop and get a pizza?"

"I don't like pizza."

"Stop right here. Turn right. To the parking lot. We can have a steak at Tahoe T's."

The Rolls-Royce pulled into the parking lot. It was the best fast-food place in town. All of Laurie's friends hung out there. She was hoping one of them, Kevin or Denise, *someone* would see her with Nick Dimani. She had never been *outside the motel* with him. Tonight was so different. He had introduced her to his associates. And now she wanted her buddies to meet *him*.

"Aren't you a little dressed up for Tahoe T's?" Nick asked.

"No. All kinds of people eat there. People from the highest walks of life to the lowest."

Nick froze. He hated when she talked like that. "Highest walks and lowest walks." He wondered who she thought *she* was. At least Rita didn't use banalities when she spoke. He liked the way Rita used English. She manipulated language so that it sounded as if everything in life was *cheerful.* You had to hand it to the English. With all their "nifty" expressions, their "chins-up" philosophy, their upper-class Spartan manners, they made him feel quite cheerful and good. Sometimes he could slap Laurie. Why was he angry with her? He didn't understand. Just a moment ago he wanted to make love to her. They walked into the restaurant and each got a tray. They stood on line in front of the grill. It was an open grill that faced out on a window. The woman behind the stove was grilling steaks; they were all grilled on charcoal and smelled delicious. Suddenly he wasn't angry at Laurie. He was hungry. He wanted a steak. He wasn't able to find the words to tell her what he had to tell her. So he allowed himself to be admired. To hear the usual, "May I have your autograph?" and he smiled and gave autographs graciously. He was admired. He had the loveliest girl in Tahoe on his arm. He was about to have a steak dinner. They moved slowly through the line. Nick wondered why he felt so unhappy.

Across from Laurie at the table, Nick began eating. A lot of people, mostly gamblers, moved back and forth in the restaurant for their second helpings. The food was fresh and good. "When are we going to Paris?" Laurie asked. *Careful Nick, don't be a prick. Don't lead her on, but don't be a prick either.*

"We're not going."

"What do you mean?" she asked. She was on the verge of tears. He knew this would happen.

"Look, Laurie, I'm going through a difficult moment."

She looked at him with a face that did not register what he meant. *"A difficult moment."* He was screaming. People started to look at them. "Please," she whispered with compassion. "My friends come here. I'm *known* here, Nick. Don't be angry. I didn't mean anything. I just don't know what you mean. Tell me."

"I'm not leaving my wife. I'm never buying a boat. And we aren't going to Paris, baby. I've thought about it a lot. I want to see you a lot. I want you to be my girlfriend, whenever we are in Tahoe, whenever I play Tahoe. But that's it. If you can accept my conditions, I'll be with you the rest of my life. Our life. If you can't accept my conditions, I'm not going to go through with our plans. Don't you see? I'm a prisoner of my life. I can't leave Rita. Think of the publicity. It'll ruin me."

"There doesn't have to be publicity. We could be discreet," she said softly.

Nick got up. Stood on line. Came back with a baked potato. Perhaps the potato would help him. Cure him of his nerves. She wasn't able to understand. He was dumping her.

"Look Laurie, I'm leaving Tahoe after the party."

"What party?"

"The party. Didn't you hear Thimble and Colesman talk about it?"

"Yes. But they didn't invite me."

"Of course they didn't invite you. You're not my public girlfriend. I can't be seen with you, you idiot."

"What about tonight?"

"Tonight was business. You could have been with Thimble. Or one of Colesman's friends. That was different. But Rita will be at the party. The whole world will be at the party. You can't come. That's it."

"Where is it going to be held?"

"At the villa."

"That's all right, darling. If you don't want me there, I won't be there. But I want to know about—Paris. I've quit my job, Nick. I can't wait to leave Tahoe. I've been studying French. Taking lessons. And how are we going to arrange it?"

"Arrange what?"

"Privately—arrange Paris."

"Paris?"

"Nick." She was hurt.

"Forget it."

"Listen to me, Nick, we've taken hours talking about being together. About going around the world on a boat. About Paris. About the Bateau Mouche."

"I work too hard to send you to Paris. What are you? A golddigger? A little tramp? I can't afford Paris."

"But you said so. It was *you* who suggested it."

"I never said so."

"Yes, you did. I heard you. You told me you were going to take me to Paris. That we were going to have an apartment——"

"You can just take Paris and shove it up your ass. I don't need *you,* Laurie. There are a million other tramps I can buy in this town. Tramps with taste and brains. Lay off me." He got up from the table, threw his napkin on the floor, and ran to the car. She watched him. She didn't move. She tried to move. But she couldn't move. It was as if a spring inside a clock had just broken. She could not speak. Could not tick tock. Could not even feel. She watched him going out of the door of Tahoe T's Steak House. A moment later she heard the engine of the Rolls-

Royce turn. She heard the tires on the snow. And then her life was gone. All she could think of was, "My life has driven away." She sat there looking at nothing but red flocked wallpaper. He had left her sitting by herself in a fast-foods restaurant. How could he do that? She would never forget this moment. Sitting in her new dress, her new shoes, all dressed up, for loneliness.

Nick drove back to the villa. When he got there, the lights were on. Rita was home. He opened the door with his key. She must be sleeping. He poured himself a drink and sat in the living room listening to one of his records. He hoped Laurie wouldn't jump in the lake, drown herself, do anything foolish. He *had* lost his temper. That was not what he had planned to do. He would call her the next day. Give her a check. Shut her up with money. Or would he? Sometimes he thought it would be easier if all the broads he dumped killed themselves. He admired Rita. At least she knew how to hang on to him. He wondered for a moment if she was really sleeping, if he could just go into her room and make love to her. No. He was tired. He felt that he had abandoned Laurie and on one level he was sure she was hurting inside.

"It was an escapade," he said to himself. "One that had to end badly." The trouble was that he didn't even *feel* badly. Once, a long time ago, he would have felt bad. Now, he reflected that it was easy for him to say to someone, even to someone he was as fond of as he was of Laurie— good-bye. If they wanted too much. If they got too demanding. If they seemed dangerous. He was better off without her. It was better for her, too. He had been too loving and led her on. But she could take care of herself. He wanted her to know that he wasn't responsible. He wasn't. He hoped she wouldn't cause a scene. Or in some way make it known to the public that what she had called love was only depravity. Her mother would shut her up. He was sure of that. Nobody who worked in Tahoe wanted a run-in with Nick Dimani. Laurie had dreams of glory. Too bad.

76. *Revelation*

THE STEAKS were cooked on the flames. The people wandered in and out carrying trays. But Laurie sat in the chair of Tahoe T's as if it were an electric chair. She could not move. Nick had left her sitting that way in the restaurant. Please don't leave me alone, she had wanted to say. Don't leave me here. But instead she said nothing. She didn't even have her car with her. The woman who ran the restaurant was a friend of her mom's and she knew she could borrow her car. Slowly, she wandered to the telephone. She called her mother. "Praise the Lord," her mother said.

An hour later, Laurie was home. She was sitting with her mom in the house and spilling out the story. "I told you he was the devil," the older woman said. Suddenly and almost for the first time, Laurie looked at her mom. The familiarity of her face disappeared and she saw the *authentic* face of her mother. As if the real saint locked in the beautician, locked in the nag, locked in the Jesus Freak, came out. The charismatic natural face of Laurie's mother made Laurie weep. She loved her mom. She had never known that.

"Praise the Lord," Laurie's mom said. *Throw up your hands,* a voice inside Laurie said. And she obeyed. Following her mother, she threw up her arms to God. "Praise be to the Lord."

"Get down on your knees, child."

Laurie obeyed.

"Now to be a Christian, all you have to do is to ask God to forgive you for your sins. There's a simple A and a B

and a C, Laurie. Ask God to forgive. Begin to Confess.
And Cross God in your heart. All of your life you have
been ignoring Jesus, who has always been inside you. You
have been a stranger and walked around with God in your
heart. Now it's time to let the natural Laurie talk with her
natural friend. Praise be to God! He will hear your
prayers. A simple voice is what God hears. A voice that is
pure."

Laurie saw the tears in her mother's eyes. She was kneeling next to her mother. She was suddenly lighter than she
had ever been. The weight of her feelings for Nick, the
feelings that she had once called love but she realized now
had only weighted her down, instantly left her. Nick was
no longer a burden in her heart.

"I confess, dear God, that I have made a mistake. I have
loved and coveted a man who did not belong to me. I have
sinned by doing to his wife what I would not want done to
me, and I beg your forgiveness, dear God. What I want
more than anything on earth is the pure life of following
your word. Hear me, oh God, from where you are and lift
me to the newness of life. Forgive me and allow each day
to be filled with your kindness and joy. Hear the flapping
of my heart's wings, the fluttering of my soul, dear God.
Make me into a dove that I may fly to you. Let me be
reborn in your love, dear God."

Laurie turned to her mother. She was also on her knees.

"Am I saying the right thing, Mother?" she asked.

Her mother had tears in her eyes. "Keep giving yourself
to God," her mother said. "It's a miracle. Keep talking to
God. Jesus will hear you. Praise be to God!"

"What shall I say to Him?" Laurie asked. Suddenly she
felt so comfortable on her knees, so happy to be loving
God, to be giving to God what she had once wanted to give
to Nick Dimani but which Nick Dimani had rejected so
cruelly. "I gave to Nick what I should have only given to
you, dear God. I gave him my heart. Now, with all my soul
and all my heart, I ask you to forgive me. I want to start

again, God, to live a Christian life. A life that follows your example, Jesus. I want to live a life not like the Gnostics and the blind Madonnas, the blind Christs in the brothels treating the flesh as secular and fleeting, not as the blind Christ inside of me lived without seeing the truth. Lift me, God, to the sky of another world, where true love is the air, where true Christian love is everywhere. It is almost as if all my life, God, I wanted to fly to find you, but I never could find wings, never could reject what I have always known was not real. Give me a chance, dear God, to be the best woman that I can be, to live with my soul wide open, to fly beyond the world of cards and casinos and the wrong choices of the soul. The love that I felt for Nick was fleeting, but it was not wrong if it was a symbol which led me to love of you, dear God. I forgive Nick for what he did just as I forgive myself. The hater only hates himself. I forgive Nick for all that was not kind or right. I forgive him. I wish only to carry love inside my heart so I can fly to you, dear God, my love and friend, my father and my life. Thank you, dear God, for giving me the wisdom not to blame him for my sufferings but to look inside my pain to find my own soul. Let me spend the rest of my life, dear God, understanding the words of love which you brought to this earth and telling others of my love for you."

Laurie rose from her knees. Tears were streaming down the face of her mother. They looked at each other. Laurie was also weeping. "Thank you, Mother."

"Praise be to the Lord, child. You're a Christian. The most important thing, child, is to be a good Christian. A simple Christian. Not a Christian that goes to a fine church only. Although a church can be a good place to pray and to think. But it's not churches and Sundays that make Christians. No, my darling, my daughter. What makes a Christian is the lack of shame to confess and to give your heart as you just did, my love."

"The pain is gone, Mother. The pain is gone."

"Praise be to the Lord!"

Laurie embraced her mother. It was the first time in her life that she had held her mother in her arms and kissed her with all her might. "Thank you, God," she whispered, "for taking my pain and turning it into love."

"Praise be to God!" Laurie said again.

"Praise be to God," the two women said together.

"Mother?"

"Yes, child."

"I will never see that man again."

"That is your decision."

"Mother, Nick Dimani was a terrible mistake."

"I know, child."

"Do you think God will forgive me?"

"He already has."

"Mother, I want so badly to be happy."

"I know that."

"I feel happy now. Peaceful. As if I have flown out of myself into another place where the air is good again."

"People laugh at this. Pay them no mind. To find God means to lose the weight that is inside of you. To find God is to find wings. To become weightless.

"You can only find happiness in yourself, child. You can only find happiness when you give to others without destroying what is good within you. God gave us the example of his life. Follow that example, child. To be a Christian is such a simple thing. It requires love and more love. To be a Christian as far as I know, and I believe this with all my heart, is to love passionately. To love others. To love others with all your heart."

"I feel so happy now, Mother."

"Good. I love you, Laurie."

She said the words she had never said in her life, "I love you too, Mother. Thank you, God."

77. *The Last Party at Tahoe*

LIONEL, THE host, welcomed everyone to the party for Nick Dimani. Nobody knew it, but it was a party to celebrate the death of rock and roll. It started out being high cock but because it was for Nick Dimani, it turned out to be low cock. Lionel, by accident, was celebrating the death of the rock and roll generation. Rock and roll—the history of America in the fifties, sixties, and seventies—was both high cock and low cock at the same time.

Around Christmas 1969, Donald Pond's party in his home for Janis Joplin was the first publicized celebrity party for the rock world. It was his idea to cross over celebrities and rock stars to make rock not only groovy and profitable but legitimate. That was after Janis Joplin sold out her Madison Square Garden concert, and it reportedly was one of the few happy moments in her life. The second party, the second big one, was given by Pond for The Grateful Dead at Tavern on the Green. But this one didn't work as well. It didn't reflect profit, which is the purpose of these parties. The last crossover party was one Ethel Kennedy gave at Hickory Hill for Neil Diamond, in which politics and society corroded and crossed over (whichever term you prefer) the Kennedys, the athletes, society, and politicians with show biz and then (still low man on the totem pole) rock. Lionel Colesman was to give the fourth big party.

The last party at Tahoe was meant to crossover show biz celebrities, high society, and representatives of the record world with another dimension: Western celebrities. All of the people at Tahoe Airlines, Harrah's in Reno, Idaho bigwigs, a few Kennedys, and the record world were to be gathered with the local politicians of Tahoe and Reno. Beautiful people. The party was ballyhooed in *Variety, New*

West, Women's Wear Daily, as well as *The New York Times.*
Ten years later it was to be the party of the decade, for
what purpose? To show the world Lionel Colesman was
even more important, in his own way, than Donald Pond.
The really big difference between Colesman and Pond was
that Colesman had his own money. He wasn't a lackey for
CBS or Gulf and Western or a lousy record conglomerate.
Colesman controlled his own fortune and he didn't mind
the boogie-woogie money spent on showing the Western
World just where it was at. The *pièce de résistance* at the
party was to be The B-52s, whom Colesman was introduc-
ing to Tahoe. In addition to this, he was going to show off
his writer/composer Nick Dimani as well as lyricist Sylvia
Lundholm, proving that even though they might be doing
an album independently, they were still the money-makers
at Mecca, turning out the songs that Mecca artists sang.
Another *pièce de résistance* was to be Barry Manilow, and
from the middle of the road, Sammy baby. Peter Hampton was flown in on Lionel's private plane. Ron Thimble
was in a tizzy. He had to screen the fag list. This wasn't to
be some queer costume party. He had to make sure that
not too many switch-hitters and gays were invited. He had
to mix up gays, blacks, Jews, feminists, Third World, un-
derground, establishment, society, high cock, low cock,
and local Mafia and still make sure that the superstars all
saw their friends. He was given the job of charting out the
party. Drawing from personal information, gossip sheets,
Billboard, he had to know who was "in" and who was "out."
Who was passé and who was coming up. He took names
off cards in his index file and planned the strategy of the
party as if his life depended on it, which, as it so happened,
it did. (He was into Lionel for a thou and Lionel was not
one to take his markers lightly.) No airplane tickets were
sent out. His private plane was sent to Chicago, Atlanta,
New York, Los Angeles, Burbank, Washington, and
Hyannisport. No one who knew about the party wanted to
miss it. Especially since only a hundred people were in-

vited. This was not to be a no-frills flight. There were all the frills on board the plane. Tape decks with all the Mecca hits playing throughout the special stereo amps on the plane, cases of Moët et Chandon, American caviar, West Coast salmon, Chung King mini eggrolls, not to mention the South African lobster. When Nancy heard about the apartheid lobsters, she was glad she had gone back to New York a day early.

Everyone arrived at the Tahoe airport; special porters and limousines were on hand to speed everyone from the airport (called the most beautiful airport in the world by the local Chamber of Commerce). All the porters wore special ski sweaters with the Mecca logo in back. (Ron Thimble thought of things like that even before the party was announced.) The guests were then led by a busy hostess to their rooms at Harrah's, all of which had views of the lake or the mountains. There, thousands of feet above sea level, the guests were treated to the Sierra views. Several of the guests who had never "played Tahoe" or been divorced there were surprised to see the breathtaking beauty of the resort. But many of them felt at home. It was better than Saint Moritz. It was the Palace Hotel at Saint Moritz without Greeks, French spoken, horse-drawn carriages, and dumbwaiters. Everyone said, "How ya doin'?" and they knew they were in America. Cold champagne was kept refurbished in every room. Ron Thimble made sure that every guest received a handwritten program of the events. He had actually written all hundred of them himself, not only to save money, but because he was the only person in Tahoe who knew calligraphy. Also, he didn't want any slips—everything had to be perfect. Or no Thimble.

The night of the party everyone set out from Harrah's to the villa on the lake in Skyland. It wasn't really a mansion because it was only on one level. It looked like a mausoleum. It had housed a few of Harrah's five wives when he was alive, and now belonged to his widow and children.

It had seen Bobbie Gentry move in as an overwhelmed waitress-turned-rock star and then move out. It had housed all of the greats from old Blue Eyes, to Wayne Newton and John Denver, when they were appearing at Harrah's club. It was dark black rock on the outside, almost as large as a small hotel. And in the dark, lit up by a thousand tiny lights which Ron Thimble had attached to the pine trees so that the house glistened in the snow, the guests were able to look out on the lake. The large forbidding doors were thrown open and the guests arrived. Lionel stood at the door greeting everyone in his black tuxedo. The less obnoxious paparazzi had been invited. Candy Bergen was taking pictures for *Paris Match,* a photographer was there from *People,* Jann Wenner and selected photographers from the *Times* and the *Washington Post.* The rest were the cream of the crop: John Denver stood out next to pert little Lee Radziwill, Wayne Newton talked cars with Sammy Davis, Jr. The reporter from Tahoe was a small-town girl from the *Tahoe News* who found herself talking about jewels and the Jewelry Factory with Sammy Davis, Jr. She counted the chains on his neck and he spoke, casually, about charities and black consciousness and the necessity of giving to help black colleges survive. Everyone drank champagne, listened to the Dimani/Lundholm songs on the tape, and stood around quietly while The B-52s jammed and gave a fifteen-minute set.

The guests helped Lionel cut a huge cake which had been sculpted to resemble, in white icing, the Sierras. Some guests were in ski clothes, mostly the townies and the Kennedys; others were dressed up and wearing jewels. Sylvia met Dr. Jerry Lynn, the New York dentist and producer. They spoke about a film he wanted her and Nick to write the songs for. Elizabeth Taylor Warner and husband showed up at the last moment and were excited to see so many of their friends from Europe that Lionel had flown over. The people, the food, the music—the setting of the night stars over the lake which shone in the dark—it made Lionel sick with excitement. This was certainly the party of his life, not just because rock had come of age and was as respectable a stock as A T & T, but also because it was only in Tahoe that talent and nature could mix so easily. He had lived all his life trying to be somebody and now, at this party, he had achieved what he wanted. It was more than power. He was known as an aesthetic person; his party did not have the vulgarity of a Donald Pond party. Here were ballet dancers, Third Worlds, great artists, and people of influence. He was not a businessman but a statesman. And the first to bring the beauty of Tahoe into world focus. From this party on, Tahoe would be on the map, not only as the most beautiful place in America, or a place for entertainment, or a place to get a quickie divorce, it would have connected it to the aroma of culture and aesthetics, for the party made Tahoe as well as rock come of age. They had both been twenty years in the coming, the town and the music; they were both the best and the most aristocratic of America's offerings: the earth, the Sierras, and the music. He was content for the first time ever. He decided to smoke a joint out by the lake, to smoke, to look at the stars, to make himself feel even higher. Was there any higher that anyone could be? As he looked at the Little Dipper and the night stars, the whole galaxy seemed to reach down to touch him on the head. It was as if he were being anointed as some prince, a snow prince, in a watery world of ice and blue water and high mountains. The world was good and everyone was good. Even Nick Dimani, with all of his ambition, was good. Wasn't it Nick and Sylvia who made all of this possible for him? Hadn't they written the music and poetry which had linked his name to the century? Hadn't he "gone after them" the way he went after all artists—an entrepreneur looking for money, a hunter poised for the kill? Didn't he bring it all back home? He. Donald Pond. Richmond Schneider. They had brought it all back home to make money. And they had turned pain into money. Richmond with black pain; Donald with white pain. And he, with black and white pain. He had taken soul and bewilderment and confession and turned all that into dollars. Pain led to money. That was America. And the more things hurt, the more money they made.

Lionel looked for Sylvia. He was attracted to her pain. He wanted to own it. To understand it. To get deeper into it. He didn't just want to touch her breasts and the wet tiny beads of perspiration on her lovely face. He wanted to smell her pain, understand what it was like to be her, and in some way he wanted to own her pain so that it would take away his own feelings of bewilderment. Under it all, under the tan and the tuxedo and the perfect body which he exercised so carefully, under the tight little ass and the perfectly exercised thigh muscles, was the toe of loneliness. And bewilderment. He wanted Sylvia to pass on some of her guts and energy and talent, *and* pain to him. And so he went to look for her. He found her standing by one of the walls alone, looking out at the lake. He went over and kissed her on the mouth. He kissed her as if he meant to wipe off her lipstick with his lips. Rev saw this and it troubled him. He also saw Sylvia pull away from Lionel.

It wasn't just that everyone was there, Sylvia wanted to say to her masseur, *it wasn't just that Lionel kissed me. It wasn't just that Rev didn't want to go. It was just that at that party, in Tahoe, I realized that I didn't have to be afraid of anything anymore. The fears are gone. I just understood a lot of things about Jimi Hendrix. I understand that everyone carries within them the time and place where they are born. Carries it around with them like an explosion of loneliness. That's what Hendrix was. An explosion. A great electric turned-on explosion. That's what rock was. Once upon a time. It was a turn-on. There is just parties that people give left. People like Lionel. Within one performance, Jimi Hendrix gave you his whole life. Now there are just parties. There's no more rock and roll. Just performances. And parties like the one at Harrah's villa that Lionel gave. It's clear to me. You have to lose yourself to find yourself. You want to know what I was afraid of all these years? Of finding out who Sylvia was, of finding out there is no such thing as 'too emotional.' No such thing as 'Just like a girl.' No such thing as loving too much. All things are possible. In one performance, Jimi Hendrix traveled the whole path that it takes an ordinary person a whole lifetime to discover. I realized that the absurd is the whole of a person's lifetime.*

A party is only a perfection of appearances. But what was missing from the party was the truth. Any kind. There was no life at the party. Just the celebration of death. I have to tell you, the celebration of death.

78. Stunts

NICK PUT on his six-thousand-dollar cowboy boots. The morning after the party was one of those perfect winter days in Tahoe that make tourists rise early and head for the ski slopes. The snow was powder and shone under the sun like huge white silken cloth that someone had thrown down over the mountains. All the casinos were deserted. Everyone was sleeping or out on the slopes. Tahoe sparkled.

The album was finished. It was the last day Nick and Sylvia would meet in Harrah's where the Steinway piano stood against the wall. Nick played through the album. It was with mixed sadness that he acknowledged the end of the songs. His feeling on this morning for Sylvia was Rabelaisian, one of carousing friendship as it was in the old days. He ran through the songs, singing them in his own arrangement. They all sounded good. His original concept, that the album have a brilliance to it, was giving *Playing Tahoe* a unique sound.

"It's a breakthrough," Nick said after he played the last song on the piano.

Oh God, Sylvia thought, everything's a breakthrough.

"I guess there's no more material needed," she said. She was proud that the songs sounded good. She had worked particularly hard on "Keep Dancin'," a sad and touching song about a woman who dances in front of a mirror with a comb. It was a song about being thirteen and misunderstood. It was her best song. "I know that when you get in the studio, you and Arthur will do something fabulous with it," she said. She wasn't good at saying good-bye, so when the set was over, she said to Nick, "I'm going to rest, sweetheart," and left. They were to meet again for small technical things with Morris later that evening. He was arriving in Tahoe at five and then there would be the run-through. The next day Sylvia was leaving.

Nick sat alone in the room after she left. He ran through a tape of one of the songs and got that high that he had hearing his own material. These were the best songs. He knew he couldn't do any better. He left the cassette and walked toward the window. He needed air. Out in the pastures of snow in front of the hotel he could see some young kids cross-country skiing. He left and walked out in the fresh air.

Rev was waiting for his Trans Am. "Want a lift, Bobby?" Nick asked. Rev seemed to take him in as if he were a stranger. He stood in front of Harrah's in the sunshine in front of a large sign advertising Don Rickles as the next attraction at Harrah's South Shore Room in Reno.

"Where are you going?" Rev asked. It was sunny and Rev couldn't quite see Nick's eyes.

"I thought I'd drive down to the airport," Nick said.

"Expecting anyone?"

"Just want to get out of here. Want to drive my Trans Am?"

"Sounds good."

Rev got in the driver's seat and opened the passenger door for Nick.

"Sylvia told me you used to work on a tuna boat. Is that so?"

"Yeah." Rev strapped on his black vertical seat belt.

"What did you do on the boat?"

"I was a speedboat driver chasing dolphins."

"What's that?" Nick looked at him strangely. He was manic. Something in his frantic energy made Rev think he was on uppers.

"You herd the dolphins and, hopefully, the tuna follow."

Fish didn't interest Nick Dimani. "Listen, that party made me sick," he said. "I can understand how Sylvia wants to take a rest. I'm fed up with the star-making machinery myself. It's been twenty years. But you have to understand my point of view. I've been knocking around all my life. Do you have any idea what it's like to be a musician? An artist? Most civilians have no idea. They think it's all good times, big money, and applause. Even to get to be an asshole like Barry Manilow, you have to do a lot of sucking. You know what I mean, Rev? I made everything easy for Sylvia. That's the part I'm sure she never told you about. I'm sure she never told you how I smoothed the way. Of course, she had a unique talent. But she wasn't the type to kick ass, to bang down doors, to get involved in law suits and a lot of other dirty business. No. Sylvia Lundholm's hands are clean. It's Nick who's the heavy. Right? It's like the old joke: Girls who think they'll hate themselves in the morning should sleep till noon. Well, Sylvia slept till noon all through her career with Nick Dimani. I'm the one who got up early. I'm the one who dealt with Lionel Colesman and the pricks at ABC and NBC." It was a litany of self-blame and self-pity.

Rev began driving the car faster. They were going around the curves at ninety miles an hour. The engine seemed to make no noise at all. Nick didn't notice. "Yeah, I know what you mean," Rev said.

"Sylvia loves you."

"I guess so."

"You guess so? You fickle little fucking Wasp! Are you out of your mind? You guess so? Is that supposed to be your idea of cool? Is that a putdown? You're taking Sylvia Lundholm away from me, from the album, from her career, and you 'guess so'!"

"So she likes me, what's the big deal?"

"And what the fuck do you think is going to happen to her after you dump her? Don't fool me, Mister Cranwell, with your super cool. I know you've been making it with Nancy and Laurie. I'm sure that's just the beginning."

Rev was listening with his eyes focused on the road. Concentrating on the snowy road. He laughed. "The beginning of what?"

"The fucking over of Sylvia Lundholm."

"She can take care of herself. It's not my idea for her to leave. It's hers."

"Listen man, this is the worst moment of my life. I'm finished without her. For you, she's a meal ticket or a piece of ass. For me, she's a troubadour. All right, I had her for twenty years and now it's your turn. Just tell me when she gets tired of tuna and I know I can always talk her into working with me again." The car was accelerating. "Hey, aren't you driving a little too fast, Stirling Moss?"

"I used to be a stunt driver."

"Listen, you've heard a lot of bullshit from Sylvia. Did you ever hear Richard Rightman's idea of his side of the story? She did a job on him. There's something about Sylvia that's so lost and helpless. He tried to put his life in order. It was a horrible day in his life when Sylvia left him. He had a nervous breakdown. Ideas left his mind."

"So?" The car was now going swiftly through the trees and around the bends. Rev handled the car easily. Suspension parts, engine mountings, and brake parts were all in control. He now gunned the motor up to a hundred miles an hour. The speedometer stopped showing the speed. Nick felt as if he were flying through a wind tunnel.

"Hey, slow down."

"I'm going faster."

"Are you a maniac?"

Rev asked himself the question. *Am I?*

"Wait until you see what Sylvia is like when she's not working. She'll lie in bed until two in the afternoon. I've seen her sleep all day. She won't shed her nightgown or change her clothes. You'll see her start drinking."

"She doesn't drink much."

"Not now, when she's working. And if you have any idea of going on a tuna boat with Madame Lundholm, forget it. The only boat she travels on is *Queen Elizabeth II*. And then she likes taking fourteen Vuitton bags, her entourage, and her dogs. You'll love bumming around the world with that group." Nick was screaming. The wind came through the windows. "And you don't know her anger. I do. She wears her anger—hey, man, slow down! You're going too fast. What do you think you're doing?"

"I'm driving as fast as I can."

"Listen, you little gentile faggot, slow down. You're going to kill us."

"I don't think so," Rev said carefully. "I don't like you."

"What are you doing?"

"I'm accelerating. And I do plan to kill *you*. It's a stunt I learned in the Skip Barber Racing School. It was actually for assassins. I'm going to bring this car right against that building that you see up there in front of us. You see that office building standing up in the snow? I'm going to take this car at a hundred and fifteen miles and I'm going to move it right into the building so that the building cuts through the car and you're smashed into the garbage heap that I think you are. I'm going to kill you."

Rev took the car even faster. "I'm going to kill you for no reason," he added.

.

"Don't do it," Nick begged. But the car did exactly what the driver intended it to do. It murdered cleanly. The terror of death was taken out of the murder. The car at a hundred and ten miles an hour went into the sharp edge of the building so the right part of the car was taken off and in it was Nick Dimani. The building sliced through the man and the car like a knife, a huge buzz saw compressing Nick Dimani and recycling him into nothing but the remnants of a person. When the police came, Rev's head was against the wheel. He pretended to be half-conscious when they put him into an ambulance and carried him off to the hospital where he was treated for a concussion. It was the perfect murder and even in the ambulance, with his eyelids half closed, Rev seemed to be smiling. Rev laughed and laughed to himself. It was a good stunt.

79. *Rev's Secret*

LYING IN the ambulance, Rev was fully conscious. He looked down at the Cartier watch that Sylvia had given him. The golden screws shone in the sun that came through the windows. "I've screwed Nick Dimani," he thought. "I've screwed something bigger than Dimani, I've screwed the major rip-off industry in America that uses so-called talent as a front, the macabre makeshift world of concert promoters. I've screwed gold/platinum studios, the image of the good guy, digital recording, promotional T-shirts, studios in suburban garage operations. I've screwed the mustang voice publishers, the big band, rockabilly, the fifties, the L.A. Sound axis, manufacturing and packaging and shipping of units. I've screwed ABC and NBC and the record business with its conventional multinational policies. I've screwed music's quasi-industry leadership, and the generous estimate of points per digit. Most of all, I've screwed that imbecile. Death is the final screwup."

He heard the siren. That was a kind of music, too. A kind that Nick Dimani had never appreciated. Had he screwed Nick? Or saved Sylvia? He looked down at the face of the watch. Time would tell. It was a perfect murder. And it had no reason. It simply eliminated from the world one long-playing digit that was annoying. There was a certain arrogance in the meaninglessness of the act. Was he so deeply in love with Sylvia? Was he trying to save her life? Not really. He listened to the ambulance siren. Death jazz. He had studied terrorist stunt driving. Was this a stunt? It had been so simple. He had that one second of excitement when he wasn't sure if the car could really splice so perfectly in half. Everything worked perfectly. It was a textbook-perfect stunt. The precision and the timing had made it so easy. But for what? It had been so simple. *Hell is other people,* Sartre had said. He had studied that phrase. It was the phrase of the loner, the tuna fisherman, the stunt driver. If only Dimani had not wanted to make *Playing Tahoe,* he might be alive. Death was the final groove on the album. This was a secret he would keep the rest of his life and play it back the way you play back a record. A track of silence. He had felt happy like this once before, driving his motorcycle into the sea. He had been stoned. The police had lifted him out of the sea and taken away his bike. This time he'd be lifting Sylvia out of the sea. The thought that he had silenced Nick Dimani made him feel light as helium. He just didn't like being called Bobby by Nick. The name annoyed him. Nick's ignition system had just been switched off and an endless shuffle of bad vibes had been silenced.

80. *The Funeral*

THE FUNERAL was actually everything Lionel had hoped his party would be. Even grander. Even Ron Thimble was amazed to see how death was the great entertainer, the great star; the people who were bored by Nick's live act were interested and fascinated by his death. Nick's casket was served up to the press and made a bigger splash than Lionel's poached salmon.

Lionel Colesman had been horrified to hear of the accident. The day after the party he had been relaxing in his Sulka pajamas in his suite, watching television, when word of the accident came over the news. All the wire services had picked it up. He immediately went to see Sylvia. His horror turned to bottom-line thinking. She was crying in her suite. She had just gotten the news that Rev was safe and she was dressing quickly to go to the hospital. "This is a mess."

"Morris is due at the airport," Lionel said.

"Can't you think of Nick? Dead! Can't you think of his death rather than Morris's arrival?"

"Someone has to be practical. I want to make sure that he learns this news from me."

"I'm sorry. I know you're thinking of everything. It's just that, I'm so shocked. Nick's dead. It's hard to realize."

Lionel put his arms around her. "There's nothing we can do about it. Ron Thimble is helping Rita with the funeral. They want me to be one of the ushers. It's going to be exactly the way Nick would have wanted it."

"That's absurd. Nick wouldn't have wanted it. He never thought of dying."

"No one does."

"I'm going to make this funeral something the world will always remember. As memorable as Spider Savitch's funeral, as dignified as Bobby Kennedy's. I think I can get Bernstein to play Mahler and Andy Williams to sing."

Sylvia began laughing through her tears, "Lionel, stop producing! For God's sake, this isn't a media event!"

"To you, it's personal. But to the world, it's something else. One of the best-selling musicians of all time is dead. In the Sierras. Mozart had no one at his funeral. A dog followed behind his casket. Things are different now. Dimani was someone everyone loved. I'm already thinking of Commander Cody and the Lost Planet Airmen leading the casket from the funeral home through the snow to a small place where S.G. has given a unique piece of land for the burial. Rita said that Nick always wanted to be buried in the mountains, and this will make him happy."

"So it's to be a real estate deal, too? What's S.G. planning? To sell condominiums overlooking the grave?"

Lionel ignored this. "I've asked Barbara Hepworth to the funeral. She's flying in from London. I plan to commission a simple piece of sculpture for the grave."

"Oh God, not a marble piano."

"Don't you know my aesthetics better than that? I want something abstract."

"I'm too tired and drained to talk. I'm going to the hospital, but first, I want to see if there's anything I can do to help Rita."

The details of the death were exactly the details Ron Thimble knew how to handle. Whereas the press hadn't really given the right coverage to the party, this time all the major television networks were covering the funeral. It was to be a combination of all things; a march through town just like the old-fashioned Dixieland funerals in New Orleans. A rabbi and a senator would say the oration. Carly Simon would sing some of the Dimani hits. Andy Williams would sing, "Glory, Glory Hallelujah." The Airmen were going to play "Roller Queen" and The B-52s were also marching through the snow. The networks were tipped off about the talent. Actually, all the party guests had remained and were milling around Tahoe talking about the accident. A discreet gentleman from Harrah's Automobile Collection had offered a large sum for Nick's favorite charity if he could add the death car to the Harrah's Automobile Collection. Ron Thimble enjoyed these details. He was a party-giver that appreciated the nature of celebration in a funeral.

"That's what I want," said Nick's widow. "Not a death mass, but a celebration of life." Since Rita was an Anglican, there was to be a mass in an Episcopal church as well as the rabbi speaking over the grave.

"All we need is a few Tahoe American Indians," Ron Thimble said to Lionel over the phone. Lionel was not amused. It was Lionel's idea to meet Morris at the Tahoe airport. Morris had heard the news from the captain of his plane. He looked tired when he disembarked. Lionel walked with him through the snow to the coffee bar in the upper part of the airport. "It's terrible," Morris said, "Such a talent. Dimani loved life. He had everything to live for. He was so excited about this album. At least he finished it."

There was a silence. "You're lucky. I'm going to let you do the program notes."

"What do you mean?" Morris asked. He lit a cigar as he waited impatiently for his luggage. Was Colesman kidding?

"I mean that Dimani respected you. He would have wanted you to put your stamp on the album."

"Fucking A, I'm putting my stamp on it by producing it," Morris said in a low tone that Lionel had never heard. At least not from Morris. He looked at Morris. A fat man with a black beard, a man who dealt with extraordinary things easily. He wondered how he was going to deal with what he was about to say.

"You can't have the record, Morris; I spoke to my lawyer this morning. According to the contract between you and

Dimani dated January 6, 1979, hereinafter called 'The Agreement,' as amended, supplemented, and extended, Dimani was to give his next album to me. And since there will not be a next album, you are herewith notified that this album is mine and the agreement is now null and void."

"Are you going to tell me that there is a deficiency in the delivery of the product?"

"I'm telling you that I have the lead sheets, I have the work tapes, I am paying the nominal cost of the master, and I am releasing the last Dimani/Lundholm album."

"This point is dubious. Let's agree to slow down. Why can't we work out a percentage deal where you distribute under the Mecca label and I produce? And you waive the rights to the *Hits of Dimani and Lundholm* and I produce that also. I don't want any heavy-handed litigation. My policy is to forget about the options, avoid litigation, and comply with the specific terms of the agreement."

The two men looked at each other.

"I'm agreeable to your producing as long as I promote and distribute. I'll even be willing to give you a producer's royalty. But I'm planning to do a TV spinoff on the life of Nick Dimani. I'm also planning to re-release the entire catalogue."

"Who's going to write the TV film?"

"Sylvia Lundholm. She's talking about working on a novel about the rock years. I think I can persuade her to write it."

"There's nothing like a dead celebrity," Morris said.

"America is celebrity-hungry. A dead one is like a fish you stuff and put over the mantlepiece. A James Dean, a Nick Dimani killed violently in a Trans Am—these are the heroics the country loves. There is no royalty in America. Every girl who sees a movie wants what is larger than life. A shoe salesman who fits the shoes for Dustin Hoffman has a story that justifies his work forever. He may have had athlete's foot, he may have had bunions, but the cancer of celebrity made his feet perfect. The toe hold on celebrities is more than anything else in America. And a dead hero is someone you can lay your fantasies on without seeing the hero age and fade into a mere wrinkled human."

"Nick Dimani's *Playing Tahoe* is going to go gold," said Morris.

"Platinum."

"Pink."

Lionel looked at him. "Only joking. Poor guy. He was just about to flex his muscles. All the chicken-shit punks who sang his songs will watch the funeral. His lawyers and accountants will clean up."

"So will we," Colesman said.

The two men finished their coffee and entered Lionel's limousine, which would take them to the funeral.

81. Trans Am Blues

AFTER RETURNING from the hospital, Sylvia Lundholm went back to Harrah's and dressed in black. Rev had regained only semi-consciousness when she saw him. *Thank God he wasn't killed,* was all she could think. The accident had stunned the world. To have Nick crushed in a heap like a sardine in a can was disturbing enough. For one terrible moment before the news was broadcast in its ghastly entirety, she thought she had lost her love as well. Now her mind flashed back to the old days, the early friends, her first songs. Lionel had mentioned something about her writing a script on their life together and the history of rock and roll. One of the directors was interested in packaging it for television, but it was to have a documentary approach. She thought about it and put it out of her mind for the moment. Lionel had quoted his famous "MNO" line—"Money No Object." He meant it. Whatever price she named, he would give it to her. This was a man who had offered Robert Redford a quarter of a million dollars to his favorite charity, C.A.N., if Redford would have lunch with his granddaughter. "But Redford wasn't available and I didn't think my granddaughter would want to have lunch with anyone else," Lionel said. "I would have gone up to a million. When it comes to what I want, it's MNO." Payola. Drugola. Now fameola. She was going to have the job of making the legend real.

"He was a legend in his own time," she would have to say. In the goddamn moviemaking business or record business, everyone was a fucking legend. It was a bore. She wanted to be a nonlegend for a change. When Rev got out of the hospital, she was going to pursue anonymity with such ambition—the way a starfucker pursues a star. She wondered what would happen to Tahoe after the funeral. It was now going to be the center of world attention. People were being flown in from all over the world. The funeral was going to be bizarre. All this fuss over a songmaker. All this fuss over someone who sat down at the keyboard when he was a kid in Brooklyn and picked out the sharps from the flats to please his own ear. Would Nick's funeral go gold?

Lionel was "recording" the funeral. Nick's funeral would be on record. A video tape. And finally, as a series on television, broadcast live via satellite to the world. Was a funeral the kind of intelligence the fans wanted? Ron Thimble was approaching the funeral as if it were going to be *reviewed*. He was putting the acts together. "Love Love Blues" and "No Real Love" were the two songs Thimble had chosen to lead the mass in church after Mahler. The price of stock at Mecca had gone up. Nick shoveled into the earth and stock shooting sky high and Rev somewhere on white sheets recovering. It wasn't a death now. It was a deal.

Lionel was already dealing with the major networks, with publishers, and with paperback people for the rights. A young executive from Warner had already flown out for negotiations on all the rights. She had told Sylvia she had missed out on all the rights to the people who ate each other in the air crash in Chile, missing out on the millions made on the film, *Survival.* As she pointed out, this time she wasn't going to miss anything big. She had cash. This was the age of overbuy. If a tragedy happened, it was immediately a "property." There were no tragedies anymore. Merely future properties. Lionel had the copyright on Nick's death. No cannibal-hunting young story editor was going to miss out on this one. If only there could have been a playback of the crash: a film for television. But it was already being simulated. Revson Cranwell was a media star. His background as a tuna fisherman was just the romantic touch for America. Yes. Nick was the big fish. Good enough to be stuffed. He was for the moment America's trophy.

After the funeral, Rev listened to her. They had to leave. She told him something. She said to him, "Our estrangement from nature will end only after we have remade nature. Without our refining influence, nature is crude and rotten. We must divest nature of all its ugliness, all its cruelties, its tyranny."

"Sounds good," he said.

She talked to him. Was she talking about machines? Or what people could do with them? Was she talking about technology, or a spiritual search? "You see, Rev, we have been attempting this from primordial times. We will continue to alter ourselves and nature until no sea can drown us, no cold can freeze us, no fall can maim us, no violence can destroy us."

She spoke to him about these things. While they packed. As they prepared to leave Tahoe. She spoke to him about hidden knowledge. About Indians. About taming nature.

She spoke to him, for the first time, about her search. And how what she was looking for was beyond her experience. And he understood. All her life, she told him, she had been searching for some truth. Was it in energy? Music? In the eye of the sun? In silence? In poems and songs? In the body moving perfectly in its own alphabet? Was it a truth or a new alphabet? A new speed? Clans? Groups? Dialects? There was so much alienation. There had to be some place beyond the snow where she could go.

"I know what you mean," Rev said in his flat voice.

In the cold white weather of the Sierras that winter, they drove out of Tahoe, Rev and Sylvia, in the rented black Trans Am. They were following a map that Rev had marked which led past Mason Valley into the desert. It was almost as if leaving were a special ritual. Behind the wheel, Sylvia thought of how much she had learned in her encounter with Nick. In the world of music that she had explored. That world was dead to her now. Her eyes were blazing with excitement. It was as if she were driving with Rev into a remote unheard-of place not shown on any map. It was a new odyssey in her lifelong search for truth, in her search for who she was. That was the magic of Rev. He could lead her straight into the mystery of snow and sea and desert, into a new crossing of a desert of the heart. He was, to her, at that moment, a scholar of the occult, a mythic American whose bond of friendship would take her further in her search above sea level, take her to a place of forgotten knowledge. He had within him the cowboy and the Indian and the prince and the mystic. He was part foundling and part fuck-up and he seemed to have some forgotten knowledge that bordered on insanity. She realized not how much she loved him, but how deep her bond was with him. It was as if she had to follow him to find out something that he had learned not from experience but from opening his life to being, just being.

As they left the Sierra country, winding on the road that led from Tahoe, she looked at the lake, so deep it would not freeze. There were thousands of bodies at the bottom of that lake and none of them bloated or rose to the top. That was why the water was so motionless. It was so cold that nothing came out of the water. If someone drowned, they stayed at the bottom and never came up. *Tahoe.* The Indian word for "cold water." Without looking back, her face was calm. She had gone through an intensive initiation with Nick and when he died, it was for her the beginning of a new life. She suddenly felt the newness of life. She remembered reading about it in the New Testament: giving praise to the newness of life. They drove at the bottom of the Sierras, those remarkable peaks that seemed like gates to her old life. It was almost as if she heard old instruments vibrating from the mountains, the old knowledge of things she once knew but would now forget. Only people who have changed their lives and followed a madman could understand her search. She saw the skiers and the children on sleds. They were seeking knowledge too, she thought. They were after their own truths near the cold waters. She wondered, as she breathed in the air from the slit above the window, if Rev was her guide to life and if so, where he would lead her, when he would dump her. She didn't care. She forgot her old fears as she strove to breathe in her new life and a new understanding of what her meaning was on that funny map of her life which led from Tahoe and the big lake. They drove down from the Sierras in the rented black car. She felt excited. On the tape deck in her car, on cassette, was Jimi Hendrix singing, " 'Scuse me while I kiss the sky."

She knew she would stay with Rev as long as she could, and that it probably wouldn't be very long. With her mind's eye, her poet's eye, she felt the innocence and the beauty inside of him that his parents had tried so hard to destroy. To her, he was her electric Buddha-buddy. With his lack of feeling and emotion, he was able to teach her the lesson of detachment and of enlightenment. But she could never tell him how much she loved him. To begin with, he would be unimpressed.